Janet Broomfield was born and brought up in Lancashire and went to school in Liverpool. She was educated at Edinburgh and Glasgow Universities before settling in Edinburgh where, in addition to training as a teacher and having a family, she has had jobs as various as auxiliary nurse, cleaner and civil servant. Always a writer as a child, her professional writing career began with a chance encounter which led to her enrolment on a correspondent course. Though many of her short stories have been published, *A Fallen Land*, which won the 1990 Historical Novel Prize in Memory of Georgette Heyer, is her first published novel.

Janet Broomfield first heard the story of the collapse of the tenement in Paisley Close, which provides the background to *The Fallen Land*, when she was at Moray House, the education college in Edinburgh's Royal Mile. The story is known at least in vague outline to most people in Edinburgh because of the incident of a trapped boy who called out to his rescuers, 'Heave awa' lads, I'm no deid yet'. The carving of a boy's head over the rebuilt close marks the event.

A FALLEN LAND

Janet Broomfield

CORGI BOOKS

1

A midsummer evening, the close of a hot day. Impassive under the soft rain, the Castle crouches on its rock, the steep roofs of the Old Town dampen to gleaming darkness. Jostling, struggling, the tenements claw upwards for air, seven storeys and more, the tallest housing in Europe, and among the worst.

In those wynds and closes, clinging to the narrow ridge which joins the Castle and the Palace, lairds once lived. Now, in 1860, the spacious rooms they deserted have been divided, and partitioned, and subdivided yet again, into ever smaller cells. And there, hidden from view, the poor are packed in their unconsidered thousands.

Laying the dust, the rain speckles the pavements of Princes Street, abandoned now by the fashionable and the respectable. The shops are closed; the grand thoroughfare is haunted by those who come to practise a different trade. They shelter from the drizzle, their silk gowns, thin, over-bright, draggled with the dirt of the street. Even in the shadows they will be sought out. A word, a furtive look, the contract is made, although the transaction will be completed elsewhere, in the Georgian squalor of St James Square or the tumbledown tenements, the unholy 'lands' of Leith Wynd.

To the north, through the gently stirring trees which bring the illusion of rural peace to the New Town, the rain patters lightly. It soaks into the parched soil of gardens enclosed by neat, geometric squares and places. It brings a breathing freshness to the grass, which trembles unseen at the impact of each separate drop.

With the rain, across the gardens in the heart of Drummond Place drift the muted strains of laughter and music, from a tall house in the terrace. Its stone facade, like that of all its kind, is restrained, discreet. Against its bright windows the spattering rain taps unheard . . .

Helen Lambert stood at the window, a little apart, fanning herself lightly. The drawing-room was full, and warm, but not too crowded for ease of movement. Her father had doubted whether so many could be accommodated with comfort. Helen had known otherwise.

She sought her father's eye, looking for a smile of approval. Even among the whirling confusion of couples her gaze found him at once. Tall, erect, Edward Lambert was sweeping his partner along in the breathless dash of the polka as vigorously as any younger man. She fixed her eyes on him, willing him to sense her look and exchange with her a glance of secret understanding. But his gaze never wavered from his partner's face. Susan Raymond seemed to engage his full attention; she was looking up at him with a sidelong smile. Some trifling banter must be passing between them. Her father's face was flushed and animated, from the dance. Helen could not catch his eye for even a second. She frowned.

'Not dancing, Helen?'

She turned. 'Oh, Doctor Cairns! I must be allowed to sit out a dance or two, if I am to be the gracious hostess to the very end.' She shut up her fan with a quick flick of her wrist, and tapped it lightly on his sleeve. 'Are you not ashamed to be neglecting your duty? Even married men have to be pressed into service on these occasions!'

To her surprise, her teasing drew no answering response. Indeed, his eyes narrowed, as if in sudden pain.

'Doctor Cairns?'

'Oh, don't mind me, Helen. I've had a sad, tiresome day, that's all.'

'It was good of you to come this evening in that case.'

'I could not stay away,' he said seriously, 'but I shan't dance. Surely my advancing years will exempt me?'

2

'Advancing years! How can you say so? Look at Papa!'

He followed her gaze, and shrugged. 'We are not all gifted with Lambert's wonderful energy, or with his appetite for pleasure.'

She seemed about to make some protest; if so, she thought better of it. She half turned from him, to scan the room, a commander scrutinising manoeuvring troops.

'There's Sophie . . . won't you stand up with her? It would be a work of mercy, at her first dance. Look at her face! How she is longing to be up! Can't you exert your failing strength even so far?'

'Sophie here tonight? You'll be telling me next that Kitty has escaped from the nursery too!'

'Another four or five years . . .'

'When I see a child I brought into the world at an evening party I really shall feel my years.' His brooding gaze followed the ruddy, greying man energetically whirling his partner through the dance. 'A hard time your mother had of it, too. I thought we would lose her then.'

She flicked her fan abruptly open, moving it quickly, to cool, perhaps to conceal her heated face.

'Poor Mama would have so wished to see this day. If only she had been spared . . .'

'Spared indeed!' He turned with an expression of distaste from his contemplation of his host, and the smiling young woman in his arms.

There was a moment of silence. 'Did you not think Rosemary and Harry a perfect couple?' she said brightly.

'A perfect couple? What a question! Do you mean any more than that he is tall and dark, and she six inches shorter and fair? The combination is popularly supposed an ideal recipe for married bliss, is it not? If it is the only qualification, they must be as well matched a pair as ever entered a bridal carriage.'

'Really, you seem determined to be provoking! What an ill-humour to bring to a wedding dance!'

3

'I'm hot, and the room is noisy, and the crush is insufferable.' He offered her his arm. 'Take me away from this rout, and I shall be prepared to see all manner of delights in store for your sister and Harry Robertson.'

He moved purposefully towards the door. She allowed him to guide her, pausing in the doorway for a lingering glance of appraisal about the room.

'How many ices and glasses of wine-cup will be needed to restore you to your cool, civil self? With that dismal scowl you could be taken for a disappointed suitor of Rosemary's instead of a staid married man! When we come back up you must do the agreeable and dance with Sophie, as a penance if you won't allow it to be a pleasure.'

They began to negotiate the spiral stair. He paused, watching her slender, slippered foot emerge from beneath her spreading crinoline, and feel for the first step.

'Helen, I hope you aren't trying to manage me? You have enough for any ordinary mortal already, with your father and eight youngsters . . .'

'Seven, now!'

'Seven, then . . . don't try to add me to the number of your charges as make-weight for Rosemary.'

They had reached the foot of the stair. She tapped her fan against his broad chest. 'A make-weight indeed!'

'Your father's elegant frame is not given to all.'

'But Papa holds himself so well! You will stoop, Doctor Cairns!'

'You will have me strapped to a back-board before I leave the house!'

The dining-room was almost deserted, save for the servants standing patiently by the refreshments. The doctor smiled sympathetically at a weary housemaid who was collecting together the dirty plates and glasses from supper. With a nod and a quiet word to the housekeeper who presided over the wine he picked up two glasses, and moved over to the far side of the room, through the folding doors which usually separated it into two.

4

He carried the wine with curious delicacy, unexpected in a man of his heavy build.

'Here, Helen, by the window.' He waited for her to come up; she had paused for a word with the servants, to reassure herself that the supply of wine was in no danger of failing.

'Is this cool enough for you?' she asked.

'If I had my way, I'd throw up that window!'

'And risk a scandalous misrepresentation of your motives? What a fine crop of chills to be doctored! The ladies are scarcely dressed for your austere notions of a comfortable temperature!'

His strained expression relaxed into a smile as he looked at her. 'If I didn't know you to be above such vanity I would think you were angling for a compliment. Here, you shall have it: I never saw you in better looks, or wearing a more becoming gown. Will that do?'

'A passable attempt . . . as a reward, you may raise the window an inch, now that we are alone. I am quite immune to chills.'

'Indeed. If I relied on your ailments to keep me in guinea fees, I should have been a pauper long since.'

The window was stiff. His evening coat strained across his shoulders as he exerted his full strength to pull it up. It opened with a sudden jerk, and the damp freshness of the garden under a soft summer shower drifted into the room. He leaned out a moment, breathing the cool evening air with a sigh of pleasure. Then, gently, he pulled down the sash to within an inch of the frame, and turned back to Helen.

As though exhausted, she was sitting back in a moment of snatched repose, eyes closed. His deep-set eyes were fixed on her as he stood, pulling off his white gloves, with an absent, distracted air.

The Lamberts were a good-looking family, Helen as much as the rest. Fair like all her brothers and sisters, she had a wide, open face, her skin glowing with the bloom of youth and health. Now that her eyes were closed it was her mouth which drew the attention, full and generous. It was a good-humoured face, but there was a stubborn set to her lips, despite their easy curve. He looked down at her, frowning.

Her stillness was short-lived. Her lids flew open, and at once her expression took on its habitual eager vivacity. She smiled up at him, seeming as refreshed by the few seconds of rest as by hours of slumber. He reached out and touched her bare arm in a deliberate, almost professional gesture.

For a fraction of a second his hand lay on her skin, the soft white skin inside the crook of her arm. She shivered. At once, his hand flew away. He closed the window.

'Forgive me. I don't know what I was thinking of.'

'Really, I was not cold. I can't think why I shivered.'

He remained by the window, his hands clasped behind his back. 'So the wedding passed off well?' he asked abruptly.

'Perfectly. I could see that Rosemary was nervous, but her responses were quite clear. She looked so lovely on Harry's arm . . . poor Rosemary.'

'Poor Rosemary? The girl has married the man of her choice. He has a promising career before him, and a comfortable home ready for her. Exactly why should I pity her?'

Eyes downcast, she trifled with her fan. 'A man could not understand . . .' she murmured.

'No, and perhaps a woman could not, either,' he said briskly. 'Harry Robertson is a genial man, with a taste for domesticity, I should say. I doubt if your sister will have any grounds for complaint, in any respect.'

He plucked at the knees of his trousers and seated himself, leaning forward a little in his chair, his elbows on the arms. 'You will miss Rosemary.'

'Sophie will be an excellent replacement. She's such a dear; I shan't allow her to follow Rosemary's example, at least until Kitty is well up . . . wasn't that Jack's voice?' She turned quickly, to look through the ferns which screened their secluded corner. 'He sounds quite excited . . . excuse me a moment.'

His gaze followed her as she moved swiftly away. Tall, upright, she carried herself superbly, with the perfect naturalness which is free of either coquetry or self-consciousness. Her evening gown was of sea-green satin, with a foam of lace at the low-cut neck. Naked and unadorned, her shoulders rose from the rich fabric, the graceful curve of her neck emphasised by her hair, drawn high up onto her head. Pearls were twined in its thick coils, and a few half-open rosebuds of ivory just tinged with pink.

Close beside the table where the housekeeper dispensed the wine stood her brother, swaying slightly. Flushed, his eyes at once bright and vague, his neckcloth askew, he shook off the hand Helen laid on his arm, staggering as he did so.

'Let me alone, can't you? Or if you must interfere as usual, tell Beattie to give me another glass of wine.'

'Mrs Beattie is quite right,' she said firmly, smiling in encouragement to the housekeeper who stood, ill at ease but resolute, pleating her apron into small folds. 'You have had too much wine already, Jack, and you're the worse for it. You'd best go to bed.'

'Like a good boy! Helen, I'm nineteen years old! How long will you try to treat me like an infant?'

'For just as long as you behave like one. Now, do you really want to spoil Rosemary's wedding day? Shall I see you up to your room? You're not yourself tonight.'

'Not myself?' He lurched towards her, his eyes staring. 'I'll never be myself, if you can help it! I can't breathe in this place for all your everlasting fussing and managing! Keep your concern for the nursery, where it belongs!' He turned towards the housekeeper again with a rough, uncontrolled gesture. His hand caught an empty glass, sending it flying. It fell onto the thick carpet, unbroken, rolled, and was still.

'Jack, you don't know what you're doing.'

'Beattie, give me more wine or I shall serve myself.'
He addressed the housekeeper, but he kept his eyes on his sister, unsure defiance on his face.

In the taut moment of silence that followed as he awaited her response she felt a touch at her elbow. Doctor Cairns moved past her, and stooped to pick up the fallen glass. He set it gently down on the table.

'Now, Jack, what's to do? Your sister's wedding isn't the place for a student brawl, is it? Would you just take a turn outside with me? It's so confoundedly stuffy in here, I'm gasping for air, though Helen will swear it's just my usual crotchets . . .'

Talking easily, soothing, cajoling, he drew his arm through Jack Lambert's, and led him unresisting to the door. As they left the room, Helen sighed, and turned to the housekeeper.

'Mrs Beattie, I'm so sorry you have been troubled. You were quite right; I'm sure my brother will thank you for it when he is himself again.'

The housekeeper nodded, still flustered.

'The evening is nearly at an end,' Helen continued, with a glance at the clock over the mantel. 'I doubt if any more refreshments will be needed; you might clear away . . .'

A sudden burst of laughter at the door interrupted her. Her father was entering, Susan Raymond clinging to his arm. With them, although a little distance apart, was a man whom Helen could not place. He must have been one of the bewildering throng of Harry's relations whom as hostess she had greeted with a ready smile, and as readily forgotten. In any less hectic setting he would have been memorable enough. He was tall, with hair of a reddish brown, parted fashionably in the centre, but, unusually, he was clean-shaven, with neither moustache nor whiskers.

'Nell, here you are! I thought I didn't see you upstairs . . . deserting your post already?'

For once, her father's high spirits grated on her, still

preoccupied by Jack's indiscretion. She shot a warning glance at Mrs Beattie before replying.

'I came down for a moment to see that all was in order.'

'That's Nell for you, Miss Raymond,' he said, patting the hand which clasped his arm. 'Always something to fret about, eh Nell?'

His teasing seemed to her to have passed into mockery; her lips parted in silent protest, but he was smiling down at his companion, not watching his daughter's face.

'Won't you let me get you a glass of wine, Miss Lambert? This must have been a trying day for you, however happy.'

Her unknown guest had approached her; she turned a grateful smile upon him. 'No, thank you.' She looked over to her father, hoping that he would realise her difficulty and contrive to mention the stranger's name. He was engaged in getting wine for himself and Miss Raymond. There was no help for it; she smiled, and candidly owned her lapse.

'We've been introduced, I'm sure, but I'm afraid that in all the confusion . . .'

He bowed. 'Francis Bethune. I am a cousin of Harry Robertson.'

'Thank you. I hope you can forgive such a shameful confession. You must think me a most discourteous hostess.'

He murmured a polite disclaimer. 'I regret to say that I was unable to attend the wedding ceremony as I had hoped. I was detained by a matter of some importance.'

'Oh? I'm sorry . . .' As she spoke, her attention was distracted from him by the sight of her father, bearing two glasses, strolling with Miss Raymond over to the ferny seclusion of the corner she had so recently occupied with Doctor Cairns. Through the screening greenery she saw her father stand until his partner was settled, then seat himself beside her, bending forward a little, as in some intimate conversation. In an impulse of involuntary irritation, Helen stepped to one side, so that the arched doorway blocked the bower from her view.

She suddenly realised that her companion had fallen silent. His words had passed her by unheard. She struggled to recall any wisp of what he had said. Had there not been something about the law?

'You are a lawyer, then?' she hazarded.

His half-smile broadened. She felt uncomfortably sure that her inattention had not escaped his notice, although he might be too well-bred to reveal as much.

'I am an Advocate-Depute.'

'Oh? What does that entail? I am absolutely ignorant of the law.' Despite herself, she looked uneasily towards that distant corner. Low, conspiratorial, her father's voice reached her straining ears, but not his words.

'Perhaps you will allow me to explain a little of our legal system, when you are more at leisure.'

'Yes, of course,' she said vaguely. Could she break into that confidential intercourse? Irresolute, she took a step towards the folded-back doors.

'I hear the music resuming. May I beg the honour of the next dance?'

'Dance? Oh, thank you, but you must excuse me. I am waiting here to see someone . . . I'm sorry.'

'Can I be of service?'

'None, thank you.' She smiled, with an effort. 'Pray don't allow me to detain you here when you might be dancing. There are one or two matters which require my presence here a little longer. I do apologise,' she added, with a belated recognition of the poor figure she must be cutting before Harry's cousin.

He bowed, and moved to the door. Something in his tall, elegant bearing recalled her father. Sophie would be delighted with such a partner. She must see to it when she returned upstairs.

Where were Doctor Cairns and her brother? She roamed restlessly about the room. By the garden window, a girlish ripple of laughter told of the continuing conversation. She passed before the arched doorway, and glanced furtively through it. Half hidden behind the luxuriant foliage, her shoulders drooping so that she seemed to be crouching submissively, Susan Raymond was fanning herself slowly, with an exaggerated undulation of her slender wrist. Over the edge of the fan, her black eyes gazed up at Helen's father.

Just beyond the doorway, Helen hesitated. There was no reason why she should not join them; she did not. Suddenly a wave of louder music and laughter washed into the room. The door had opened.

'Doctor Cairns!' she ran to his side, her gown rustling softly. 'Where's Jack?'

'In his bed. He'll be very sorry for himself tomorrow.'

'I can't thank you enough! When I think of what might have happened . . .'

'I've a word or two to say to you,' he said, raising a hand to deprecate her thanks. 'Is there anywhere we can talk?'

'Would not tomorrow . . . ?'

'It's important. Why not step outside a moment? The rain is hardly anything now. Mrs Beattie, will you fetch Miss Lambert a wrap?'

'Really, I hardly like to absent myself. It will look so strange.'

'Everyone is too intent upon their own pleasure to miss you, and if there is any real difficulty, your father is here. Let him take some responsibility for once.'

The arrival of Mrs Beattie with a shawl silenced any rejoinder. He took it from her with a smile of thanks, and folded it about Helen's naked shoulders. He offered his arm; with a parting, uneasy glance about the room, she was led out.

After the warmth and glare of the house, the evening was a shock to the senses; it was another world. As he had said, the rain had all but stopped. The pavements were scarcely damp. Beneath her thin slippers they felt unyielding and strange.

11

'What was it that you wished to say? I really must not be absent for long.'

He guided her along the western edge of the square, past the long broad stretch of Great King Street, deserted at this hour.

'I scarcely know. Can I use the freedom of an old friend?'

'What candid friend always says what is welcome? Speak your mind; I shall not blame you.'

'Very well. Jack needs careful handling. He didn't say very much, but I could see that he is not happy.'

'Jack? Nonsense! He was elevated tonight; you can't judge him by his behaviour under such circumstances. Usually he's the same sweet-tempered boy he's always been. I hope you will allow that I know my own brother!'

He made a small sound of annoyance. 'There, I knew how it would be! You will never admit to any want of perfection in anything or anyone relating to your family!'

'I certainly won't admit that my brother's behaviour is anything more than youthful imprudence. Remember, this is Rosemary's wedding day, the first break in our family circle. Is it to be wondered at if he said and did a few thoughtless things?'

'I tell you, you don't know the half of what passes in his mind.' He patted her hand. 'How should you know? It would be unreasonable to expect it. I gather that he is considering a move.'

'A move?' She could not conceal her astonishment. She halted abruptly. The pale gleam of the gas-lamp beneath which they stood fell on her lifted face, her wide, wondering eyes. 'Away from Edinburgh?'

'He mentioned your uncle in Canada. He is eager to go.'

'Jack?' They might have been speaking of two different people.

'If it is what he wishes, I think it might be advisable.'

'But Papa would never sanction it! Jack cannot abandon his studies!'

'Your father may be a man of letters, but Jack can't be expected to share his talents. Why must he complete his studies, if he has no taste for the life?'

They began to walk again, crossing the shining cobbles towards the gardens. Beneath the trees overhanging the railings the ground was drier. Overhead, the leaves rustled, unheard.

'What makes you think it might be wise to let him go?'

'It is nothing I can put into words. He said nothing definite. Sometimes a doctor learns as much from a patient's bearing as from what is openly avowed, from his whole tone, his silence, even. I think something is troubling your brother, something which he wishes to escape.'

'Jack is not ill! And he is no coward; if something is troubling him, he will not run away.'

'Helen, you are a dear girl . . .'

'You are abusing the words! You mean that I am blind, ignorant, unable to imagine the temptations to which a young man may be exposed in a city such as this.'

'I was not aware of meaning anything of the sort. But after all, would it be so strange if a part of your brother's life was a mystery to you? Don't take fire at the very thought – I am far from meaning to insult you.'

'Whatever Jack's difficulties may be, I know my own brother. He is incapable of a mean or a base action. He will have done nothing of which he needs to be ashamed.'

He sighed. 'Helen, I tell you plainly, Jack at home with you and your sisters, and Jack abroad with his student friends, to name no worse companions, are two very different creatures. As you love him, if he approaches your father with a request to try his luck in Canada, support him. You know how much your father relies on your judgement in all that concerns his family.'

'I most certainly would not give him my support! To abandon his studies, and barely nineteen! To send a boy of that age half way across the world! No!'

'He does not consider himself a boy. If you continue to treat him like one he will hate you for it. Did you not see as much earlier this evening?'

'I saw nothing but a boy who had taken more drink than was wise. You don't know Jack as I do. He and I have been everything to each other. Hate me? Impossible!'

'I'm not denying his affection . . . or yours. But you don't see him as he is.'

'It's getting late, Doctor Cairns. We shan't agree, and I don't wish to quarrel with you.' She paused, and added more cordially, as if regretting her abrupt tone, 'Thank you for all you've done tonight, and for all you tried to do. Jack is going away next week to the Highlands, a reading party. He's going to be away until the middle of August. I'm sure he will have forgotten all this nonsense by then.'

They had followed the line of the gardens, beneath the overhanging trees which expanded their scentless freshness on the mild air. The tall bright windows of the house came into sight again. Sweet and sad, the muted strains of music reached them. As they crossed the cobbles, from the unseen depths of the garden came the sound of a sudden scuffle, a thin shriek, a tiny, desperate tragedy.

2

A mile away, a world away, a girl crossed the cobbles of the High Street, picking her way through the decaying refuse, holding up her skirts as best she could to keep them from contamination. The rain was not heavy enough to wash the street clean; it had served only to compound the rotting cabbage-stalks, the fish guts and buckie shells, the stinking rubbish of scores of street-hawkers, the ordure, animal and human, into a noxious, semi-liquid slush, pulped by the wheels of passing carriages.

Wrapped in her shawl a baby slept, its rapt face pressed close to her shoulder. On her arm hung a basket, far from full, but a burden: she moved her arm uneasily, trying to shift the weight dragging at her elbow. It would have been less painful to have carried the basket in her hand, and let her skirts drag in the filth. She glanced down at the crossing, and hitched her skirt higher.

Before her gaped the black arch of the close, flanked by the bright windows of Cairns's grocery shop and Brown's the victual dealer. She paused outside the grocer's. In the window, crossed by a long gas-pipe with numerous burners, were crowded eggs, cheese, a side of bacon, rich yellow butter, and a boiled ham. A slice was cut; thick, reddish-pink, it lay close beside the ham, curving slightly, for it was still attached at the bottom.

The child on her arm stirred. She shifted its position without taking her eyes from the slice of meat. Its edge was ragged where it had not been cleanly cut from the joint. Delicate white fat, gilded with an outer rind of light brown, glistened round the meat, good and deep. She swallowed. Her right hand released her skirt and moved slowly to her pocket. She told over the few coppers there, as though she did not already know their exact sum and what they must be made to buy. She took a step away, towards the dark close, but still the flaring gaslit window exercised its fascination; she looked back.

A shop-lad, staggering beneath the weight of the shutters he was bringing into the street, hailed her.

'Are ye wanting messages, Lizzie? Ye'd best look sharp, hen!'

She turned quickly away, her fingers dropping the pennies into her pocket as though they had become red-hot.

'Lizzie!'

She looked back. The lad was beckoning to her, glancing over his shoulder into the shop.

'The old man's down the stair,' he said in a hurried undertone. 'A couple of chipped eggs any good to ye?'

'Aye,' she said, without enthusiasm.

He followed her eyes. 'The ham?' Another furtive glance into the shop. 'Hold on the now, Lizzie.'

He was back within moments, hands tucked casually beneath his long apron. He approached the shutters, motioning her close with a tiny inclination of his head. She felt him slip something in amongst the other messages in her basket, then he busied himself once more with his task. She did not linger.

'Tell Tam I was speering after him,' he called, as he struggled with the unwieldy shutters. 'He's a wee while to go still, eh no?'

'He gets out in February,' she said, already at the close. He nodded sympathetically, as she turned off the street.

She walked through the low-arched tunnel as quickly as its treacherous surface permitted. The passage was cut through the heart of the seven-storey tenement. Now, at nearly midnight, its drainage channel was piled with refuse and filth awaiting the scavenger's broom. In the enclosed space the smell was overpowering. She would have run, had she not feared to slip.

The close gave onto a court surrounded by tenements. A stair opened into it; at the foot a group of men were idling.

'How's the bairn, Lizzie?'

She stopped, and nodded to the man who had spoken.

'No bad, Mr Shannon. Your lassies?'

'Oh, ill weeds wax weel,' he said, raising a laugh from one or two of the other men. He straightened himself up from the wall against which he had been leaning, and knocked out his pipe. Its glowing contents fell to the ground and were extinguished with a hiss.

'I'll get ye up the stair, hen. Give me your messages.'

'They're no that heavy.'

He silently reached for the basket. She allowed him to take it, and with a sigh of relief settled the child more comfortably on her shoulder.

'Ye didna need to see me up the stair, Mr Shannon,' she said, with an inflection of proud independence.

'Ken, but I was ready to go in anyway. The lassies'll be in their beds. I like to give them a minute to sort themselves, it's only decent.' He paused, more for her sake than his, as they reached a landing. 'I was only saying to Minnie the day, I miss a good crack with your father at the foot of the stair. My pipe doesna taste the same since Rab went . . . How's he doing?'

'Still on the tramp.'

'No work yet?' He whistled softly. 'A man with his skill . . . I never saw the joiner his equal, Lizzie.'

'Aye.' Her tone did not invite further question, or sympathy. He said no more. They continued the long, weary climb. It was a spiral stair, its stone treads worn so thin near the newel that the effort of the ascent was doubled. In many places the stone was wet, perhaps from water carried up, but more likely, to judge from the smell, from slops spilt on the long journey down to the close.

As they rounded a curve in the stair, Lizzie's companion made a sound of disgust. 'See the bairn!'

He was pointing to a ragged girl of perhaps ten or eleven, lying huddled at the top of the flight, her arm pillowing her head. She seemed to be asleep despite her uncomfortable posture, but as they approached she roused, and looked at them with vacant eyes.

'Ye'll take your death out here,' he said, with rough kindness. 'Why are ye no in your bed?'

The girl shook her head, her matted hair sticking to her cheek where tears had wet it. 'My ma'll no let me ben.'

'What for no?'

'She's got a friend with her ben the house.'

Shannon cast a meaning look at Lizzie; they understood, although the girl might not. He passed on. Lizzie seemed as though she might linger, speak further to the child. But if so, she thought better of it. She hitched her burden higher on her aching shoulder, and toiled up the stair. The outcast stolidly resumed her former position, seeking some sort of ease on the unyielding stone.

Shannon was waiting for her on the next landing. 'I wonder the mother's no put her to the same trade,' he said, looking back down the stair, in pity and distaste.

'The poor bairn,' Lizzie said softly, and then, drawing herself up, she held out her hand for her basket.

'Aye.' He handed her the basket, frowning as he hefted its all too light weight. 'Mind, Minnie's aye got a wee drop broth in the pot, if ye're short . . .'

'I'm sure we're obliged to ye,' she put in quickly.

'I couldna see Rab Crearie's weans want . . .' he said apologetically. 'Good night to ye, Lizzie.'

Shannon went along the passage. Lizzie continued up the stair, stumbling a little in sheer fatigue as she neared its end.

The room into which she let herself was in darkness, but for the wavering firelight. She entered softly, almost stealthily, and moved silently over to the bed-recess. Her features lost something of their strained weariness as she looked down on the three children sleeping there; Joseph had returned during her absence, then, and was safe beside his sisters. She waited a moment by the bed, but although May coughed fretfully, there was no sign that her entry had disturbed them.

With infinite care, scarcely daring to breathe, she eased the baby from her cradling arm and laid him, still wrapped in her plaid, on the mattress which lay on the floor by the bed. He flung one tiny fist in the air as she settled him, but the protest or alarm subsided without a single cry, as his arm slowly sank down.

Lizzie crept away from the recess to the fire. She looked doubtfully at the embers, as though wondering whether she dare stir them, and risk the cry, the cough, the appeal which would summon her once more to her responsibilities. Fearfully, she set the kettle to boil over the fire, and began to unpack her few messages. A little oatmeal, some potatoes, a broken smoked herring or two, half an ounce of tea, a screw of sugar. She disposed of them on the shelf which served as larder.

The kettle was boiling. She made tea with a tiny pinch of leaves, so cheap that they were little more than dust. Then, at last, she seated herself by the dying fire, and drew out the slice of ham. Watching the children, freezing in shame and guilt whenever one of them stirred, she ate the meat, desperately surrendering to the craving for something tasty for a treat, for anything but the everlasting potatoes and oatmeal.

She was fourteen years old.

Her hand resting on Doctor Cairns's arm, Helen climbed the steps to the street door where MacRoberts yawned at his post.

'I must go up to see that the dancing is going as it ought,' she said, removing her hand. He detained it.

'Won't you give me a dance, Helen?'

'What, Methuselah? I thought your dancing days were long past!'

'If you throw a man's words in his teeth, how is he ever to mend his ways?'

'I suppose any last remaining youthful impulses must be fostered . . . I accept with pleasure!' She gathered up her skirts, and lightly mounted the stair.

A waltz had just begun as they entered the drawing-room. She placed her hand on his shoulder, his arm encircling her waist with its heavy warmth. They waited a moment to catch the rhythm, and then glided into the slowly eddying stream of the dance.

'You dance better than I would have expected. With practice you would waltz as well as any man of your age . . . except Papa, of course!'

His arm tightened about her waist as he looked down in mingled amusement and exasperation. Almost, the marks of strain on his face were erased.

Sophie was dancing too, she noted with pleasure. She and Francis Bethune made a handsome couple. There was a formality, a precision in his movements which made them a perfect foil for Sophie's girlish vivacity. She watched them over her partner's shoulder, seeing with satisfaction her sister's excited smile.

The shifting kaleidoscope of the dance carried her away. Another couple drew her eye; the smile froze on her lips. Her father and Miss Raymond. The attention he was paying her was highly indiscreet. She absolved her father of any guilt: he was so good-natured, so impractical. It was like him not to realise how his unthinking courtesy might be misconstrued. To some, his attentions to Miss Raymond might seem too particular. It was a pity that Miss Raymond had not shown a little more prudence. Her father might be no more than a child in these matters, but his partner looked to Helen far from naive.

'I may be given that practice in waltzing sooner than we anticipated, Helen. Another wedding may be no great distance away.'

With unconsidered grace she turned to look at her sister, her head swaying on its slender white neck. 'Perhaps. We must not be premature, though. Is Mr Bethune unmarried?'

20

'That tailor's dummy? Oh, I wasn't thinking of him,' he said, and nodded with a meaning smile towards her father.

Helen faltered in her step, losing the rhythm of the dance. She quickly recovered herself. 'Papa? What are you thinking of? He will never marry again. Why should he?'

His brows rose quizzically. 'When a man's wife dies in presenting him with a tenth pledge of mutual affection, he has shown a certain taste for the conjugal state. I'm only surprised that he has been six years a widower. I wonder he hasn't sought consolation long since.'

'Papa has consolation, in his home and family!'

'How old is Lambert? Forty-five? Less, probably. He'll not remain single much longer.'

'You're being perfectly odious. Papa has his writing, his editorial responsibilities, his studies. He has his children, and me to take almost every household care from him and act as his hostess. I'm sure I'm able to do more for him in that respect than poor Mama, ill as she always was. He doesn't need a wife!'

'Helen, are you wilfully shutting your eyes to my meaning? Don't make me lose all respect for your understanding!'

'Not even the oldest of friends can be allowed such licence!'

He looked at her flushed, troubled face, and his arm made to draw her closer. It met with a sullen stiffness.

'I meant nothing improper,' he said more softly, 'but you will allow that you cannot entirely replace a wife. Don't pretend to be ignorant of what you know quite well. If I try to speak to you as to a sensible woman there's no need to fancy yourself insulted.'

'Unlike you, Doctor Cairns, I do not see coarseness and sensuality in everything I meet!'

'Coarseness and sensuality? Is that how it appears to you?' His hand moved at her waist in a tiny, gentling caress. If it was a plea for forgiveness, she ignored it.

'Don't ever revert to the subject again!'

'Very well.' He paused. 'I beg your pardon if I've hurt you. I'm sorry for it — but I can't retract the opinion I expressed, mind!'

'I suppose that is meant to pass for an apology?' she asked, her eyes still flashing, but her tone less hostile.

'I suppose it is.'

'Well. It's best forgotten.' He felt her relax in his arms; the waltz was ending. He detained her as she moved away. 'Friends, Helen?'

'Old friends,' she said, wryly.

Engrossed in her thoughts, she started as a voice addressed her. 'Are you engaged for the next dance, Miss Lambert?'

For an instant she gazed at him without recognition. 'Mr Bethune . . . really, I don't . . .' She checked herself. 'Thank you. I should be delighted.' She gave him her hand, nodding coolly to Doctor Cairns.

'I hope you have not been distressed by bad news?'

'Oh, nothing of any importance.'

The next dance was to be a quadrille. There was a pause to allow the couples to gather. Helen, feeling some compunction at the scant attention she had paid her brother-in-law's connection, set herself to make amends.

'I'm so glad you were introduced to my sister. She adores dancing.'

'And you?'

'Oh, I like it well enough.'

'But not waltzing?'

She coloured, lost for a reply.

'You were detained downstairs for quite a long period. No serious difficulty?'

'Doctor Cairns was able to manage things perfectly.'

'Our families are linked now. Perhaps in future I may

claim the privilege of assisting you, even if I cannot pretend to so longstanding an acquaintance as Cairns.'

She smiled her thanks. To talk to him was as different as could well be from her ugly, disturbing conversation with the doctor. Urbane, self-possessed, as he adjusted a button of his white gloves and pulled down his shirt cuffs a fraction, he seemed the embodiment of discreet, civilised virtues. It was a relief to converse with him.

'Your sister will be much missed at home, no doubt?'

'Yes, but we shall see a good deal of Rosemary still. Even over the summer we will not be far apart. We always go out of town about this time, for the children's sake, you know. This summer we are to go down to Melrose. Rosemary and Harry will be only a short distance away, at Newtown St Boswells. We will probably see almost as much of her as ever.'

'I may well be in the Borders at some point during the summer myself. Harry has invited me down for a weekend's fishing.'

'I hope you will call on us, if you are so close.'

He half bowed. 'Thank you. I shall most certainly do so.'

The sets had formed, the music was beginning again, putting an end to the exchange. Brief as it had been, it had restored her to composure. As second couple, she and Francis Bethune had no part to play in the opening bars of the first figure. At liberty to look about her, she saw Doctor Cairns lounging in the doorway, his frowning gaze fixed on her. She looked away, unsmiling, with a toss of her head. When, in the course of the Chain, she passed by the door again, he had gone.

As the quadrille progressed, Helen's pleasure in the dance increased. She was fortunate in her partner. Francis Bethune moved faultlessly through the figures, without either hesitation or display. Even when he stood unoccupied, some sense of presence drew her eyes to him. It seemed impossible to imagine him lounging, or

23

slouching, as other men did when they were at rest. In those passages which he danced alone, the attention of the whole set upon him, he carried himself with a cool composure which won her approval. To many men, it was painfully clear, such moments were an embarrassment, a torment, even, to be shuffled through with an agonised or a fatuous expression. He, however, conveyed a rare sense of the courtly, of unassailable self-possession.

She watched him advancing towards her, and at the very second when it seemed that he must encroach upon her outstretched skirts, retreating again, his steps precise and perfectly controlled. He was of an athletic build, his shoulders broad and straight, his waist neat. She found something pleasing in his appearance; the unstrained dignity of his bearing must contribute to the striking effect he produced, she supposed, for his features were not, in themselves, remarkable.

Beneath the brighter lights of the ballroom she could now see that his hair was redder than she had at first thought. As a child he might well have been quite ginger. Although it was cut short, his hair clearly had a tendency to curl. He had the fair skin typical of his colouring, with light brows and lashes. His eyes seemed to be brown; she suspected, from a trick she observed in him of frowning slightly when he looked at anything more than a few feet away, that he might be short-sighted.

He would, she supposed, be recognisable in any part of Britain as a Scot. He had the high cheekbones, the long face and blunt chin, the wide mouth characteristic of a certain type more commonly found there than elsewhere.

His eyes were alert and watchful, but it was his mouth which held her attention. His teeth were unusually good, she noticed. Above his upper lip, in the centre, was a hollow of the sort which always suggested to her the imprint of a silencing finger when the skin was still in a malleable state. The lower lip was rather full. The absence of either moustache or whiskers emphasised the graceful, ambiguous curve of his lips, of which the natural, or at least the habitual expression appeared to be a half-smile. And yet the effect was not that of a humorous mind, but of a rueful, ironic inner commentary.

In the shifting evolution of the figures they joined hands and promenaded, were separated, changed partners. The women clustered together in the centre, like the petals of an exotic flower, and gently dropped apart once more. But at the end of every configuration, however complex, the partners were reunited in their original positions. She noted with amusement the compelling force of habit, establishing itself even in a single dance, so that there was a curious relief to find herself opposite him again, and greet him with a smile.

The final figure was concluded by a brief waltz. The touch of his hand at her waist was so light that she almost doubted whether he held her at all. His left hand barely curled about the fingers of her right. She compared his delicacy favourably with Doctor Cairns's hearty grip, and yet, by some paradox, his restraint had the effect of inducing in her a self-consciousness of which she had never before been aware. She found it difficult to look him naturally in the face, much to her annoyance. She scarcely knew, when the dance ended, whether or not she was relieved that the pretended intimacy was over.

The midsummer night was greying into dawn before Helen finally went to her bed, the bed in which she could never remember sleeping alone. Reminding herself to speak to Sophie about her move from Kitty's room to replace Rosemary, she fell easily asleep, while outside in the gardens the first light was greeted by an uncertain discordant croaking from the still drowsy birds.

Helen slept deeply, but beneath the same roof, in his small room not far from hers, her brother tossed and flailed in his disordered bed, grinding his teeth in tormented slumber.

The birdsong had tuned itself to harmony before Francis Bethune reached home in Heriot Row after a leisurely stroll along the north side of Queen Street gardens in the pearly cool of the morning. He paused on the steps of his house and looked about him with an air of satisfaction, not marred by the blur into which more distant objects melted; he could see his own solid house well enough, for it lay within his immediate field of vision.

He found his key, and let himself in. He was a considerate master, and would not have kept a servant from sleep to wait up for him. He was crossing the passage to the stair when he stopped, and went instead to the library. Some legal oddity had presented itself to his mind as he walked home; he found at once the reference work which would settle the quibble. He read two or three pages with keen attention, holding the book close to his eyes. The frown of concentration cleared from his brow. He closed and replaced the book, and made his way up to bed, confident of sleep.

Long after Francis Bethune had neatly laid aside his evening clothes and retired the gas still burned, sickly in the midsummer dawn, in the sitting-room of Doctor Cairns's house in George Square. Daylight filtered through the curtains, unheeded by the burly figure slumped, round-shouldered, in his chair. Still in his dress coat he sat as he had sat for many hours, his face buried in the outspread fingers of one hand while the other clutched a crumpled sheet of writing paper, edged with black.

He had scarcely moved since his return from the Lamberts'. He had not even reread the letter edged in black; he had not needed to. The words had already branded themselves on his mind, before he left for Drummond Place.

And in the stifling, crowded room whose dingy yellow panelling had witnessed such a strange procession of the mighty and the humble, Lizzie lay wakeful, her mind endlessly calculating, rent money and coal, milk for Danny, shoes for May . . .

3

It was a matter of some pride with Helen that no matter how late she had been in retiring she would always be the first down to breakfast, ready to pour her father's tea precisely as he liked it. In fact it was no hardship to her to rise early; her own prompt habits were no less instinctive than Rosemary's sluggish awakenings, much scorned by Helen.

On the morning after the wedding dance she was left in solitary occupation of the breakfast table for some considerable time before her father appeared. She essayed a light-hearted comment on the lateness of the hour. His grunted rejoinder did not invite further conversation. She rang for fresh tea, and devoted herself to another piece of toast. She was always particularly hungry after dancing.

She plied her father with tea, solicitously selected for him bacon cooked to precisely the degree of crispness he favoured, and generally cosseted him until she saw the signs of returning good humour in his brow. Despite all her efforts, however, he remained unusually silent, as though his thoughts were elsewhere.

'Really, Papa, it's as well you don't see a daughter married every day of the week!' she said, smiling at him, as he stared absently at the window. 'Papa?'

'Yes, Nell?' He turned to her with a sigh, as if recalled from a pleasant dream to dull reality. 'What is it now?'

The resignation in his manner hurt her; her idle pleasantry seemed too weak to repeat. She searched hurriedly for something to interest him, worthy of his attention. 'Doctor Cairns seemed in poor spirits yesterday,' she hazarded.

'Cairns? Working too hard, probably. He has a sentimental attachment to the poor Irish in the Cowgate. If he devoted himself more to his fashionable practice he could make ten times the money at a quarter the effort. He's hard-headed enough in most ways, but with his precious cinder-women and troggers he's as soft-hearted as a girl . . . Nell, isn't that his brougham outside now? You've not sent for him?'

'No . . . I believe it is only Donald, delivering a note . . . there, he's away again. It can be nothing of any importance, he hasn't waited for a reply.'

As Helen expected, MacRoberts entered within a few seconds bearing a letter for her father.

'Oh, Papa!' She gazed at him in consternation. He lifted the black-bordered envelope from the salver.

The note seemed brief; he read it swiftly, and laid it down. 'I'm sure you will be sorry to hear that Margaret Cairns has gone at last, poor soul,' he said, and reached for another piece of toast.

'Mrs Cairns? Oh! When was it?'

'He says that it was yesterday, but that he learned of it only by first post this morning. Really, it's a happy release, under the circumstances, for both of them.'

'I'm sure that Doctor Cairns won't see it in that light, Papa.'

'No?' He shrugged, and held out his cup to her. 'Thank you. I wouldn't admit as much to anyone else, Nell, but to be honest about it, Margaret Cairns has been a millstone about his neck ever since I've known him.'

Helen shifted uneasily in her chair. 'She may have been an invalid, but I'm sure . . .'

'Invalid? For Heaven's sake, the woman was mad. Why pretend otherwise? She lived in the country, with a keeper!'

He looked at her speculatively from beneath his finely arched brows, still dark although his hair had long been grey. The piquant contrast made him seem younger than his years, as though he had greyed prematurely.

29

'Between you and me, Nell, it's the best thing that could happen as far as he's concerned. He's already been a widower for years, for all practical purposes . . .' The insensitive phrase drew a reproachful look, but he was continuing, oblivious, '. . . believe me, Patrick Cairns will be married again as soon as his year's mourning is up, if he even waits so long.'

'Perhaps, but I suppose it's no concern of ours,' she said, with a placatory smile to soften the implied criticism.

'I don't know so much about that, Nell. I've thought more than once that he's the sort of man who might suit you.' His tone was so casual that at first she did not fully grasp his meaning. But as the significance of his off-hand remark struck her, the colour rose in her cheeks.

'The sort of man? What might that be?' She checked herself, and attempted a lighter tone. 'Besides, I don't know that I want to be suited, as you put it. I feel quite well suited in my present life!'

She roused no answering smile. Indeed, he frowned a little, and set down his cup with a chink of disapproval. She continued hurriedly. 'Such a thing would be quite impossible in any case. Who would take care of the house, the children, preside over your table? Sophie is far too young. I could not think of abandoning my duty when I am so much needed here.'

He wiped his lips with his napkin. 'You musn't allow such considerations too much weight, you know,' he said slowly. 'I'm sure you're invaluable here, but that ought to be the last thing thought of where your happiness is at stake . . .'

'But my happiness is to be here with you and the children!' she exclaimed.

She broke off, as a shade of impatience passed over his face. His mouth, usually set in a curve of good-humoured indulgence, twisted as at some gauche blunder.

'Quite, quite . . . all very well and proper, my dear girl, but all the same don't let your copy-book sentiments blind you to your own best interests. You could do worse than Pat Cairns.'

'My best interests are quite satisfied by remaining here! And Doctor Cairns must be at least fifteen years older than I am!'

'If it were twenty, it need not signify.' He rose abruptly, pushing back his chair with a force which set the tea-spoons clattering in the saucers. 'By the bye, while I think of it – you might just call on Miss Raymond. They still know very few families in Edinburgh.'

'Certainly, Papa. I shall attend to it on our return from Melrose.'

'Need it be put off? What's to prevent an earlier date – today, for that matter? I hardly think some little show of attention to the granddaughter of my publisher and oldest friend need require three months' notice.'

She recognised his tone; he would not be managed. 'I'll call this morning.'

'Good girl!' He put his arm about her shoulder in his easy way. For once, the affectionate gesture gave her no pleasure.

Helen dressed for the call with unusual care. In general, although she had a natural sureness of taste in colour and line, she devoted little time to her appearance. The simplicity of effect which resulted was far from unflattering to one of her tall build.

This morning, however, her swift, instinctive judgement deserted her. She was still not completely dressed when Sophie hurried into the room.

'I'm sorry to keep you waiting, Helen . . . Mrs Beattie thinks my lilac gloves may clean . . . why, you're not ready!'

'I beg your pardon, Sophie. I've been standing here these ten minutes and I'm still no further forward; what shall it be, the hat or the bonnet? Decide for me!'

Sophie picked up the bonnet and regarded it, her head on one side. It was a pretty straw with broad ribbon-ties of blue satin, trimmed inside the brim with blonde lace. She looked from it to the wide-awake Helen had put on. She was turning her head from side to side before the glass, anxious to see herself from every angle.

'I like the hat better. Bonnets are so fearfully proper.' Sophie tossed down the despised headgear. 'That's a darling of a feather. I must get myself a hat exactly the same for Melrose.'

Helen pursed her lips doubtfully and laid aside the dashing little hat. She picked up the bonnet again, and this time tied the ribbons with a purposeful air.

'What, the bonnet after all?'

'I think its propriety has won the day.'

'What a fuss for a morning call! There will be no gentlemen at home, I don't suppose?' Sophie replaced her sister before the pier-glass, and settled her neat Zouave jacket more snugly at the shoulder. She stroked its braided fronts with a smile of satisfaction.

'Sophie, how can you be so . . . so fast!'

'Fast? I would have to be very slow indeed to look forward with any relish to our morning's entertainment! All women together, sitting dutifully for ten minutes, Miss Raymond wishing us away just as heartily as we wish to be gone, and never a man or boy in sight to liven us up!' She gazed mischievously into the glass, watching her sister.

'Sophie, you're a tease,' Helen said calmly, drawing on her gloves. Sophie pouted, watching the effect in the glass. She tried the expression again, studying the shape of her lips. It struck her as not without its possibilities.

Helen picked up her shawl. 'Will you help me with this?'

Her sister deftly folded the soft cream square bordered with a pine-cone design. 'Mama's Indian shawl? My word, you are doing the magnificent!'

Helen made no reply. She was adjusting the folds of the shawl with frowning concentration, twisting round in a vain attempt to judge of the effect from behind.

'Really, Helen, let's be gone before I fall asleep! Indeed, I don't know why we're going today. Next week would have been time enough.'

'Papa wished it.'

'Oh, if Papa wished it, it's a different question!' she said, with a shrewd look at Helen. But engrossed in a final doubtful consultation before the glass, Helen did not respond, if she heard.

Susan Raymond lived no great distance away, in Castle Street. The morning was fair, and it was a pleasant walk through the New Town. The sisters made a striking pair, Sophie shorter, with quick lively movements, Helen more womanly in figure, carrying herself with a stately grace.

'I never thought Doctor Cairns would dance,' Sophie began, with an appraising glance at her sister's face. The shallow bonnet, worn far back on the head, as though slipping off, revealed her profile, framed by the smooth sweep of her hair. She seemed thoughtful.

'He is surprisingly light on his feet.'

'He seemed much in earnest about something during the waltz,' Sophie continued.

Helen frowned, remembering what had given rise to that unpleasant conversation – the sight of Susan Raymond almost lying back against her father's supporting arm, he bending eagerly forward over her upturned face, the flowers entwined in her hair beginning to tumble down in wilting disarray.

'Poor Doctor Cairns,' she said quickly, to dispel the vivid image, 'even as he danced, his wife lay dead.'

'It was fortunate that he didn't know. He would have been obliged to stay away.'

'Obliged! Sophie! His own feelings would not have permitted him to attend!' Perhaps her indignation was not the less warm because Sophie had voiced a thought which had already presented itself to her.

'One has to be reasonable. I never met the poor woman, any more than you did, but I'm sure her life was mere wretchedness to her, and no doubt to him too.'

'Oh, you're quite heartless!'

Sophie squeezed her arm. 'Helen, you're too good for this life! I may not be long out of the schoolroom but even I know that life's a scramble, and the Devil takes the hindermost. That particular gentleman won't catch me!'

'A scramble? After what? No, Sophie! Where would that leave compassion, and pity for the weak, and . . .'

'Oh, a sermon on such a beautiful morning!'

'What a pagan you are, Sophie!'

'An honest one, then, like Papa. In his case it comes of his precious Greek. I wonder that you haven't gone the same way. Why you ever induced him to teach you I can't imagine.'

'I wanted to be a help to him. I couldn't have made the fair copy of his book on Theognis without some knowledge of the language.'

'How you do sacrifice yourself!' Sophie said slyly.

Helen was honest enough to laugh. 'Of course, I enjoy it. Papa says I read Greek as well as any first-year student at the University, and better than many. I don't do so much prose-writing, but perhaps in time . . .'

'In time, you may find something else to occupy your thoughts,' Sophie interrupted briskly. She continued, apparently at random, 'Did you find Mr Bethune agreeable? I believe he never took his eyes off the door until you came back upstairs, and then he asked you to dance the moment you were disengaged.'

'Mr Bethune?' Helen said, a secret pleasure mingling with her surprise, as at unexpected flattery. 'He seemed pleasant enough. You danced with him, I noticed.'

'He waltzed tolerably, but he wasn't a very lively partner, was he? He held me as though he were afraid I might explode in his arms on the slightest provocation.'

'Really, I couldn't say,' Helen replied loftily, but not quite ingenuously. She knew very well what Sophie meant. 'I did wonder whether you might not think him personable?'

'Personable? With that hair? And sandy eyebrows?

Besides,' she added, with a little toss of her ringlets, 'didn't you find him rather dull?'

'Dull?'

'So correct! He spoke to me as though he were addressing a deaf, doitered old judge, or an exceptionally stupid jury. I'm surprised that he didn't appear in his wig; it might have improved him, at that!'

'You are perfectly wicked this morning,' Helen said, pulling her arm away from her sister's hand. 'You seem to feel justified in giving a wonderfully detailed reading of the poor man's character on the strength of a single waltz!'

'But waltzes are very revealing, don't you find? A warm arm about your waist, a pair of dark eyes gazing tenderly down . . .'

'Sophie, you are incorrigible. I'm sure I don't know what you mean.'

'You should have danced with Tom Hewitt,' said Sophie, with a smile.

Helen observed with some relief that Castle Street was in sight.

They handed their cards to a neat maidservant. As she carried them away, they exchanged a hopeful glance. Alas, the answer was favourable. Mrs Raymond was indisposed, and Miss Raymond was at present with her, but would be down directly, if the Miss Lamberts would be kind enough to wait . . .

There was no help for it. The Miss Lamberts were duly conducted into a morning-room to await their hostess.

During the constrained silence which followed upon the housemaid's departure Helen gazed about the room, the only diversion open to her. Spacious, with the high ceiling, the elaborate cornice, the indefinable rightness of proportion in doors and windows common to housing in the New Town, it had the confident, understated elegance of all such interiors.

What particular quality did the Raymonds bring to the almost indestructible grace of the room? There was the usual carefully negligent arrangement of books and ornaments, to suggest the clutter of a cultivated family. Was there perhaps a greater hollowness than usual in the fashionable pretence? The artifice in the display was visible; the effect was not of thoughtless disarray, but of calculation. To Helen, there was affectation in the neat clutter of netting silks spilling from the work-bag in such pretty confusion; they might have been arranged purposely, to figure in some still-life. She saw only contrivance in the music lying artlessly open on a side table as if for interrupted study, in the tasselled bookmark showing a considerable advance through a ponderous volume.

Seeing this, Helen's lips curled in disdain. She made it a point of some pride to read her Greek in the library only, scorning the easy triumph of leaving her books to be wondered at in the sitting-room. Her modesty won her much favourable comment amongst those visitors — the majority — who knew of her studies.

A rustle of silk along the passage gave the sisters warning; they composed their expressions before Miss Raymond entered in a flurry of apologies and exclamations of delight.

Seeing her in a less elaborate toilette, Helen realised that she was even smaller than she had thought, tiny almost. The word 'stunted' rose uncharitably in her mind; she pushed it aside, but it left a glow of reprehensible pleasure. Her complexion was pale, a strong contrast to her abundant black hair. Her face was heart-shaped, with a pointed chin and an enviably small mouth. In compensation, Helen noted, her teeth were poor. She seemed generally to smile without revealing them. The effect, to Helen's eyes, was singularly unappealing.

'Miss Lambert! And Miss Sophie! How sweet of you to call, and after such a fatiguing day, too!' She seated herself, with a silvery chime of chains and bracelets, of which she seemed inordinately fond. She took up that crouching, submissive-seeming posture which had affected Helen so disagreeably the previous night. It recalled to her a cat, gathering itself for mischief. 'What a delightful evening it was! I enjoyed it excessively, I do assure you.'

'I'm glad,' Helen replied shortly. Miss Raymond smiled, mouth coyly closed, and said nothing, as if to punish Helen's coldness. Her eyes, so dark that they seemed rather to absorb than to reflect light, never wavered from Helen's face, with predatory patience. Helen's innate courtesy betrayed her; as the silence grew to alarming proportions, she felt obliged to speak. 'You have not long lived in Edinburgh, I understand?'

'Since Easter only. My mother belonged to Edinburgh, of course; Grandpapa is Douglas Morton . . .'

'My father's publisher. Papa mentioned as much.'

'I was born here, but we left when I was quite a baby. Such perfect gypsies as we have been! But I believe we are settled at last. How it would have pleased my poor mother; she did so love Edinburgh.'

'Did your mother die quite recently, Miss Raymond?' Helen asked, in a softened tone. 'I see you are in half mourning.'

'Over a year ago,' she replied, with a sigh of the correct melancholy, absently smoothing the folds of her violet-coloured gown with her fine, taper fingers. The gesture displayed to perfection her white hands. 'Papa has remarried, you know,' she added, with a brave smile. 'I hope you will forgive my step-mother for not receiving you. She is in an interesting condition . . .' and she accompanied the words with a meaning glance.

'Oh, quite,' Helen murmured. She felt her eyes straying to the ormolu clock on the mantelpiece, and rallied her forces with a feeling of desperation. 'Do you enjoy living in Edinburgh?'

'Oh, more than anything! Such a quantity of social engagements! Really, it exceeds anything we have known before.' She adjusted a bracelet, her long nails trifling delicately with the clasp. 'Do you find the amount of entertaining to be undertaken a difficulty, Miss Lambert?'

'By no means. Papa moves largely amongst a set of literary men, artists, some of the University circle. It is not an ostentatious society.'

'You are a large family?'

'Nine. Only Kitty, Julia and little Phoebe are still in the nursery now. Philip and Andrew are at the Academy.'

'I believe I met your eldest brother last night. A charming young man, so high-spirited, and so like Mr Lambert!' Black, calculating, her eyes assessed the effect of the remark on her visitor. Helen made a sound of vague assent. She had no wish to enter into the subject of Jack's condition at the wedding.

As if following up her advantage, Susan Raymond continued playfully, 'So your sister has given you the green garter, Miss Lambert?'

'If the expression refers to any supposed envy on the part of the unmarried older sister, it was never so ill applied as in my case, I assure you.'

'I never thought such a thing! And no doubt you will soon be following her example . . . ?'

'I have no such intention.'

'Oh, I know how to estimate such denials, eh, Miss Sophie?' she said, nodding archly to the younger girl. 'I have seen it happen over and over again. Once the first break is made in the ranks, one marriage follows hot upon the other in a family.'

'Not in this family.'

'The management of so large an establishment must be a great responsibility to you,' Susan Raymond said, turning the subject slightly.

'I am so used to it that I scarcely think of it.' Another pause. It did not appear to discompose Miss Raymond. Little hands neatly folded, she watched Helen, who turned in silent desperation to Sophie, without response. Unnaturally demure, she sat with her eyes downcast.

'You cannot have known many of the guests last night,' was the best Helen could manage, in a frantic effort to scrabble together fuel to keep alive the last sparks of polite conversation for the requisite minutes.

'Oh, Mr Lambert was so kind that I did not feel a stranger for above a moment. He quite took me under his wing. And then there were some familiar faces. Doctor Cairns is quite an old friend, I assure you. Such a very Irish look as he has, don't you think? That black hair and blue eyes . . .'

'I did not know that you were acquainted,' Helen said, with an effort.

'Oh yes. Such a sad loss for the good doctor, is it not? He is bearing up bravely, though, as all his friends would wish.'

Helen's face showed her surprise.

'He was here this morning; what manly composure! If you had seen him, Miss Lambert. I did my best to offer what words of consolation I could . . . it was a delicate task, under the circumstances.' She leaned forward towards Helen, her pale face glowing with eager curiosity. 'I understand that his wife had been for many years an invalid?'

Helen rose, drawing herself up to her full height with the cold hauteur which always expressed her very fiercest anger. 'I'm sure that like all Doctor Cairns's friends – his true friends – you have too lively a respect for his domestic misfortune to wish to make them the subject of idle chat.'

The other woman, small and blackbrowed, smiled as though she had not perceived the snub. 'Must you go? I declare, I never knew a call to pass so quickly . . . I hope we may soon be able to repay your hospitality of last night, Miss Lambert. As soon as my step-mother is equal to it . . .'

'We shall be out of Edinburgh for three months.' Helen scarcely attempted to soften the rebuff.

'And Mr Lambert? Can he be spared for so long?'

'No,' Helen replied, with obscure unease. 'Papa usually remains here for much of the summer. Melrose is near enough for him to come down for the day or at the weekends, as his work allows.'

'Then we must invite him for dinner one evening. It would be quite a work of charity to attempt in our poor way to replace the joys of his family circle.'

Helen managed a smile of thanks. She left Castle Street in the throes of an emotion as novel as it was disagreeable, the uneasy sense that she had been outmanoeuvred.

She could hardly contain herself until they were a respectable distance from the house.

'Well!'

Sophie laughed.

'It's no laughing matter! What a little cat!'

'Why, Helen!'

'I'm sorry, but if I don't speak plainly to someone I shall . . . I shall burst!'

'Well then, have your say. I liked her no better than you.'

But despite her declared intention, Helen walked on in silence for a moment. At last she turned a troubled face to her sister. 'You don't think . . . ?'

'Papa?'

Helen nodded.

'"A charming young man, and so like Mr Lambert!" I only wonder it wasn't "Edward"!'

'Don't!'

'If she is making a play for Papa . . .'

'What an expression!'

'What else should I say? If she is, then she will succeed. I feel no doubt of that.'

'But why should she? After all, what can she be? Twenty-four or five, scarcely older than I am. Why should she wish to establish herself as step-mother to eight children still at home, with a widower twenty years her senior? She is not ill-looking, in her way,' Helen continued, suddenly finding remarkable comfort in a fact which, ten minutes before, she would have hotly disputed. 'I'm sure that she could hope for a more eligible match, without Papa's encumbrances.'

'Perhaps she has fallen in love with him,' Sophie suggested with a shrug.

'Now you're being simply ridiculous! How could she? He's . . . he's . . . ' She stopped, struggling for expression. 'At his age, most men are old.'

'Is he?'

'You know he's not!'

'Men far older than Papa marry, don't they? All that can be said is that she seemed to show an equal interest in her old friend, Doctor Cairns.'

'I don't believe they can be such friends as she gave out!'

'He had already told her of his loss,' Sophie pointed out acutely.

Helen frowned, then she cried in triumph, 'Mrs Raymond! She was indisposed; no doubt he had paid a professional call! It would be like him, not to give way to his private grief when his duties called.'

'No doubt he is bearing his sufferings patiently.'

Helen ignored her sister's dry tone. 'Did you see the look on her face when she asked about his wife? Oh, Sophie, how she would have loved to talk scandal!'

'Who doesn't?' Sophie asked calmly. 'For my part, I don't blame her if she's trying to establish herself. What's a woman to do, after all?'

'But that's so humiliating! To fish for a husband; is that all we live for? Thank Heavens I have no need to seek happiness in that way, like most women!'

'No?'

'I could not be happier than I already am,' she replied, with a shade of defiance. Only the day before, her tone would have been quite unclouded.

'Perhaps.' Sophie hesitated, as though even she scarcely dared tell Helen what was in her mind. She squeezed her arm, and said with unusual diffidence, 'Don't be vexed with me, Helen, but you will try not to take one of your pets against Miss Raymond, won't you?'

'One of my pets! What do you mean?'

'I only wanted to say that it might be prudent to conceal your feelings a little more. Miss Raymond can have been in no doubt as to your dislike just now.'

'Conceal my feelings? Why should I? She's a sly, underhand schemer. I don't like her and I see no reason to pretend to.'

Sophie sighed. 'And if she can persuade Papa that she can make him happy? Be like the rest of us, Helen, and don't make your dislikes quite so plain. It makes life so much easier.'

She glanced up at her sister. Her lips were set in the stubborn line which proclaimed how useless further argument would be. Sophie, a realist, said no more.

The approaching departure for Melrose occasioned as great an upheaval as a full-scale flitting. There were endless consultations with Mrs Beattie and the nursemaid over what was to be taken, and what left. The children's clothes had to be checked; at the last minute Helen decided that the girls really must have new straw bonnets, and Philip's elbows finally burst through his much-tried jacket. Every day brought some fresh requirement to light, and saw Helen and Sophie hurrying between shops, milliners and dressmakers.

They were at least spared Susan Raymond's return call. They came home from a visit to the boys' outfitters on South Bridge to find her card.

Sophie was a considerable help. Helen found herself relying upon her far more than she had ever been able to depend upon Rosemary, always so lazy, so bored by household concerns. As the very last days in Edinburgh approached, however, Sophie increasingly absented herself in a round of farewell visits to her friends. Chief among them was Margaret Hewitt. She appeared to have become Sophie's bosom friend since Rosemary's wedding.

In the general stir Jack's departure on his reading party passed almost unnoticed. He had been subdued since his outburst, and rarely at home. He told Helen that he was much engaged with the Grants, whose son he had been coaching for some months. She wondered at times whether he could in fact be spending his time on so innocent and praiseworthy an activity. Certainly, he had at times a hang-dog, wretched air which made his absence a source of relief, if not absolutely of pleasure.

But neither her puzzled concern over Jack nor the confusion of last-minute commissions kept Helen from the engagement which was for her the jewel of the week, her hour of Greek with her father.

Since he had acceded to her eager pleading and begun to teach her, ten years before, a Tuesday evening was held sacred for their lesson. Only the most urgent crises over unfinished articles and rapidly advancing publication dates were ever allowed to encroach upon that precious hour, which usually stretched to at least twice that. It held in her week a significance of which she would scarcely have known how to speak.

That week, Helen took her place beside her father at the library table as usual, her pleasure dimmed by the awareness that this must be their last lesson for weeks, months. During his visits to Melrose it might be difficult for her to claim so much of his undivided attention.

She had, as ever, prepared her work with scrupulous care despite all the pressing domestic duties of the past days. She opened her Aeschylus at the place where they had left off the previous week, and glanced at the passage before her. To her annoyance, she noticed an optative which had not struck her before; she frowned at the unexpected difficulty.

'Really, Helen, if you will scowl so, I shall begin to think that Greek is a mistake for your sex after all; you look exactly like an ill-tempered spinster governess.'

She looked up, scarcely believing that it could be

her father who was addressing her with such careless unkindness.

'I'm sure I didn't mean to scowl, Papa, only the optative in line 203 has thrown me rather.'

He glanced at it indifferently, and tossed the book aside. He rose and wandered over to the window.

'You might leave Sophie here for a week,' he said suddenly, looking out towards the gardens, his hands clasped behind his back, straight and elegant in his dress coat. 'I could run down with her next weekend, when you're settled in, and all that,' he continued, without turning. 'We could bring Miss Raymond with us, perhaps, if she would care to come. It's only a thought, she may be engaged. The poor girl doesn't get much diversion, I fancy. Her step-mother is all but confined to the house just at present. What do you think, Nell?' He turned towards her, his charming smile subtly constrained.

Her heart thudded in her breast. 'Shall I be frank, Papa?'

He frowned. 'By all means.'

'She is not the companion I would choose.'

His frown deepened. 'And why not?' Usually light and musical, his voice was taut with displeasure.

She stared wretchedly at the Greek letters before her. Normally she loved their fluid elegance, now they seemed alien, incomprehensible. Should she retract? No. A defiant honesty drove her on.

'To me she seems shallow, lacking in delicacy of feeling, in true refinement,' she said, trembling but determined.

'Not another word!' His voice was choked with an anger she had never heard before. 'Miss Raymond is a charming young woman. She may not have that superficial cleverness on which you pride yourself, quite excessively, I fear . . .' the hateful script distorted beneath her swimming gaze, 'but I can assure you that a knowledge of Greek is not essential if a girl is to be an ornament to society. I regret ever being persuaded to instruct you, if as a result you affect to despise another woman as shallow.

Shallow!' He turned abruptly away from her once more, his hands contorting behind his back.

'Indeed, Papa, you misunderstand me . . .' She could not continue her defence, her throat aching with the struggle to keep back her tears. Surely he could not really believe that it was Susan Raymond's ignorance of Greek which she found objectionable!

He spun round to face her. 'As for delicacy of feeling, refinement, it is possible for a girl to be not delicate but artificial, over-strained. Miss Raymond is a natural, lively young woman, most agreeable company. I would even go so far as to say that you might yourself learn from her. At times your own manner could with advantage be less cold. Take Rosemary's wedding; I saw you dancing with Cairns. You looked as if you hated the poor man! An ice-maiden! Pat Cairns is our oldest acquaintance, for Heaven's sake! Where's the harm in a little laughter, even a little nonsense? I tell you, Helen, it would do you more good than all the Greek in the Lexicon when it comes to finding a husband – though you seem to consider yourself above such things. I am sorry to say it,' he ended, with vicious righteousness, 'but there is nothing in all nature more objectionable than an unsexed, crabbed old maid, affecting to despise what others rightly prize.'

She fumbled for her book and fled from the room, stumbling against the arm of a chair in her blind haste.

Sophie was away from home, at a musical evening at the Hewitts'. Helen fell onto the white satin quilt of their bed and wept until her head ached. Her father's brutality had in a few moments betrayed a bond on the strength of which she would have staked her life. Good-humoured, easy in his temper, how could he have spoken to her so contemptuously?

All the pleasure she had ever found in their shared study of Greek seemed devalued; had she deceived herself in believing that he had liked to teach her?

Surely it had not all been false, the words of praise, the smiles as she mastered some new difficulty, the light

45

of appreciation in his eyes when she found some apt translation for a passage of particular beauty? How often he had said that Jack should show her quickness, her application! It had pleased him, once. Why had he changed?

Into her mind came the black, unreadable eyes, the drooping shoulders and small, smiling mouth of Susan Raymond. It was Helen's too-honest criticism of her which had brought down his wrath upon her head.

Her distress giving way to resentment, she roused herself and prepared for bed, fearing Sophie's imminent return. When at last her light steps were heard on the stair Helen feigned sleep, her face turned to the wall.

The next morning at breakfast her father treated her with coolness, as though she, not he, had been at fault. It wounded her, but stubbornness came to her aid. She tilted her chin defiantly, and replied coldly to his cold enquiries. For the first time in her life she saw her father leave the house and did not lift her cheek to him for a kiss.

4

None of Doctor Cairns's patients had cause to complain of neglect, despite his bereavement. In the days which followed his wife's death Mrs Raymond was not the only sufferer to see him by her bedside as usual. It was true that his mourning seemed to intensify the resigned sadness never far from his eyes, but his gentleness to those in need of his ministrations seemed to increase in the same proportion. He spoke to no one of his loss, although his departure from many a sickroom was the signal for prolonged discussion on the interesting question of his wife's history, and her likely successor.

As Edward Lambert had said, a great part of the doctor's practice, although the least profitable, lay amongst the poor of the Lawnmarket, the Canongate, the Cowgate and the Grassmarket, the unspeakable squalor of Leith Wynd and the packed lands of the Tron. At 314 per acre the density of population in such areas exceeded that of any town in Britain, with a death rate to match.

If the daily, senseless slaughter continued it was not owing to any want of effort on the part of Doctor Cairns. He fought death every inch of the way for every consumptive child, every fever-racked mother, every syphilitic prostitute and rickety infant. He grieved at every defeat, although to some, seeing the conditions under which his patients struggled to live, existence might have seemed to have little but familiarity to commend itself to the sufferer.

The Crearies were amongst his patients, although he stood towards them in an ambiguous relation, between doctor and guardian. Any fee would be far beyond Lizzie's means, as he well knew. He had attended Mrs

Crearie in her fatal illness, but Rab Crearie had been in work and money more plentiful in those days. Now, he called as often as he could without offending Lizzie's quick pride, touchy as that of any dowager for all her youth. When he could, he mingled a little gossip with his professional interest, making it as near a social call as he could, hoping to lessen her sense of indebtedness.

Within two days of his wife's funeral Doctor Cairns ventured to pay one of his infrequent calls, introducing himself as usual with the remark that, happening to be passing the close mouth, he thought he would just look in to see how the wean was coming along . . . And as usual, Lizzie stood thin and forbidding at the door, showing none of the pleasure she felt at seeing him, only her suspicion that he was about to give what she could never repay: his skill, his time, and very probably his remedies.

This time, as the moment of silence lengthened, it seemed that her independence would positively refuse him admission. From within came the sound of a cough, all too familiar to him. He renewed his efforts.

'Come, Lizzie, won't you let me come ben?' he coaxed. 'Here I've been thinking I'll get to take the weight off my feet for a minute or two, in a house kept so trig it's a pleasure to look about me . . .'

Despite herself the girl smiled, and stood aside to let him in.

His praise had been no more than the truth. Although it was still not much past nine in the morning the hearth was redded up, the bed neatly made and the mattress tucked away beneath it, all traces of breakfast had been cleared away and a pail of water stood in the corner. He glanced around him with genuine pleasure as he twitched at the knees of his trousers and seated himself by the fire.

'Now, where's the wee man himself?' He stretched out his hands as Lizzie brought the infant. For a moment, the child seemed to swither between fear and recognition, his eyes fixed doubtfully on the man's face.

48

Then, suddenly, uncertainty gave way to smiles, wide and toothless.

'As fine a baby as any in Edinburgh!' he said, looking up at the girl who hovered close by, seeming reluctant to leave her brother in any other hands, even his. 'He's a credit to you, Lizzie.'

For a second, pure delight lit her plain, unremarkable face. He dandled the baby on his knee a little while longer, talking solemn nonsense to him interspersed with questions to Lizzie which, in an off-hand way, elicited more information than many a more formal examination.

'You're a picture of health, Danny,' he concluded, handing the child back to his sister. 'You're a grand mother to him, Lizzie. Only show that child and any lady in the town would be running after you for a nursemaid . . .' Idly chatting, he got to his feet and looked around the room. 'And where's my wee favourite? Is that May, that great girl? What have you been feeding these bairns on, to make them grow?'

He patted first one pocket then another in a show of absent-minded bewilderment that brought May, pale and timid, stealing over from the bed-recess where she had been engrossed with a peg doll and a few scraps of calico.

'There! I knew I had them in one pocket or another! May, you'll find a home for these, I daresay?' He handed her a bulging paper poke. 'You'll give Joseph and Nettie their share, won't you? Even Lizzie, if she's not too grown up for sugar bools . . .' He continued to pat at his pockets, and drew out a stethoscope. 'You remember this, don't you? Shall we just listen to that chest of yours, now I've found it? Lizzie, if you don't mind . . . ?'

Lizzie propped the baby in a corner of the battered armchair, and began to help her sister to unbutton her bodice. The child stood patiently, still clutching the sweeties, breathing in and out as he told her to, while the stethoscope moved dispassionately over her thin chest. Her ribs rose and fell, showing with a fatal, delicate beauty like that of the stripped veins of a winter leaf. Trusting, mild, her eyes rested gravely on him.

He turned abruptly away, his examination complete. While Lizzie busied herself with May's dress he amused the baby, swinging his watch gently before him. Danny crowed and waved his podgy fists after the elusive glittering circle.

'Well?'

He turned to face Lizzie, and cleared his throat. 'Has your father found work yet?'

'No yet.'

'He's up north?'

'Aye. Seemingly there's railways being built; he'll no want for work much longer.'

'Good. And he'll send for you?'

'Aye, aye,' she said impatiently, 'but what's all this to do with the wee lassie?'

He looked cautiously over to where May was absorbed in dividing out the sugar bools. She stopped her task, watching them, knowing that she was the subject of their discussion.

He smiled reassuringly at her and said lightly, 'That cough of May's won't mend in the town, with all the smoke, the gasworks and tanneries and so on. She would do better in purer air. In a smaller town you might be able to find more than one room, that would help, too. The sooner your father can get settled work in a healthy situation and send for you all, the better.'

Lizzie shrugged. 'That's as may be, but what can I do?'

He considered his reply, passing his hand slowly over his cheeks, concealing his mouth. When he did answer it was cheerfully.

'Just carry on as you are doing, Lizzie, keeping the place sweet and clean, opening the window to give a good circulation of air whenever you can. Give May as much milk as you can manage, and nourishing food . . .' His cheerful tone faltered, then he resumed, almost as though he were ashamed of his own advice. 'When winter comes on try to keep her from chills; she should have warm clothing, strong shoes . . .' With every word his embarrassment grew, for he knew what a burden he was placing on the girl. Every one of his recommendations meant one thing to her, cruelly simple: money. 'Don't forget, though, about the window. The more ventilation the better.'

'More ventilation!' She flung herself across the room to the window, the fury and scorn in her voice telling him of her impotent misery, seizing on a tangible outlet.

'See this!' He looked at the window, so warped from the true that at one side the sash hung down a good half inch from the frame. 'Who needs to open windows? We get all the ventilation we want, aye, and more, whether they're open or no!'

He frowned, and scrutinised the ceiling. There was a crack, faint but distinct, running over the window. But what of it? He had seen far worse in these old tenements.

He picked up his bag and moved over to the door. It was always the most awkward moment, for it was then, he suspected, that the question of payment recurred most forcibly to Lizzie.

'How's your brother?' he asked, as she opened the door.

'Tam? He's fine, what for no?' she replied sharply.

'Will he be home soon? It wasn't so heavy a sentence this time, was it?'

'He'll be back after the Year, February.'

He nodded, knowing better than to pursue the subject, and stepped into the dim passage. Anyone observing him might well have wondered at how much his bereavement had aged him, for his shoulders were stooping more than ever, his walk even more shambling, as he left the Crearies' door.

Although by the time of their departure for Melrose relations between Helen and her father appeared to have improved, she at least was aware of a difference. Politeness had replaced familiarity. It was with a sense of relief that she felt the train drawing away at last from the station, and saw, minutes later, the startling mass of Arthur's Seat rising above the haze of smoke which hung over the Old Town.

She sorely missed Sophie's good humour during the journey. Even with the help of Miss Edgar, the ageing governess, it was no easy matter to quell the exuberance of five children in a railway carriage for almost two hours.

The house they had taken for the summer was situated not far from Melrose, to the east. It was a pleasant, substantial building, of reddish stone. It struck Helen as agreeably colourful, used as she was to Edinburgh's greys and duns. The grounds were extensive, and surrounded by a stout wall. Within them even Julia and Phoebe could be allowed complete freedom. The Tweed was a few minutes' walk away, and from the south-facing windows the Eildons were visible.

Despite the children's unquenchable excitement, chiefly expressed in clattering in and out of the house and up and down the stairs, whooping with delight at each new discovery, despite the doubtfully aired beds and the unaccountable want of milk, so particularly ordered, Helen's spirits began to lift as she explored her domain. Her father, she was sure, would relish their summer retreat. As eagerly as her brothers and sisters, though more decorously, she set herself to the congenial task of discovery and organisation.

The first full day of their stay in Melrose had been set aside for a visit to Rosemary, a little over two miles away at Newtown St Boswells. They took the train after breakfast; if the weather held, even Phoebe might be able to manage the walk back.

The Robertsons had taken a cottage a short distance from Newtown, on the road to Maxpoffle. It was a pleasant walk from the station, the road following the

Bowden Burn some way beneath. The boys raced ahead, their boots raising puffs of dust. Their bonnets hanging slackly back on their heads, Julia and Phoebe wandered along, bickering amicably; it seemed to be their preferred pastime.

Kitty, as usual, was left out. She hung heavily on Helen's arm, discoursing ponderously on the relative merits of the previous day's two sermons. Helen listened with half an ear, irritated. Big, clumsy, well-meaning, Kitty was painfully eager to win adult approval, her oldest sister's above all. With a sigh, Helen forced herself to express some opinion, selected at random, on the curate's delivery. Pleased by the show of interest, Kitty babbled on.

The Robertsons' cottage was considerably smaller than the house the Lamberts had taken. It had a small but pretty garden, where Rosemary was engaged in the lady-like and far from arduous task of cutting flowers.

'Helen!' She tilted back her head, in its suitably rural broad straw, and put out a plump cheek for a kiss. She looked about at her young brothers and sisters, already scattering over the garden. 'I don't know why you brought them all, I'm sure. There's no room for them indoors.'

'Of course I brought them all! Really, Rosemary!' Her sister's familiar querulous discontent was working its usual mischief on Helen's temper. She checked herself. 'They so much wanted to see you, dear. They'll be quite happy in the garden; perhaps you could have something cool brought out for them to drink?'

Rosemary sniffed. 'I have only the one cook-general, you know, and a girl for the rough . . .' She caught sight of her older sister's expression, and added pettishly, 'Oh, I'll see what Shaw can do. You have no conception of the difficulties of living in the country and keeping up a reasonable standard for one's husband.' Leaving her barbed comment to find its mark she turned on her heel and led the way into the cottage. Kitty began to

53

trail in after Helen. She always believed that her place lay with the older portion of the family, despite every discouragement.

Helen turned to her, flatteringly confidential. 'Kitty dear, I know I can rely on you to keep an eye on the children for me, can't I?' Kitty responded readily to the appeal, as Helen had known she would. Thankfully, Helen escaped into the dim coolness of the cottage.

'In there.' Rosemary gestured towards a room to the right of the passage. 'I'll go and have a word with Mrs Shaw. Perhaps she'll see her way to bringing us some tea; we may be lucky.'

Rosemary was absent for some time. When she returned she soused down in an armchair with an aggrieved air, as after some exceptional but unappreciated effort. 'Servants!' she muttered.

'Where's Harry?' asked Helen hurriedly, to forestall a tale of woe all too easy to predict.

'Out fishing. His cousin is down for the week. There won't be a salmon left in the Tweed soon.'

'His cousin?'

'Oh, Francis Bethune. Really, Helen, for a first visit to your newly married sister you aren't showing much interest in me. Don't you think marriage suits me?'

'I'm sorry? Oh, indeed. I don't think I ever saw you in better looks.' It was true. Although Rosemary's tendency to put on flesh was evident, it gave an opulence to her form which suited her. She was wearing a new blue skirt, trimmed at the hem with a broad band of darker blue. Her bodice was V-necked, filled by a lace-trimmed chemisette. With her Swiss belt of black velvet, her florid complexion and thick blonde hair she had the look of a healthy Tyrolean peasant, Helen thought with sisterly malice.

'I can recommend the state of matrimony,' Rosemary said, leaning back in her chair, and yawning. She eyed her older, unmarried sister speculatively, as though awaiting an enquiry which Helen had no intention of making. There was a heavy pause; Helen felt her colour rise.

'Matrimony is all very well, no doubt, for those who have no other duties. But who would look after Papa and the children?'

'Let Sophie take her turn. Where is she, by the way?'

'Still in Edinburgh. She comes down on Friday with Papa, and Miss Raymond.' She did her best to add the last words in a tone of unconcern, but Rosemary's face lit up at once.

'Miss Raymond? Really? Francis Bethune said something concerning the attention Papa paid her at our wedding dance. Oh, Helen, how extraordinary!'

Helen eyed her sister with some distaste. 'Mr Bethune must have seen more than I did.'

'I'm sure you were far too busy to notice such things, dear.'

Rosemary's patronising tone seemed to be one of the less desirable effects of matrimony. Helen cast about for a way to turn the subject. 'Is Mr Bethune enjoying his stay?' she asked, glancing out into the garden at the children.

'I assume he is. It's not always easy to discover quite what his feelings are.'

'Oh?'

'Perhaps he unbends when he's out with Harry, but with me he's polite to a fault. There's no ease in his manner at all.' She leaned forward and added with conspiratorial relish, 'There's a secret there, I believe.'

Dignity struggled with curiosity, briefly. 'Whatever do you mean?'

'If you look so very superior, I shan't tell you! You know you love a gossip as well as I do, so there's no need to pretend to be above such things,' said Rosemary calmly.

'I certainly do not wish to gossip about Mr Bethune, or anyone else,' Helen replied in her loftiest manner. 'On the other hand, I should be loath to trespass on some painful subject, out of ignorance . . .'

'Ah, I see!' Rosemary raised her brows in mocking comprehension. 'High-minded as ever, Helen; it's not idle curiosity, after all! Well, I'll not tease. Harry won't tell me the full story, if he knows it, but seemingly old Mr Bethune would have nothing to do with Francis after his wife's death. Francis was not more than eight at the time, his only son and only surviving child. They were never again under the same roof until Arthur Bethune was on his deathbed. Even then, it was only his sister's urging – Harry's mother – which persuaded him to see his son. Can you imagine?'

'But it's terrible! How could a man use his own son so cruelly! He could scarcely have been sane!'

Rosemary shrugged. 'Perhaps not. I suppose there was a reason of some sort behind it, but it cannot have been sufficient for such coldness.'

'What a sad life for a little boy! Where did he live?'

'He was sent to school in Edinburgh, and lived as a boarder in a lodging house, I believe. Harry's family were living through in the west at that time, but he went to them for holidays. That's why he and Harry are so close . . . at least, as close as anyone can be to such a model of correctness.'

'I am glad that you mentioned this, Rosemary. Only think, what unfortunate questions I might have asked, in all innocence!'

'Perhaps you should ask them anyway; I'll never get the full story from Harry.'

'I will do no such thing! Oh, listen to that! Whatever can the boys be at? Heavens, that branch will be broken in another second!' and Helen darted from the room before her sister had even risen to her feet.

Not without making Helen fully sensible of the effort involved, Rosemary, or rather her cook, produced a plain but adequate luncheon for the children, and was even induced to join them that afternoon in a stroll, if not absolutely up the Eildons at least between them. From there Helen could easily have taken the children home on foot, but she allowed herself to be persuaded that it would be better to accompany Rosemary back to Bowden Cottage, and indulge the boys with another train journey.

Harry and his cousin had not arrived home in their absence, nor did they put in an an appearance during the hour or so which elapsed before Helen considered the little girls sufficiently rested for the walk back to the station.

'We must be going, if we are to catch the train,' she said at last, pulling on her gloves with something of reluctance. 'You must come to us for dinner one evening. When shall it be?'

'Friday or Saturday? I should so like to meet the fascinating Miss Raymond!'

'I don't know whether we could entertain so large a party before we are well settled in,' Helen said, frowning in concentration as she busied herself with buttoning her glove. 'You will be bringing Mr Bethune, I suppose?'

'Oh, we wouldn't strain your domestic resources so far!' Rosemary said, with some asperity. 'I'll explain your difficulties, and he can dine here alone, off a chop and a piece of pie. It will be all one to him . . . '

'He will do no such thing! The very idea! Bring him by all means, but let it be tomorrow, or even better, Thursday.'

'Thursday then, if it can't be the weekend,' Rosemary agreed, still in a huff. 'The six o'clock train? You can arrange for a fly to bring us back, I suppose.'

It was settled. Helen gathered her brothers and sisters for the dusty walk back into Newtown. Beside her Kitty poured out her artless confidences, unheeded as the rippling burn at the foot of the slope. Helen's eyes, and all her attention, were fixed on the road ahead although they met not a single traveller to reward her concentration.

Helen devoted herself to planning the coming dinner with real pleasure. Long accustomed to managing her father's hospitality in Edinburgh, entertaining held no terrors for her, although in a strange house there was the challenge of a kitchen less well equipped and servants not all habituated to her ways. Mrs Beattie was with them, and the cook, but MacRoberts remained in Edinburgh. Helen debated whether to make enquiries in Melrose for a man to wait at table for the occasion, but decided against it. After all, there was no need to impress Rosemary and Harry, or Francis Bethune for that matter.

Nevertheless, she held long discussions with her own and the locally recruited kitchen staff. She conducted a full inventory of fish-kettles and shapes, and examined the potential of the local grocers, butchers and pastry-cooks with ruthless urban eyes. Finally, after many modifications, a menu was devised which seemed safely within the capabilities of Mrs Beattie and her untried assistants, and a generous order was placed at the wine-merchants'. Helen had seen many an indifferent meal redeemed by their produce.

There remained the difficulty of dress. It occupied Helen's thoughts little less than the food. On the one hand, Mr Bethune's presence raised the occasion above the ranks of quiet family dinners. On the other, the small numbers and his near relationship to her brother-in-law made her doubt the suitability of too showy a dinner gown.

Eventually she arrived at what she hoped would be an acceptable toilette. She wore a gown of pale rose pink, in a light velvet, but added a deep lace bertha to moderate its décolletage.

She had her hair dressed something in the Madonna style, parted in the centre and looped back from her face at the sides in smooth, shining waves. She was amused to find how anxiously she scrutinised her appearance. It was the effect of a rustication of less than a week, she supposed, that she should feel such nervousness before so trifling an engagement. In Edinburgh she had faced without a qualm far grander parties than Harry and Rosemary, and Francis Bethune.

From the drawing-room window she could command a view of the gravel sweep and, beyond the wall, the road to Melrose. She stood in the embrasure, watching for her guests' arrival. It would be the first occasion on which she would have to cede precedence to Rosemary as a married woman. Her lips compressed; it was a galling thought. Rosemary would enjoy it.

Still, her heart lifted, with a little stirring of pleasurable apprehension at the thought of the evening ahead. She envisaged herself calmly crossing the drawing-room to greet her guests, smiling in welcome . . . She turned to the door; Mrs Beattie, hot and flustered, was hurrying in.

'Oh, Miss Lambert, that fish that came down by the early train is stinking; you couldn't give it to a cat! And the cream's been left in the sun . . . shall I send out for more? Or shall I serve the dessert without the meringues?'

'I'll come down,' said Helen in dismay, hastily running through the depleted menu in her mind.

The kitchen was far from the well-ordered scene of activity she expected. The little kitchenmaid's tear-stained face suggested her guilt in the matter of the cream; she was still sobbing as she stirred the white sauce, destined for the sweetbreads. The cook looked truculent, there was an ominous smell of burning from the range, and no very close approach to the fish was necessary to persuade Helen that Mrs Beattie's diagnosis had been correct.

'There's nothing to be done about the fish; let me taste the cream . . . no, that won't do. We'll not use the meringues. Didn't we bring down a jar of bottled apricots? The ones Miss Anderson gave us, preserved in brandy?'

'I have them in my room, Miss Lambert.'

'Bring them, then, if you would be so kind, Mrs Beattie. They will be useful in the dessert . . . is the kail not catching, Mrs Lowther?'

59

In the middle of the new crisis, as Helen hurried to prevent the cook from scraping the burnt kail into the redeemable, the bell rang. Helen jumped; she was not accustomed to hearing its summons from such close quarters.

'Don't touch the kail until Mrs Beattie comes back!' she said, picking up her skirts and turning to go. 'And mind and check the apricots for mould!'

Her guests had already been shown into the drawing-room when she reached it. Her cheeks, as she could feel only too well by their warmth, were flushed from the heat of the kitchen. She passed her hand nervously over her lips as she entered, seized by the sudden fear that a trace of cream might be lingering there. It was all she could do to prevent herself from dusting off her velvet skirts from any flour which might be adhering to them.

She saw Rosemary's smile of greeting broaden into amusement at the sight of her older sister, the practised hostess, caught in a last-minute flurry of activity, scurrying red-faced up the stairs like any scatterbrained housemaid.

'How warm you look, Helen!' she said deliberately, destroying any tenuous hope that her colour might escape notice. In her annoyance, Helen's manner took on a distant hauteur, very far from the friendly composure of the welcome she had planned.

'Helen!' Harry Robertson stepped forward, and kissed her heartily, it being their first meeting since the wedding. 'You know my cousin, of course?' He put his arm about Francis Bethune's shoulders and drew him forward. He seemed to bear the easy affection stiffly, almost pulling away from Harry. Helen gave him her hand; he barely touched it, half bowing. She could have wept in vexation at the awkwardness of the moment to which she had so looked forward.

It soon became clear, however, that no party of which Harry Robertson made one could be for long ill at ease. Good-humoured, good-natured, he devoted himself with equal gusto to his dinner and the conversation. At first Helen was too much under the shadow of her early embarrassment to second his attempts at sociability. Fortunately, he seemed happy to run on without assistance, for Francis Bethune said little and Rosemary's attention was chiefly given to her plate.

Rosemary, Helen observed, had scorned the reticence of a bertha. Her gown, of magenta, the queen of colours, was startlingly low-cut, it seemed to Helen. She felt oddly uncomfortable at the sight of her sister's plump white shoulders and unashamedly swelling breasts. Her own confusion puzzled her; she must have sat at the same table as Rosemary a hundred times in gowns as revealing, and thought nothing of it. But tonight, somehow, she could have wished her sister had been more discreet.

As the meal progressed without a flaw Helen gradually regained her confidence. She was quite happy to listen to Harry talking, and smile at his anecdotes. She looked from him to his cousin, as Harry carved the saddle of mutton. There seemed little resemblance between the two men either in appearance or disposition. Harry's hair was dark and curling; he wore flourishing whiskers, almost meeting under his chin. His features were irregular, so that in repose he might have seemed ugly but for the good nature and animal spirits which enlivened them. Bluff, ruddy, energetic, he seemed to throw himself with gusto into whatever he did.

Beside his cousin's exuberance, Francis Bethune's manner appeared all the more restrained and lacking in spontaneity. He was not, she noticed, absolutely free from the besetting masculine fault, a tendency to treat conversation as a duel. Harry was not, it was true, always perfectly consistent in the ideas and opinions he voiced with such rapidity. So infectious were his enthusiasms that she would not have been aware of any contradictions, but for Francis Bethune's cool interventions. With invariable logic he pointed out here a flaw in his cousin's argument, there a discrepancy with what he had already said.

At first Harry took the corrections in good part, but eventually even his patience was ruffled.

'Really, Francis! Can't a man express his opinions over a family dinner without feeling on trial for his life?' he said, only half joking. 'You should lay aside your professional character with your wig, you know.'

Francis Bethune shrugged. 'You must own that you contradicted yourself quite plainly. You say that there is a shortage of housing and in the next breath you tell us that much of the accommodation already available in the Old Town should be razed to the ground. Will that lessen overcrowding? I am no architect, but I should have predicted quite a different result.'

'Of course new houses must be built to replace the old!' Harry laid aside his knife and fork in his eager pursuit of the argument. 'Decent housing at a price the labouring classes can afford; that's the need, not the genteel villas in the Grange which is all that Robertson's, or any other architects in the city, are being asked to produce!'

'And why? Because there is a demand for houses of the better sort: they sell. It is the operation of market forces, pure and simple. If a building project offers a profitable return it will be undertaken. Houses for artisans do not.'

'And so nothing is to be done? The Canongate, the Cowgate and the rest are to remain for ever what they are now, full of hovels in which you would not kennel a dog? No, Francis!'

Francis Bethune shrugged. 'What would you do, then? Reduce the present housing stock and increase overcrowding? Tamper with the rights of property owners to let their rooms as they choose? Introduce the foreign element of benevolence into the market by philanthropic schemes? Do so, and you deflect the natural impetus of capital, and it is capital alone, in its search for profitable investment, which can build in any quantity.'

Harry ran his fingers impatiently through his hair, and

leaned forward over the table to his cousin, still imperturbably eating his mutton. 'Well, where are the houses built by private capital? Look at all the tenements which have been demolished in recent years. Decent accommodation destroyed on the Castlehill to build three churches; two hundred dwellings taken down for the erection of George IV Bridge – how many more for Lord Cockburn Street? Housing removed at Holyrood to improve the amenities of a royal park; displaced for railway stations, for public buildings . . . has the market rushed to replace them? You know it has not!'

'Oh, Harry, eat your dinner, do!' his wife interposed fretfully. 'Keep your arguments for the claret.'

'No, please! I'm sure it is a subject which ought to concern us, although it is so rarely discussed,' Helen said, speaking to the two men without distinction, Harry flushed and vehement, his cousin still cool, seeming to treat the question as a purely abstract exercise. 'Harry, as an architect you must have an understanding of the facts which few can equal.'

'There are thousands in the closes off the High Street who understand it far better!'

Francis Bethune made a sound of stifled annoyance. 'Are you not being sentimental? You are judging these people by your own standards. Because you are accustomed to calm and regularity you imagine that others long for it; because you like to be clean you do not believe that others may be indifferent to dirt.'

'Francis, if I didn't know that your heart is better than your head you and I should fall out! Indifferent to dirt! How highly would you value cleanliness if you were a poor woman with seven of a family living six storeys up, and no water in the house? Every drop to be fetched from a public well, every drop to be queued for whatever the weather, and then hauled up a long stair, perhaps with one bairn at your skirts and another in your arms? You can't imagine it because you daren't. If you did, your complacency would be shattered. You, and all the comfortable, respectable folk in the city are wilfully blind to the festering sore in our midst . . .'

'Harry, really!' His wife's protest was more severe now. 'Is that the language for the dinner table?'

'Language? Words would fail me if I were to try and tell you what I saw in my student days, five or six years ago. I went with a surveyor, investigating the drainage of Leith Wynd. We entered cellar dwellings flooded by sewage: human beings actually lived there! There was not a soil-pipe in the tenement. All the refuse, all the filth of the building was flung down into the court.'

He paused, and looked at his cousin. The same intellectual pleasure in debate was visible in the latter's keen, half-smiling face. Harry resumed, deliberately. 'I looked out through a window on the ground flat. There was a roof projecting immediately outside. It received the impact of what was thrown down. On it hung accretions of filth, the accumulations of years, like stalactites . . .'

'Harry, you are forgetting that there are ladies present,' his cousin broke in, the first signs of anger in his voice.

'No, it's not to be spoken of before my wife and her sister! But other men's wives and sisters live in such degradation, and die in it often enough!' He clenched his fist, and for a second Helen feared for the wine glasses. But when he spoke again, it was in a calmer tone, his gravity all the more impressive for the contrast with his habitual good humour.

'I tell you in all seriousness, Francis: not long after I had seen those cellars some of the tenements in Leith Wynd were condemned as unsafe and pulled down. The Happy Land, do you recall? It would have been in '54, I think. The ruins are there to this day, where the penny theatre is. Private capital has not replaced them by decent housing, by the way. The timbers were rotten, the walls were cracked from top to bottom. They leaned so badly that it was a wonder they still stood. But do you know, when I heard that the tenants had been given notice to quit and that demolition was to begin, I was almost sorry.'

He paused, to allow his hearers to appreciate the full significance of his words. 'Perhaps if that land had fallen, and its wretched inhabitants had been killed in sufficient numbers, perhaps that might have woken douce, well-doing Edinburgh from its complacency. It will take nothing less, I fear. Just suppose that some such catastrophe had occurred six years ago, and improvements had resulted. I wonder how many lives would have been saved since then? How many have died each week of those six years from the diseases of dirt and overcrowding? Think of it, a silent execution each week, from cholera and fever and phthisis; but who cares?'

There was a silence. Harry picked up his neglected knife and fork and applied himself to his congealing mutton. Helen saw Mrs Beattie regard her guest with a mixture of awe and disapproval as she waited to remove the plates. Heaven only knew what reputation Rosemary's husband would now bear in the kitchen.

5

As if by common consent the subject was dropped and they spoke of less contentious things. Only Rosemary, however, seemed able to devote herself with any relish to the food or the conversation. An air of unreality pervaded whatever other topic was started, hung over the spotless table-linen, the rose-filled epergne, the wine which glowed in their glasses.

At last the dessert was brought, the cloth removed, and Mrs Beattie and her assistant dismissed. There was a pause as the dessert wines circulated. Helen looked at Francis Bethune with a sense of anticipation. He had allowed Harry the last word, and yet she felt sure that he was not the man to be worsted in debate.

He sat back from the table a little, upright in his chair, and slowly turned the glass before him by its stem, as though he had never before seen so rich a red, or perhaps was not seeing it at all.

'I come back to my point, Harry,' he said, with an abruptness which was only apparent; the interrupted talk was fresh in everyone's mind. 'You take too simple a view of the matter. You can't coddle the working man. Try it, and you destroy his dignity, you pauperise him. Those who find the conditions you so graphically depicted unbearable will exert themselves to improve their lot. Those of a grosser sensibility will remain, the clartier the cosier, in the telling old phrase.'

'What a neat appointment on the part of Providence! How fortunate for us! We can leave it to nature! Those who feel the little inconveniences of their situation will leave; we need waste no sympathy on the callous wretches who remain, because they are quite insensible to dirt and overcrowding. We can safely leave them to wallow in their own filth, happy as pigs on a midden. There is no problem, after all!'

Francis Bethune showed no sign of discomposure at his cousin's sarcasm. He replied calmly, as though to a child who was querying the operation of some natural law.

'You exaggerate the effect of such conditions on those who live in them. Don't forget, our grandparents, even the finest of them, lived in these same tenements. They contrived to get along in the most perfect contentment without the conveniences we now enjoy. A hundred years ago who felt themselves outraged by the arrangements for street cleaning in the Old Town? And since the cholera, they are much improved from those days . . . I tell you, Harry, better men – and women – than your profligates in Leith Wynd endured the same regulations without complaint.'

'There is no comparison! I don't deny that the lands of the Lawnmarket and the Canongate were once accommodation as fine as any in the kingdom, but what has happened to them since the gentry flocked north to the New Town and now south to the Grange? Apartments which were once spacious have been divided over and over again, to cram in as many bodies as possible, packed like herrings in a barrel!'

'But do you think they feel it a hardship? There is no shortage of takers for rooms, I can assure you. The closer they huddle together the better they must like it. You're judging them by an alien standard; they live as they choose, not as you think they should. Consider, for example, the enormous sums expended by the labouring classes on alcohol. With thrift, how many of those now living in a single room in the Grassmarket could not instead occupy a larger property, in one of the humbler streets of the New Town perhaps? Rose Street, Jamaica Street . . . But if they choose to dissipate on drink what they could spend on better housing why should more prudent folk save them from the clear consequences of their indulgence?'

'You enjoy a good claret, as I do myself. Why should you begrudge a coal-heaver, a navvy, a scavenger, his beer or his dram at the end of a day's work?'

'I don't begrudge them whatever they may choose to spend their money on. I'm not a temperance reformer. I don't abstain, nor do I urge abstention on others. But to be blunt, I can afford it and they cannot. If for any reason I could no longer maintain the standards usual among our class, then I would cease to have my table supplied with wine. If economy were necessary I would make the saving without repining.'

'I'm sure you would. You're young and gifted, and free from family responsibilities. You would retrench, and work for better days. But if you saw no hope of those days? If what you would save by denying yourself that pleasure were so pitifully small that it offered no real prospect of improvement? Would it not be unbearably tempting to seize on at least one certain immediate escape from the everyday grind? Secure in all that makes life pleasant, you're preaching virtues to the poor which you're unlikely to be required to practise yourself.'

'You would say I am a hypocrite, in fact?' Bethune said, quite dispassionately.

'I was speaking of attitudes all too commonly found amongst our class, even amongst those with consciences more tender than yours. Many will mouth some benevolent platitude or other, but how many are ready to give the poor, the industrious classes, what they truly need: not charity, but justice?'

'Take care, Harry, you are on dangerous ground. I am no authority on soil-pipes and domestic economy, but I can claim some expertise in the legal department!'

'Let's suppose that a man build a house without proper foundations, without effective support for the walls, using inferior materials and unskilled workmen. Suppose that house fall and kill its inhabitants; he would be liable for culpable neglect, would he not? But if his wretched tenants die instead from diseases born of insanitary conditions and an entire absence of ventilation? He can hold up his head, enjoy his comfortable dinner in his stone-built villa — paid for by the grossly inflated returns on his investment. I tell you, some of these slum landlords are paid in blood! It may be legal, but is it just?'

For the first time a certain unease was showing in Francis Bethune's manner. He was fidgeting with his collar, and seemed to Helen to wish to be done with the subject. 'It's impossible to discuss the question in such terms, Harry. Capital has a right to a return on outlay . . .'

'Capital has a right?' Harry thrust his chair back from the table; for a second Helen thought he would seize his cousin and shake him. Instead, his anger found vent in his voice, raised almost to a shout. 'What right do tenants have? Not a one, in your precious law!'

'Really, Harry,' Rosemary put in crossly, dabbing at her skirt. 'Need you be so warm? My skirt is quite spoiled with madeira splashing on it; must you hurl the table about so?'

'Well, you have described what you see as the problem. What is your solution?' Francis Bethune asked, as Harry hushed his wife with a distracted gesture.

'I would oblige the owner of every dwelling in the city to install proper conveniences and an adequate water supply. They have been raking in their profits for long enough, let them face the outlay. Make no mistake about it, these tumbledown tenements bring in a higher return on capital than buildings of a better sort. If you calculate by area the poor pay from twenty to fifty per cent more for their miserable holes than the more prosperous . . .'

'But the fact remains that in a free market prices are set by the willingness of the purchaser to pay. So long as there are tenants willing to give the rents . . .'

'Willing? What else can they do? Where else can they go? Housing is not to be had as easily as you seem to think. If you were bringing up a family on twelve shillings a week, you would not have many choices!'

'Helen, shall we go up?' Rosemary said, rising abruptly to her feet. 'I positively refuse to endure another moment!'

Harry laughed. 'Poor Rosie, how we've neglected you! What do you say to an after-dinner stroll with the ladies, Frank?'

'I don't believe I could lift a glass of Miss Lambert's excellent claret to my lips without uneasy thoughts of coal-heavers and worthy scavengers. A walk would be delightful.'

'For my part, I can admire the grounds quite adequately from the drawing-room windows,' said Rosemary, already at the door. 'Come along, Helen; I'm sure the evening air will be horrid and unwholesome, so near the river as you are.'

'We needn't stay out long . . .' Helen murmured, looking wistfully out at the garden.

'Come, Rosie, the exercise will do you good.'

His wife glowered at Harry, her mouth set in a mutinous pout. He should have known better than to make even so indirect a reference to her corpulence.

'I am going up to the drawing-room. I have no wish to catch a chill in the damp evening air, dressed as I am,' and she glanced down at her full breasts, half exposed by her low dress, startlingly white against its rich magenta, and raised her eyes to her husband, with a smile which struck Helen as peculiarly vulgar.

She felt a moment of anger. 'You won't mind waiting for your tea? I shall go out at any rate.' She looked to her brother-in-law for support. He glanced uncertainly at his wife.

'Harry?' Rosemary paused in the doorway, her gaze lingering on his face.

'Another evening perhaps, Helen . . .' he said with a shrug of resignation.

She was about to follow Rosemary's triumphant white

70

shoulders when she felt a touch at her elbow. She turned in surprise. Francis Bethune was offering her his arm.

'If Miss Lambert would be satisfied with my company I should be delighted to see the grounds.'

The thought of keeping Rosemary waiting for her tea had a certain reprehensible charm. 'Thank you. I shall just get a shawl . . . tell Rosemary we shan't be long, Harry.'

In fact the evening was still so warm that she scarcely needed her wrap. She allowed it to hang loosely open, luxuriating in the sensation of the mild, still air against her exposed neck and arms.

'It is a beautiful evening.'

'Most unlike Edinburgh.' She rested her hand lightly on his arm as they began to stroll down the gravel sweep. 'Rosemary has missed herself, as they say.'

'To the newly married the beauties of nature are very small beer, no doubt.'

'Rosemary never was an enthusiast for them. Marriage hasn't changed her,' she said, rather more severely than she had intended.

'You and she are very different.'

'As different as you and Harry, perhaps?'

'We are only cousins, but as children we were as much together as some brothers. Yes, we differ in almost every respect. It does not destroy our good relations, though. It is one of the great blessings of a family, I suppose.'

The light was still good, the sky a serene ocean dotted with islets of cloud. She watched his face as he spoke; it showed a resignation, almost a sadness which recalled to her Rosemary's story of his lonely childhood. She cast about for a question which might encourage him to say more, but he was already continuing on a new train of thought.

'I hope our discussion was not tedious to you?'

'By no means. Such issues should be given every consideration.'

'And your opinion?'

71

She was surprised, and pleased. It was not an idle question; he was regarding her as earnestly as though he really cared what answer she would make. 'You were both able advocates. Really, I was swayed by the last speaker.'

'I know that it is easy to sympathise with the indignation Harry expressed. He really feels it, to his credit.'

'But?'

He laughed, the delicate skin crinkling pleasantly about his eyes. 'You are very perceptive. My objection, then, is this: sentiment ought not to be the only or even the main influence on action, as individuals or corporately. If we allow ourselves to be washed away on a tide of emotion we soon lose our sense of direction, and our ability to control events. However appalled we may be by conditions of the sort Harry described we owe it to the poor not to seek a remedy which would only worsen their plight.' He paused, and she saw again the look of awkwardness which she had already marked. 'I feel that I should confess an interest; I believe I am myself one of the rapacious landlords of whom Harry spoke so feelingly. I could almost have looked at my hands expecting to see them dabbled in gore.' He laughed again, less easily.

'You *believe* you are a landlord?'

'I'm sorry, I should have explained. I have not myself ever made any purchases of old property but I did inherit some from my father. It is in the hands of a factor. I take no active part in its management, and am certainly far from any design to grind the faces of the poor, whatever Harry may choose to believe.'

'And are your holdings as bad . . . I mean, are they of the sort Harry mentioned?'

He cleared his throat. 'To be quite candid, I don't know anything of their condition. I have given MacGregor — the factor — standing instructions to see that they are kept weatherproof. I can say no more; I could not even tell you where the properties are situated, or even how many I possess. Do you find that strange? I don't

72

know whether surprise or horror is uppermost in your countenance.'

'I'm sorry.' She hastily composed her expression, feeling herself colour beneath his gaze. 'Yes, to be honest with you, I do find it strange that you should know so little of your property, and yet, after all, it is not uncommon, I suppose. My father has investments, but I have never enquired further into the question. I believe that he leaves such matters in the hands of his man of business, as you do.'

'So you, at least, will pardon my negligence?' he asked lightly. 'I should not wish to lose your good opinion so early in our acquaintance.'

It was the sort of mock-serious compliment which the young men of her father's circle had paid her at the dining table and in the drawingroom for the past seven years. She was well practised in accepting such idle banter with an equally light-hearted response, but now she was silent, for a moment as tongue-tied as the most bashful miss fresh from the schoolroom.

'I may add, although I would not have admitted as much to Harry, that I will take an early opportunity of seeing MacGregor and making some enquiry concerning the management of my properties. To that extent at least his rhetoric has been victorious. But you are smiling?'

'I was merely remembering Harry's remark, that your heart was better than your head.'

'Well might he say so, since my heart agrees with Harry in his outrage, but unlike him I don't consider that impulse to be a sound basis for action.'

'Who is to say that the instant, unreflecting response is not at times the correct one? Should we not be spurred to action by the sight of squalor and degradation? Are you not – forgive me – trying to reason away what you know in your heart?' As if to soften the criticism she placed her free hand on his sleeve, and then quickly removed it, reddening. His eyes fixed thoughtfully on the path ahead, he appeared not to observe the gesture.

They had reached the end of the drive. Before them was the gate, unlocked for the fly which had been ordered for eleven thirty. He stretched out his hand tentatively to the handle. 'Yes?' She nodded.

They turned to the right, towards the river, following the wall which enclosed the garden. Helen felt a surge of reckless delight. She was behaving badly, she supposed, in neglecting her sister by so prolonging their stroll. It was her duty to return; defiantly she turned away from the gate.

They walked on in silence for a moment. Overhead the trees which lined the garden within the wall swayed in a breeze so slight that it could almost have been created by their passage. Here and there a drooping branch over-hung the path; with a little laughing confusion Francis Bethune reached across to hold back the luxuriant greenery. The chance pressure of his shoulders against her arm, the momentary brush of her breast against him as she squeezed beneath his arm, uplifted to raise a sprawling branch, heavy with foliage, suddenly brought into her mind a sense of their unobserved companionship.

A blackbird interrupted its leisurely song, breaking off in a harsh clatter of alarm. They turned the corner of the wall. Before them, a short distance away, the tranquil sweep of the river.

'For scenes such as these I suppose you will allow the emotions free play?' she said, with a smile of greater freedom than she had used before, a smile Doctor Cairns would have recognised, or her father, vivacious, teasing.

'However great the beauty which surrounds us,' he said, with an emphasis which raised a flattering conjecture in her mind, 'I really cannot say that the emotions can be given absolute freedom. In the Garden of Eden it was possible, perhaps, but mankind has never found its way back to the Garden, alas.'

'You don't trust the emotions, in fact?'

'They must be held in check.' He gestured towards the river, running fast and deep, while swifts screamed and swooped over its waters. 'What, for example, would you think of me if, overcome by these pastoral charms, I were to fall into transports of joy, weeping uncontrollably?'

'And yet, where would the harm be?'

'In making the most intolerable exhibition of myself, in wallowing in sensibility without regard for the feelings of anyone else, like an infant, conscious only of its own imperious demands. How repulsive such a man would be!'

'As repulsive, perhaps, as one who never acted on impulse? Who was in all things cool and deliberate?' She spoke without realising that her words might be taken in a more personal sense than she had intended; only when she saw a frown gathering on his brow, his lips compressing in pain or displeasure did she understand her mistake. 'Oh, I did not of course mean any particular application . . .' She faltered into silence, dreading that she was making a bad case worse.

Her evident confusion, the distress in her eyes, must have spoken for her. His mouth relaxed into its habitual smile of rueful detachment. The moment passed, but left some residue of self-consciousness, as though they had unintentionally moved towards a greater intimacy than was quite comfortable.

'Is your whole family with you in Melrose?' he asked politely. She greeted the topic with relief.

'My brother Jack is away in the north with a reading party. He will return to Edinburgh, I believe, although we may see him in Melrose for a day or two. I hope he will come; his younger brothers adore him.'

'And Miss Sophie?'

'She is still in Edinburgh with Papa. They are to travel down on Friday.' She remembered what a striking couple Sophie and he had made in the waltz. It was curiously displeasing to picture; she shivered.

'You're cold?' he said instantly. 'Shall we turn?'

She looked at the path stretching temptingly before them, and sighed. 'Not in the slightest, but perhaps we should make our way back. Rosemary will be wondering what has happened to me . . .' Again, she ended awkwardly. She, usually so much at ease, seemed constantly to blunder, to feel herself clumsy and inept, in his company and his alone. Did he have the same effect on his every acquaintance, she wondered.

'Do you have no brothers or sisters?' she asked, not without hesitation although it was no very unusual question.

He did not answer at once, busying himself with smoothing the lining of his hat which he was turning between his hands. His head was slightly bowed and he devoted his full attention to the trifling task. On his reddish-brown hair where it was brushed back from his temples was the faintest of indentations, made by the brim of his hat. Her eye traced the line, just visible on his forehead. He had the delicacy of skin often found in those with red or chestnut hair.

When he did reply, his voice was so low and muffled that she could barely catch his words. His head was still bowed to attend to his troublesome hat-band: that must have made the difference, for his voice was usually clear, as befitted a man whose profession depended on his powers of speech.

'I had a sister. She died. It was within a week of my mother.'

'How terrible that must have been for you and your father!' She might have said more, but for the memory of Rosemary's hints.

'It was. I was eight years old. It was the end of my childhood, or at any rate of the happy portion of it.' He replaced his hat, settling it with the precision which seemed to mark his every movement. 'I was fortunate in receiving from the Robertsons the warmest of welcomes during holidays. There were six children; I was made a seventh. At least . . . it was my own fault if I was not. Only children are apt to be awkward, prickly creatures.'

She waited for him to continue, but he added nothing

to what he had said. Already the gate was in view; he held it open for her. The spreading skirts of her crinoline swept against his legs as she manoeuvred through the entrance, for he had opened only half of the double gate. Under any other circumstances she would scarcely have noticed the insignificant incident, but with him she had a vexing, half-pleasurable consciousness of any contact, however trifling. Her every sense seemed sharper.

As they moved up the drive beneath the shadowing trees she realised how dark it was becoming. In the open, by the river, she had not been aware of the fading light.

'How late it must be!' she exclaimed.

He reached for his watch, in the pocket of his waistcoat. Beneath the trees the light was so poor that they drew to a halt while he scrutinised the dial, holding it close to his face. She dropped her hand from his arm to allow him greater freedom.

'It is not far off ten,' he said, preparing to return the watch to its pocket. He was already offering her his arm once more when to her horror an indistinct white shape lurched across their path, so close that she felt on her skin the breeze of its passing. She gave an involuntary cry of alarm, almost a scream, and threw up her hands to her face.

In the same second she felt his arms about her, holding her close against his chest. Before she was aware of what she did, her face was buried against his shoulder. Against her cheek she felt the velvet of his collar, at once soft and resistant, as she breathed in the smell of the fine cloth of his dress coat. With it mingled another, faint, indescribable, the wholesome, pleasing smell of another human body. Alien, alluring, it filled her senses, strangely disturbing.

For a fraction of a second, she thought his arms were tightening about her, but it must have been an illusion for he released her, with some abruptness, before she had scarcely formed the thought.

'It was an owl.' His voice was gentle, but not quite steady. Was he laughing at her?

'How could I be so stupid?' She raised her eyes to his face, and hurriedly dropped them again. In the dusk his face was a dim white blur. His expression was unreadable, but he appeared to be regarding her with peculiar intentness. Certainly, he was not laughing.

He moved towards her, as though he would renew their embrace. She felt a curious stirring in her breast, as if her heart had turned over. He offered her his arm. She took it stiffly, barely laying the tips of her fingers on his sleeve. They walked on quickly, in constrained silence.

He raised his free hand to straighten his collar. 'I hope you can forgive the familiarity . . . it was not intentional . . .'

'Oh, please . . . don't give it another thought . . . I was most grateful . . . for the protection you meant to offer, that is . . .'

The phrases were as awkward, as embarrassed as his. They lapsed into silence again, she at least glad of the merciful darkness to conceal her heated cheeks.

On entering the house, they went at once to the drawing-room. The door was slightly ajar. He pushed it open for her, and stood aside. She entered, and stopped dead where she stood.

On the sofa near the fireplace sprawled her sister, half sitting, half reclining. Harry, seated beside her, was leaning over her. They were kissing; Rosemary's hands were moving in a slow caress over his back, and Harry's . . . Helen recoiled a step, catching her breath in shock at the sight of Harry's hand on her sister's opulent breast, his fingers almost lost to view where they plunged down beneath the bold magenta of her bodice.

At her gasp of horror, Harry spun round, ludicrous dismay in his flushed face.

'For Heaven's sake, Harry!' Francis Bethune strode across the drawing-room to the empty grate, his tread setting the dried grasses which hid the hearth trembling.

He stood with his back to the cold fireplace, looking down on his cousin.

Harry Robertson got to his feet, attempting ineffectually to smooth down his tousled hair. Helen was glad to see that he looked extremely sheepish. Not so her sister.

'Aren't you going to ring for tea now you're here at last?' she said coolly, not a whit abashed. 'I can't think what kept you so long.' The meaning smile which accompanied her words suggested that she had very definite ideas on that subject.

Helen rung the bell with angry energy, glaring down at her sister in disgust.

'Really, Helen,' Rosemary protested slyly. '*We* are married, after all.' The emphasis was almost more than Helen could bear.

'Not a day too soon, either!' she retorted, her composure vanishing at the sight of Rosemary's lazy, sensual smile. Her fingers itched to slap that plump, highly coloured cheek as they had done more than once in nursery days.

The timely arrival of the tea things imposed a truce. Helen devoted herself with relief to the homely ritual. It gave her temper the opportunity to settle, although she wished Rosemary's three lumps of sugar might give her toothache.

Helen had never in her life felt less inclined for conversation. If only the fly had been ordered for an hour earlier! But there was no help for it. The time must be got through somehow until half past eleven. With an effort she recalled herself to her duties as hostess.

'Mr Bethune, do you care for cards? Or music, perhaps? You may not have heard Rosemary sing. She has a fine contralto, if she would but practise.'

'Oh, I've given up my music altogether now. What use is it to me? But you must sing for us, Helen. I'm sure Francis would enjoy it.'

'You know I have no voice at all, beside you,' Helen said quickly, rising to take Francis Bethune's empty cup, her only desire to distract attention from Rosemary's insinuation. 'I certainly could not sing unaccompanied, and my playing is no use . . .'

'May I offer my services?'

She stopped, in the act of turning away with his cup. There was real kindness in his voice, as though he guessed something of her feelings, and sympathised.

'Do you play?'

'As a child I was boarded with a family which was remarkable for its musical gifts. It was natural to pass the time as they did. I am as tolerable a performer on the pianoforte as anyone can be without any real talent.'

Helen hesitated, and turned to her sister with some impulse of reconciliation. 'Rosemary, won't you sing? You know how much better you are than I . . . well then. I will see what music there is, Mr Bethune.'

There was a selection of ballads and Scottish songs – Helen hurriedly passed over any more ambitious pieces. As Francis Bethune had said, he played well enough to be an adequate accompanist, his style correct rather than expressive.

She had elected to sing purely to avoid conversation, but soon she found herself enjoying the music. There was a certain charm in watching his impassive, regular features as she awaited her entry; in seeing him nod to her, smiling, at the end of his introduction; in the companionship as they concentrated on the same purpose. One ballad followed another and it was with surprise, almost with disappointment, that she heard the pealing of the bell which could only announce the arrival of the fly.

Helen escorted her guests down to the door, and stood in the drive before the portico to speed them on their way. The evening was chill now; she hugged her bare arms, feeling them roughen with goose-flesh.

The horse was scuffing its hooves restlessly in the gravel, but still the fly did not move. From within, Helen caught her sister's voice, at some length. Suddenly the glass was let down and Rosemary's head appeared. She seemed uncommonly pleased with herself.

'Helen, Harry and I have been discussing the question, and we believe we could accommodate the whole of your party without too great a crush. Will you bring Papa and Miss Raymond to dine on Saturday?'

'What, and Sophie too?'

'Why not? What's one more?'

Helen was too astonished for words. Really, Rosemary's curiosity must be overwhelming.

'But . . . I'm sure it's kind of you to propose it, but where will you put so many?'

'Oh, we'll squeeze in somehow; Francis will have gone by then, I should think,' she added, in a whisper.

'If you're quite sure . . . the six o'clock train, then?'

Rosemary nodded, and withdrew her hand. An instant later the fly set off, its wheels crunching on the dimly glimmering gravel. Shivering, Helen turned back to the house.

6

Normally, Helen would have looked forward to her father's arrival and her reunion with Sophie the next day, but at the recollection that Susan Raymond would be with them all her pleasure was doused. In her preoccupation she even found herself returning sharp answers to tiresome, innocent Kitty. Then, seeing her hurt face, her uncomprehending round blue eyes, she would make amends by asking Kitty's help with some task, a secret penance for her unkindness.

It was at least some comfort that Susan Raymond's stay would be brief; she was to return on Monday morning. It might even prove a blessing of sorts. Perhaps in the uninspiring setting of a family weekend, away from the excitement of a dance or a grand dinner, her father might become aware of the sly, tawdry ways which had set Helen's teeth on edge.

If there were a heavy and continuous downpour on Sunday? A wet Scottish Sabbath, with five children to be kept indoors and an embargo on every diversion: could the romance of Romeo and Juliet themselves have survived such an ordeal?

Helen was in her room, nervously scrutinising her appearance for the tenth time that afternoon, when Philip and Andrew raced up the drive to announce the arrival of the travellers. She peeped round the curtains. The little group had just emerged from the obscurity of the trees. Miss Raymond, small and slight, was leaning heavily on Edward Lambert's arm. Sophie walked alone.

Helen went down. The children clustered about her, excited but shy, to greet their father. In other years she had vied with her sisters for his first kiss; now,

82

constrained by the presence of a stranger, even Phoebe hung back.

'So quiet?' Her father turned to Miss Raymond. 'That won't last, I assure you!' He looked at Helen, his smile losing something of its warmth. 'Is everything in order? The house is satisfactory, and all that?'

'Perfectly.'

'And who are these pretty little girls?' Susan Raymond put her head to one side in an arch pretence of bewilderment. The children exchanged a look, giggling and scuffing their toes. 'Let me guess now . . . yes, surely this must be Julia? And can this be Phoebe? Oh, they are so like you!' She looked up at her companion; Helen thought she had never seen so foolish a smile on her father's face.

'Most people who remember my mother consider that they favour her,' Helen said ungraciously. 'Papa, won't you introduce Kitty? And the boys?'

Leaving Miss Raymond to her pretty enthusiasm for the children, Helen edged closer to Sophie. They embraced silently.

'Let Miss Raymond into the house, children! Helen, show our guest to her room, if you would; the fly will be here shortly with the baggage. Now, is this the sitting-room? I will wait for you here, Helen. We may as well settle any domestic business at once.'

Helen obeyed. She had at least an excuse for interrupting the little cries of rapture with which Susan Raymond greeted the sight of her room.

She found her father in front of the looking-glass which hung over the mantel; he was adjusting his neck-tie.

'You wished to see me, Papa?'

'Ah, Helen.' He finished his minute improvements and turned around. 'There was nothing very particular. I simply thought it might be as well to give you another supply of money for household expenses while I'm here. It will save the need for sending money orders when the bills come in. Here, twenty pounds should keep you going for a while, I suppose?'

'Of course, but there is really no need. You will be down here long before I have exhausted what you have already given me.'

His eyes slid away from hers. 'No doubt, no doubt, but still, I would be happier knowing that you are comfortably supplied . . . I have no hesitation in leaving you with large sums, such an excellent manager as you are, Nell. I never have a moment's anxiety that you will be led into extravagance.'

She said nothing. Something in his manner jarred. Surely this false heartiness was new? Or had she not noticed it before?

'And the children? All well and happy?'

'Yes. They have been looking forward to your visit.'

'Hmm.' He began to play with his watch-chain, half withdrew his watch, dropped it back. 'You mustn't let them make a nuisance of themselves to Miss Raymond, you know. Keep them in order, won't you? She hasn't come down to be bothered by Kitty's tedious nonsense and the boys' rampaging, although she would be too unselfish to object.'

What has she come down for? she thought mutinously, but she only said, 'I see.'

He looked at her, as though puzzled by her cold tone. He produced a smile. 'Where would we be without you, Nell? I know I can leave the children absolutely to you. You can't think what a comfort it is to have no vexation on that score.'

Had such compliments pleased her once? Did he think they would please her now? 'It's no easy matter, to be down here alone with the responsibility for five children,' she said, hearing with horror an acid, querulous note in her voice.

'You will have Sophie.'

'Yes . . . and I suppose you will manage a week or two with us in September? The boys are longing to go fishing with you.'

'Very probably . . .' he murmured, strolling over to the

window. She waited for further information on his plans. He turned with sudden decision, and rang the bell.

'Ah, Hamilton,' he said to the servant who answered. 'Could you just step up to Miss Raymond's room and ask her if she would care to see the grounds before dinner? I shall be in the hall.'

There seemed to be nothing else to say; her father clearly had no further interest in the details of the household.

'Rosemary? Have you seen her?' he asked, as though recalling his thoughts with an effort.

'We are all to dine there tomorrow.'

'Miss Raymond is included? It would not do to leave her out.'

'Rosemary most particularly included her.'

'Good. There will be no difficulty then.' There was the sound of light steps on the stair, a whisper of silk, a tiny chiming of jewelery. His face lit up, he sprang towards the door. She heard him greet Susan Raymond with unfeigned delight; as they left the house she remained in the sitting-room, forgotten.

Within a few moments, she saw them pass the window of the sitting-room. Her father was smiling, a boyish eagerness on his face. He was bare-headed; the wind ruffled his thick grey hair. Susan Raymond's tiny hands were clasped about his arm. They walked with deliberate slowness, it seemed to Helen; Papa was always such a quick, impatient walker. Only she and Jack had ever been able to keep pace with him.

'Helen!'

She opened her arms thankfully as Sophie ran to her. 'I'm so very glad you're here!' To her horror, her voice was trembling.

'Oh, Helen, have the children been beastly?'

'No . . . really, it's nothing. How was your journey?'

Sophie rolled her eyes to heaven. 'I felt exactly as Aunt Jeannie must when she chaperones us! Such meaning glances, such tender compliments, such a significance in unfinished sentences, such speaking silences. And I, of course, to appear blind, and deaf, and half-witted!'

'You're exaggerating!'

'Not a bit! I would have been happier sitting on the roof with the luggage, I assure you. Miss Raymond and her father came to dinner on Tuesday, by the bye. Aunt Jeannie came to help me preside – it takes two of us to replace you, Helen! Papa is to dine there next week.'

From the garden came the sound of laughter, low and intimate. Helen glanced down. They were strolling before the house, a parasol of pale green over Miss Raymond's shoulder. It had long tassels, like the fronds of a sea anemone drifting in the hidden currents of the ocean. Helen turned hurriedly away from the sight.

'We go to Rosemary's tomorrow. I don't know how she will manage so many. It's quite a small house. She would have it so; you know how inquisitive she is. I think Mr Bethune told her some nonsense about Papa's behaviour at the wedding.'

'Mr Bethune?'

'He was there this week, for the fishing. They dined here yesterday.'

'Will he be there tomorrow?'

Helen frowned. 'If you mean Mr Bethune, he will not. He is to return to Edinburgh today.'

'Thank Heavens!'

'I don't know why you should say so. He's a most agreeable companion.'

'You sound almost as starchy as he did at the dance. It must be catching!'

'Really, Sophie! Must you be so giddy?'

'At least you're laughing again,' Sophie said, her arm stealing around her sister's waist. 'Say you forgive me and I'll see any virtue you care to mention in Mr Bethune. I'll even try to believe that he can speak in words of less than five syllables when he chooses!'

Exasperated, charmed, Helen felt her spirits rise. Whatever would she do without Sophie?

'I'm so glad you are only seventeen,' she said, in mock severity. 'It will give me the opportunity to teach you some decorum before some unfortunate man makes you his wife.' She led the way from the room, and did not see the expression on her sister's face, or her contentment might have been short-lived.

If Helen had been honest with herself she must have asked whether her father's presence did in fact contribute to the happiness of the household. Had he always been so eager that she should suppress any show of high spirits on the part of the children? Was it reasonable in him to expect healthy young creatures never to raise their voices at play? Were muddy boots and torn pinafores such heinous crimes on a country holiday?

To Kitty his manner was off-hand to the point of cruelty. He seemed reluctant to allow her within sight of Susan Raymond, and scarcely spoke to her but in tones of irritation. Julia and Phoebe were more favoured. Phoebe, a delicate, elfin child, was made a particular pet and even allowed to walk about the garden with her father and his guest. She was a decorative little girl, unlike the rather lumpish, red-faced Kitty, freckled and flat-footed, who seemed always on the verge of bursting out of her clothes.

To compensate for his neglect, Helen forced herself to make as much of her as she could. She sought her help in cutting flowers for the table, and in picking gooseberries in the well-stocked kitchen garden. The scratches she incurred in the process were as nothing to the thousand pinpricks inflicted by poor Kitty's endless, pointless chatter.

Altogether, Helen could not recall Papa as ever before being so disagreeable. She blamed Miss Raymond, or rather, his wish to impress her. Susan Raymond's own attitude to the children seemed to her cloying and insincere, but that was often true of childless women. It was her father's selfishness that she found unforgivable. She even voiced her criticism to Sophie, alone in bed that Friday night.

'Papa selfish? Showing no interest in the children? Why, Helen, he's treating them exactly as he always does,' Sophie said, yawning. 'When has he ever had any time for them?'

Helen wished that she could disbelieve her, or even deny her own judgement. Nothing could be more painful than the growing suspicion that her father was not the god-like being she had been so willing to worship.

After a long, hot day, spent as it seemed largely in keeping her father from being disturbed by his own off-spring, Helen was far from feeling any enthusiasm for a dinner in company with Susan Raymond, Rosemary and her father. Almost she excused herself on the plea of a headache; it would have been true enough. But Sophie urged her not to abandon her, and so she consented.

She dressed for dinner at the last minute, feeling no interest in her appearance. She wore an old muslin, limp from much washing, which had long since been relegated to the least dressy of occasions. She had always been fond of it. The fabric was embroidered with tiny bouquets of flowers; ribbons of the same design looped up the skirt over a blue silk slip.

'You look charming, Helen,' said Sophie, with her usual ready generosity, 'but are you not going to dress your hair? There is still time; let me ring for Hamilton. She must have finished with Miss Raymond by now.'

'Oh, it will do very well as it is. I can't be fussed with having my hair tugged and pulled about. It is neat enough, I suppose?'

'Yes . . . but so plain. Here, let me see . . . even this single row of pearls will add a little interest, if I pass it over your hair, between the bandeaux.'

Helen let her do as she wished. Add interest? For whom? she thought bitterly. She remembered her nerv-ous preparations before Thursday's dinner almost with disbelief.

During the brief train journey to Newtown St Boswells Helen scarcely spoke. She stared out of the smeared glass at the Eildons, which dominated the landscape for miles about Melrose. She heard her father telling Miss Raymond the legend of how they came into being, a single peak split into three by the Devil in the course of a night, at the bidding of the magician Michael Scott. Miss Raymond seemed suitably impressed. It was a pity that he had never seen fit to amuse Kitty with the tale.

Sophie and Helen drew ahead a little on the walk from the station to Bowden Cottage. Helen began to feel her headache lifting under the soothing influence of the quiet countryside and Sophie's tactful silence. She turned to her sister with a smile, meaning to beg her pardon for her dullness. She surprised on Sophie's young face a look of such thoughtfulness that her trifling remark remained unspoken. It struck her that Sophie might not have been consulting anything but her own wishes in avoiding conversation.

Sophie and Helen were shown up to Rosemary's room to lay aside their shawls and brush the dust from their gowns. Susan Raymond soon joined them.

There was a moment of awkwardness, before Helen's innate courtesy forced her to speak.

'May I be of help? Your skirts are a little marked at the back . . . Sophie, have you the brush?'

Helen performed the little service to the best of her ability, and straightened. She felt her hand caught in a soft, purposeful clutch.

'How kind you are! I do so wish we may be friends! I feel that I know you so well, from all that Mr Lambert has told me of his clever, clever daughter . . . now I've displeased you! You shrink from praise, but you shall hear it.' She detained Helen's hand, which in an instinctive movement was pulling away from hers. 'Must we be so formal? Can it not be Helen and Susan . . . and Sophie, of course, my dear!' Her winning smile was turned on Sophie.

There was an embarrassing pause. Helen cleared her throat.

'By all means. I . . . I am glad that you proposed it . . . Susan.'

'You see, it wasn't so difficult, was it?' Her black eyes lingered on Helen's face in a look of disturbing acuteness, beneath which Helen felt uncomfortably defenceless. 'There is nothing to prevent our friendship, you know, Helen.'

'No. Sophie, if you're ready? Shall we go down?' She had intended to call Susan Raymond by her name once more but she absolutely could not. If she noted the omission and her abrupt manner, Susan Raymond gave no sign of it. She released Helen's hand and began to manoeuvre her crinoline through the door.

In the flurry of introductions and welcome which centred upon Miss Raymond, Helen and Sophie entered the drawing-room almost unremarked. Sophie lingered to greet Rosemary and Harry for the first time since their marriage. Helen moved away, towards the window, and stopped. There, watching her, half smiling, was Francis Bethune. She made no attempt to hide the delight she felt; his smile relaxed into genuine pleasure.

'Mr Bethune! I thought you were to return today?'

He shrugged. 'Harry was good enough to press me to stay. A solitary dinner at home had little to commend it.'

The dinner bell put an end to conversation, as Rosemary swept up to claim his arm, in all the pre-eminence of her married state. To no one's surprise, Miss Raymond fell to Edward Lambert's lot.

At the table, rather too crowded for comfort, Helen was placed diagonally opposite Francis Bethune. He was devoting himself politely to his neighbour, Sophie. Helen found herself glancing anxiously towards them more than once across the prettily arranged flowers in the centre of the table. She hoped her sister might not be teasing the poor man; certainly, he was showing no sign of unease.

He was listening attentively to Sophie, nodding from time to time, in approval or understanding. Seen thus, from a position of detachment, it was the intelligence of his expression which most struck her, quick and alert. It was vexing to be excluded from what appeared to be an interesting conversation by the noisy hubbub about her.

At length, quite suddenly, one of those general silences occurred which fall so oddly when everyone in a group ceases to speak at exactly the same moment, as though by command. It was broken by Francis Bethune. He addressed Helen across the table, wishing perhaps to prompt a less fragmented discussion. As always in such circumstances, his remarks seemed painfully laboured.

'Your sister has been telling me of your Greek studies, Miss Lambert. In one respect at least I hope you will allow that our modern practice is a great improvement on the ancient: ladies never graced their convivial gatherings. What a loss to society that must have been!'

'Ladies may not have been included, Bethune,' her father replied drily, 'but female company was not entirely absent. There were slave girls to provide music, and diversion of another sort from . . . it would be as well to leave their title in its decent obscurity, perhaps, and call them *hetairai*.'

'I'm sure we can't imagine what you could mean, can we, Sophie?' said Susan Raymond coyly. 'Don't enlighten us, Helen! How wonderful, Mr Lambert, to have a daughter of such talent, a masculine mind, almost!' Helen felt her cheeks begin to burn at the apparent compliment. 'I'm sure my poor brain could never have mastered such a language,' Susan Raymond concluded, looking across to Edward Lambert with a droll little shake of her head, suggestive of pretty, helpless femininity.

'You don't do yourself justice, Miss Raymond,' Edward Lambert said gallantly. 'And in any case, a woman is no worse for an ignorance of the dead languages.'

'But you have often said that there is no reason why a girl should not cultivate her mind as well as a boy!'

Helen cried, angered by what seemed to her a betrayal. 'Have you not told us over and again that a well-educated woman is capable of being a true companion to her husband if ever she should marry?'

'If ever she should marry . . . but how many men would not be alarmed by such a woman . . . so intimidating . . . of course, Helen,' Susan added, with wide-eyed sincerity, 'I need hardly say that I mean no personal reference.'

'No one could possibly impute such an intention to you,' broke in Francis Bethune. 'Miss Lambert is living proof that intellectual excellence is entirely compatible with every other feminine attribute.'

'What a pretty compliment! So eloquently turned! I declare, you will make Miss Lambert blush! How the colour becomes you, Helen dear, quite charming!'

'How's Jack?' asked Rosemary suddenly, with some instinct to protect her sister, perhaps, or an equally sisterly disinclination to hear Helen praised. 'Is he not coming down this year?'

'Jack? Still away on his reading party,' Edward Lambert replied carelessly. 'By the bye, Nell, did he mention to you his notion to go off to Canada? He approached me about it before he left, seemed much in earnest. I said I'd turn the matter over and let him have an answer on his return – if he hasn't changed his mind, of course. To be quite candid, I have not given it a thought from that moment to this.'

'I knew that he had some such scheme,' Helen replied slowly, remembering Doctor Cairns's warning. 'Will you allow it?'

'I really am in two minds,' he said, describing intricate patterns on the tablecloth with his glass. 'He has a certain talent for mathematics, but he's no scholar. He'd be all the better for seeing a little of the world; it might be the making of him. On the other hand, it doesn't look good for a young man to throw up his studies on a whim. He might live to regret it.'

'I'm sure he would!' Helen said eagerly. 'Surely Jack

is far too young for such an undertaking – he's barely more than a boy! Let him finish his studies, it is only another two years, after all. Let him go to Canada then, if he still wishes it.'

'Helen, I'm sure your reluctance to part with your brother does you every credit,' Susan Raymond said, offering her opinion with a becoming show of diffidence. 'To me, an ignorant, simple woman . . .' Edward Lambert duly made a murmur of dissent, ' . . . it seems that a young man may do very well in a country such as Canada, without a piece of paper or parchment or whatever it is to say that he has scraped through some exams or other. If he wishes to go, let him!'

'I believe that Miss Lambert's point remains valid,' said Francis Bethune, apparently unmoved. 'To abandon one's studies after a year is a poor thing. A man of any pluck will continue, whether it takes his fancy or not. He will be all the better for persevering, even more so if he is not a natural scholar. Good steady application will always be a virtue, though not a showy one.'

'There's a lot in that, Bethune,' said Edward Lambert, pursing his lips. 'I'd be the last man to encourage any student to throw everything up and chase off to the other end of the world on an idle distaste for work.'

'But may he not choose his own work? In her brother's place, I'm sure Helen would ask nothing better than to pore over dusty books in a fusty library!' Susan Raymond shuddered, with a little flutter of her fingers which set the bracelets tinkling on her slender wrist. 'But think, Helen, is he not of a different nature? We are not all gifted with your wonderful talent! Let the young man find his own way to excel . . . so cruel, to tie him to a life he hates!' and her eyes softened, as though she would positively shed tears in her quick sympathy for a youth whom, Helen calculated, she had seen once, drunk, at a ball.

'I think I may be allowed to know something of my own brother.' The cold arrogance of her extremest anger was in Helen's voice. 'Jack has always been impetuous.

This will be no more than a passing fancy. It would be tragic if Papa were to let him ruin his entire future for some notion he will have forgotten in a month.'

Her father sighed. 'Well, you may be right, Nell. If I tell him to wait even another year . . . ?' He looked across to Susan Raymond, as if in appeal. 'He could write to Richard in Quebec in the meantime. That may content him.'

Rosemary, to whom the subject was of little importance, had been waiting with evident impatience for the discussion to end. Now, gathering the eyes of the ladies, she rose and led them to the door. She turned to her husband who had leapt to open it. 'Don't keep us waiting, will you?' she said, a little pettishly.

In fact, they had scarcely settled themselves in the tiny drawing-room before steps were heard in the passage. Susan Raymond addressed Rosemary with a show of wide-eyed admiration. 'What a model of obedience your husband is, Mrs Robertson! How delightful to see such devotion!' she said, quite loud enough for the newcomer to hear.

Harry Robertson did not seem well pleased by the praise. 'Francis suggested that we might walk over to Melrose, view the Abbey by moonlight, if you ladies care to walk so far. It's a sight not to be missed.'

Rosemary pouted. 'I'm sure I've seen the ruins often enough by daylight, and very tedious they are too. I doubt whether they are any more interesting by night, only less visible.'

'Oh, don't be such a wet blanket, Rosie,' her husband replied, frowning. 'It's a charming sight, romantic, everyone says so. Everyone else would like it.'

'Then everyone else may go,' she said, crossing her plump hands in her lap. 'I shall save my energy for serving you tea when you return, hot and weary and even more ill-tempered.'

He turned sharply on his heel. 'Helen, Sophie, will you come? Miss Raymond?'

Nobody chose to share Rosemary's indolent solitude – at least, not once it was realised that all the men were resolved upon the excursion. They set off as a compact group, but soon, without apparent decision, the party was strung out along the path which led to Melrose, following the west flank of the Eildons.

Sophie, quick and eager, was soon far ahead with Harry Robertson. Susan Raymond was slower. She and Edward Lambert imperceptibly drifted behind; he appeared to have lost his distaste for dragging, rambling walks. In the centre Helen and Francis Bethune strolled together at a comfortable pace.

'The Eildons are very tempting,' he said, looking towards the conical peaks to their right.

'If I had brought my Balmorals, I would agree,' she said, smiling ruefully down at her light shoes.

'There may be another occasion?'

'I hope so. Will you be down again?'

'If I am on the South Circuit this autumn I would be coming to Jedburgh in September. I might impose myself on Harry and your sister for a day or two before the Circuit begins.'

'We may see you, then. We will be here until October when the boys have to go back to the Academy.'

'You are finding your stay enjoyable?'

'On the whole. It will be better now that Sophie is here.'

'Your sister is to stay?'

'Of course.'

'I must have misunderstood her, then. She mentioned the hope that she might return to Edinburgh in the near future.'

'I think you must be mistaken, Mr Bethune,' she said, frowning.

'Very probably.'

Mollified, she turned the subject. 'The Southern Circuit? What is that? My ignorance on the law is encyclopaedic, I warn you.'

'To be brief, I am an Advocate-Depute. We appear for the Crown, as public prosecutors. We act in criminal cases, in the High Court of Justiciary, and in Circuit Courts, outwith Edinburgh, when cases are tried there during the Spring and Autumn Circuits. There is also a Winter Circuit, held only in Glasgow.'

'So you are a Public Accuser? How very alarming!'

'The unruly elements which give rise to crime must be suppressed, deterred, and where necessary punished. The prosecutor performs for the body politic a service similar to that of the surgeon in the case of the physical body, or of the sensitive conscience in the moral organism, if I may use the phrase.'

'Have you always held this post?'

'No. I was several years on the left side of the table – appearing for the defence, in criminal cases at least – before I received my present appointment. As it happens, I find myself better suited to prosecuting. You often find it so; a man has a greater aptitude, or perhaps simply a greater liking for the one branch of the profession than the other.'

'I can more easily imagine an attachment to the defence.'

He laughed. 'Oh, I suppose these things really are beyond the rational understanding; they rest on the very foundations of the personality. But perhaps in my own case I could point to a liking for order and regularity, a passion for the truth at any cost, a desire to maintain the fabric of society undisturbed.'

'So you enjoy your profession?'

'I find it a satisfying one. It helps to support the structure of a decent society.'

'I wonder what Harry would say to that? He might question whether the structure of society deserves to be supported in its entirety.'

He said, not unkindly, 'I have not followed my profession for the last ten years without learning a certain amount about crime, at any rate. I can take no very sanguine view of human nature in its unredeemed state, as it appears in the High Court.'

'And what redeems it?'

'Education, the civilising influence of religion, the escape of individuals by the force of their own efforts from the squalor which contents their fellows.'

'I wonder if I would fare well, if such an effort were demanded of me? It is as well that only the poor are divided into those who are "deserving" and those who are not.'

'I honour you for your sympathies. A hard, severe mind is an unnatural thing in a woman. But those of us who have to engage with harsh reality cannot afford the luxury of a compassion which forgives all, makes every allowance, seeks no retribution for offence.'

'Do you feel the want of that luxury very severely, Mr Bethune?'

He was spared from the need to reply by a call from Edward Lambert. He was hurrying towards them, alone. Miss Raymond was barely visible in the gathering twilight, her dress a pale blur.

'Papa! Is something wrong?'

He did not answer until he drew closer. 'I've been calling for nearly five minutes, didn't you hear? Well, never mind it now . . . Miss Raymond is a little fatigued. She wishes to return; what will you do? If you don't turn soon, you'll be nearer to Melrose than Bowden. You might as well carry on home, instead of returning to Rosemary's.'

'I could scarcely do that, Papa. It would mean that Mr Bethune would be obliged to walk back from Melrose . . . and Harry, too.'

'I'm sure Harry will think as little of the walk as I do,' Francis Bethune put in quickly.

'Very good, very good,' said Edward Lambert impatiently, with an anxious glance over to where Susan Raymond stood. 'Make up your mind, do, Helen. I can't have Miss Raymond kept standing.'

'Then we will go on to see the Abbey from close at hand, and continue home. Please present our apologies to Rosemary . . .' He was away before she had ended her sentence.

They walked on in silence for a while; Francis Bethune glanced at her troubled, averted face. 'Miss Lambert?'

'I'm sorry . . . I have quite lost the thread of what we were saying.'

'You had hinted in the kindest possible way that compassion is a virtue alien to me.'

'Oh, I'm sure I meant no such thing!'

'Perhaps there is some truth in it, all the same. I see so much of human viciousness in the course of my work. If I were to tell you of some of the cowardly assaults and murders, carried out for the sake of a few pence, perhaps, or in a drunken fury, or for no motive at all . . . some cases haunt me for years. I recall one brute who broke into an old woman's cottage down the chimney, violated and killed her. The thought of her last moments gave me no rest for long enough, I can assure you.'

She looked up at him in some surprise. It was not the speech of the dispassionate, even unfeeling man she had taken him for, the man he seemed to wish to appear.

'Did you obtain a conviction in that case?'

'Yes. I took care to conceal my feelings, of course. Personal considerations must never be allowed to interfere with the most effective conduct of a prosecution. Prosecution is a cleaner business than defence, I often feel. No advocate can refuse a defence brief, let his private opinion of his client be what it may. Faced with a hopeless case the defence must look for quibbles in the law or procedure, or try to shake reputable witnesses, or fall back on emotional appeals. It's all permissible, of course. I've done it myself in my junior days, but it doesn't bear much relation to truth, and that, it seems to me, is the great object.'

'Forensically speaking?'

'In every aspect of human existence. Absolute truthfulness, a candour which cannot lie, that is the indispensable virtue for me.'

'But are there not situations in which it is excusable to lie? To save a friend's life in time of war? To comfort the last moments of the dying?'

'Excusable perhaps, but still a sordid compromise.'

'You are very exacting. Not many people could satisfy so high a standard.'

'Very few, but those few all the more valued for that.'

The conversation made her obscurely uneasy. She did not reply.

'The moon will be bright enough to illumine the Abbey in quite the desired romantic style by the time we reach Melrose,' he said, more lightly, as if sensitive to her mood.

'Rosemary should have stirred herself. It will repay the effort of the walk,' she answered, gesturing to the clear disc of the moon, which seemed to float above the hills in a sea of flawless blue.

'Your sister is not a creature for the moonlight,' he said unexpectedly. 'Mrs Robertson's natural hour is noon, in some more exotic clime than ours, where nothing stirs under a merciless sun.'

'Where nothing stirs . . . that would suit Rosemary famously,' she said, amused. 'Sophie, now: what is her hour?'

He considered briefly. 'Dawn perhaps? In early summer, fresh and expectant?'

'And Miss Raymond?'

'Dusk, when the light is becoming uncertain and nothing is quite what it seems. That is the best I can do . . . and since you are too modest to ask about yourself, I would say that your hour is exactly this, a tranquil summer night when the stars are just emerging and the moon looks down, serene and indifferent, on a world which cannot sully her.'

She was not sure how to receive this playful fancy. Did she really appear to him so distant, so impassive? And yet he clearly meant only what was complimentary.

'And what of yourself? You can't be allowed to escape your own system.'

'Well, if you won't allow me any mercy, I will say about two in the morning, on a clouded, moonless night, and perhaps throw in a good thick fog to complete my concealment.'

'How very unsporting! . . . And Doctor Cairns?'

'An overcast afternoon, about four o'clock, with more than a hint of thunder in the air.'

'No, really!' she said, laughing in spite of herself.

'Cairns will glower so. When he looks at me and draws down his brows like a bull about to charge I never know whether he thinks worse of my bodily health or my spiritual,' he replied, with unusual asperity.

She was silent, and lowered her gaze.

'I'm sorry,' he said, almost at once. 'It was a stupid thing to say. Cairns has never done me any harm. In fact he once did me a great service, but that doesn't make me like him any the better, human nature being what it is, or my own portion of it at least. I find him antipathetic, that's all.'

They had reached Melrose, and were approaching the ruined Abbey. The austere moonlight, revealing form but not colour, seemed the perfect medium to illumine the soaring arches, the broken tracery of the windows, the roofless walls where, high above the deserted aisles and chancel, ferns had managed to grow.

'How sad it looks!' she said softly, as they began to walk slowly around the perimeter of the site. 'When it was built, with such confidence, who would have believed that it could ever be so fallen?'

'Don't forget, it was the fall of superstition and corruption.'

'But this is so noble, so beautiful! You must concede

some good to a faith which expressed itself in such sublimity.'

He hesitated. 'I envy the Catholics one thing. Their Madonna.'

'You surprise me. To most people the veneration of the Virgin is the most alien of Roman practices.'

They left the ruins and began to walk towards the river. Now that the end of their journey was in sight they walked more slowly. The road soon left the houses of Melrose behind. She had a sudden sense of their shared solitude. Perhaps he experienced something of the same feeling, for when he began to speak again it was in a lower, less confident tone.

'My mother was a sort of Madonna to me. When she died I was so young . . . For years afterwards, in bed at night I would shut my eyes and try to imagine her leaning over me, as she used. She had never let a night go by without coming up to kiss us before we went to sleep. Sometimes I could almost persuade myself that her death had been a terrible dream, that if I were to open my eyes and look up I would see her bending over my bed, smiling down at me . . . I used to long to open my eyes, but I never dared. The illusion was too precious to destroy.'

She pressed his arm, not wishing to break his mood by speech; what, in any case, could she say?

'I can still remember one night, not long before . . . before she took ill. She had guests, I suppose. She must have excused herself from the dinner-table to come up to my sister and me. I was drowsy, the rustle of her silk skirts awakened me. She was so beautiful! She was breathing quickly; I expect she had run up the stairs to us. She teased me for falling asleep without her kiss, I put my arms up to her neck and drew her down to my pillow. I remember the touch of her ringlets against my cheek, and the scent of cloves from the carnations at her bosom, and my pride that she was my mother, this glorious laughing vision.'

His eyes were fixed on the path before them, although she doubted whether he saw it. In his face she traced a wistful yearning far removed from his habitual smile of detachment and self-sufficiency. Suddenly, his expression changed, his lips set once more in their ironic curve, he became once more the urbane, assured legal man.

'Is that Harry approaching?' he asked.

'Yes. He must have left Sophie in the house.'

'He seems to be in some haste. Do you think he fears for his reception on his return?'

Whatever his apprehensions, Harry insisted on retracing his footsteps to escort Helen to her door. The two cousins then set off at once on their return journey, refusing all refreshment.

As they prepared for bed Sophie showed some curiosity as to how Helen and Francis Bethune had fared during their walk. Helen answered vaguely. Often the greatest charm of a social engagement lay in the leisurely discussion of it with Rosemary or Sophie in the privacy of their room, as they lingered over the brushing of their hair. But this was different. She jealously hugged to herself all that he had said. To pick it over with her sister would be a desecration.

7

Sunday passed in the usual uneventful routine of church-going. Helen took the children to the Episcopal chapel in the Weirhill district. It was a lovely building, but during the morning service Helen found herself studying the congregation rather than the window, the pulpit or, least of all, the sermon. She had thought that Rosemary might be there, but it appeared that she had conformed to Harry's religion and abandoned the whistle-kirk in favour of the Presbyterian, unless indeed she had remained at home, resolving religious differences by apathy.

That evening, however, at the second service, she did see the Bowden party. They were already seated when Helen led her brothers and sisters into the church: Miss Raymond had pleaded a headache, and Edward Lambert, always a reluctant church-goer, had remained with his guest.

Helen was a few rows behind her sister's pew. She found her eyes straying frequently in Rosemary's direction, or more accurately in Francis Bethune's. The sun was striking full on his hair; it seemed the only patch of living brightness in the church. She had never seen him before in full daylight. She was fascinated by the varying effect of the light; at times, when the sun was overshadowed, his hair would be almost brown. Then, illuminated once more, it shone coppery red.

After the service, Helen hurried over to her sister's little group.

'We missed you this morning!' she said, speaking to Rosemary, but with a smile which included Francis Bethune. 'Will you not come back with us for tea?'

Rosemary looked at her husband. 'Yes?'

'By all means. Frank, you'll come?'

'Thank you, no,' he said, with the faintest of bows to Helen.

At the blank refusal, unsoftened by any excuse, at his stiff, unsmiling formality and unfriendly tone her mouth dropped open in astonishment.

'Oh, Mr Bethune!' she said in dismay, then recovering herself a little added, 'Don't disappoint us, please. You are most welcome.'

Again, a cold bow, a repeated refusal, with a few murmured words concerning the need to prepare for an early departure the next morning.

She did not press him further. His reluctance was too plain, too inexplicable. He seemed to have become suddenly not merely a stranger but an enemy. Sophie and Kitty bore the burden of the conversation as they returned home with the Robertsons; Helen, silent, turned this way and that at the rebuff she had received. She would have willingly accepted the blame, if she could but see how she had erred.

Her father and Miss Raymond left by the early train the following morning. Helen was glad that the hour excused her from accompanying them to the station. Francis Bethune, she supposed, would be travelling up by the same train. She had no wish to encounter again the coldness which had so puzzled and distressed, almost angered her, in the churchyard.

Her parting from her father was uneasy. The constraint which had been growing between them since Rosemary's wedding seemed to be changing to something more like estrangement. When she remembered what they had once been to each other the contrast was so painful that she made, in the last minutes, an effort to restore their closeness. It was not easy, with Susan Raymond hovering near.

'I scarcely seem to have seen you, Papa!' she said lightly. 'You will come down again soon, promise me! We all look forward to it so much, and it will do you good, I know . . . the country is paradise at this time of year when Edinburgh is so unwholesome. You will come, please?'

'Of course, of course,' he replied, bending to kiss her hastily on the cheek. 'Early in September, if not before . . . I'll write. Jack will be down before then, no doubt. Now, we mustn't be late for the train . . .'

Helen watched her father and Susan Raymond seat themselves in the waiting fly and rattle off down the drive. His visit had brought little but vexation and yet she resented his departure, and the long time which she suspected would elapse before his return.

She had prided herself on her devotion to her family, had found pleasure in knowing herself to be useful, had spoken of duty and sacrifice quite contentedly. She would have laughed, only a month before, if anyone had suggested that she did not know the meaning of the words.

Duty and sacrifice. As she watched the fly round the curve of the sweep, she began dimly to realise that the fine-sounding words she had used so easily had a significance she had never guessed. Now she began to feel their full force, and beside that felt experience her former understanding was lifeless and pale.

Rab Crearie may have been absent from his family, but he did all that he could to assist them. Even while on the tramp he sent what money he could from odd jobs he picked up, it seemed, in almost every village, every farmstead that he passed through.

By August, however, came more reliable work, on the Elgin to Rothes railway. The money was good, he wrote, and the line would not be complete for at least a year. Every week, faithfully, he sent Lizzie a money order to be cashed at the Post Office; he even promised more when he should have paid off the sums he had laid out on boots and working clothes.

There was not, though, any mention of the family

moving up to be with him. Doctor Cairns's remarks had made their impression on Lizzie. She knew him well enough to be sure that if he recommended the move, it must be necessary for May's health. Like many girls, Lizzie had been given schooling enough to be able to read but not to write. Her replies to her father were penned by Joseph, at eight years old already the family scribe.

And so, through Joseph, a letter was sent to Rab Crearie, expressing in guarded terms Lizzie's concern for May's health and her wish that the family should join her father as soon as possible.

The reply, eagerly awaited, was not encouraging. Her father was having some difficulties with the foreman in the joinery shop; there was feeling against the Irish workers on the line, with whom Crearie, despite fifteen years' residence in Scotland, was still classed; he did not know how long he would remain on that line, or whether he might try his luck on one of the other railways then being built in the north-east.

The conclusion was clear. Until her father felt more settled, he had no intention of sending for them. His reasons were sound, but Lizzie was not convinced that they told the whole story. Her father never kept a job for long. He liked his freedom, freedom to answer back to an unjust or brutal overseer, freedom to do a piece of work his own way when he knew that was the best way, freedom to try his luck at another shop when he became restless. And his freedom was greater if Lizzie remained in Edinburgh, looking after the children.

There was nothing Lizzie could do. Certainly, her father was earning good money, better than he would get in a joiner's shop in a town. Always at the back of her mind, even in the stifling days of August, was the fear of the winter to come and the expenses it would bring. They would need more coal. May at least must have shoes, and Joseph and Nettie too, if it could be managed. A warm jacket for him, and thicker clothes for the girls; more bedding, more substantial food.

It seemed at first that it would be the easiest thing in the world to put aside something each week for clothes and shoes; her father was sending her almost a pound a week. She had never been so rich in her life. And yet, after so many weeks of worrying and pinching while her father was on the tramp, able to send only dribs and drabs of money, Lizzie found herself almost unable to save.

When she was out shopping and the sun was warm, it was all too easy to look only to the demands of the moment. She would treat the children to a relish for their tea, relaxing her caution and indulging their craving for something tasty: a rasher of bacon to go with their potatoes, a few ham ribs to make a good pot of soup.

Gradually, what had been luxuries became daily fare. She tempted May to eat with white bread and butter, bought eggs and milk for Danny, gave Nettie a penny for buckies or Joseph a bawbee for gingerbread, treated them all to a supper of whiting on a Saturday night. She could see the children gaining health and strength with the good, abundant food. They were less fractious, and even May's colour improved. But somehow, week by week, every penny of the money orders was spent on ordinary living expenses and the little treats which it was so hard to deny the children, or herself, while she had money in her purse. She redeemed bedding which had been pawned when things were at their worst, bought a few extra blankets and began to lay in a supply of coal against the winter, but that was all.

Early in September came a few days of autumn weather, cooler, wet, a foretaste of what was to come. Nettie, caught in the rain in her thin cotton dress, took a bad chill. She worked as scullery maid over in Lauriston Place; her journeys to and from her work in all weathers often left her soaked to the very skin. Although Lizzie did not allow May past the door during the bad weather, she rapidly came down with Nettie's cold. Long after her sister had recovered, May remained ailing.

Lizzie could put off the question of warm clothing and shoes no longer. Long after the younger children had gone to bed she would sit by the cooling embers, turning over the problem in her mind. Then, one evening, as though she had reached a decision at last, she wrapped the sleeping Danny in her plaid and with the infant in her arms slipped out, along the passage and down the stair to the back tenement, to the Shannons' door.

Stout and florid, Mrs Shannon opened the door a cautious crack, then seeing Lizzie, flung it hospitably open.

'Lizzie! Come ben! Here, George, get the lassie a seat! Will ye take a dish of tea?'

Lizzie hesitated, then nodded. She seated herself in the chair George Shannon drew up to the fire for her, and looked about her with a curiosity not unmixed with envy. The Shannons' kitchen was smaller than her room, but they had another room forbye the kitchen; the three Shannon girls must sleep there. There was no sign of them, at any rate.

George Shannon had a steady job at the gas works close by; the signs of their comfortable position were plain to see. On the mantel a clock stood. There was a birdcage hanging at the window, where a jaunty yellow bird darted from one perch to another. The table was covered by a thick chenille cloth, and a heavy curtain of the same rich material screened off the bed-recess from the rest of the kitchen. There was a brightly coloured print on one wall; Lizzie suspected that it was the Prince of Wales. On another wall was ranged a gleaming row of pans, bright and clear as a new sixpence. Lizzie sighed, and received from Minnie Shannon her tea in a cup so thin and pretty that she almost feared to touch it.

A speaking look passed between husband and wife. George Shannon rose, and reached his tobacco pouch down from the chimney-piece.

'If ye dinna mind, hen, I'll away down to the close for a pipe and a crack,' he said, and left them alone.

Mrs Shannon drew her chair closer to Lizzie's. She bent forward, her dress creasing over her fat arms. 'Was there anything special?' she asked, wheezing a little. 'No that ye're no welcome, ken, only Geordie'll no be that long . . .'

Lizzie coloured. 'It wasna anything very great, Mrs Shannon,' she began, and saw a shade of disappointment pass over the older woman's face, for all its good nature. 'It's only . . . ye're in a menage, are ye no?'

'Aye, a clothes menage, from Cooper's, on the South Bridge.'

'How much?'

'Shilling a week. Gillanders is the menage man. He's a sleekit wee man, but no ill to deal with, if ye keep up with the shillings.'

'And shoes?'

'Ye'll no get shoes from Cooper's. But Gillanders would oblige ye with a pound. Ye'd need to pay sixpence a week for the twelve month. I'll put in a word for ye, if ye like.'

'A sixpence forbye the shilling for clothes . . .' Lizzie frowned. Her father had been sending at least eighteen shillings a week. The rent was one and nine; even allowing for extra coal during the winter the sum should be well within her reach.

She put down the fragile cup with extraordinary care. 'Ask him to chap my door the next time he's round, will ye?' she said, standing up. 'I'll need to get back. Our May's no so very great just now.'

Mrs Shannon grunted as she heaved herself to her feet, her gown creasing across her vast bosom. 'Watch yourself with Gillanders, mind,' she said, as she led Lizzie over to the door.

'Oh?'

'He's aye been all right with me, dinna get me wrong, only ye hear the wifies clash, ken . . .' She nodded knowingly.

'Let them clash,' Lizzie said scornfully. 'I've more to do with my house and my bairns than listen.'

Footsteps drew closer out in the passage; a warning cough told of George Shannon's tactful approach.

'Aweel, just dinna fall behind with your menage, and ye'll no need to worry,' Mrs Shannon said, a little huffily perhaps; Lizzie knew well enough her fondness for a tasty blether.

As George Shannon entered his own house like a shamefaced sheriff's man at a warrant sale, Lizzie took her leave and hurried back to her own house. Secure in the knowledge that May's shoes and the family's winter clothes were provided for at last, she fell quickly asleep, not disturbed either by Danny's restlessness or May's weary, relentless cough.

As if to amplify Helen's new sense of the burden of family responsibility, the weather changed with her father's departure. Their first week in Melrose had been glorious. Now, heavy skies and drizzling rain replaced the sunshine she had come to expect of the Borders, and the Eildons were muffled in low misty clouds.

The children had to be kept indoors, day after day. By Wednesday, in sheer despair Helen allowed the boys out to fish. Even the risk of chills and coughs seemed preferable to enduring their banging, bumping, clattering ways in the house for another twenty-four hours.

Sophie was a great help in amusing the little ones and absorbing some of Kitty's earnest, blameless babble, but even there Helen was conscious of some cloud. Her sister was bright enough in company, but she seemed to be developing a tendency to daydream when not called upon to entertain her younger brothers and sisters. Seeing her features rapt in some inner vision which was never communicated to her, Helen felt a pang of something she did not care to examine too closely.

The enforced confinement was not helpful in keeping

at bay thoughts which Helen had no wish to entertain. Despite herself, she found herself recalling Francis Bethune, his conversation, his manner to her on the last occasion of their meeting, his appearance. She had great difficulty in summoning his features to her mind. This bothered her, as did so much these days.

Thursday brought no improvement in the weather, but there was at least consolation in the form of a letter from Edinburgh, lying beside Helen's plate when she came down to breakfast.

'Who's been writing to you?' Sophie asked, raising her eyes from a letter of her own. 'It's a man's hand; no woman would write so badly.'

The cover was directed in a large, sprawling script, hasty but not without a certain style. Helen opened the letter with a pleasurable sense of anticipation.

'Oh!' she cried, vexed at her own disappointment. 'It's only from Doctor Cairns!'

Sophie raised her brows at the 'only', but she said nothing. Helen's face was clearing.

'How nice that will be! He proposes to come down on Saturday for the day. Papa suggested it when they met by chance.'

'Salving his conscience, no doubt.'

'Well, never mind, we have Doctor Cairns to look forward to; perhaps we may persuade him to stay!'

'Here?'

'Well, with Rosemary perhaps?' she suggested. 'I suppose you're right, it would not be quite correct for him to stay here in Papa's absence. I'll write to him directly . . . who is your letter from, by the bye?'

'Oh, Margaret Hewitt,' Sophie said, with studied carelessness. 'They are still in Edinburgh, until the beginning of September. Margaret is very insistent that I should manage to stay with her for a few days before they go across to Fife; she says Edinburgh is so dull with everyone away . . . what do you think?' she ended, with a self-conscious little laugh.

Helen frowned. Philip and Andrew were kicking each other under the table in pursuit of some obscure joke, and Julia and Phoebe were absorbed in biting their bread and butter in the tiniest possible mouthfuls, but Kitty's earnest eyes were missing nothing of the exchange between her older sisters.

'We can discuss it after breakfast,' she said, folding Doctor Cairns's letter. 'I shall be in the sitting-room, writing to the doctor.'

The letter took no time to compose. She was addressing it when Sophie entered, with a nervousness which surprised Helen.

'Another moment . . . there! Now, Sophie, what's all this about Margaret Hewitt? Surely she can live a month in Edinburgh without you?' she said, twining her arm affectionately in her sister's, and giving it a playful shake. Sophie smiled in response, but as though by an effort.

'To be honest, Margaret wants me to spend a week or so with them at home, and then go over to Elie with them for another week.'

'A fortnight! And what do you want?'

Sophie kept her gaze lowered to her bodice, where her fingers were twiddling a button. 'I've never been to Elie,' she murmured.

'But Sophie, you are scarcely so intimate with Margaret Hewitt that you should . . .' She stopped, as she suddenly recalled something which had lodged in her mind despite its apparent insignificance. 'Rosemary's wedding . . . it was Tom Hewitt you danced with, was it not? I remember you teased me about it . . . Sophie?'

'Oh, Helen!'

'It is that, isn't it?'

Sophie hung her head. It was answer enough.

'But you are so young . . . you scarcely know him . . . do his parents know of your attachment? Has he spoken to you without any possibility of misunderstanding?'

Under the barrage of questions Sophie moved distractedly to the window. Beneath the steady rain the garden was a glossy, dripping green. She began to speak, in a soft dreamy tone Helen barely recognised. Even to talk of him seemed a pleasure to be savoured.

'I can't explain it to you. I saw Tom at the Hewitts' nearly two years ago. He was so good-natured and kind to us when I visited Margaret. He never teased or if he did, in such a funny way . . . I always liked him. Then at Rosemary's wedding, everything changed. I think it was the first time he thought of me as more than a girl,' she said, innocently proud. 'I was down at the Hewitts' almost every night when you were away with the children. The last time . . .'

Helen saw with a sort of dread the smile which lit her young sister's face. 'Yes?'

'We were in the garden together, alone. He asked me if I thought I could care for him. When I told him . . .' She fell silent. Helen said nothing for a moment.

'His parents, do they know?'

'Not yet. Tom will be twenty-one in December. He wants to wait until then to tell them.'

'But is it right for you to spend a fortnight with the family if they are unaware of your position? Might they not object, when they do discover it?'

'Why should they? They are both as kind as can be to me, and Margaret knows everything, of course; she has done from the very first.'

Margaret Hewitt knew; I did not. The thought was a sudden pain. When Helen spoke again her tone was colder. 'I'm afraid I can't think it proper that you should go. It is deceitful. Papa would agree with me.'

'Oh, Helen, you know he wouldn't care a button, as long as no one bothered him about it! He'd be glad if we eloped and saved him the fuss of another wedding!'

'That's a terrible thing to say!'

'It's true, though! Anyway, Papa's far too busy on his own account to want to be troubled with my concerns.'

'That has nothing to do with it. What are we to reply

to Margaret Hewitt's invitation? That's what we have to decide.'

'I have decided,' said Sophie, turning squarely to face her sister. 'I shall accept.'

The cool defiance took Helen aback, used as she was to deference from the younger members of the family. Not even Rosemary had ever ventured beyond grumbling to an open flouting of her authority. Nevertheless, her real affection for Sophie made her seek conciliation; she scarcely knew what else to do.

'Sophie, please, for my sake, won't you deny yourself this pleasure? Does it mean so much to you? We will soon be back in Edinburgh, another six or seven weeks . . . you can't think how much I hated being here without you. Is it too much to ask?'

Clearly, Sophie was disarmed. She hesitated, as though having steeled herself to rebellion she was outflanked by the unexpected appeal. She sighed, exasperated.

'Oh, Helen, I didn't mean you to suffer . . . Rosemary is here, after all . . .'

'Rosemary?' Helen said scornfully. She needed to make no other comment.

'Oh, it's all Papa's fault! Why can't he take on his responsibility for the children?' Sophie walked quickly away from the window, to the empty grate with its gaudy pink shavings hanging down as a substitute for living flames. 'It's suited him too well all these years to have you taking everything on your own shoulders. You've spoilt him, and now that it's too late, you are starting to find it all a burden, aren't you?'

The shrewd comment was nearer to the truth than Helen quite cared to admit.

'Whatever the reason, I am here with five children to care for until the end of September; don't abandon me, Sophie dear!' She thought she saw her sister weakening, and pressed home her advantage. 'After all, you will see Tom soon enough; you can surely wait for less than two months?'

'No!' Sophie burst out in a sort of anguish. 'You don't understand; how can you? Have you ever been in love? Do you know what it means?'

'Of course I know what it means,' she said briskly.

'But you don't! Have you ever felt your heart beat faster when someone enters the room? Have you ever been happy to walk, saying little or nothing perhaps, but looking at the man you love, and know you are loved in return? Have you ever felt his arms around you, and been drawn close to him, and kissed . . .'

'Stop it!' Helen cried, in a panic she could not understand, knowing only that she wished to silence that exultant young voice.

'I did not mean to hurt you,' Sophie said, more gently. 'You have devoted yourself to us, without a thought for yourself. You have never allowed yourself to think beyond the family. We owe you a great deal, Helen, but I'm not willing to do the same thing. I can't sacrifice my life for Papa and the little ones. If I tried, I would end by being sour and crabbit, I know I should,' She looked at her sister, as if wondering whether she dare say more, but she remained silent.

Helen paced the small, cluttered room, irresolute. She felt that she had received some bruising blow, of which the full pain was yet to come. She wanted desperately to settle the question and end this interview.

'If you were to go to Elie for a week?' she said at last. 'I would wish to have a formal invitation from Mrs Hewitt, of course . . . would that satisfy you?' A note of scorn crept into her voice despite all her efforts at calm.

Sophie's arms were about her neck in a moment. 'Oh, Helen, how good you are! You can't think what this means to me! A whole week together . . .'

The arrival of the butcher's boy put an end to the scene, to Helen's immense relief. It was almost soothing to discuss with the cook the household requirements for the next few days, including a good joint of beef for Saturday.

Try as she might – she sensed that Sophie was trying too – relations between the two sisters were not what they had been after Sophie's disclosure. The world which had seemed so secure to Helen was proving a shifting, illusory place. She wished passionately that she could put back the clock, to the spring, before all the changes began which undermined the stability of her family, and even more painful, the position she held within it.

8

In Edinburgh a visit from Doctor Cairns was so common as to occasion no particular excitement. In Melrose, at the end of a week of wet days and solitary evenings, it was a great event. Waking that morning and seeing even through the curtains that the sun was shining once more, Helen felt as light-hearted as if she were no older than Phoebe, and the holiday just beginning.

She allowed the children out into the garden after breakfast, under strict instructions to keep to the paths, although the bright sun promised to dry the grass quickly. From the sitting-room she watched them running and shouting with all the delight of young animals newly released from confinement. Sophie was chasing about among the rest, as though no such creature as Tom Hewitt existed. Seeing Helen at the window she beckoned to her, laughing. Helen hesitated, but only for a moment. They were not in Edinburgh, after all; why should she not forget her dignity for once?

The children were playing tig. In her walking skirt, cut fashionably short to reveal brightly striped stockings, Helen was able to run as fleetly as any. She dodged and twisted, forgetting all her cares in the exhilaration of the chase and of sinking thought in vigorous action.

Philip and Sophie were her swiftest pursuers; Andrew, a more stolid, lumbering boy, she could easily outpace, but they had more than once come within a hairsbreadth of catching her. Breathless with laughter and excitement she fled down the drive, looking back over her shoulder to see if they were gaining on her.

'Helen!'

Amongst the shrieks of the children she didn't hear the

cry. Her first warning that their guest had arrived came when she cannoned into a substantial form, bringing her to a sudden halt.

'Doctor Cairns!' Flushed, eyes bright from the exercise, she smiled up at him with unmixed delight, without a trace of embarrassment.

'No need to ask if the Borders' air is agreeing with you, Helen!'

'You wouldn't say so if you had seen us yesterday. This is the first dry day of the week.'

She drew her hand easily through his arm and they began to walk back to the house, the doctor joking with the children who skirmished noisily on their flanks. At the entrance he paused to distribute amongst them the brown sugar candy he had brought.

'You don't mind, Helen?' he asked, looking up from where he squatted on a level with the little girls. 'It's wholesome enough in its way.'

'At least we will have medical advice to hand if it isn't,' she said, leading him into the house. If only her father had taken the trouble to give his children such a treat!

In the sitting-room she rang for fresh tea and established him in an easy chair, with a cup drawn just as he liked it.

'Am I an absolute fright?' she asked ruefully, consulting the glass over the mantel. 'You might have told me . . . my hair isn't fit to be seen. This is what comes of romping with the children at my age!'

'I have no complaints.'

She glanced at him quickly, her fingers pausing in their work. Something in his tone struck her as odd, but before she could define it the moment had passed.

'I haven't had a minute to say how very sorry we were to hear . . . your loss,' she said awkwardly.

'Thank you. You needn't try to say any more. I know how difficult it is.'

'That is like you!' she exclaimed, turning from the glass. 'Even at such a time you can think of others.'

'Don't!' he cried, almost angrily. 'You must not put me on a pedestal, Helen.'

'No man better deserves it,' she began, then seeing his expression added, 'but I won't praise you if it vexes you. I am on my very best behaviour today. A visit from Edinburgh is too precious to waste.'

'Oh? Are things so bad?'

'I think I must be growing very cross-grained with age . . . but what are we doing indoors on such a perfect day?' she said, with a sudden return of her former vigour. 'Won't you come down to the river for a walk with the children before luncheon? I mustn't monopolise you. Andrew is longing to show you a rabbit's skull he found. We have to make the most of you, you know!'

Laughing, she gave him her hand to pull him to his feet. It would have been difficult to say whether the gesture pleased him or not, but she was already leading him to the garden, and did not see his troubled glance.

The morning passed more pleasantly than any she had known in Melrose. The Tweed was swollen by the week's rain. She found a curious fascination in watching its swift, silent flow, always changing, always the same. The children clustered around the doctor, subjecting him to a barrage of questions, interrupting each other to claim the privilege of telling him some story, or to correct the teller in some trifling, vital particular.

He bore his popularity easily. Her practised eye could see in him a man who genuinely enjoyed the company of children. It struck her for the first time that it might have been a sorrow to him that he and his wife had been childless. He had never spoken of it, or indeed, of his marriage. He would have made an excellent father, she reflected, hearing him indulge in some mock-serious banter with Andrew which struck just the right note of mingled sense and absurdity. When did Papa ever take so much notice of his own children? Even in her own mind she no longer attempted to make excuses for him.

Helen had taken care that luncheon should be substantial; Doctor Cairns's fondness for good cooking was well known. 'What plans do you have for me this afternoon?' he said at last, pushing away his empty plate with a sigh of mingled satisfaction and regret. 'Give me half an hour's respite and I'll be yours to command.'

'The Lammas Fair!' Philip broke in at once, before Helen could say a word. Doctor Cairns looked at her for an explanation.

'It is held a mile or so away from Melrose, on the side of the Eildons. If you are agreeable, we may take a walk there?'

'Why not?' he said, with a smile to the children's delighted faces. 'Will there be gingerbread, do you think? Gingerbread eaten at a fair is always twice as good as any other.'

There was indeed gingerbread, and a host of other treats, which Doctor Cairns seemed to relish as much as his young companions. There were stalls for toys, for ribbons and handkerchiefs, for ornaments and trinkets, for pottery figurines of a naive gaudiness. The children darted from one delight to the next, calling on Helen and Doctor Cairns to admire some new discovery, or to advise on the purchase of some trifle.

Helen was happy to wander through the crowd, Phoebe's hand in hers. It was a good-natured gathering; there were drinking booths, but no rowdiness, at least not so early in the day. Some of the stalls appeared to be kept by country folk, others by tinkers, drawn by the main business of the fair, the sale of livestock.

After losing sight of them in the throng for a while, Helen came upon Doctor Cairns with Sophie and the two other girls, outside a canvas tent clumsily daubed with mysterious symbols.

'Well, are you going in, Doctor Cairns?' she asked gaily. 'Don't you want to know what the future holds for you?'

'No. I would rather keep my dreams intact, thank you,'

he said. It struck her as a sad rejoinder, although he smiled as he spoke. 'Shall we hunt for the boys? They're over by the shows, I think. I hope you are fond of coconuts; Philip has won enough at the shies to supply the Zoological Gardens all winter!'

Not without a struggle, they persuaded her brothers to abandon the charms of the swings and the wrestling booths. They were beginning to make their way off the hill, when the doctor stopped.

'Sophie, you could take the family home from here, I suppose? I've a great fancy to see a little more of the Eildons while I'm here; Helen, are you too tired to stay out a little longer?'

'By no means,' she answered readily. 'It would be a pleasure to take some exercise, after a week of confinement.'

The boys pleaded to come too, but Doctor Cairns was firm in refusing. 'I shall see you when we come back, and perhaps there may be surprises in store,' he said patting the breast pocket of his jacket.

'The boys were disappointed,' she said as they moved off alone, towards the saddle which separated one hill from the next.

'They'll get over it. I must have my treat too,' he replied, watching her to see how she received the remark.

'To be sure, it would be a pity to go back to Edinburgh without seeing the Eildons except as a fairground,' she said, with no trace of confusion. 'Shall we attempt the climb? My Balmoral boots are stout enough, if you will lend me your arm.'

'With all my heart!'

She smiled, and they began to walk up the slope.

'Your father told me that Francis Bethune was down last weekend,' he began.

'Yes.' She frowned, and then added, in a burst of candour, 'I find him difficult to understand. I would not say as much to anyone else, of course, but you are different . . .' She looked up, and surprised on his heavy, likeable features a look of such suffering that she stopped walking. 'I'm sorry . . . is something wrong?'

'Nothing . . . I feel my age sometimes, that's all. If we walk a little more slowly . . . You were saying, about Bethune?'

'Oh, yes . . . it was so strange; we dined together twice. I found him agreeable, friendly even. Then we met a third time, at church. He was so cold that I could almost have believed I had offended him in some way, and yet we had parted the previous night on the best of terms. I can't understand it.'

He shrugged. 'Don't blame yourself. He treated me in much the same way once.'

'You?'

'Yes. I did him a service; he has scarcely addressed a word to me since.'

'He did mention that he was indebted to you,' she said, a little self consciously, as she remembered his other comments concerning her companion.

'It was over ten years ago, fifteen probably. His father had come up to Edinburgh on some business matter. He was staying with his sister, Harry Robertson's mother, when he was taken ill. She sent for me. I saw at once how things stood, and told her that she must expect the worst. I did what I could to make him comfortable, and left. When I called in the next day, she was in a state of great agitation.'

'He had died?'

'No, although he was barely conscious. She had been trying since my last visit to get him to receive his son, Francis. She had summoned him as soon as I told her what the outcome must be. He'd spent the night there, in a chair outside his father's room. Arthur Bethune would not have him cross the threshold, would have barred him from the house, if it had been his. Fanny Robertson didn't dare gainsay him, ill as he was. She begged me to do what I could to persuade him.'

'And did you?'

'I promised to try. Young Bethune was still outside his father's room. I shall never forget his face that morning. He could have had no sleep, he was sheet-white. He tried to speak to me as I passed him; he had to turn away, he couldn't utter a word. When I see him now cultivating his superior smile and his stilted law-court language, I remember that ghastly-faced youth fighting to hide his tears. Everything else is only a wall he's thrown up to protect the self he showed that day.'

'Were you successful?'

He was breathing more heavily as they plodded up the hill. He spoke slowly, choosing his words with care. 'I sent everyone from the room. Only a few minutes after I entered, Arthur Bethune sank into a stupor. I knew he would never rouse from it this side of the grave.' There was a pause before he added, in a carefully dispassionate tone, 'I told Francis that his father had asked me to summon him, his last conscious wish before he sank into a coma. He was with him to the end, a few hours later.'

'You told him . . . but was it true?'

'Can't a look convey as much meaning as a sentence? I interpreted Arthur Bethune's dying gaze as a desire to see his son. Who can say that I was wrong?'

'Not I, for one,' she said softly.

'When it was over, Francis Bethune thanked me for my advocacy. He was moved, as you can imagine, and genuinely grateful. We parted on excellent terms. The next time we met, at dinner at the Robertsons' some months later, he all but cut me. It puzzled me at first, and even hurt me, to be honest. You know how it is in Edinburgh, our paths have crossed more than once since, over the years. He's kept his distance from me, but I've watched him, and drawn my own conclusions.'

'And?'

'Anyone who has seen his real self is a danger to the facade he wishes to present. If you have had a glimpse of what lies behind it he will never forgive you.'

'But who could live like that? How lonely he must be!'

'Lonely? That's nothing unusual, is it? Bethune at least has the advantage of a comfortable income, a profession in which he's likely to prosper, a sound constitution and a decorative enough person. Some of us have fewer sources of consolation,' he ended, with a wry smile which would have made it impossible for her to discern how seriously he was speaking, even if she had been fully attentive.

'Why did his father treat him so badly?' she asked, following her own train of thought.

'Oh, Arthur Bethune was an odd character,' he replied evasively. 'Can you manage this last scramble? Here, hold tight!'

The view from the top of the hill repaid all their effort. In every direction hills folded into each other like interlaced fingers. Here and there, through their greens and browns, ran the grey-blue strand of the Tweed, sweeping in a great loop through the countryside. Clouds glided through the sky in stately towering masses, like galleons under full sail, while their shadows sped effortlessly over the hills beneath.

Breathless from the climb, she rested against him with a freedom she would have used with no other man. A vainer or a more foolish man might have been deceived by her ease.

'How petty all our cares seem up here!'

'And what cares do you have in mind?'

'Oh, nothing worth talking of. I think I have allowed my spirits to be sunk by a few days of rain. Everything will be quite as usual once we see Papa here again. He brought Miss Raymond with him the last time, and the presence of a stranger always makes things strained and artificial.'

'And when do you expect him?' he asked, with a gentleness which struck her as curious.

'In a week or two, at the beginning of September,' she replied carelessly. 'Why do you ask?'

He sighed, and gave her his hand to begin the descent. 'Take care, the grass is slippery.'

'You haven't answered my question,' she said, more sharply. 'What are you keeping from me?'

'Perhaps I misunderstood Lambert but I thought he spoke of spending his weekends in Balerno this summer. That was one reason for my visit today. He said he would take it as a kindness if I would run down to see you, as he would be unable to return. I hardly needed urging.'

'Balerno? Papa knows no one in Balerno!'

He did not answer, all his attention seemingly taken up by handing her down a difficult patch. At last, he said quietly, 'Douglas Morton has taken a house there for the summer. His granddaughter is with him. Miss Raymond.'

'But Papa can't intend to go out there every weekend! He wouldn't!'

'It was what I thought he said, Helen,' he said, almost apologetically. They walked on in silence, half slipping, half running down the slope. When it levelled out, he added, more decisively, 'You may not like what I'm going to say. Would it really be so terrible if your father were to remarry? No – listen to me – might it not be best for you all?'

'I'm sure you will explain exactly how?'

'For one thing, try to put yourself in your father's place. He's been a widower these six or seven years. Will it not make him happier?'

'And have I not done everything to make him happy?'

'Everything a daughter could.'

'You are very honest, at least.'

'Someone has to make you see it,' he said, watching her averted face. 'But think of yourself, Helen. Won't it be best for you to be free to lead your own life? How much longer could you sacrifice yourself for your family?'

'It was no sacrifice!' she said angrily.

'It was, even if you were not aware of it. A sacrifice of your future, of what you might have been in some other relation than daughter and sister. You were – are – in a false position, a sort of limbo. While it was necessary it was admirable, but now that freedom may be in sight, why cling to your chains and resent your liberator?'

'It is my life! The only life I know! What am I, if I am not the mistress of the household, a mother of sorts to the little ones? What other existence have I known since I was sixteen, or even younger? Mama was able for so little that last two years . . .'

'Except bearing her tenth child,' he said grimly. 'I'll say no more, but perhaps you'll reflect on what we've discussed. Susan Raymond is not very much to my taste, I'll admit, but she's a sensible enough woman at bottom. She would make a reasonable wife to your father, and she doesn't lack common sense, whatever you may think of her tiresome ways. Try to make a friend of her, or you may regret it.'

'Thank you, the ground is so level now that I can dispense with your assistance,' she said, withdrawing her arm from his.

'I would be no friend to you if I had not spoken my mind,' he said, catching her hand and holding it tight. 'Am I to be punished for telling you what seems to me the truth?'

'Who is punishing you?' she said sulkily.

'Then give me your arm again.'

Still not looking at him, she stiffly rested her hand on his arm. He pressed it close to his side. 'Helen!' he said reproachfully. Her frown relaxed into a reluctant smile.

The remainder of Doctor Cairns's visit passed without friction. The whole family escorted him to the station. As they awaited the train, he had a final surprise in store. From the Lammas Fair there was a little memento for every child, knives for the boys, trinkets for the girls. Helen was included, with a pretty locket, a moss-agate in its centre.

'But it's beautiful!' she exclaimed. 'Really, you should not have bothered with me.'

'Oh, you must have your fairing too,' he said lightly. 'I see the train coming; Phoebe, a goodbye kiss?'

Even Phoebe, usually so shy, willingly proffered the requested kiss, followed by the other girls. With a moment's hesitation, laughing, but scarcely more self-conscious than her sisters, Helen lightly brushed her lips against his cheek. She could almost have fancied that the gesture displeased him, so gravely did he regard her, but already the train was bearing down on the station in a fury which seemed an assault on every sense. She gave the little incident not another thought.

After Doctor Cairns's visit the days settled into a rhythm pleasant enough in its quiet way. There were walks in plenty to explore if the weather were kind, sometimes with the added delight of a picnic. There was always the trip to Rosemary's, and from there the excitement of the ferry over the river to view the ruins of Dryburgh Abbey, or the coach out to Abbotsford, or a walk along the Allan Water, the so-called 'Fairy Dean'.

Every weekend Helen looked for her father, but his letters spoke of unduly heavy commitments, his excuses becoming ever weaker with repetition. She duly reported them to the children, with all the conviction she could muster. They seemed little disturbed by his absence, apart from Kitty, whom he never treated with anything better than suppressed irritation.

She and Sophie never again referred to the subject of Tom Hewitt. Sophie gave her, without comment, a letter of invitation from Mrs Hewitt, warmly urging her to join their family party in Elie, for a week or as long as she chose. Helen communicated the letter to her father. Somewhat against her better judgement, she added that Sophie very much wished to go, and that she herself saw no argument against a week's stay. In return, as she had expected, she received a hasty note telling her to arrange it all as she saw fit.

It was two weeks after the doctor's visit, at the end of August, that Jack, newly returned from his reading party, came down for the weekend. Sophie was to accompany him back to Edinburgh, and from there go on to Elie with the Hewitts.

Helen was not absolutely easy in her mind as Jack's arrival approached. She had scarcely seen him since his outrageous behaviour had threatened to bring Rosemary's wedding day to a distasteful end. Although she would not have admitted as much, she felt a little apprehensive at receiving him into the household.

In fact, when Jack arrived shortly before dinner on Friday, Helen positively failed to recognise him. 'Jack?' she asked, in unconcealed dismay.

'Don't you like them?' he said, a little huffily, pulling at the flourishing whiskers which now framed his face, leaving only the point of his chin exposed. He seemed changed utterly from the fresh-faced youth she liked to remember.

'Wasn't a moustache enough?' she asked, as she kissed him. 'It at least was neat . . .'

'All the men have full whiskers now,' he replied, with a dignity which amused her. 'You find that funny? I suppose you would like to see me still in sailor suits?'

'You were the sweetest creature imaginable . . . but no doubt I'll come to like the whiskers, with time. Now will you go up and change your coat? Dinner is only waiting for you.'

In honour of Jack's visit, all but the two youngest children were allowed to dine. Julia and Phoebe had their tea as usual, but came in for dessert. Helen had given some thought to the question of wine. Eventually she decided to provide it as usual, and allow Philip to take a little. At fifteen it seemed reasonable to include him in the adult privilege, and she calculated that Jack would be all the more abstemious for the need to give his brother a good example.

Her tactics worked admirably. She doubted whether Philip positively enjoyed his half-glass, although he sipped it with a lordly indifference, but the consciousness that his eyes were upon his admired elder brother did appear to exert a restraining influence on Jack. She saw him look at the wine with longing, but he drank no more than Helen herself. The meal passed off agreeably. Jack was always at his best in the company of the younger children. She was happy to let him absorb their full attention with his stories of the reading party. They appeared to have devoted such a large amount of their time to walking, fishing, climbing and larking that she wondered how much reading could have occurred.

But despite the good humour with which he kept his brothers and sisters entertained, something in Jack's manner left Helen uneasy. She might not have noticed anything amiss had she not been anxious from his behaviour at the wedding, but now it seemed to her that there was a sense of strain under his undeniable high spirits, that his gaiety was forced. Although the meal was a success she was glad when it was over and the children despatched to bed.

'Helen, will you come into the garden to keep me company while I smoke?' he asked, a little self-consciously.

'When did you start smoking? Really, Jack . . .' She checked herself. 'Let me get my shawl, and I will be with you.'

It was a still, warm evening. In the air hung the scent of stock, sweet with childhood memories, until put to flight by the cloud of pungent smoke which Jack perseveringly produced. She thought the expression on his face not unlike Philip's faced with his wine, but she was wise enough to say nothing.

'I asked Papa about Canada when I got back to Edinburgh.'

It was what she had been expecting, but she felt a tremor of alarm at his tone, so abrupt and brittle. 'What did he say?'

'He scarcely listened to me, as usual. I wouldn't be put off, so he told me to apply to you. If you approved, he said, he would consider it. It all depends on you, Helen.'

'You're quite sure he said so?'

'Quite. I would not make a mistake. It's too important.'

She was silent, furious at her father's shuffling of responsibility onto her shoulders. Disconcertingly, she remembered the time when to spare Papa trouble had been her sole ambition. If he were spoilt, who had spoiled him?

'It was my understanding that Papa and I had discussed the matter, and he had decided in favour of at least one more year at your studies. He suggested that you might write to Uncle Richard in the meantime.'

He made an exclamation of impatience and disgust. 'You know Papa! He'll not stick to that if it causes him any annoyance. He has no real concern for me, for you, for any of us! He wants not to be bothered, that's all, so that he can concentrate on being the charming man of letters, the *bon viveur*, the ardent suitor!'

The concentrated bitterness shocked her, but even more shocking was the suspicion that some truth underlay the venom.

'Papa may have his failings, but that's not to the point. If he asked my opinion, it would have to be unchanged. I think you are too young to go so far – no, hear me out – and I think that you would regret for the rest of your life not taking your degree. What will you lose by waiting another two years? Think how much you have changed in even one year, since leaving the Academy! The boys you knew there would scarcely know you! In another two years you will be so much more prepared to face the challenge. Why go now, and risk failure?'

'Look, Nell, I'm sure that's all very well and I won't deny that you mean it for the best, but you don't understand. I've got to get away!'

'Why?'

He threw away his cigar. The glowing tip described a transient arch through the gathering dusk, and was extinguished. 'I can't answer you. Won't you trust me, when I tell you that it's essential?'

'Have you done anything of which you need to be ashamed?'

'No!'

'Are you in debt? Gambling?'

'No . . . if it were only that! Don't ask me, Nell. You must take my word for it when I tell you that I have to get away. Please, believe me!'

'And what good will it do if you go? Whatever you're running away from, won't it go with you? How can I say that it would be a wise move?'

'It would be better than staying, a thousand times better, for me and for all of you!'

'Jack, aren't you being a little dramatic? Perhaps your troubles seem very important to you just now, but if you won't confide in me how can I help you?' She hesitated, then added boldly, 'If you drink to excess, why, it's scarcely uncommon amongst young men, is it?'

He groaned, seeming to despair of conveying his urgent need to her. 'Drink has nothing to do with it. Nell, you can get Papa to agree to anything: ask him to let me go, I beg you! I was never more in earnest in my life!'

The exaggerated whiskers trailing onto his collar were an incongruous frame for an expression of such misery. She began to waver. 'You can get Papa to agree to anything.' It had been true, at Rosemary's dinner party. Susan Raymond had argued then in favour of Jack's wishes. Was she, after all, to admit that Susan Raymond had been right?

Not even her affection for her brother could bring her to so humiliating a concession. She patted his arm.

'Cheer up, Jack. In six months you won't take such a dismal view of life here. You'll be glad that I recommended that you stay, believe me.'

She was braced for further argument, but he remained silent. When he did speak, his voice was muted, defeated.

'I've done all I can. Remember how much I wanted to go away, if the worst should happen.'

'The worst? What a prophet of doom!'

'We shall see. Shall we go in? I don't suppose there's such a thing as brandy in the house?'

She followed her brother in, sure that she had won a victory for prudence, yet by no means as easy in her mind as she would have expected.

Her sense of unease never quite left her during the remainder of Jack's stay, and yet his behaviour was impossible to fault. He kept himself constantly involved in the younger children's games and expeditions; to Helen he was courteous and helpful, seeming to bear no grudge for her refusal. He was calm, resigned. She was at a loss to understand, unless by assuming that his wish to leave, though sincere, had been a desperate struggle against an equally strong temptation to remain.

His younger brothers and sisters greeted the prospect of Jack's departure on Monday morning with such distress that Helen urged him to delay his return, if only by a day.

'I can't. I have an engagement this afternoon.' He walked to the door, and stared down the drive. 'Where is that fly? We shall miss the train at this rate.'

'Is it anything important? Could Sophie not make your apologies? We have so enjoyed having you here.'

'I'm coaching Grant. I can't put it off.'

'Is that all? I'm sure it won't make the slightest difference to James Grant whether you give him a lesson this afternoon or another day. Let Sophie take a note of apology; stay until tomorrow!'

The children took up the cry with enthusiasm but he was immovable. 'I can't let him down. It will be our first lesson since I went up north. I'm sorry, but it can't be changed, and that's an end to it.'

Helen said no more, secretly approving his firmness in a matter which, she thought, offered him so little pleasure. His devotion to duty was none the less admirable for being so unexpected. As the fly approached, he snatched up his carpet-bag and one of Sophie's and began a hurried round of farewell kisses.

She watched the fly down the drive with a sense of real loss. She wondered how she would pass the time until her sister's return. She was quite sure that Sophie was not asking herself a similar question.

9

The Monday following Lizzie's visit to the Shannons brought Nicholas Gillanders to her door. She greeted him with a heightening of the guarded manner habitual in her; Mrs Shannon's hints had not passed her by quite unheeded.

He seemed, though, harmless enough. Small, with the red-veined cheeks and nose of the whisky drinker, he was an old man to her merciless young eyes. His greying hair, long and lank at the sides, was strained unconvincingly across his bald head, the thin strands looking strangely wet. He was dressed more showily than most of the men she had encountered, with loudly patterned trousers which seemed to her not in keeping with his age.

His manner was kind enough; he seemed eager to accommodate her. She found herself explaining her needs more freely than she had intended as he listened, head held sympathetically to one side, nodding in encouragement, while his eyes, moist and slightly bloodshot, rested on her with fatherly interest.

'You can join the clothing club at Cooper's this very morning, and go along with credit of two pounds – that's a shilling a week for a year. You could get some fine warm dresses for your sister, and pay for them without noticing it.'

His voice was soft and coaxing, and to Lizzie almost alarmingly English in speech. She wondered if he had perhaps been in service in the south, to learn to talk so properly.

'But the shoes . . . that's a different matter,' he continued, pursing his lips. 'Cooper's don't keep shoes, you see.'

'Minnie Shannon said ye'd maybe give me a loan of a pound,' she said, concealing her awe of him; she had not looked for anyone so genteel, so respectable.

'Not me, oh, dear me no!' he said, shaking his head sadly. 'I only wish it were possible, believe me, but I am not in a position . . .' He watched her face fall, and waited a moment, as her disappointment made itself felt.

'I wouldna be speering, only Minnie Shannon said . . .' she murmured.

'Yes . . .' he said, rubbing his chin, 'I wonder . . . she heard perhaps that in one or two instances I have been able to prevail on a friend of mine to oblige a customer with a loan. I don't do it for everyone, of course. I have to be able to guarantee to my friend that the payments will be kept up; usually, it's only as a favour to a special customer . . .' He eyed her speculatively. She was too proud to beg for any favour, but she could not conceal her anxiety from those calculating, watery eyes.

'It's not every day that I come across a situation which affects me so much as yours; I tell you what I'll do. I'll see my friend, and speak up for you, and see if he won't let you have a pound. I'll need to stretch the truth, of course, and say that I've known your family for a good while, but I'll do it, this once. If he's agreeable, you shall have the money by the end of the week. There, how's that?'

Lizzie's joy was all the more intense for its rarity. She could barely speak.

'And I can trust you to be regular in your payments? Sixpence a week for a year, you know.'

'Without fail,' she said proudly.

'It's a bargain, then?' He took her hand, still damp from the washing in which he had interrupted her.

'Aye,' she said, looking at him with a trustfulness far from common in her.

'We'll sort out your club card just now, anyway,' he said, drawing out his pocket-book. 'Your menage runs for a year, see?' She felt a sudden stirring of alarm at the

135

fifty-two spaces on the club card. She had not realised that they would seem so many.

'Don't forget, you can go to Cooper's this very day, with as good as two pounds in your pocket,' he urged, as if he had noted her momentary panic.

She nodded, taking heart.

'You can pay me your first shilling just now, if you like . . . yes? See, there's one down already!' He marked her card with ostentatious care, and handed it back to her. 'I usually call on a Monday, like the rent man,' he said, with a laugh. 'It's as well to take all your medicine in the one dose, don't you think? But this week I'll try to come over again, with the pound from my friend – if I can persuade him, that is.'

He left, seeming well pleased with his morning's work. Lizzie, now that the bargain was struck, looked less sure of its wisdom. The fifty-one blank spaces on the card spoke of an eternity, of uncertainty and risk. She sighed, and fingered the card doubtfully. Her eyes fell on May's patient, listless face.

Lizzie straightened her shoulders. 'We'll get ye a braw dress for the winter, ye'll see,' she said, and put the card out of sight.

The week of Sophie's absence passed. Helen threw herself into the task of amusing the children. It was at least a distraction from the self-pity, a weakness new to her, which seemed to be awaiting any moment of unguarded reflection.

Images of Tom Hewitt and Sophie would steal into her mind. They were all in all to each other, she supposed. Who cared so much for her? She dismissed the thought whenever it put itself into words, but it coloured her mood. And yet she had seen Rosemary marry without a tremor of regret for her own lot, with indeed a flicker of pitying superiority.

Even when Sophie returned things were not much better. Her native high spirits were replaced by a dreamy absence of mind, as if the present moment were of value to her only if spent in recalling the past or imagining the future. She was of little help to Helen. Try as she might, she could not but resent Sophie's moping.

A letter from her father announcing that he might be expected in Melrose for a brief visit on the Saturday following Sophie's return raised Helen's spirits. To be sure, a day was not much, but she was ready to see it as a proof of his concern.

From the first moment of his arrival it was clear that her father was making an effort to please. There was a little gift from Edinburgh for everyone, chosen with surprising thoughtfulness. Helen kissed him with an affection all the warmer for the secret resentment she had allowed herself to cherish against him.

'You're so kind, Papa!' she said, winding her arms about his waist with her old, unthinking freedom. 'How did you manage to choose such a love of a parasol? I didn't know you could be so clever; it will be the perfect set-off to my walking dress.'

He looked uncomfortable at her praise, but said nothing as she drew him into the house, laughing and chattering.

'Now, Papa, shall I ring for you some tea?' she asked, her hand already on the bell. 'You must have been up at some unthinkable hour to reach us so early. Would you like something to eat, or will you wait for luncheon?'

'Nothing just now. Don't ring for tea quite yet. I have some news, some very good news. I came down to tell you, and to see you all, of course. Sit down, Nell. You make me nervous standing there in front of me like an erring housemaid.'

Obediently, she sat, eyes fixed on him. He remained standing before the empty hearth. As he half turned to rest his elbow on the mantel, he caught sight of himself in the glass. As though he were alone, he examined his reflection and carefully swept back a stray lock of his springing grey hair which had fallen onto his forehead.

As she waited for him to speak, she really expected that he was about to tell her of some literary success to justify, triumphantly, so many weekends away from his family. Docile, eager, she waited to share his delight.

He cleared his throat and began, as though repeating a prepared text. 'I'm sure that you will share my joy, Helen, when you learn that Susan Raymond has agreed to become my wife. We are to be married next week . . .'

'Ah!' The cry escaped her despite her vigilance, a cry of pain, and disgust, and anger. He continued, ignoring or not noticing her reaction.

'That will allow us three weeks together before you need to return to Edinburgh. There should be no difficulty in getting the house here for the extra week. If you leave here the day before the boys are due back at the Academy it will be time enough . . .'

Helen let him talk on. The blow was not absolutely unexpected, and yet it crushed her. She was scarcely capable of thought.

'It will be a change, of course. We' – at the word she looked at him in sudden anguish – 'we understand that you will find things strange for a while. Susan and I have discussed it, and she expressed the most perfect delicacy on the question of your feelings. She entertains the very kindest regard for you. She often speaks of you, indeed one of her anxieties was the fear, foolish though natural, that you might not welcome a step-mother. I was able to reassure her on that point, I need hardly add.'

'Of course.' Her throat was so constricted that the words were barely audible.

He was continuing, either wishing to allow her to recover her composure, or unaware of her distress. 'It will be a great thing for you, Helen. I could see on our last visit how the strain of family responsibility was beginning to tell on you. It would have been selfish in me to ask you to continue . . . indeed, I may even go so far as to say that not least among the considerations urging me to this step was the wish to provide my

138

children with a mother.' He smiled at her, sublimely complacent.

She rose to her feet with the innate dignity which survived even this shock. 'If you will excuse me . . . I will be back for luncheon.' Further explanation was beyond her. He held the door for her.

'Be sure to take your parasol,' he called after her, with a show of concern which touched her despite everything. 'Susan will be pleased to know that you used it. She took great pains over selecting it.' Tears blurring her eyes, she just managed to pick out the hated parasol, and fled.

Without giving any thought to her destination, wanting only to avoid Melrose and its inhabitants, she struck out along the banks of the Tweed, downstream. One thought circled in her mind with the futile angry persistence of a wasp on a window pane: How will I share a house with that woman? See her every day, sit at table with her, spend every evening with her? She gritted her teeth, walking so quickly that she was almost running.

The thoughts she sought to dismiss were not so easily outpaced. To hear her address him as Edward! To see her kiss him goodbye; to know that nothing which was said to him might not be coaxed from him by that insinuating creature at night, when his head lay beside hers on the pillow in an intimacy from which Helen was for ever debarred . . .

It was only when she heard a voice calling her name that she came to herself. She looked about her, with the confusion of an awakened dreamer. She had almost reached the village of Newstead, although she could not recall a single feature of her journey. Walking towards her, bearing fishing tackle, were her brother-in-law and Francis Bethune, Harry smiling, his cousin hanging back, aloof.

'What brings you here, Helen?' Harry began cheerily. 'No children? Have you run away from them for a moment's peace?'

A tremulous smile was all the response she could make

to his teasing. He continued, seeming not to notice anything amiss, 'Why not come and view our efforts? You might bring us luck; the fish are proving very shy.'

'No . . . not this time, thank you,' she murmured, already breaking away from them, past caring what her brother-in-law might think of her manner. To Francis Bethune she gave not a thought; she barely glanced at him.

At first, he had held back from the encounter with the same wary coolness which had so wounded her at their last meeting. But as he watched her speaking to his cousin, his expression softened, and when Helen hurried on, he spoke in a hasty undertone to Harry Robertson, and thrust his fishing rod into his hands.

Even in the few seconds which this demanded Helen had covered a good distance. She did not hear his footsteps as he came in pursuit of her. Only when he had twice called her name did she stop and turn to him a face of desperate dazed unhappiness.

'Miss Lambert — may I walk with you?'

'I would prefer to be alone,' she said simply.

'Please . . . I shan't bother you with talk. You won't need to be polite.'

She looked at him with vague bewilderment, as though some memory of his indifference on their last meeting had suggested itself to her. 'As you wish,' she said dully. He offered her his arm. She hesitated, but took it. They continued along the river, more slowly than before. True to his promise he remained silent, except to suggest that at Newstead they should turn to the south, towards the Eildons, as the banks were beginning to rise in the great scar above the Tweed. She allowed herself to be guided away from the river, not caring where she went.

By degrees the first shock of her father's news lessened. As it did, she became more aware of her present situation, and of her silent companion, whose arm, she realised, she was gripping tightly. At once she relaxed her hand.

'You have been most kind. I scarcely know how to thank you.'

'I could not help but observe that you appeared to have received a shock of some sort. It did not seem to me proper that you should be alone.'

He expressed himself awkwardly, his manner was stiff, but she sensed the kindness underlying the lack of ease. For the first time she spoke in something like her natural tone.

'You were quite right. You may as well know: my father is to marry Susan Raymond, almost immediately. I shall return to Edinburgh to a step-mother.'

'Forgive me, but was this not expected?'

'Not by me. It is not merely that I feel a want of sympathy with Miss Raymond; what has been so painful is my father's attitude. I have been used while it suited him and now I am to be supplanted, with the sham that it is in my interests, that he is acting for us, and not for himself . . .'

Irrational, passionate, her grievances poured out like a river in spate, carrying with it waste and detritus in swirling confusion. And when her words faltered, tears replaced them. She fought for self-control, but it was useless. She threw her hands up to her contorted face.

'Don't! Please, Miss Lambert, I beg you! Don't distress yourself!'

He took a tentative step towards her, and put his arm about her shoulders, as uncertainly as though he were following dimly heard instructions. At the touch of his arm, clumsy and unsure, she turned blindly to him, concealing her face against his shoulder, and sobbed in childlike abandon.

His left arm encircled her waist. He held her close, more naturally than at first. His head bowed towards hers, so that his cheek rested against her hair.

It was the caressing, soothing movement of his hands on her back which recalled her to herself. She became alarmingly aware of the impropriety of their situation, and even worse, of a stirring of pleasure, almost a desire to prolong the chance embrace. At once she raised her face from the comforting darkness of his shoulder, seeing with embarrassment the damp trace of her tears on his jacket.

'Here.' He gave her a handkerchief, and stooped to pick up her forgotten parasol while she wiped her eyes and, more prosaically but equally necessary, blew her nose. He studiously busied himself with opening the parasol, either from tact or inexperience taking so long that she had almost recovered her composure before he succeeded.

'Thank you.' She took it eagerly to shade her face from view, blotched and reddened as it must be. They walked in merciful quiet, the breeze refreshing her swollen eyes as it gently agitated the fringe of her parasol. As the silence lengthened she realised that he would not be the one to break it, from delicacy, or fear.

She cleared her throat. 'I can't tell you how sorry I am, Mr Bethune. I have made the most appalling fool of myself. I don't know what could have induced me to . . .'

'There's no need to say another word.' His hurried interruption suggested the dread of another breakdown. Mortified, she relapsed into silence again. As if realising, too late, his ineptness, he added in a gentler tone, 'You may be quite assured, Miss Lambert, that no one will hear of this from me.'

'You are very kind. I am more indebted to you than I can well express.'

'I am glad if I have been able to be of service. I am not, you know, well suited to such a role, temperamentally, that is.'

She would have liked to protest, but the awkwardness of the situation kept her speechless. Conscious of her tear-stained eyes, she did not even dare to give him a reassuring glance.

'I am far from wishing to curtail our walk, but under

the circumstances do you not think it advisable to return before your absence occasions comment?' he suggested, with the same disjunction between the stilted language and the genuine good feeling it expressed so pompously which she had observed before. She could see why many people thought him cold and artificial, but she saw what they did not, that the complicated formality of his speech had, concealed at its heart, a timid impulse of simple kindness.

'You're probably right,' she said with a sigh. 'Could we sit for a moment, do you think? I can't quite face the thought of going back yet.'

He followed her gaze. 'The sheep fold? Well, why not?' They walked over to the tumble of rough stones just retaining the suggestion of its original function. He removed the loose pea jacket which served as overcoat on his fishing expedition, and spread it on the most level portion of the ruined wall. She seated herself, keeping the parasol between them to hide her face. He hesitated, and joined her at a distance of several feet, separated by the spreading skirts of her walking dress.

She contemplated the homecoming which awaited her. 'I shall never forgive my father,' she said suddenly.

'You must not say that!' he cried, as though shocked out of his formality. 'Whatever the cost, don't allow a lasting estrangement to develop. You would regret it to your last hour, I can assure you.'

Beneath the fringe of her parasol she could see his ungloved right hand resting on his knee. As he spoke, she saw his fingers clench into a fist with such vehemence that his knuckles showed white. She scarcely dared reply.

'No estrangement is likely. I expressed myself badly. I should have said that my feelings towards him will be changed.'

'Not even that, if you can help it! Believe me, nothing exceeds the misery of prolonged coldness in a family.'

'You seem to speak with particular feeling,' she ventured. From beyond the screening parasol she heard him sigh, and reluctantly answer.

'It is an old story now, and of no interest to any but myself. Yes, I can claim excellent authority for presuming to advise you on the subject. My own father was a stranger to me from my early childhood until almost his dying breath. It was no wish of mine that it should be so, but I have often asked myself whether I could have done more to repair the breach, even though it was none of my making. I did make one overture to my father, when I entered the University. I met with a mere acknowledgement that my letter had been received. A communication from his lawyer; can you imagine it? A letter from which I had looked for so much, full of my hopes for my future career, telling him of the little triumphs which marked the end of my school days, a letter into which I had poured my whole heart, I may say . . . and in return? A legal document acknowledging receipt, as though I were a creditor making some unwelcome demand upon him! I never wrote to him again; it will be long before I ever write another letter from the heart, and risk such a rebuff.'

'Why did he treat you so unnaturally?'

She thought he was not going to reply. When he did, it was in a carefully unemotional tone, as though he were describing something which had happened to a different self.

'My father was a solitary, friendless man. I can see now that he had a tendency to melancholia. We saw little of him as children. He was happiest amongst his books; to be honest, my sister and I were rather afraid of him. He adored my mother. I think she was the one being whom he ever loved. She was in every aspect his opposite, sociable, gay, loving, always thinking how to make life pleasant for all about her. I have wondered since how she came to marry a man so different to herself. I think perhaps she felt a sort of pity for him, or perhaps she recognised in his attachment a love beyond the ordinary.' He shrugged. 'In his way he was a strikingly good-looking man, I have often heard my aunt say so. Perhaps that alone accounts for it.'

Helen listened, her own troubles forgotten, scarcely daring to breathe, lest in attracting his attention she interrupt his confidence.

'My sister was older than I by a year or two. There had been two other boys after me, but they did not survive infancy. I was, I suppose, my mother's baby. I was inseparable from her. I can remember that she used to tease me about my devotion, calling me her little spaniel. I was an unusually affectionate child, I believe.

'When I became ill during the summer of my eighth year there was no reason to suspect anything worse than some childish ailment. I was unwell, complained of a sore throat, had a heavy head, wanted only to lie in my mother's arms and be soothed to sleep. She wasn't anxious over the illness. We were staying in the country, near St Andrews. She didn't summon the doctor, and nursed me herself, as I wanted. I can just remember one tearful scene, I clinging to her, my father protesting vehemently, wanting her to leave me to the nursemaid. She stayed with me, promising not to leave me until I was better. I think she was vexed by his intervention.

'I was fortunate. I recovered quickly, never having been seriously unwell. It soon became clear that my mother had succumbed to the same illness. In her case it rapidly assumed so severe a character that my father himself drove to St Andrews for a doctor.'

There was a lengthy pause. 'It was diphtheria. I had escaped with a mild infection, as sometimes happens, whether by chance or constitutional vagary. My mother, and my sister who was already showing the same disturbing symptoms, were not so lucky. Within a fortnight they were both dead. My father had never stirred from her bedside; he remained unscathed, although I have no doubt he would gladly have died with her.

'I did not see him again until he lay on his own death-bed, twelve years later. A week after her death I was sent away. My nursemaid told me that the change of air was to help me recover my strength. I thought I would return home when I was better. It never happened. After convalescence I was sent to school in Edinburgh, boarding with strangers. My holidays I spent in the charge of my landlady, or with the Robertsons. When I grew older I realised the truth. My father could not forgive me; he blamed me for my mother's death. Her love for me had killed her. The very sight of me was hateful to him.'

She shifted her parasol, and gazed at him in self-forgetful sympathy. She saw by the bleak set of his face what the recital had cost him.

'In its way it was not the worst of preparations for life, perhaps. From the age of eight I have learned to stand alone. I need no one. I have often wondered if that was the lesson my father wished to teach me. He needed my mother. Without her, his sole support, he was a broken man. He became a total recluse, I believe.'

He stood, and offered her his hand to rise. 'If you are rested, shall we think of returning?' Once more the self-contained, impassive public man, he shook his jacket, and folded it neatly over his arm as they began to stroll back towards Melrose. Overhead a crow flapped laboriously past, its wing tips splayed out like fingers as it beat its way along, with infinite effort, against the breeze.

'Will you be with Harry and Rosemary for long?' she asked, with some thought of turning the conversation to more mundane channels.

'I leave for Jedburgh early on Monday morning. The Circuit begins there. We move on to Dumfries and Ayr.'

'I'm sorry that we shall see so little of you.'

'You will be returning to Edinburgh, I suppose?'

'In another four weeks or so. Papa wishes us to stay until the very last possible day.' It was said resentfully, but with no stronger emotion. An hour ago she could not have spoken so calmly.

'Is that so difficult to understand?'

'Oh, perhaps not, but we are his children. It hurts to be so plainly regarded as an encumbrance. He has even contrived to shuffle off onto my shoulders the responsibility for Jack.'

'I thought that was settled?'

'When Jack pressed him, he told him to apply to me for a decision. I repeated what was agreed at dinner last month. I'm sure I was right, and yet I'm concerned about him.'

'Is he in some financial difficulty? Or some imprudent entanglement? At his age, it is not uncommon.'

'Entanglement?' she said coldly. 'My brother would do nothing dishonourable, I assure you.'

'That must depend upon your definition of what is dishonourable. Your opinion might well differ from his.'

'Or yours?'

'Since you ask me, yes. A man may, I would almost say must, see these things in another light from a modest woman.'

'I don't see why. The virtue of chastity, for that is what is at issue, I suppose, is the same for man or woman, is it not? A man is required to be pure, as is a woman?'

'Yes, but . . . the cases are not absolutely the same,' he said, with a slight frown.

'Theft is theft, whether committed by a man or a woman? You would not allow a man to plead his sex in mitigation of a robbery or murder? Why make an exception of unchastity?'

'The rules are made by society, by nature, even, not by me. It is undeniable that society regards with amused tolerance lapses on a man's part which would sink a woman without hope of return.'

He hesitated, and added, 'Miss Lambert, you don't know the temptations to which a young man is exposed in a city such as ours. You are not out, alone, being solicited on every street corner, along every major thoroughfare. You cannot, thank Heavens, have any idea of the repeated assaults upon his self-control which a man encounters in even the briefest walk along Princes Street after dusk, to say nothing of the High Street. It is a crying scandal, but is it any wonder if a young man should succumb?'

'I repeat, Mr Bethune, you do not know my brother as I do. I believe he is worrying unnecessarily over some peccadillo. If he were to confide in me, or Papa, or even Doctor Cairns, I'm sure his alarm would prove to be groundless.'

'I hope so, but who does not have his secret life, and a face which cannot be shown to even the dearest of sisters?'

She was surprised, and even annoyed. She had looked to him as an ally, but his attitude struck her as ambiguous, and more nearly cynical than she would have expected. As if sensing her displeasure, he turned the conversation to indifferent subjects.

They talked of music, and public lectures, and books, with just enough difference of opinion to give zest to the discussion. It was the type of debate she had conducted with countless young men who had dined with her father, but never before with such enjoyment.

As they neared the gate, a sudden sense of nervousness overcame her. 'Will you come in to meet Papa?'

'Would you prefer to see him alone? Or would the presence of a stranger be of use?'

'I would be grateful if you would come in, even for a moment. I scarcely like to add to the obligations under which I already . . .'

'Not another word, please,' he protested, and opened the gate.

If her father found anything strange in her return on the arm of Francis Bethune, it was outweighed by his relief at the clearing of her mood. His first swift glance betrayed a certain disquiet, but seeing her smile, his momentary unease was at once allayed. He accepted Francis Bethune's congratulations on his forthcoming marriage and pressed him to stay to luncheon, seeming genuinely sorry when his offer was refused, on the grounds that Harry Robertson would be looking for his cousin to join him by the river.

Helen went to the door to bid him farewell. He took his hat, and turned it uncertainly by the brim, lingering over the parting.

'I hope you won't forget us when you return to Edinburgh. Anyone of Harry's connection will always be welcome in Drummond Place.' Even as she spoke, she remembered with a pang of misgiving that she would not then be the mistress of her father's house.

'Thank you.' He adjusted his hat, and set off down the drive. From the portico she watched until he had vanished from view.

10

Helen was surprised and oddly hurt by the indifference with which the children heard that they were to have a new mama. Kitty, indeed, with her invariable desire to please her father, expressed a gushing enthusiasm at the news; as usual, she merely succeeded in setting his teeth on edge. She earned herself a rebuke which she was sensitive enough to feel although never to avoid. For once Helen found it difficult to feel any compassion for her.

To Helen's considerable irritation, her father proposed that Sophie might usefully return to Edinburgh the following weekend.

'We will be away in Chester for two weeks on our wedding trip,' he said, as the family sat at dinner before he left for the evening train. 'There should be someone at home for Jack, and to keep an eye on Aunt Jeannie, I suppose. You're more use here, Nell, but Sophie could come.'

'Why is anyone needed to keep an eye on Aunt Jeannie?' Helen asked, swallowing her resentment.

'Didn't I mention it? It must have slipped my mind in all the excitement. She had a seizure a few days ago. Cairns thought it was apoplectic in origin.'

'But how is she? Has it left her with paralysis? I do wish you had told me, Papa. I would have come up to town to see her, if only for an hour or so.'

'Oh, there was no danger,' he said, with the easy confidence of a man who has never known a day's ill health in his life. 'Cairns says she may never suffer another. She won't get about as much, that's all. You don't need to worry; you won't need to look far for a chaperon now, girls!'

With that Helen had to be content. She wrote to her

aunt that same evening, explaining that she had only just been informed of her illness. She made no attempt at excusing her father's negligence.

Sophie at least was heartened by the prospect of her early return to Edinburgh. In normal circumstances Helen would have rejoiced to see her so restored to her usual high spirits. Knowing as she did the cause, it only increased her sense of isolation.

By the end of the first week in October, when the house in Melrose was given up, Helen scarcely knew whether or not she was glad to be going. The good weather they had enjoyed was beginning to give way to damp, dismal chills. The children were restless, tired of their own company. Helen felt the last extra week drag, and yet when the cab finally rattled over the greasy cobbles to Drummond Place, and drew up outside her home, the dun stone facade seemed to her as grim and alien as a prison.

Helen descended from the cab first, and waited for the children to disentangle themselves. Heavy drizzle was reducing sky, houses, pavement to a sullen grey monochrome. Around the railings of the garden, the first fallen leaves lay pulped into a sodden mess. Her face stiff with apprehension, Helen clutched Phoebe's hand, ostensibly to help her up the steps, glistening dark with the rain.

In the hall, beneath its columned archway, stood her father, his new wife on his arm. Instinctively, Helen moved quickly towards him, meaning to embrace him as she had done every other year on returning home after a summer apart. He made no answering movement; Susan Lambert did not release his arm. Helen faltered to a halt, and held out her hand instead, offering it first, by a conscious effort, to her step-mother. As soon as she made the gesture, Mrs Lambert took her hand from her husband's arm.

'Oh, so formal, Helen my dear! Won't you let me kiss

you? Please?' She stood on tiptoe with a pretty laugh, and kissed her with graceful competence, so much more becoming, to the onlooker, than the muddled embrace of real feeling.

It had been cleverly done, Helen recognised. She had been put in the wrong before she had spoken a word. Already, not a minute beneath her father's roof, she was outmanoeuvred, made to appear to him less generous, less affectionate than her step-mother.

She turned to him, the first impulse of happiness at their reunion now crippled and flightless. She felt his lips just touch her burning cheek. It was so painful a contrast to other homecomings, to his exuberant welcome, the excitement of the children at recognising the familiar, forgotten delights of home, that Helen felt a treacherous lump rising in her throat.

It was a relief to escape to her old room, so well known and yet so strange after her long absence. It was soothing to begin to arrange her things, to re-establish herself. She sensed already that the little room would be a refuge in a house whose security no longer seemed a matter to be accepted unquestioningly.

Helen had assumed that dinner would be a family affair. At the second bell, she descended to the drawing-room, to find Tom Hewitt standing by the fire, eyes fixed eagerly on the door. At her entry he started forward; seeing who it was, his face fell.

'Be patient a little longer, Tom!' Mrs Lambert shook a playful finger at the young man. She was seated on a chaise-longue near the fire. Helen stared at it stupidly, knowing that something was wrong, too disorientated to say what. Then she realised. She looked about the room in angry disbelief.

'Mama's sofa — where is it?' she asked abruptly.

Mrs Lambert raised a taper finger to her cheek, and considered. 'Do you mean that old thing which used to stand between the windows? It was grown so shabby that I was quite ashamed of it. Perhaps you didn't realise its condition, seeing it every day, but it was such an eyesore, and never used.' She smiled up at Helen, her eyes steady. 'I got rid of it.'

The door opened. Helen spun round. Her father was entering, fiddling with his shirt cuffs, smiling determinedly.

'Papa!' Helen turned on him. 'Mama's sofa! Could you not have waited until I came home? I would have kept it in my room if it was not wanted anywhere else, now.'

'Helen, for Heaven's sake, calm yourself!' he replied, with a warning glance over to where Tom Hewitt had developed a sudden, improbable interest in an anaemic watercolour.

'Edward dear, you must not blame Helen,' put in Mrs Lambert, stretching out her small hand in a placatory gesture. 'How very touching, to see such devotion to a mother's memory! Believe me, I can understand it all too well . . . but life must continue, however hard that may sound. It doesn't do to be sentimental over trifles. We are beginning afresh, after all, and we must put the sad old days behind us.' She rose, as if on sudden impulse, and floated over to Helen, with a rustle of her green watered silk and a fairy chiming of bangles and bracelets.

She laid her hand with ostentatious fondness on her step-daughter's rigid arm. 'I am to be your mama now, darling, and I do so wish to do my best – not to replace her – no, but to supply the want you must all have felt. So we won't begin by falling out over a worn old couch, will we?' and she gazed up at Helen's set, sullen face, putting her head to one side in a winning, birdlike attitude.

'Well said, Susan!' her father cried, pat on cue as Helen thought savagely. 'You musn't mind it, you know, Nell,' he added in a lower tone. 'It was a melancholy sight, when you come to think of it. The room is more cheerful without it.'

'And besides,' said Mrs Lambert, regarding her new acquisition with satisfaction, 'it matches the curtains so well, don't you think?'

Helen did not deign to reply; fortunately the omission was not noticed, for Sophie entered at that moment.

'Sophie dear, you would not have been so late if you had known who was waiting!' Mrs Lambert cried archly, as Sophie stopped, in evident confusion and delight. Recovering herself, she gave Tom Hewitt her hand. Helen's heart constricted in pain as she saw the look which passed between them.

It was impossible not to realise that Sophie's manner to her step-mother was warm, affectionate even. She's bought Sophie off! she thought scornfully, seeing the grateful little squeeze of the hand with which her sister silently thanked Susan Lambert for her surprise.

But was it right to put so harsh a construction on what might have been a sympathetic wish to further Sophie's happiness? Uncomfortable honesty forced Helen to admit to herself that if Sophie had confided in her step-mother nothing could be more natural than that she should do what she could to help the affair to a satisfactory conclusion. There was nothing objectionable in the match, except Sophie's youth. Had Helen herself not taken pride in smoothing Rosemary's path to the altar with just such discreet efficiency?

She was fair-minded enough to concede so much, and yet reason seemed powerless to dissolve the resentment which made her instinctive reaction to her step-mother's every word, every gesture, one of contempt. She had to force a smile when, in a secret storm of self-doubt and stubborn hostility, she stepped aside to allow Susan Lambert the *pas* as a married woman. For the first time since her mother died she would have to see another woman preside at her father's table.

Dinner was intolerably dull to Helen. At first she barely spoke, until her pride rose to her aid. She would not let her father think that she begrudged his new wife her position. She exerted herself, but found that nobody seemed to care very much whether she spoke or remained silent. What real interest could there be in her polite attempts at conversation, in a company consisting of one couple recently married, and another who longed to be?

'I had hoped to see Jack this evening,' she remarked. He at least would be an ally of sort.

'Oh, Jack rarely dines at home these days,' her father remarked indifferently. 'He's at the Grants, as usual.'

'The Grants? But that's merely a matter of some coaching, surely?'

'He's struck up a friendship with young Grant. The boy isn't strong, that's the reason for the coaching in the first place, of course. He missed almost the whole of last year at school. He's only a year or two younger than Jack, but through illness he's missed so much that he's in a lower class than his age. He's often confined to the house.'

'The Grants must be glad of Jack's companionship for him. To be honest, I can imagine that more readily than I can his coaching.'

'Oh, I don't know, Jack's no fool, if he would only apply himself. Who can say, perhaps this will rouse him to enthusiasm for his studies at last. He seems quite reconciled to staying in Edinburgh, at any rate. You were right, Nell, Canada was no more than a whim on his part.'

She smiled at her father, thanking him for his praise, but a sense of unease remained. Jack had been so terribly in earnest.

'Helen is sceptical of her brother's sudden devotion to mathematics, perhaps?' said Mrs Lambert acutely. 'Perhaps she suspects, like me, that there's a pair of blue eyes in the case?'

'Such a thought has never crossed my mind!'

'But I wonder whether James Grant has a sister, all the same,' Susan said, pushing a bracelet up from her wrist. Would she make such eternal play with those bangles, those ruby-eyed serpents and turquoise-set coils, if she did not have such tiny hands and slender wrists, Helen wondered spitefully, and instantly hated herself for it.

'How is Aunt Jeannie, Papa?' she asked, to turn the subject.

'Much the same, I understand. To be honest I've hardly seen her.'

'I'll call on her tomorrow, if I'm not needed here, that is.'

'Indeed you must, dear,' her step-mother interposed archly. 'Rich maiden aunts are to be petted and made much of by their dutiful nephews and nieces; why else did Providence create them?'

Edward Lambert laughed, and even Sophie and Tom Hewitt smiled. Helen turned on them. 'Is it inconceivable that anyone might choose to visit a lonely, ailing old woman without having an eye to her will? Must every human act be reduced to its basest motive?' she added, looking directly at her step-mother, and making no attempt to keep the contempt from her face.

'Why, Helen, how sharply you take me up!' Susan Lambert was the picture of misunderstood innocence. 'As if I would breathe a word against you, my dear, so noble and disinterested, and such a very particular favourite of Miss Anderson's, I believe?'

'Aunt Jeannie has been kind to all of us. She has been our chaperon since my mother's death, although it often involved her in going into society when she would have been happier by her own fireside.'

'How fortunate that I can now take that role upon myself! A married woman is so much more proper a chaperon, I always think. I hope I will not be too severe a duenna!' She smiled knowingly at Sophie. 'My heart will always be with lovers, I confess,' she added, with a sentimental sigh.

Helen wondered how her sister could endure such stuff. To her, Susan Lambert seemed to cheapen everything she touched. In Sophie's position, she vowed, she would have died unmarried before she would have entrusted her secret to that odious woman, clever as she might be.

In the drawing-room, as they waited for the gentlemen, Helen betook herself unasked to the pianoforte. It offered a respectable refuge from conversation. Alas, her intention no sooner appeared than it was thwarted.

'Sophie, dear, won't you let me hear those charming Mendelssohn pieces again? I'm sure Helen will not grudge me the pleasure of hearing you.'

Sophie glanced uncertainly at her sister. 'Did you want to play very particularly . . . ?'

'You know that I would far sooner listen to you than play myself,' she replied, with a smile of reassurance. She would not allow the slight to cause ill-feeling between them, if that was Mrs Lambert's intention.

'How delightful, to see sisters so united! Now, Helen, sit by me, here on the chaise-longue, and let us have a moment of cosy chat together . . . Sophie, you will excuse us for a minute or two, won't you?'

Sophie obediently began to play, as Helen was led a captive to the new, hard, bright chaise-longue. She sat beside her step-mother, reduced to a child again, but in an irksome submission she had never known as a child.

'Now, dear, let me open my heart to you.' Susan Lambert's eyes coolly studied her victim's face. 'I am the fondest of creatures – it is quite a fault in me, I confess it – where I love, I dote to excess. I cannot live with coldness or disapproval. It wounds my foolish affections, makes me wretched. You and I must be friends, we must agree, or life will be no better than a torment to me, and I am the very last person to be able to conceal my feelings. How I would hate your darling papa to see my unhappiness, and guess the cause!'

She paused, watching Helen's set, proud expression until she was sure that the sweet venom was taking effect. 'I could be such a true friend to you; I know so well all the secret heartache a young girl suffers . . . only think how happy I have been able to make dear Sophie, by asking Tom Hewitt to dinner tonight. Won't you let me assist you in the same way? Do, do let me help you!'

She bent forward confidentially, grasping Helen's wrist. 'Such opportunities are precious, Helen, and can easily be managed. You have only to whisper a name, and I shall not say a word of it even to your papa – men are such poor hands at this work, don't you think? – but we will see if I don't contrive to arrange our guest lists in a way to suit . . .'

She sat back a little, with a smile of satisfaction, tight-lipped, concealing her unattractive teeth.

She could scarcely have devised a more exquisite torment for her step-daughter. The temptation she offered could not have been more alluring if she had been privy to thoughts of which Helen herself was hardly conscious. A word, and Francis Bethune could become a familiar guest. She wanted so little. If she could look forward to renewing the long conversations they had begun in Melrose, her new life would not be absolutely without its compensations. To see him, to find in him a friend, a brother, was all she asked, she told herself.

But in her step-mother's calculating eyes she saw the price she would have to pay. To confess to a woman she despised that she felt such an interest, a thing of the spirit and intellect rather than of any grosser fabric, would be to defile it at once. She would become an accomplice in a tawdry scheme, a party to arch comments and knowing glances. Her soul revolted in its stubborn, unworldly pride at a compact with such an ally.

'I am greatly obliged to you, but you must make up your guest lists just as you choose,' she said coldly. 'I am perfectly indifferent to their content.'

'Truly? Oh, how glad I am that I mentioned the matter! You have quite put my mind at rest! You will laugh at me when I tell you that in my foolish way I had imagined there might have been the merest *tendresse* between you and Mr Bethune! See, the very idea makes you colour! How could I be so mistaken? Only think, fancying it would please you I had been planning to invite him for next Thursday! But if you have no preference in that line,

I will spare myself the trouble. *Entre nous*, I find him far from agreeable — so cold and superior! But of course, if ever you should wish any other particular friend to be invited, you have only to murmur his name and the thing is done.'

The arrival of her father and Tom Hewitt spared Helen the necessity of answering.

'I must say a word of praise to poor Sophie for her music,' Susan Lambert whispered confidentially, 'but I declare I haven't heard a note, our little chat has been so absorbing, hasn't it? I'm so glad that we understand each other . . . Sophie, that was quite exquisite, my dear! I never heard those pieces played so well!'

Helen could find no better resource than to plead a headache brought on by the travelling and retire to her room. She crept wretchedly between the sheets, and when Sophie finally came up she feigned sleep rather than speak. Her joy in the evening would have been more than Helen could bear.

The next morning she was glad to be able to escape to her aunt's. She went alone; Sophie had already promised to accompany her step-mother to the milliner's.

Helen did not linger at the breakfast table. She had hoped to see Jack, but early rising, it seemed, was no more attractive to him than of old.

It was a fine morning, which by its sparkling brightness might have been spring, but for an indefinable sense in the air, of completion, of the drawing of all things to an end, of changes to come. From the gardens in the centre of Drummond Place a hazy blue smoke drifted towards the houses; they were burning fallen leaves. There was a curious poignancy in the thought, as Helen remembered the night of Rosemary's wedding, and the fresh greenness of the gardens after the midsummer rain. Although the brave sunshine denied it, summer was gone.

Although she hoped she concealed it Helen was shocked at the change in her aunt. Her left hand seemed almost useless, and her breathing was more laboured than Helen remembered it. Twenty years older than her sister, Edward Lambert's first wife, she had never seemed her age. But now, active and bustling no more, she sat inert in her chair, an old woman. It was almost impossible to believe that only a few months before she had been chaperoning her nieces to balls and evening parties.

'Aunt Jeannie! How are you?' Helen bent to kiss her. "We came back to Edinburgh yesterday – Sophie sends her apologies, she'll come as soon as she can. We thought you might enjoy seeing us more in small doses.'

'Oh, Sophie must make her own excuses.' The voice was weaker than before, but there was no distortion in the speech. In a sudden access of relief she kissed her aunt again, more warmly, before seating herself opposite her beside the fire.

'Well, you're a sight for sore eyes, Helen, there's no gainsaying it,' her aunt said, with the briskness which Helen knew concealed her affection. 'Now, let's have a good crack; it's about the only pleasure age and the doctor have left me. What's all this nonsense about Sophie and Tom Hewitt? I hope your father isn't in such a hurry to get rid of his daughters that he lets her marry at eighteen, like your poor mother. Much good it did her! Nine bairns in sixteen years, and a tenth that killed her!'

'I . . . I . . .'

'Heaven bless the girl! Red as fire! Plain speaking was the rule in my day, Helen, and none the worse we were for it, either. But I'll spare your blushes, since we're grown so proper, though no doubt folly is a gay dog yet. Rosemary? You'll have seen her over the summer?'

'Indeed, often. She seems happy. I think she and Harry Robertson are well suited.'

'Is she in the hopeful way yet?'

'I'm sure I couldn't say.'

'It'll be a near-run thing between your sister and your new mama. You'll be laying in the baby linen by the bale before the year's out . . . there, I'm a wicked old woman to provoke you, never heed it, Helen.'

Bessie, the ageing maid, as white-haired as her mistress, thrust her head around the door. 'It's the doctor, Miss Anderson,' she announced, although the precaution was scarcely necessary, for he was at her heels, and had entered before the words were well out of her mouth.

'Just in time to save my niece from her outspoken old aunt, Doctor Cairns. I hope you're grateful to the man, Helen!'

'Helen?' As he caught sight of her for the first time, his heavy features lit up. 'It's good to see you back.'

'You'll know her again, that's for sure,' Miss Anderson commented drily, and indeed his eyes had rested on Helen with a sort of thirst. 'Now I suppose I may as well have my guinea's worth out of you while you're here; Helen, on you go down to the kitchen and see if you can wheedle her new receipt for tea-loaf out of Mrs Blair. I'll ring when the doctor's done with me.'

Helen was not sorry to be dismissed. When her aunt was in this humour, she delighted in the outrageous. It was pleasant to sit for a while in the kitchen with its gleaming copper saucepans in diminishing rank, its black-leaded range and scrubbed deal table where Mrs Blair, a thin, bustling little body, was deftly rolling pastry. Helen had always enjoyed discussing domestic affairs with her; many of her father's favourite dishes had originated in Mrs Blair's spotless kitchen.

All too soon the bell jangled. When Helen reached the sitting-room, Doctor Cairns was taking his leave.

'Can't you stay for a blether?'

'Not this morning, Miss Anderson; next time, perhaps . . . Helen, are you going home? If so, I'll send Donald on and get you up the road. I've a call to make in Fettes Row and the exercise would do me no harm.'

'I've not long since arrived, and I intended going from here to see Rosemary. She and Harry have been back for a week or two, you know.'

'They're in the new place now, in the Grange? Well, I'll give you a cast; I'm going back to George Square myself after my next call.'

'That would suit me very well, if it doesn't put you to any inconvenience . . . ?'

'I'll be back within the hour, then. Don't trouble Bessie, Miss Anderson! I should think I know my own way out by now.'

'How nice it is to see an old friend,' Helen said as the door closed behind him. 'Even one look at his face and his patients must feel better . . . forgive me, I didn't ask whether he was able to give you a good report?'

'Oh, at my age one doesn't expect much,' her aunt replied cheerfully. 'A day without pain, seeing a friendly face or two, enjoying a nice little dinner, I don't look for more than that. I'm not afraid to meet my Maker, dear, although I'm beginning to think he's quite forgotten to call me home.'

'Don't!'

'Well, give me some good gossip and take my thoughts off my latter end,' her aunt said, the gleam of mischief returning to her eyes. The old-fashioned cap tied under her plump chin framed a face which retained, despite age and ill-health, something of the innocent naughtiness of childhood. However often Helen had been shocked by her aunt, she had never been able to maintain her displeasure for long, faced with her unashamed zest for life and blunt kindness.

'I've only been back in Edinburgh for a day, I haven't had time to pick up the threads yet,' she temporised, in vain. Her aunt swept the feeble defence away with a single exclamation.

'Your step-mother! Come on, draw in your chair and tell me all about her.'

Helen shifted uncomfortably in her seat. 'Have you met her?'

'Once. More slate than coal, I should say. You can't like her, so don't pretend to.'

'Well then, we don't seem quite to take to each other. But Sophie likes her well enough,' she added quickly, at the prompting of her stern sense of honesty.

'Are you jealous, do you think?' her aunt asked, as easily as if she had been asking about the weather.

'Jealous? Really, Aunt Jeannie!'

'Don't ruffle your feathers! What could be more natural? Only a saint would relish giving way to another woman after ruling a household and a family for years as you have – and a man, too. Edward looked to you in everything, as you well know.'

'Oh, perhaps I'm deluding myself, but I think I could have handed over my keys with a good grace to someone whom I could respect, a woman more of Papa's age, a widow even, with a sensible manner and a kind heart . . .'

Her aunt was laughing so heartily that Helen had to stop, puzzled and no little annoyed. 'What have I said?'

'Bless your heart, can you imagine your father looking for some widow with a sensible manner? She could have the kindest heart in the Lowlands, but if she had thick ankles and thin shoulders do you think he'd have given her a second glance? What a great baby you are, Helen, for all your brains!'

Helen stood up in a sudden movement of anger and mortification. 'I'll wait outside for Doctor Cairns!'

'Sit down again, do! Flouncing off in a huff won't alter facts. Your father's like all men, a fool for a pretty face. She makes him young again; would a middle-aged widow? She'll have him round her little finger. If you take my advice, you'll leave the love-birds to their nest, and make your own life.'

'Make my own life?'

'Perhaps you'll have plans to follow Rosemary's example? No? Well, you've more sense than she has! Not every woman needs to find the purpose of existence in being a kind of superior servant to some man or other – although a servant can at least give in her notice and suit herself better elsewhere! I was never afraid to be called an old maid . . . see how your face falls at the words! But I tell you, there's more to life than sewing buttons on Jock Tamson's shirt and presenting him with another wean every year!'

'Oh, Aunt Jeannie, how you will tease me!'

'Of course, but there's some truth in it, all the same . . . is that the doctor's brougham? He must have despatched his business – or his patient – more quickly than he expected. Here, give me a kiss to forgive me, and away you go. Come back soon, now, with plenty of scandal about your wicked step-mother!'

Doctor Cairns cast a shrewd glance at her burning cheeks as he handed her into the carriage, but he made no comment.

'If crinolines continue to expand at this rate,' he grumbled, squeezing himself in beside her, 'you ladies will require a travelling chariot apiece soon.'

'Ever the candid friend, Doctor! Between you and Aunt Jeannie I shall have a very clear picture of my own failings.'

'You know perfectly well that Miss Anderson dotes on you, in her way,' he said carefully.

'A very robust way she has of showing it.'

'She's one of a dying breed. She may be more forthright than our niminy-piminy days approve, but she's got a heart of pure gold. She doesn't like to have it talked of, but I have standing instructions to call on her purse for the relief of any of my patients who need extra little comforts which are beyond their means. Many a fatherless bairn owes its every stitch of clothing to her, though I am never to mention her name.'

'She means well, no doubt.'

He looked at her searchingly, as though his quick ear had caught the constraint in her voice. 'I know it is early days yet, Helen, but how are things in Drummond Place? It must be strange to you, I fancy?'

'Of course.'

'You are not happy?'

She made no reply, too proud to lie or to admit the truth. Even in the dim light of the carriage, he saw in her guarded expression the answer to his question. He sighed.

'Have you ever considered making your home elsewhere? With Rosemary, I mean, or Miss Anderson?'

'Such a thought has never crossed my mind! Rosemary? No. It wouldn't do. Aunt Jeannie? Really, I don't know that I could . . .'

'It's only an idea which seemed worth mentioning. Think it over. If you feel it might suit, let me know and I'll sound Miss Anderson out for you if you like. I'll tell you my own opinion at once: I can't see you living beneath the same roof as your step-mother with any real contentment. I would even go further, and say that it would be better for all of you if you left.'

'Well, that's plain enough speaking!' she said, with a lightness which could not conceal her sense of dismay, of terror even.

The pause lengthened into a silence before he spoke again. 'Apart from any other consideration, Miss Anderson will remain an invalid now. If you wished to make your home with her, it could be managed in the most natural way possible, without any open break with your step-mother. If you neglect this opportunity, I don't know how else it could be done so painlessly . . . unless, of course, you follow Rosemary's example.'

She remained silent as she considered the good sense of what he suggested.

'Is there any likelihood of that, in the near future, that is?' he asked abruptly.

'Oh, no . . . unless you would like to offer, Doctor Cairns,' she said with a flash of the old teasing, revenge for the unexpectedly blunt question.

'I would offer tomorrow, but you would laugh in my face.'

Sure of understanding him, she smiled as at a joke, and they spoke of other things.

They were not long in reaching the Robertsons'. The doctor refused to come in, pleading the pressure of work. Rosemary had never been a particular favourite with him.

Helen remained with her sister until it was time to return home for dinner. Rosemary's company with all its irritation was preferable to Susan Lambert's. The time passed not unpleasantly with the house to view and its new furnishings to admire.

'It's a pity that I didn't know quite when you were expected back in Edinburgh,' Rosemary said, unusually gracious with the after-glow of Helen's praise of her establishment. 'You might just as well have stayed and dined with us. It's only a small party; we already have a woman in excess, otherwise you would have been welcome. Harry's quite fond of you, he wouldn't have minded a bit.'

'There will be other times, I hope.'

'Yes. You must come when we have got up a more interesting party than tonight. You would only have known Francis. I suppose you will easily console yourself for missing him.'

'Francis?' She allowed herself the question, curious to hear her own voice pronounce his name. It gave her a secret, almost guilty pleasure.

'Bethune, of course. Really, Helen! The poor man clearly didn't make any very great impression on you for all his finicky manners and pompous speeches.'

'I remember him perfectly,' she said, bending her head as she concentrated on smoothing on her gloves. 'I would be quite happy to meet him again, if the case were to arise.' For a second she feared that her sister might read more into the remark than she wished, but Rosemary's indifference was undisturbed.

Jack dined at home that night. She found him alone in the drawing-room when she went down. He stood in the window embrasure, holding back the curtain with one hand and staring out into the dusk.

'Jack! What an age since I saw you!' On a sudden impulse she kissed his cheek, and tugged at his silky whiskers in playful disapproval. 'Papa tells me you are quite reconciled to Edinburgh now,' she continued, drawing her arm through his and strolling with him into the sheltered recess, the short arm of the L-shaped drawing-room. 'I never thought that mathematics could have so happy an effect,' she ended, looking at him with teasing fondness. To her surprise she met with no answering smile, indeed for a second she would almost have said that he seemed alarmed, furtive.

'Why are you looking so uncomfortable? I was delighted to hear that you were persevering with your coaching, and giving the Grant boy your companionship too. It is so like you; you were always so kind to younger children . . .'

'Don't!'

She looked at him in bewilderment. 'What is it? Have I said something amiss? Nothing was further from my thoughts!'

He forced a smile. 'You shouldn't praise a fellow up so, that's all. I can't bear to hear it. And James – Grant – isn't a boy. He's almost eighteen. But for ill-health he would not still be at school.'

'Yes, so Papa said,' she replied negligently. 'But it is such a relief to know that you are reconciled to giving up the Canada scheme. I was sure in my own mind that I was right to oppose it, but it worried me all the same to see you so unhappy. That's all in the past now, isn't it?'

'Oh, yes,' he replied, his fingers restlessly combing and stroking his absurd trailing whiskers. She frowned. His manner did not reassure.

The click of the door opening and Susan Lambert's low ripple of laughter put an end to their *tête-à-tête*, but as they moved back into the main body of the room he detained her for a second.

'I shall stay here now, and I'm happier than I ever thought possible, but all the same, it would have been better to have let me go.' In his fatalism there was something more disquieting than in all his former blustering.

She observed him carefully over dinner. He had declared himself happy, but he gave an overwhelming sense of nervousness. His eyes flickered uneasily from speaker to speaker, like a duellist facing several adversaries, from any one of whom an attack might come. He drank little, she was glad to note, but that with an avidity painful to see. Only the conscious exercise of the will produced his moderation, she was sure.

To Susan Lambert his manner was distant almost to the point of rudeness, as Helen noted with guilty satisfaction. On him at least the pretty feminine ways which had ensnared his father's heart had no appreciable effect, unless it were that of revulsion.

As the meal progressed, Helen detected in Jack signs of growing impatience. When at length MacRoberts had removed the cloth, brought the dessert and retired, Jack stood.

'If you will excuse me, I'll just call in at the Grants for a while. James Grant was unwell earlier today and it would be civil to enquire after him.'

'It would be equally civil to wait until the meal is well over before leaving,' Edward Lambert said, with unusual sharpness. Helen suspected that her brother's thinly veiled distaste for Susan Lambert had not escaped their father's attention.

'It's impossible. He will retire early. He had very little sleep last night. The rest of the household will be in the same state, I suspect.'

'But it seems almost an insult to poor Helen, to rush away as soon as you can on the first evening you are both at home,' put in Susan Lambert, although how her enjoyment could be augmented by Jack's presence, treating her as he did, was more than Helen knew.

'Don't mind me, Jack!' Helen said quickly. 'Go if you wish, by all means.'

He cast her a single look of thanks and apology, and hurried from the room.

'How painful for you, my dear! I'm sure Jack doesn't mean any unkindness, although I know you must feel it.'

'Not in the slightest,' said Helen, turning coolly on her step-mother. 'Jack and I understand each other far too well to fall out over such a trifle.' She spoke boldly, but in her heart she was far from confident of understanding him at all.

11

After leaving Helen in the golden-leaved drive of the
Robertsons' villa with its Doric-columned portico and
adjoining coach-house, Doctor Cairns had instructed
Donald to return to George Square. The order was soon
countermanded. A longer time than usual had elapsed
since last he saw the Crearies. Soon his brougham, plain
and shabby, was drawing to a halt outside Paisley Close.

It was no easy matter for him to maintain a cheerful
manner after examining May Crearie. The signs in her
chest brought a frown to his brow when he turned
away from the bed on which she lay, Danny kicking
and crowing beside her. He walked over to where Lizzie
was adding potatoes to the broth which was simmering
over the fire.

'How's Nettie keeping these days?' he asked, as casually as he could.

'No bad. She's hoasting, but no so sore as May.'

At the news his frown deepened. 'How long since she
took the cough?'

'A month or more.'

'Is she well otherwise? Eating as usual, and so on?'

'Aye, she eats more than me.'

'Hmm.' He looked over to the bed again. May, and
Nettie and Joseph, lying close together there every night
in the ill-ventilated room, while May coughed . . . 'Is
Nettie still in the same place? Not living in yet?'

'No. She likes it fine where she is, for all she gets so
droukit going to and fro.'

'How old is she now, eleven? Haven't you thought of
getting her a live-in place, Lizzie? She's a rare wee worker,
I'll be bound, if she's anything like her sister.'

'She'll do.'

He smiled at her dry tone. 'Would you like me to ask about for a place for her? Somewhere not too far away?' In some house like the Robertsons', perhaps, surrounded by greenery, a healthy, still rural setting, away from the stink and smoke of the densely packed Old Town, away from that single room where five youngsters breathed the same exhausted tainted air. He watched her closely. Her face showed no enthusiasm for his suggestion.

'Lizzie? It would be best, you know. She would earn more as a live-in kitchenmaid. She wouldn't need to be fed here, she wouldn't get soaked trailing back and forth in all weathers. What is there against it?'

She glanced over to the bed. May had drifted asleep. 'Nettie's a help in the house, but it's no that. May would break her heart. Nettie's awf'y good with her. She's more tender-like than me; I canna be.'

He nodded.

'And forbye that, she's only a wee lassie, for all she's shot up like an ill weed. Ye hear such things . . . how would I ken it was a fit place for the bairn?'

As a medical man he knew better than to pretend that Nettie's youth would protect her against the hazards Lizzie feared. 'You are quite right to be concerned, but I would not recommend a situation in which I thought she would be in any danger. She would probably be only a couple of miles from home, too. That would help to set your mind at rest, would it not?'

'Aye.' He knew that she was unconvinced. She looked again at the sleeping child.

'Why can Nettie no stay as she is?' she said stubbornly. 'We're doing fine, are we no?'

He replied very gently. 'Some doctors believe that when one member of a family has a weakness such as May's, there is a danger of others, children in particular, developing the same illness if they are much together, breathing the same air.'

'Some doctors? And what do ye think yourself?' Her voice was challenging, almost hostile.

He sighed. 'I think it would be better for Nettie to find a place as a live-in maid.'

In the heavy silence she walked over to the window, beaded with moisture from the pot simmering on the fire. She stood by the clouded glass as though looking out; he knew that she could see nothing. He waited, suffering with her, until she said, as he had known she would, 'I would take it kindly if ye would speer after a place for our Nettie, Doctor.'

'Of course. Believe me, you've done the right thing.' He dared not say more. For once, she did not see him to the door, but remained, face averted, staring sightlessly at the running window.

For the remainder of that week, Helen busied herself in resuming the threads of Edinburgh life, and in repairing the rents in its fabric caused by her father's remarriage. She tried to spend as little time as was decently possible with her step-mother. She involved herself in the schoolroom and enjoyed it more than she expected. It was a task for which she had never had time before. Now, at least, she had time in plenty.

She found Sophie's company strangely unsatisfying. Her sister seemed to be turning increasingly to Susan Lambert as confidante and comforter. An atmosphere of plots and secrets, of whispered conferences which ended with significant glances whenever Helen disturbed the conspirators, and half-suppressed hints as to Sophie's fate, left her feeling in equal parts irritated and excluded. She was too proud to ask her sister what was happening, and yet Sophie's reticence hurt her.

Although the worst of the ostentatious secrecy was dropped in her father's presence, she felt sure that he did not care for the atmosphere any more than she did. She found in this trace of their former sympathy a glimmer of solace. She would be satisfied with very little, she told herself. If only there remained one area, however tiny or insignificant, which they, and they alone could share, if only she could know herself still important to him, she could bear all the rest. Would it be too much to hope, that she might claim one hour a week of his undivided attention? As Tuesday approached, she laid her plans to fight for that privilege, their old, treasured hour of Greek.

She spent every available minute of Monday in the library, studying the next passage with obsessive care. She prepared as though her life depended upon it. For this, the first of their resumed lessons, she must be word-perfect. She felt a fierce joy, of which she was half ashamed, at the thought that on this ground at least she could claim a victory over her step-mother.

She was not sure whether he had remembered their longstanding arrangement. In the past it had always been the inviolable rule that the family dined alone on a Tuesday. This week, too, there were no guests, but that might have been chance. As it happened, Sophie was dining with the Hewitts that day, and Jack at the Grants. All through the meal, Helen hugged the knowledge of her anticipated treat to herself. It was a part of her pleasure, and some instinct warned her to give her step-mother no notice of what she intended. But when Susan Lambert rose at the end of the meal, with a glance to Helen, she turned to her father.

'Have you forgotten what day it is, Papa?'

'The day?'

'Why, Tuesday, our Greek day! I've been preparing so hard, you can't think. Shall I come with you to the library at once, as we always used?'

Her father hesitated. His handsome, florid face showed some uncertainty. He fumbled with his napkin, as though he could not fold it to his satisfaction. He looked furtively at his wife, but she stood by the door without speaking, awaiting his decision with the utmost unconcern.

'To be honest, I had quite forgotten.' He looked at

Susan Lambert again, indecisive, but as she still gave no sign, he added more confidently, 'Why not? Bring the Aeschylus along directly. Susan, my dear, you'll not object to spending an hour or so alone upstairs, will you? Nell and I have an old engagement.'

'Oh, don't apologise! It's perfectly charming to see such devotion to study in a young woman – so disinterested! In fact, it suits me very well. I would not have mentioned it for worlds, but I have the most tormenting headache. It will be a relief to be able to lie down for a while, and not need to be brave, and sit with you both in the drawing-room keeping up the conversation. Could you give me your arm upstairs, Edward? These migraines so affect my sight that I scarcely dare venture on the staircase unaided.' She turned to Helen as she reached the door, and smiled at her with suffering fortitude. 'You can spare your papa for so long? You are so wonderfully robust, dear, that you can't imagine what a martyr I am to these stupid heads. He will be down with you as soon as he has performed this little service for his foolish old wife.'

Helen's polite murmur barely concealed her scepticism, but her father seemed to entertain no doubts as to the reality of the sudden migraine. He bent solicitously over the tiny figure clinging to his arm as he guided her from the room.

'Just go through to the library, Nell,' he said, over his shoulder. 'I won't be above a moment.'

With a lightness of heart she had not felt since her return home, Helen hurried to the dark, still room which was to her the heart of the house. It was eminently a masculine room in its furnishings and atmosphere; everything was for use; comfort and practicality ranked before fashion or simple ornament. The long velvet curtains were of dull crimson, faded long since to a shade scarcely brighter than the dark wood panelling which separated the bookcases. Here and there were paintings, old, sombre almost, impossible to imagine suiting any other room so well. And everywhere books, from floor to ceiling, the topmost being accessible only by means of a curious wheeled step-ladder, one of the charms of her young world, on which her father, and he alone, would propel himself along the shelves in search of some arcane reference.

When her father came they would sit at the table together, sharing the text. He usually liked to take a glass of claret; she rang for MacRoberts to bring the wine. Everything must be perfect. It must be as it had always been, whatever the other changes since their last lesson. There, at least, in the library, the passage of time could be checked. They would share the intellectual companionship which had never included another being. Even her mother had been excluded from the love they shared for the beautiful language, preserved in its perfection by its deadness.

She checked again with eager anticipation that everything was to hand, the fire burning clearly, the gas giving a steady light. She wanted the treat to be drawn out for as long as possible; she had asked for an hour but secretly she hoped that, as so often, they would lose all sense of time, and spend twice that in their reading. It would prove to Susan Lambert that in some things, at least, there was a bond between her husband and his daughter transcending anything she could understand.

It was one of her father's quirks that he could not bear to have a clock in the library, his study. When, with a growing sense of unease, Helen drew her watch from its pocket at her waist, she was alarmed to discover that she had been waiting a full fifteen minutes. Her father was only handing his wife upstairs; did that take so long? Was she seriously ill?

In an instant the pleasure she had taken in waiting for her father was gone. She moved aimlessly about the room, straightening a book here, settling a cushion there, her gaze fixed with anxious intensity on the door at the slightest of sounds from the passage. She looked longingly at the bell handle beside the fireplace. She approached it, and forced herself to turn away. She would wait for five more minutes. At the thought, her face cleared. It was not to be conceived that he would not be down before so long a period had elapsed.

Certainly, he must not find her in such a nervous state. She sat at the table, and set herself to read through the next hundred lines of the *Prometheus*. She would not consult her watch until the end of the task, supposing that her father had not entered long before.

For all her self-command, she could not concentrate. She struggled on, until she realised that the words had long since failed to communicate any sense. She looked at her watch. Almost ten minutes had gone by since she last consulted it. She crossed to the fireplace and turned the handle of the bell.

'Ah, MacRoberts,' she said, striving for the most impossible of effects, complete naturalness. 'Could you mend the fire? You know how my father hates to be disturbed once he is at his studies.'

She caught the look of surprise on his face as he approached the fire; it scarcely needed touching. Too well trained to demur, whatever his inner mutterings, he bent to the task.

'By the bye,' she added, with studied indifference, 'has Mrs Lambert rung? I know that she was feeling unwell.'

'No, Miss Lambert,' he said, straightening. 'I would have heard for sure, seeing as I was down in the kitchen getting my dinner, until the very minute you rang yourself.'

'Thank you, MacRoberts,' she murmured. 'I'm sorry to disturb you at your meal, but you know how Mr Lambert loves a good fire . . .'

He bowed, expressionless, and withdrew. She made no attempt to resume her reading. She seated herself by the fire in baffled, fearful misery. The house might have been deserted, such was the settled silence. She wandered over to the door, opened it a fraction. A muffled laugh reached her from the kitchen; that was all.

Not until three quarters of an hour had passed did she hear her father's footsteps. She did not rise from the armchair where she sat, the text open and unregarded on her lap.

Her father entered, his handsome face flushed, his hair, in a subtly incongruous contrast, as neat as though it had been freshly combed. 'Ah, Nell,' he said, with a joviality which she instantly knew as false coin, 'I'm sorry to keep you . . . your step-mother's head, you know . . . I didn't like to leave her.'

She looked at him. His waistcoat was buttoned awry, as though he had dressed hurriedly. But when she had sat facing him at dinner it had been buttoned perfectly correctly. It was new, rather garishly patterned, Mrs Lambert's choice no doubt, and she had noted it particularly. She concealed her hands by the side of her skirt; they were literally shaking with anger.

He dropped into the armchair on the opposite side of the fire, and yawned. 'Let me just see the text, Nell,' he said without enthusiasm. 'Where the deuce were we?'

'Line 197. The beginning of Prometheus's long speech.'

'Yes . . . just read it through in Greek, will you, before we move over to the table?'

He settled himself more comfortably as she began. She read mechanically, without interest or pleasure. Suddenly she stopped. There was a profound silence. His head sagging onto his shoulder, his mouth hanging slackly open, her father was asleep.

She went to her room without wakening him, humiliation sour as nausea rising within her. She never again mentioned their Greek reading to her father. It was ignored by them as if it had never been. The following Tuesday Mrs Lambert had invited two dinner guests. Helen could have told her that it was unnecessary. Her step-mother had won a victory as crushing as it was unacknowledged.

177

As autumn wore into winter and the days shortened, it took all Helen's natural elasticity of spirits to maintain a cheerful face. Each day, as imperceptible and inexorable as the loss of a few more minutes of light, came the erosion of her position within the house. She felt herself being reduced to an irrelevance, without use or purpose.

She had always accepted the need to surrender her household responsibilities. It was an abdication which she regretted, for she had always taken a pride in the smooth running of the establishment. She noted with the secret malice which at times alarmed her that her step-mother had less success than she in managing the servants. There was a rapid exodus of staff, including the housekeeper, Mrs Beattie, who had been with the family as long as Helen could remember.

Helen could scarcely believe that Mrs Beattie would take such a step. She even tried to persuade her to change her mind, but the housekeeper remained adamant.

'No, Miss Lambert, that I won't. I've had a good place here, and I never thought to leave it, but when things are said about honesty, and I feel my word is not believed, then I have no choice.'

Helen looked at the older woman's hurt, proud expression. 'Honesty? Oh, surely you must have misunderstood Mrs Lambert! She could not have intended to question your honesty!'

'She told me in so many words that the house was to be run on very different lines from now on.' She sniffed scornfully. 'I could see that much. Now that the house had a proper mistress, she said, there would be no more cheating on bills, and tampering with stores, as she had reason to know always went on in such establishments. She was warning me, she said, out of fairness, to give me a chance to change my ways. I changed, all right. I gave her my notice on the spot. I've never been so insulted in all my days. Playing on perquisites beyond what was just, indeed! An ill-governed household!'

Mrs Lambert seemed not all discomfited by her failure

to retain staff, indeed she regarded it with some complacency. When, over the dinner table, Edward Lambert passed some idle comment on the appearance of yet another new member of the household to replace one of many years' service, she had her rejoinder ready.

'Now you see what comes of spoiling the servants, you dear naughty creature,' she said roguishly to Helen. 'Don't think for a moment that I'm blaming you – not many girls could have managed even as well as you did. But quite naturally things have been let go which a wife cannot tolerate in her domestic arrangements. And now that I am bringing a little more rigour to the checking of accounts, and the provision of food to the kitchen – the butter that is consumed there quite exceeds all that's reasonable – why, of course, the lazy, greedy creatures aren't prepared to work for their money, having got it so easily before!'

'I see. So it is all my fault?' said Helen, in cold fury.

'Now, Helen, you are misunderstanding what Susan said,' her father put in quickly, looking uneasily at his wife. 'You did a magnificent job, my dear, but as Susan said no doubt the servants did take advantage of your inexperience.'

Even more than his wife's poisoned insinuations, his betrayal drove Helen to recklessness. 'Did you ever have cause to complain about household expenses? Were you less comfortable then than now? True, I did not expect the housekeeper to show me every torn napkin before it could be replaced' – this being an innovation which had particularly incensed Mrs Beattie – 'nor did I keep a tally of every candle-end and scrap of dripping . . . some might call it rigour, others might prefer the term penny-pinching, it seems to me! I was prepared to come and go with the servants, and I didn't hear you finding fault with the results, Papa. At least I kept my staff for years, not days!'

'How warm you do grow, Helen! Of course you kept your servants for years; they knew a snug berth when they saw one! To keep a pack of idle servants for years is no great gain, however it might seem to a thoughtless girl!'

Helen dared not reply, frightened by her own rage. But even worse, because less expected, was the loss of her maternal role.

It seemed as though Susan Lambert set herself out deliberately to ingratiate herself with the children. Helen soon learned not to attempt to check their behaviour in even the slightest detail when they were brought in for dessert. Whenever she ventured to enjoin silence on Philip and Andrew, or moderation on Kitty, whose flesh, threatening to burst the seams of her sleeves and bodice, warned of the dangers of her voracious appetite, Mrs Lambert would be sure to take the children's part, with an arch smile which seemed to include herself in their naughtiness.

'Why, Helen, we're only naturally high-spirited, aren't we, boys?' or 'We won't listen to our great, solemn sister, will we, Kitty?' she would say, with a pretence of juvenile impudence which delighted the children, although Helen could have writhed in irritable disgust.

Finding herself cast in the role of humourless tyrant, Helen quickly schooled herself to ignore behaviour which no sane person could approve. Even this was turned against her. When her father chastised the boys, who were throwing walnut shells at each other across the table, Mrs Lambert interceded for them.

'Edward, please be patient with them; don't forget, it's so long since the poor children have known a mother's care . . . is it to be wondered at, if they have been denied that attention to their manners which only a mother's softening influence can give? You have been so occupied yourself, it is no blame to you if they have been neglected, but such is the case, as you see.'

'That's nothing but stuff!' said Jack contemptuously. 'Nell watched our manners as well as any mother. If the boys are larking about it's because you didn't check them when they first began flirting scraps of orange peel across the table, as she would have. She left it to you, being our mama now, I suppose.'

There was a tense silence. The younger children exchanged glances, half excited, half alarmed at the dissension amongst their elders. Helen felt a surge of gratitude to Jack for his defence. At that moment she would have laid down her life for him.

'I think you may as well go up now, children,' said her father abruptly. 'If we have any repetition of this, you won't come down again.'

That night, lying next to the sleeping Sophie, Helen thought about the future as honestly as she could. Looking back over the weeks which had passed since her return to Edinburgh she could see nothing which gave her any hope that she and Susan Lambert could ever achieve mutual respect, far less liking. She saw in herself a bitterness, a growing resentment, which threatened to corrupt her whole nature, which had already gone far towards destroying her peace of mind. What would she become, living as she was?

The next morning she delivered a note to Doctor Cairns, asking him to raise with Miss Anderson the question of her finding a home there. Within two days, the matter was settled. Helen could move from her father's house whenever she chose. For the present, even the knowledge that escape was possible whenever she wished made life more tolerable. But at the beginning of November came news which decided her on fixing a definite end to her stay in Drummond Place.

The endless confidential discussions between Sophie and Susan Lambert had borne fruit at last: Edward Lambert and the Hewitts had been brought to agree to an early marriage. On reaching his majority at the end of December Tom Hewitt was to be sent to London, to the English branch of the family wine-importing business. Sophie would go with him, as his wife. That seemed as suitable a time as any to make the break. With the new year, Sophie would be away and the three youngest girls were to go to school. The governess was to be let go, like so many other familiar members of the household. For Jack's sake Helen might have stayed a little longer, but she was sure that in offering him a refuge from Drummond Place at their aunt's she would be of far more use to him than in remaining to share his misery.

In all the happy confusion of preparations for Sophie's wedding, Helen's planned departure made little stir. Even Kitty, ecstatic at the prospect of attending a school, seemed scarcely to feel it.

Helen gladly played what part she could in the plans for the wedding and the purchase or working of the necessary items of the trousseau. She could not but be aware of how secondary a role she played beside Susan Lambert. With the cynical clarity which was replacing her idealism she suspected that her step-mother saw in the event a chance to throw Rosemary's wedding, arranged by Helen, into the shade.

Amongst the invitations which she helped to address she noted one to Francis Bethune. She could not repress a pang of disappointment when he sent his regret; during the first few days of January he was to be in Glasgow, on the Winter Circuit.

The duty of informing Rosemary of her proposed move to Northumberland Street was put off by Helen until it could no longer decently be delayed. As she had expected, Rosemary, now a prospective mother, received the news of her plans with some relish. After a girlhood spent in the shadow of her clever, managing sister she was not averse to extracting the last drop of pleasure from her triumph in being the first daughter to marry and now to be expecting a child, while Helen's fate had proved so very different.

'So you aren't finding it easy to bow the neck to our new mama?' Rosemary asked, sipping her tea. She was reclining on her couch, as she would probably recline for the next six months, Helen thought with some exasperation.

'It will be better for everyone if I leave her a clear field. We all have our own ways of running a household.'

'And Aunt Jeannie? Won't you differ from her? That household is run on principles which haven't changed in forty years. She won't give an inch where her own comfort is concerned, for all you're her favourite.'

'I don't know why you think so.'

'It's because she thinks you'll follow in her footsteps, an old maid. When Harry and I became engaged I heard her tell Papa that you would have more sense. She expects you to live as she does, you know.'

'I have no objections,' Helen said lightly, suppressing an obscure flicker of unease. Rosemary's words rang all too true.

'Has she told you that you are not to have followers, like a kitchenmaid? No? I wouldn't be surprised. You'll find it very quiet, won't you?'

'Perhaps. Shall I refill your cup?'

Rosemary nodded, a shade of malice on her plump, high-coloured face. 'Backgammon every night isn't my idea of fun. Of course, you'll have no end of time to devote to your precious Greek now.'

Helen made no answer, busying herself with the tea. She carried Rosemary's cup to her couch. The service was accepted regally, as a right. 'I hope it won't be backgammon every night,' she said mildly. 'You'll have me over to dinner from time to time, won't you?'

Unfortunately Rosemary did not miss the undertone of anxiety in her sister's voice. For once, plump, lazy, dull as she was, she had the upper hand. She set about savouring the unusual experience to the full.

'I don't suppose we will be entertaining very much, now that I'm . . . you know what.'

'Just as you choose, Rosemary dear. I hope you won't

consider me company, you know. It would be quite agreeable to me to dine perfectly quietly with you and Harry. I hope you will always feel equal to so much.'

'Yes . . .' Rosemary considered briefly. 'I suppose if ever we do entertain we could always call on you at short notice? If someone drops out at the last minute, and we are a woman short?'

She eyed her sister with almost impersonal curiosity, as though to see whether she would swallow the bitter draught to the very dregs of humiliation. But Helen's pride revolted. 'Ask, by all means. If I have nothing better to do, I may come; you would lose nothing by asking,' she replied coolly. 'Do you really think it wise to eat so much cake, dear? You know how you do run to fat, at the best of times . . .'

Rosemary's ensuing sulks quite restored Helen's spirits.

As Episcopalians the Lamberts always made rather more of Christmas than was customary in Scotland, but this year it passed almost unnoticed in the shadow cast before it by Sophie's wedding and immediate departure for the south. Despite the distance which had grown up between them, as Sophie had increasingly been drawn into Susan Lambert's orbit, Helen found herself dreading her sister's removal.

The day before the ceremony was hateful. The whole house seemed restless, irritable. Trifles assumed vast significance, Sophie's mood swung erratically between tears and brittle laughter. There was a constant stream of tradesmen and delivery boys, bringing food, flowers, clothes which had required last-minute alterations, and taking away Sophie's luggage, already ticketed with her married name.

That night Helen went to bed before Sophie, detained in final consultation with Mrs Lambert. She sat in her nightgown and wrapper, slowly brushing her hair. Its heavy weight down her back, the crackle of electricity from the long, steady strokes, the almost animal warmth against her cheek and neck, induced a strange unthinking reverie.

She looked up dreamily as Sophie entered. Sophie collapsed into a chair. 'Helen, I'm so fagged I don't know how I shall get to bed!'

'I'll help you.' She laid aside the brush. 'Let me unhook you.' She worked deftly, and suddenly stopped. 'Only think, Sophie, this will be the last time we will share a room, the last time I'll help you to undress. After tonight you'll belong with Tom, not us.'

'Don't, Helen!'

Helen held out her sister's nightdress. 'I'll brush your hair for you. It will help you to sleep.'

As she worked, she saw in the glass the marks of strain relax in Sophie's face. 'Are you afraid?' she asked softly.

'Of tomorrow? The ceremony?'

There was a silence, then Helen sighed. 'Yes, the ceremony.'

Sophie's gaze held hers in the dressing-table mirror. She raised her hand to press Helen's where it rested on her shoulder. 'I'm not afraid, of anything.'

Impulsively, Helen bent and kissed her sister's cheek. There was so much remaining unsaid between them, but they had no language for their uncertainties, their fears and doubts.

'Come to bed, Sophie, or you will be fit for nothing tomorrow.'

Sophie smiled, and obeyed. For the last time Helen felt her cuddle close to her back, warm and comforting. Sophie was soon asleep, but Helen was long in following.

Doctor Cairns's enquiries soon bore fruit. By the beginning of December Nettie Crearie was installed in the service of an eminently respectable household in Newington, comprising a minister's widow and her two daughters. The parting was a terrible wrench for May, although she did not complain.

Lizzie knew that Nettie had been to her what she herself, forced into early responsibility, could never be. Hers was not a temperament which easily showed affection. The fierce, aching love she really felt for May would express itself more readily in the sharp words of intolerable anxiety than in caresses.

She could show her feelings only in practical ways, by forcing May to drink the milk she disliked; by going for messages herself, however weary, rather than send her sister out shopping in bad weather; by sparing a copper to buy a soft white roll for her breakfast instead of the porridge which so disgusted her. And when the consciousness of Nettie's absence overwhelmed May, Lizzie set her thin shoulders, and pretended not to notice her silent tears.

To comfort her sister was more than she was able for; Lizzie had worries enough without. Fitting out Nettie for her new place had necessitated a good dress for her, costing the last of the credit at Cooper's. The clothes were all bought – her own dress, cheap and of poor quality, was already wearing thin at the elbows – but on the club card almost forty blank spaces still remained to be marked off.

Nicholas Gillanders had been as good as his word, and brought her a pound from his accommodating friend, to be laid out at once. The repayment was to be quicker than he had said, however, at a shilling a week over twenty-six weeks. Lizzie agreed, desperate for the shoes, and accepted the second card. There had seemed no difficulty, but after three months only five entries had been made. Slowly, inexorably, Lizzie was becoming lost in a quagmire of debt.

The first few weeks had been simple enough. Every Monday Gillanders called in the evening, by which time Lizzie had received and cashed the money order from her father. But on the first Monday in October the money order had not arrived. Lizzie was frantic with worry. For the first time she realised how precarious were her means of support, and above all her ability to pay off her debts.

Joseph had brought in a few pence the previous week from casual work after his attendance at the Industrial School where, with other children from the poorer families of the Old Town, he was receiving a basic education to fit him for a trade. He would do odd jobs after school in the shops of the neighbourhood, washing bottles, delivering orders, anything which would earn a copper. She had put the money by against her elder brother Tam's return; he was to be released from prison in February and, black sheep though he was, she wanted to welcome him home to a good meal. But now there were more urgent needs; Joseph's coppers were added to the proceeds of the shirts which May was beginning laboriously to sew, and the necessary two shillings were scraped together, although it left her without a penny in the house.

Lips tight with anxiety, she handed Nicholas Gillanders the two cards with the hard-won coppers from Joseph and the shilling which it had taken May all week to earn, with Lizzie's help, by sewing three shirts.

He took it, his red-veined eyes regarding her acutely. 'Now, Lizzie, tell me truly, can you manage the full two shillings this week? Am I robbing you?'

'No, no,' she said hurriedly. 'Mark the cards, and I'm straight with ye.'

'But does it leave you short? I couldn't rest easy in my bed tonight if I thought you were toiling.'

She shot him a questioning look, undecided whether he could be trusted.

'You can tell me, Lizzie,' he said, putting the money down on the table with a soft jingle of coins. 'Not a penny do I touch until you've told me honestly whether you have enough to see you through the week.'

She wavered, and succumbed; the temptation to confide in the fatherly, concerned old man was irresistible. 'The money order didna come the day.'

'No! And have you cleared the rent?'

'Aye, it was put by.'

'But if the order has gone missing in the post? How will you get through the week?'

'Dinna ken.'

'Keep your two shillings, Lizzie,' he said grandly, pushing the untidy heap of coins across the table towards her.

'But the menage!'

'I'll pay it for you myself! Where's the harm in that? It'll keep you straight with Cooper's, and we can just mark an extra two weeks on my friend's little loan, owing to me, not him. No, I won't hear a word against it, Lizzie; what's two shillings more? At least you will be sure of your food for the week.'

He brushed aside the thanks she could scarcely utter. All her habitual suspicion was swept aside by his heaven-sent kindness. From that moment he occupied in her private Pantheon a position second only to Doctor Cairns's. Practical herself, judging by deeds not words, she was conquered by that very practicality, although May shrank from even his eye.

It was Wednesday before the money order arrived, and then for a mere five shillings. Her father had been injured through the carelessness of one of his workmates, an unskilled labourer, a nephew of the foreman, who should never have been given work in the carpentry shop. The five shillings had been contributed by his fellow workmen. He promised to send what more he could, whenever it was possible, but he warned her that it would be a week, or even longer, before he could return to work. The letter was written in an unknown hand, for it was his wrist which had been damaged. It concluded with a sentence at which Lizzie burned with shame and anger, 'As I have sent you extra these last months you will I trust have something put by for times such as these.'

She was aghast; why had he not warned her to save? She had expected his good money to continue, they had been living well, as she had thought they could. Five shillings, and no guarantee of anything more, for at least a week! One and ninepence rent, and two shillings for Gillanders!

Somehow, they struggled through, relying on Joseph's coppers and May's sewing, in which Lizzzie now joined her at every spare minute and far into the night. Nettie managed to bring home kitchen scraps on her afternoon out, and fortunately Lizzie had built up a stock of coal and some little supplies of tea, sugar and meal.

She found the rent, and sank her pride sufficiently to offer Gillanders only the shilling for the clothes menage. Again, he was all kindness, and allowed her to carry over the repayment of the loan he had negotiated. He promised to consult his friend; the answer was favourable. She could defer payment until her father was fully restored and able to send his usual sums.

She accepted his help gratefully, believing that it would be an easy matter to make up the difference when the money orders were resumed. Alas, it was many weeks before she received more than a few shillings. Even when Rab Crearie went back to work, it was to a less skilled job, at a lower rate of pay. Having himself incurred debts in order to send her the little he could, he was burdened with their repayment out of his diminished wages.

The Crearies' room had never contained much beyond essential furniture and equipment. Even so, Lizzie was reduced to stripping it for the sake of raising a few shillings at the pawn shop. The very shoes which had tempted her into debt were amongst the first things to be disposed of. May went out so rarely now that the loss was felt less than others. A blanket off Lizzie's bed went the same way, and a neat, plain foot-stool her father had made for her mother before their marriage. Gone were the treats and relishes she had been providing so recklessly, as it now seemed. Not even for May was there milk.

Often, as Lizzie toiled barefoot up the damp, dirty stair, she would see her neighbour's child hanging about the landing below, barred from her home until her mother's latest friend had left. Lizzie quickened her steps as she passed that door, as though to run from what disgusted and frightened her.

12

One raw January morning a week after Sophie's wedding Helen moved to her aunt's house in Northumberland Street. The children were at school, Jack up at the College, her father at an editorial meeting which he could not miss, as he assured her with apparent regret. She said goodbye to her step-mother with no effusion of feeling on either side, and walked from the tall gracious building in which she had passed her entire life with as little ceremony as if she had been paying a morning call.

Most of Helen's clothes and possessions had been transferred piecemeal over the previous few days. It had been the most sensible way to proceed, in order to spare Miss Anderson the upheaval of a full-scale flitting, but it left Helen now with little to do.

Since her seizure, Miss Anderson had lived solely on the ground floor of her house. She allotted two rooms to Helen to the rear of the first floor: a small bedroom, and a somewhat larger room to serve as her sitting-room. Now Helen wandered aimlessly through them. When she had shared a room with Rosemary such privacy would have been unspeakably precious. Rosemary had been the untidiest creature imaginable, and careless over the use of Helen's belongings. She had often dreamed of a room of her own which she could enter in the confidence that she would not find Rosemary's hair clogging her brush, or her best stockings reduced to shreds by her sister's casual and illicit borrowing.

She arranged the last few things she had brought with her. It took minutes. Her trinkets and toilet things seemed oddly incomplete on the dressing table, no longer jostling for space with Rosemary's or Sophie's belongings. Miss

Anderson was in the back parlour downstairs, reading the *Scotsman* as she did every morning, she had told her niece. Her unmistakable emphasis warned of the impossibility of any change in this practice. Helen suspected that there would be many such rules in Aunt Jeannie's day.

Miss Anderson had given her to understand that they would meet again at luncheon, at one. It was still only half past eleven. Helen looked down into the garden. An icy drizzle was blackening the trees. Amongst their branches, contorted as by agony in the cold, a hunched, songless bird sat in bedraggled misery. A walk was out of the question.

She approached her books, neatly ranged in the new bookcases which Aunt Jeannie had ordered for her. From behind their glass doors they stared back at her. English poetry and a few good novels, some volumes of history and biography, her Greek plays and one or two of the shorter dialogues of Plato formed the bulk of her collection, with some oddments which had belonged to her mother. It was a library on which she had prided herself, but on a gloomy January morning there seemed little in all those great works to cheer or divert.

The doorbell rang. The tones of a man's voice reached her, and the sound of quick steps on the stair. At once her isolation was dispelled. It must be her father, escaped from his editorial meeting and come to see her, realising how strange she must be feeling at first. She turned a face of childlike happiness to the door as it opened to admit Doctor Cairns.

Her face fell; at once his smile of greeting faded in disappointment. She recovered herself as best she could. 'How nice to see you, Doctor Cairns! I was expecting my father, but you are a most welcome substitute.'

'I thought you might be rather lost, this first day. Here, these may brighten the room; one of my patients has a hot-house full of the things. I begged a bunch for an elderly relation, if you will believe it.'

'They are beautiful!' She bent her head over the flowers. Roses and clove-pinks, sprays of feathery fern, they brought to the room colour, fragrance, life.

She looked up from the blooms, seeking refuge from emotion in the teasing tone which had always marked her relations with him. 'How your patient would have quizzed you, if he had seen your elderly relation! What misunderstandings might arise!' His answering smile was tinged with constraint.

'You have a delightful room here.'

'I feel as much out of my proper sphere as these poor flowers would be, if they had been uprooted from their warm beds and planted out in that garden, and left to fend for themselves in the sleet.'

She distanced herself from the confession by the elaborate comparison, but the feeling was none the less real. He nodded. 'Take each day as it comes, and get out as much as you can. Things will improve with the better weather.' He strolled to the bookcase. 'You'll not want for reading matter.'

'No. I've often longed for the chance to spend more time on study, and now that I have it I don't feel inclined to open a book.'

'These are your mother's, aren't they? I have a copy of one of the volumes of Lamartine. Your father allowed me to take something from her things as a keep-sake. I chose it because it was a duplicate, and one of her favourites.'

'I don't think I've ever opened one of her books since Papa gave them to me.' Seeing the ready sympathy in his face she added quickly, 'Oh, not because it would have been too painful. I never liked French very much, that's all.'

'Perhaps you could try it again now, and see if your tastes have changed? One of my patients has a Frenchwoman lodging with her. She gives lessons, and seems a decent young woman. I can give you the address, if you like. It would be an interest, and help the teacher too, no doubt.'

She did not reply at once. She opened the bookcase and picked out one of her mother's books at random. It fell open at what must have been a favourite poem. In a clear, correct hand English words were pencilled into the broad margins, with here and there a little line at the side of the text marking what must have struck her mother as verses of particular beauty, or difficulty, perhaps. She passed her fingers gently over the page. She turned to the front cover. In the same girlish hand was written her mother's name, Margaret Anderson, and a date in 1832.

'Eighteen thirty-two . . . I suppose she would have been living here then. I didn't think of it before.'

'It is very likely. I didn't know her until more than ten years later, of course, when she was already married. I attended her throughout her fifth confinement, and from then onwards.' He stretched out his hand for the book. He turned a few pages, his stubby fingers curiously delicate.

'She was a remarkable woman,' he said unexpectedly.

'Mama?' At once she felt ashamed of her unconcealed surprise.

'There was no one I have ever known with a greater gift for friendship. I often wished I had known her when she had her full strength. Your father was always so full of energy, so enthusiastic about some notion or other, he overshadowed her. But even so, she had a wicked sense of fun at times. And none of her friends ever went to her with a great sorrow and came away unconsoled.'

His praise made her uncomfortable, as though it were a reproach to her. 'You must have missed her,' she said, almost at random.

'Oh, I missed her.' He gently closed the book and returned it to her. 'You favour your father, of course, but at times you have a look of her, about the eyes.' He paused, and added more briskly, 'Shall I write down that address for you?'

'Why not? I think I might like a new interest.'

'Here, then . . . now I must go down to see your aunt.

There's a poor old woman I think she might wish to hear of; don't come down. Miss Anderson likes her good deeds to be as secret as though they were bad, you know.'

He was closing the door behind him when she called him back.

'Yes?'

'Thank you again for the flowers, that's all. You may tell your kind patient how much they pleased your elderly relation!'

As she set herself to arranging the flowers she heard his footsteps heavily descending the stair.

The first days with her aunt were not easy. Miss Anderson was rather pleased than not to have her favourite niece with her. She made her welcome, urging her to buy at her expense whatever she wished for her rooms, and to invite her friends and family to her sitting-room whenever she chose.

For all her undoubted generosity, however, there was never any question of Miss Anderson adapting her own habits to suit Helen. Her days followed the pattern which pleased her, and Helen soon recognised that she must learn to conform to her aunt's routine. She acknowledged that it must be so, but none the less after living in a predominantly youthful household the sense of being governed by a regime which had been unchanged in forty years, the sense of petrified, arrested life, soon became oppressive to her.

On her return from the brief walks which were all the weather allowed, even the entrance hall would strike her with dread. Nothing in it had altered since her earliest visits, as far as she could remember. The same umbrella stand was positioned in the same dim corner, still holding the ivory-handled cane which had once belonged to Miss Anderson's younger brother. A silent reminder at once of his existence and his premature death, its self-contradictory message never failed to disturb Helen.

Opposite the staircase stood a long-case clock, its

implacable ticking measuring out time into neat, identical seconds, each passing in the act of declaring itself. For over sixty years Aunt Jeannie must have heard that tick, without listening to it, just as she had lived her life without noticing it, perhaps, until an inconceivable number of seconds had lost themselves in the thick air of the passage, and a lifetime had been meted out by the deceptively innocent strokes of the ageless pendulum.

In the parlour at the rear of the house Helen would sit with Miss Anderson in the evenings. It had changed little since her father Robert Anderson had set up the home, in the days when the New Town really was new. Helen had always rather liked the room and its antiquated formality. By the standards of her own generation it was sparsely furnished, with the emphasis on spindly elegance and not comfort. As a visitor, she had been able to appreciate the stiff, faded changelessness of the room, preserved at the loss of its vitality, like the dry undecaying flowers which in summer stood in its hearth. But, living there, she would at times be overcome by a sort of panic at the sight of her aunt in her old-fashioned lace pelerine and quaint cap nodding beside the fire, protected from its blaze by a screen worked in her childhood by Helen's mother. Her aunt belonged in her fading Regency elegance, but for Helen at twenty-three it was a genteel prison.

Miss Anderson liked her to read to her in the evenings. Scott, the idol of her youth, was her choice, but before Helen had read very far, her aunt's head would droop, her hands, their fingers swollen by ill-health, would slide helplessly apart on her black satin skirts. It was the lightest of sleeps; she would awaken at the fall of a cinder in the grate, and Helen would resume as though there had been no interruption.

Such naps were the very worst moments for Helen. Sitting in enforced silence, she would begin to feel that the overheated room, as her aunt insisted on having it, was being slowly drained of air, stifling her. At times the illusion was so strong that she found herself fighting for breath; she longed to throw back the heavy curtains, fling open the shutters and let the cold night air flood the room. Sometimes her thoughts took an even wilder turn. She would imagine herself going out into the icy street, without bonnet or mantle, to feel in a sort of ecstasy the bitter wind on her cheeks, the sleet stinging her face and neck. Then, at least, she would know herself to be alive.

There was a force in such reveries which disturbed her. It was a relief when her aunt awoke, and she could try to lose herself in her reading. Supper would be brought, and she could listen to the wind beating in impotent fury against the windows, and shudder at the strangeness of her own desire to be out on the streets, struggling against the indifferent harshness of the elements. How many poor women wandering homeless through the city would not have crouched gladly by the warmth she had felt smothering her! And so the mood would pass, for the moment.

Gradually her days took on a sort of meaning. Doctor Cairns looked in for a minute or two whenever he was in the neighbourhood; Helen began her French lessons, and enjoyed them; Jack came to see her, more often than she had looked for. James Grant was away in London, it seemed, to consult a doctor renowned for the management of rheumatic complaints. Jack was subdued. She honoured him for his concern for the health of the pupil to whom he had become as much friend as teacher.

For the rest, Helen dined at Drummond Place often enough to avoid any suggestion of a family rift between her and the Lambert household. She was always received warmly by her father, and by Susan Lambert with an effusiveness which she never quite trusted.

The children seemed pleased to see her in their way, but she could not deceive herself that they missed her very severely. School concerns now took the pride of place with the girls, and in her heart Helen had to admit that Kitty in particular was much improved by the change.

Kitty was escaping from the too-close absorption in the family which, in her own case, Helen was coming to see as having been a lost but false paradise.

She called on Rosemary often, but no dinner invitation came from that quarter. It would have added very much to her enjoyment of life had she been able to mix at the Robertsons' with the varied, youthful society which, as mistress of her father's household, she had taken for granted.

For her, entertaining her father's friends had been a delight, but she had devoted no effort to building up friendships on her own account. Her sisters had satisfied any need for the companionship of other women; she had no friends such as Margaret Hewitt had been to Sophie. Lacking the wider contacts which already Kitty was making at school, looking no further than her family for interests and amusement, content with the frequent but essentially impersonal social engagements of her father's circle, she now stood alone.

In the middle of February the cold weather returned with renewed force after a long period of chill dampness more unbearable than a sharp frost. One Monday morning, as she sat in her room struggling to find something of interest to report to Sophie in exchange for a letter full of breathless details of balls and dinners and visits to the opera and London fashions and customs, she heard the bell ring as though it would be yanked from the wall.

To the echoes of the bell succeeded the clatter of boots up the stair, and excited voices calling her name. Before she could tidy away her writing desk, Philip and Andrew had burst into the room.

'What a heat in here! Come out with us, Helen, we've got a holiday for the ice!'

'Duddingston Loch is bearing!' broke in Andrew, his plump cheeks red with the cold. 'It may be the last time this winter, don't miss it!'

Their enthusiasm was irresistible. She had gone to change before she knew what she was doing, hurrying as though even the thought of vigorous exercise had roused her blood from its torpor.

The boys had planned to take an omnibus. Helen, in the holiday spirit of the day, gaily hailed a passing hackney cab, her impatience almost exceeding theirs.

The loch was already drawing a crowd, word of the ice, as always, spreading throughout the city with inexplicable speed. Schoolboys predominated, given a holiday or taking one, but older enthusiasts were not lacking. When skating was in prospect, professors forgot their gravity, judges their sobriety, even ministers their decorum.

Her fingers already nipped by the cold, Helen fumbled eagerly to put on her skates, and launched out onto the ice, uncertainly at first then gaining in confidence as she trusted her body to remember its skill.

Andrew and Philip were soon hailed by friends from the Academy. Helen urged them to go across and join them. Her sparkling eyes and smile of delight added weight to her protests that she would be quite happy alone; her brothers exchanged a questioning glace, and skated off, Philip crouching low, with fluid grace, Andrew's solid figure seeming to plod along, even on ice.

She picked her way smoothly through the crowded margin of the loch, where beginners, tottering and squealing, clung in delicious terror to their instructors, and headed out to where the ice was clearer.

She sped along, striking out in swift easy strokes. She thought of nothing, giving herself up to the physical enjoyment of the crisp air against her cheeks, and the sensation of effortless speed, the nearest approach to flight which she could imagine.

By the edge of the loch, reeds were frozen where they grew. Seeing them, jagged and stiff, it was impossible to believe that beneath the ice their roots were unharmed, that in a few months they would stir and bend in the breeze, a shelter to wild-fowl, their drowsy rustle the very soul of a dreaming summer day. Far above, the snow-spumed flanks of Arthur's Seat added to the illusion of rural isolation.

A few skaters, like Helen, were seeking out the less frequented areas, some to conceal their early errors from public amusement, others to gain a clear field for speed, or to appreciate undisturbed the austere beauty of their surroundings. Such, by unspoken agreement, paid no need to their fellows, avoiding any with whom they might naturally have come into contact.

Helen, like the rest, paid no more attention to other skaters than enabled her to avoid them. After the close confinement of the past weeks freedom of action was intoxicating. It was an exhilaration she had sometimes known in dancing; fatigue seemed impossible, the awareness of speed and movement replaced thought. She gazed about her in a near trance, conscious only of a surging well-being and the fierce joy of physical activity.

Some distance away from her, a black silhouette cut out against the ice and patchy snow, a solitary figure was gliding along, arms behind his back, holding himself uncompromisingly erect. He was turned away from her, but she knew him at once. It was Francis Bethune.

Without thinking, she set off towards him, exerting herself to the maximum speed of which she was capable. If she had stopped to consider, if she had not been so reckless with the licence of the holiday, she might have lacked the courage to break in upon the isolation of a man whom she knew so slightly, and who was so clearly avoiding company.

But the sense of unexpected freedom, so far removed from the conventions of her everyday life, swept timidity and prudence aside. She approached him fearlessly, without a thought for the distant politeness which might greet her, simply glad to see him, and naturally seeking to make herself known.

Hearing the approach of another skater, he perceptibly increased his speed and veered away into the centre of the loch. Clearly he expected his pursuer to continue without deflecting their course. When he heard the crisp hiss of skates still following him, he glanced behind him, frowning. But seeing Helen, surprise replaced annoyance, and he slowed to a halt.

She came to rest beside him, miscalculating slightly and clutching at his arm to steady herself, laughing. 'Mr Bethune! I think I must have dropped out of the race in another moment!' she said breathlessly, withdrawing her other hand from her muff to put back a stray tendril of hair from her brow.

Gazing happily about her as she recovered her breath she did not see the wonder in his eyes as he regarded her. She stood, still resting on his arm, the breath from her parted lips showing in little puffs on the frosty air. Fluffed out by her swift passage over the ice, her fair hair stood in an aureole about her face. Her eyes were sparkling with the high spirits induced by the exercise, her full breasts rose and fell as she panted, their curve emphasised by her close-fitting Zouave jacket, black, with trimming of gold braid. She wore a fur tippet round her neck; its fur lay in delicate points against her cheek, soft against her skin. Beneath her hat the tip of her ear was visible, small and neat. She was the very embodiment of life and health.

'Are you recovered? I'm sorry, if I had known . . . I didn't realise . . .' His manner, stammering, ill at ease, was so unlike his usual composure that she turned to him in sudden compunction.

'Am I intruding upon you? Would you prefer to be undisturbed? I didn't think; I saw you in the distance and knew you at once. It is so long since we met that I had to make myself known.'

'I'm glad,' he said awkwardly. 'Shall we go on? You may take a chill if we stand.' He offered her his crossed hands. She took them, laughing over the little confusion as they became entangled with her muff. They set off, more slowly, taking a little time to adjust their movements, but quickly falling into an easy partnership.

Conversation had never been wanting between them before, but now she was content to move with him in shared silence. His fair skin was somewhat flushed by the exercise, she noted. His hair seemed to have been allowed to grow slightly longer than she remembered it; it curled beneath his hat, not quite touching his collar. She thought it rather suited him, and would have liked to tell him so, but dared not.

'It must be five months since we met last,' he said.

'As long as that? And yet I don't know why I should say so; it seems as many years.'

'That usually suggests an eventful life.'

'Eventful? Hardly, but there have been changes, I suppose. I have changed my residence, Rosemary will have mentioned that?'

She felt her hands suddenly squeezed, almost painfully. 'No, she didn't . . . am I to understand, I mean, are you to be congratulated, or rather some fortunate unknown?'

At first she failed to grasp the point of his allusion, contortedly expressed. 'I have moved to my aunt's home, in Northumberland Street,' she said, still not understanding. 'She is an invalid. I think the arrangement suits us both.'

The grip on her hands slackened. Comprehension dawned. 'Did you think . . . I'm sorry, I did not express myself clearly.'

'I was being stupid.'

The exchange seemed to alter the unthinking ease which had existed on her part, at least. She became intensely aware of their closeness, of his shoulder against hers, of the momentary resting of her breast against his arm from time to time in the chance contact of their swaying motion. She looked up at him in a confusion which was half pleasurable, half fearful. She had never before noticed what a pleasant shade of brown his eyes were, nor seen them regard her so intently. She dropped her gaze.

'Should you not be in court, Mr Bethune?'

'Do you wish I were?' he said unexpectedly.

'I . . . of course not,' she replied lamely, at a loss for the joking response which would have come so readily had she been talking to Doctor Cairns.

'I have often thought it strange that our paths have never crossed. I expected that we might meet at Harry's.'

'Perhaps we might, if Rosemary were not . . . if she had felt equal to entertaining.'

'I am almost glad now that we did not; here, we could almost be in Melrose again.'

She nodded, knowing that he did not refer to the scenery alone, but the precious freedom they had enjoyed there. 'It is strange to think that we are only a mile or two from the High Street.'

'You may like to know, I saw MacGregor when I returned from Melrose.'

'Your factor?'

'Yes. I asked him his opinion of the improvement of the properties I hold in the Old Town. In his view the installation of a water supply would be a mixed blessing, since the rents would have to rise to cover the cost. He told me that many tenants would be unable to pay the increase, and that there was no wish for water on such terms.'

'And the other conveniences?'

'He doubted whether the fabric of one of the tenements in particular would stand the disruption caused by the improvement. What's more, he told me enough of the problems he has seen from the misuse of such facilities to persuade me that it is not a practical proposition. One careless tenant can cause endless difficulties, stairs flooded by sewage, and so forth. He quite convinced me.'

'So nothing is to be done?'

'What more can I do? I have consulted my man of business, and must abide by his advice. The tenants have not complained, after all. I repeated to MacGregor my standing instructions that they are to be kept wind-and-rainproof, and all repairs to be undertaken promptly.'

203

There was a silence. She felt his eyes on her. 'You are disappointed, Miss Lambert? You think the worse of me, for receiving rents from properties in the Old Town without water or sanitary conveniences, properties I have never seen?'

'Yes. If you press me, I have to say that I am sorry that you have any sort of responsibility for the scenes Harry described to us.'

'I honour you for your honesty,' he said warmly.

'I do not wish to offend you . . .'

'We differ on the question, that's all. What is offensive in that?'

She was silent, feeling obscurely that the matter was more important than some question of taste, on which any difference of opinion was utterly insignificant.

'What would you have me do?' he asked, half seriously.

'Sell your properties.'

'No. I would feel that I had betrayed my principles. It would be almost cowardice. I could not do that, even for your sake.'

At the last words, his voice dropped, suddenly intimate. Helen felt herself colour to the roots of her hair. She dared not look at him, wanted the conversation to continue, and yet hurried to change it.

'You seemed lost in thought when I burst in upon you,' she said, seizing upon the first subject which came to mind.

'It was nothing of any consequence. I was thinking of the future. I don't expect to be in Edinburgh for very much longer.'

'I didn't know that.'

'I am senior Advocate-Depute now. Unless the present Sheriffs are a particularly long-lived set I can expect to move at some time over the next year or so.'

'You did not seem to be regarding the prospect with any great satisfaction when I first saw you.'

'Oh, who is ever satisfied?'

'It is a step to further advancement, I suppose?'

'It isn't the particular piece of advancement which seems worth so little. I haven't explained myself clearly. A year ago success in my chosen career was the only good I desired in life. Now, I ask myself "Is that all?" It scarcely seems worth the effort, at times.'

'But only at times; no doubt such self-doubt plagues all but the brutally insensitive, the complacent.'

'If you will forgive my egotism, a few words about myself will explain the situation. For fifteen years I have devoted my every energy to the pursuit of excellence in my field. I began, I suppose, with some idea of pleasing my father. He had sat at the Bar for a few years although without any success. He had a poor speaking manner. My father's death removed that spur, and the financial need for success, but I worked all the harder. I surrendered other pursuits, other hopes, and told myself that they were a necessary sacrifice. And now? Has the game been worth the candle?'

'Those other pursuits can be resumed now, can they not? Can you not afford to relax your efforts and enjoy all that you have had to deny yourself until now?'

'I'm afraid that I have become as ill-suited for diversion as a man who had spent fifteen years in dissipation would be for serious study. I am accustomed to standing alone, to relying on no one but myself. And yet when I look about . . .' He fell silent.

'Yes?' she prompted gently, sure that he wished to say more, if he dared to trust her.

'Well then, if I may allow myself the self-indulgence; look about you, Miss Lambert. You will see the perfect metaphor for my life: an icy waste, lifeless and desolate.'

'No, not lifeless!' She hesitated, and drove herself on. 'There are fish still living beneath the ice, are there not? The reeds will spring up again, and look at the wild geese!' She drew to a halt, pointing up at the ever-changing patterns of the skein of wild-fowl passing overhead on their journey to the coast.

'You forget, Miss Lambert,' he said with a wry smile, 'I can't see them; I am extremely short-sighted.'

'They are there, all the same.'

'I shall believe you,' he said lightly, his hands tightening on hers as he drew her round in a smooth curve, for they had reached the furthest extent of the loch.

'Helen! Helen!'

She looked up in surprise. Her brothers were hurtling across the ice towards her, clearly in no very good humour. 'It's Philip and Andrew,' she said, with a sigh.

'Ah . . .' He sounded disappointed. Only a few seconds of privacy remained to them; already her brothers were clamorously voicing complaints, questions, demands from a distance of thirty yards away. 'Please, may I call on you – and your aunt?' he asked hurriedly.

'That would be very pleasant,' she said, smiling at him, and resolutely repressing the suspicion that her aunt might not agree with her.

'Where've you been this long? We thought you'd drowned!' 'I'm starving! Have you got money for chestnuts?' In an instant the atmosphere of the last minutes was dissipated. There was nothing for it but to cross the loch again towards the enterprising chestnut seller.

The party drifted away from Duddingston, Francis Bethune carrying Helen's skates as well as his own, the boys squabbling, devouring their chestnuts, burning their fingers, pelting each other with shells. They caught the omnibus back to town, although Francis Bethune left them with an apology at the Tron. As he got up, he muttered, 'Northumberland Street?'

She gave him the number, as quietly as she dared, conscious of her brothers' sharp ears and irreverent tongues.

As the omnibus moved away, she stared through the misted glass for a last sight of him. It was impossible. She saw only a dark, blurred outline as he turned up towards Parliament Square.

'He's not such a flat as you'd think, is he?' said Andrew,

nudging his brother, his eyes on Helen. 'He isn't a bad skater, considering his age.'

'A flat! Andrew!'

'Why, don't you think he's a flat, Helen?' Philip asked innocently.

'I would never use such a term, as well you know,' she said severely.

'He tipped us more than Harry, anyway,' said Andrew, regretfully crumpling up his empty paper bag. 'I wonder what Aunt Jeannie will make of him?'

Helen silenced him with a look; she had no need of her brother to suggest that question to her.

13

The coming of the snow and the freezing weather brought no joy to Lizzie. Bad weather and short time reduced her father's money orders; for two weeks he sent her barely enough to cover the rent. Lizzie's position would have been perilous indeed had Nettie not begged her mistress to give her her wages on a weekly basis. That, and the scraps she could bring, kept them from starvation.

For the rest, every halfpenny that Joseph could bring in was precious. Now she allowed him to stay out on the streets until well after nightfall, even in the worst weather: the worse the night, the fewer children there were looking for the odd jobs which would earn them a penny or two.

Joseph was a bright, cheerful child, quick and willing. As he pushed himself to earn the money which he knew was so badly needed, Lizzie saw the change in him, saw the fatigue which dulled his eyes and washed the colour from his cheeks. She hardened her heart, as she had to. The only way to lessen his burden was to leave him sleeping in the morning. He should be attending the Industrial School, but she could not bring herself to rouse him in time, knowing that he had been trailing the streets until midnight, watching out for cabs in the hope of a penny for carrying a bundle up a stair, or taking a letter to the post.

One week despite all her struggles she could not find the shilling for Cooper's menage; the shilling for the loan had not been paid for months.

'Look here, Lizzie, things are bad just now, aren't they?' Gillanders said, looking about him at the bare room, the wretched fire, low in the grate, barely enough to render their living quarters any warmer than the ice-bound street.

'Things will mend,' she said quickly. 'My father'll be back at his own work in another wee while, the cold doesna stop the work there, ken, and forbye that he gets a better rate. And it'll not be long afore Tam – my brother – gets home . . .'

'I'm delighted to hear it,' he broke in smoothly. 'I'm sure you'll pull through in no time, but I hate to see you having to pinch yourself, especially when things will improve so soon. This room can't be warm enough for May's cough, surely? And wouldn't she be better for another blanket on her bed?'

He paused. Anxiety tightened Lizzie's face as she looked at her sister, sewing in bed as the warmest place in the room. Sensing their attention, May struggled hopelessly not to cough.

'Here, I'll tell you what I'll do; I've been collecting a debt for my friend today. Would a sovereign be any good to you? I'll make it right with him, tell him he'll get it back soon, one way or another. That way you could keep yourself straight with Cooper's, and get in some coal and solid food.'

'I canna! I canna!'

He took out a sovereign, and pressed it into her cold hand. 'Of course you can! We'll make it all businesslike. It'll go down on the card, you'll pay my friend his interest, he won't be the loser. He's making an investment, that's all! You're happy, and he'll be happy, and when you've got that fire blazing up the chimney as though it meant it, May'll be happy too, with cheeks as rosy as an apple.'

He could not have offered a more seductive temptation. She made no further protest. After all, she told herself, with desperate optimism, in a week or two at the most her father's position would be very different from its present low ebb. If Tam went up to join him, and there were two full wages coming in, she could soon pay off even bigger debts.

And so she allowed herself to be persuaded. Nicholas Gillanders seemed even more delighted at the arrangement than she was. 'It's an excellent investment, Lizzie,' he assured her, as he pocketed his cards.

During the days which followed the skating excursion Helen found herself unsettled as never before. Uncertainty as to when she might expect a visit from Francis Bethune made every other activity seem oddly provisional; she could devote herself wholeheartedly to nothing. Even worse was the fear that he might not call, despite his declared intention. He had, it was true, seemed at their last meeting to be admitting some need for human warmth, but she sensed that habits of self-reliance built up over long, painful years would not quickly be demolished.

As day followed upon day without a visit, she tried to tell herself that she cared not at all whether he came or not. But she could not deny that he exercised some charm over her thoughts which no man had ever before possessed. Almost she resented her yearning towards him; she tried to dissect it, in the hope that understanding would destroy its power, as with some childhood fear, banished by rational explanation.

He was good-looking, in her eyes at least, but she had seen better-looking men and given them no more than dispassionate appreciation. He was intelligent, well read, conversable, but she had known other men with quicker wits, with views which more nearly approached her own, and had found in them merely agreeable dinner companions.

Try as she might, she could not account for her interest in him, any more than she could conquer it. It was the sense of another suffering human being, seen by her alone, behind the public facade of amused composure; the desire to console and encourage him as he reached, stumbling, towards the shifting light of human affection with all its dangers; it was something in his straight, neat figure, some precise grace in his movements which drew and pleased her eye; it was all these things, and still it remained, in the end, an enigma.

Now Sophie's dreamy preoccupation in Melrose was all too comprehensible. For the first time, reading failed her as a resource. She would try to settle to some French preparation in her sitting-room, but no longer could she lose herself in study. The sounds of the household distracted her, the sudden hiss of a fiercer flame in the hearth, the long whisper of wheels in the wet street, even the slow jerky progress of raindrops down the window panes, or the familiar patterns of the cornice, nothing was too insignificant to capture her wandering attention. Whenever the doorbell rang her heart thudded painfully. She always forced herself to remain seated; it might be only Doctor Cairns, she would tell herself, scarcely admitting even in her own mind the longed-for identity of the caller.

It was a grey, wretched afternoon of constant sleet, a week and more after the Duddingston excursion. Helen was reading to her aunt, although it would have been difficult to say whether the sounds she uttered made less sense to her or Miss Anderson. The latter's lace-capped head would droop, as her eyes closed, until it fell forward onto her chest with a jerk, awakening her for a few minutes, until her eyelids wavered, her chin slowly subsided, and the whole process began again.

The sudden peal of the bell awoke Miss Anderson in real earnest. She peered out at the leaden sky, the splinters of sleet lancing themselves against the window.

'Whoever can be calling on such a day? Only a debt collector would be out in such weather – or a fool of a lover.'

'Or a minister? Or a doctor?' Helen said, with enforced calm.

'I don't see Doctor Cairns's brougham, at any rate. Here's Bessie to put us out of our misery with a card.' There was a pause, as Miss Anderson fumbled to find her spectacles and then to open them, ignoring Helen's offer to read the card for her. 'So, a Francis Bethune is honouring us with a call! And he's an advocate, too! I don't know any Bethunes do I, Helen?'

'Yes, Aunt Jeannie, you remember, last week I met Harry Robertson's cousin when we were at Duddingston. He asked if he might call.'

'Well, he's either very foolish or very dutiful to pick such a day. I think we'll just deny ourselves, Helen, and let the poor man escape to his own fireside.'

'No!' Helen cried, a note of panic in her voice which brought a frown to her aunt's face. 'He . . . he is most eager to make your acquaintance, Aunt Jeannie,' she added lamely.

'How very odd! I mustn't disappoint him, in that case. Show him in, Bessie, if you would,' she said, in a tone which augured ill for her visitor's reception.

A minute or two elapsed; Bessie must be helping him off with his wet outer clothes. Helen glanced quickly about the room. Was the light dim enough to require the gas? It might be brighter, and yet there was always something mournful in the effect of gaslight by day. The flickering firelight gave a more welcoming atmosphere. She confined herself to smoothing her hair with trembling, ineffective fingers, which abandoned their useless task in sudden guilt as Francis Bethune entered.

She rose, and introduced him to her aunt. She feared that her nervousness must be all too apparent; her heart was pounding unpleasantly and her voice sounded hopelessly unnatural to her own ears.

Francis Bethune, the introduction complete, turned to her, reaching for her hand. She gave it to him, ashamed at its trembling. His hand was cold; it clasped hers with an eagerness which stilled its tremor in a moment. A sense of peace began to dispel her anxiety; she dared not look at him, but in the silent pressure of his hand, prolonged a fraction beyond the demands of politeness, there seemed a secret message of reassurance.

Miss Anderson was speaking. Helen seated herself in a little flurry of self-consciousness. He waited until she was settled, and took the chair to which Miss Anderson gestured him, by hers. Helen was opposite him. When he turned his head attentively to her aunt, she saw him in profile; his hair was dark with rain, plastered close to his temples by moisture, a curious vulnerability in the whiteness of his skin where the hair clung. He was sitting easily back in his chair, his hands lightly clasped before him, one leg crossed over the other. His foot, long and slim, swayed just perceptibly, as at the impulse of his heartbeat.

'So you are a legal man, Mr Bethune?' Miss Anderson was asking, in a voice from which her usual bluff charm was noticeably absent.

'Yes, an Advocate-Depute.'

'A criminal lawyer, then?'

'In a manner of speaking.'

'You must have fastened the noose round many a poor soul's neck.'

Helen shifted uneasily in her chair. She feared that worse would be to come.

'The verdict rests with the jury, and the sentence with the Bench. I am only a part of the process.'

'But doesn't your own responsibility ever prey on your mind, Mr Bethune?' her aunt persisted.

If he noticed the hostile tone of the question, he ignored it, and answered pleasantly enough. 'In the first place, Miss Anderson, the number of capital crimes is much smaller than thirty or so years ago. Then again, many of the sentences of death which are pronounced as a matter of form are not carried out. They are commuted almost automatically. But if you press me, I would go so far as to say that I have never regretted the condemnation of a prisoner, while I have often regretted an acquittal.'

'Well, that's honest enough, at any rate.'

'I have occasionally had more personal grounds than you might suppose for my regrets.'

'Not threats, surely?' Helen said in horror.

He looked at her, some new sense of intimacy in his gaze which made her for a second feel as though they were alone, and then wish that they might be. As he answered her question, he turned again to Miss Anderson, but his eyes kept returning to Helen.

'I have been threatened once or twice, although judges are the more usual objects of such attention. I can remember the first time, a few years ago. The panel – the defendant, that is – was a petty clerk named Gillanders, who had formerly worked for a prosperous business man but had been dismissed for drunkenness. At about the time of his dismissal, his employer lost some documents, incriminating him in underhand financial dealings. Within a few days of missing the letters, he received a demand for money as the price of their return.'

'Well, what happened?' Miss Anderson asked impatiently. Helen suspected that he was not averse to keeping her in suspense, after her unfriendly reception of him.

'You're sure I'm not boring you? Well, the employer had the courage to lay the matter in the hands of the police. They advised him to take the money to the proposed place, somewhere on Calton Hill, and leave it as instructed. They would then arrest whoever came to collect it.'

'Was the arrest made?' Helen asked, still unable to address him quite naturally.

'Yes, but not as planned. It was a dark night, and the officers' nearest place of concealment was some distance from the collection point. Nevertheless, they could see a figure approach the spot, lift the stone above the money and make off. They set off in pursuit, but at that very moment a dog which they swore had appeared out of nowhere began to attack them, barking and snapping at their legs. In the confusion the blackmailer made off, but a search was made. Gillanders, whose description had been circulated to the officers involved, was arrested on the path leading off the hill to the High Calton. In his pockets were found a couple of sovereigns from the decoy – they had been marked, and could be identified.'

'The man was guilty! Not a doubt of it!' Miss Anderson cried, interested despite herself. 'Surely you got a conviction?'

He smiled wryly. 'No. The defence exerted themselves to the utmost. There was wonderful eloquence on the dangers of police traps to ensnare unsuspecting members of the public going lawfully about their business. Juries don't like undue officiousness on the part of the police, any suspicion of *agents provocateurs* and so on, and of course the man from whom the papers were taken had been indulging in sharp practice, all but embezzlement. That alienated sympathy from the prosecution. But all the same, I think we might have succeeded, but for Donoghue.'

'Donoghue? Who was he?' Miss Anderson asked testily.

'The chief defence witness . . . in fact, as I firmly believe to this day, the instigator of the whole thing. Gillanders didn't seem to me to have the brains or the pluck to be acting alone. Donoghue was a very different type. He was Irish, but sounded as though he'd spent most of his life in England. His story was that he'd been walking his dog on Calton Hill that evening, and had seen what he took to be a cowardly and unprovoked attack, three men against one. He had set his dog on the supposed attackers, until realising too late that they were police officers he whistled it off. He then continued his walk, only to be all but knocked to the ground by a man running full tilt down the hill. The man dropped a small package when they collided, and although he picked it up at once and made off, Donoghue found a sovereign on the spot. It was produced: it was marked. The defence claimed, of course, that Gillanders had found his two quite innocently further down the path, the bag having been torn in the fall. Needless to say, Donoghue was able to provide a full description of the mysterious – fictitious,

I would say — fugitive. It corresponded with Gillanders in height and build, but differed totally in every other respect.'

'Perhaps he was telling the truth?' Helen ventured.

'He was plausible, but every instinct told me that he was acting in collusion with Gillanders, and that Gillanders had passed the money to him before arrest. We did what we could, pointing out the coincidence of a former clerk who had had access to the documents in question being in the area at that very time, but the defence produced another witness who claimed that she was to meet Gillanders on Calton Hill.'

'On Calton Hill? At night?' Miss Anderson repeated incredulously.

'Indeed. She was, if you will excuse me, a street-walker of the lowest description. I tried to shake her story, but she was immovable. Her manner was curious. She was nervous — terrified even, but not of me or the Bench. She must have passed through the sheriff's court too often for that. No, it was Donoghue who seemed to frighten her. He had already given his evidence and been cross-questioned, and had slipped back into the court onto the public benches. Her eyes kept turning to him with an expression of the most abject terror. Even now I don't care to imagine how a man achieves an influence of that sort.'

'What was Donoghue like?' Helen asked.

'I find it difficult to answer dispassionately; I have never felt such antipathy to anyone, not even to any of the convicted murderers I have encountered. Nine times out of ten, your murderer has acted under the influence of drink or anger. With Donoghue it was different. His viciousness seemed intrinsic, so to speak, innate. In person he was not ill-looking, though undersized. He had a quantity of black hair and a cocky sort of way with him which went down well with the court. I imagine he was, or thought himself to be, something of a ladies' man.'

'You can't put a man behind bars for that,' her aunt commented acidly.

'We couldn't put him behind bars for anything, there was not the shadow of a case against him. I tried to weaken his evidence in my cross-examination but he held firm.' He hesitated, and added with a rueful shrug, 'His answers were given with such cool insolence that I went beyond what was strictly proper; to be honest, the judge pulled me up once or twice. It is the only case in which I have overstepped the mark in that way. Donoghue seemed to touch some raw nerve in me.'

'And was the antipathy mutual, Mr Bethune?' Helen prompted. 'The threat?'

'He certainly seemed to dislike me as much as I did him . . . as for the threat, a week or so later I received an unsigned letter. It was admirably concise; I can quote you its entire contents. "Watch yourself, Mister Bethune. Late or soon I will pay you out." That was all.'

'And you are sure it was Donoghue?' Helen asked.

'I can think of no other likely candidate. Gillanders as defendant never appeared in the witness box, of course, and in any case he was acquitted. He could have had no quarrel with me. It was Donoghue whom I tried to break . . . with no success, as I said. It was a lesson to me never to allow my personal feelings to go into court with me.'

'What, is an Advocate-Depute not a man as other men are?' Miss Anderson asked, in a tone which Helen recognised with some alarm. 'Judges allow themselves personal feelings enough, at any rate. I'm sure you could tell us tales of many an injudicious ornament of the Bench, could you not?'

He murmured non-committally, as though doubtful of her meaning.

'My grandfather was acquainted with one of the justiciary at the turn of the century. I understood that he took good care not to leave the learned lord alone with any female member of his household, from the oldest to the youngest. He had his by-blows in every circuit town in Scotland.'

'Aunt Jeannie!' muttered Helen.

Francis Bethune cleared his throat. 'The present-day Bench is a much reformed institution. There are exceptions, but the general tone is more refined, if the stories which still circulate of the incumbents of fifty years ago are to be believed.'

'No doubt there are as many sinners now as then. Folk were more honest then, that's all the difference.'

'Even the wish to conceal misdemeanours argues an improvement in public morality, does it not?'

'Greater hypocrisy, perhaps,' Miss Anderson said briskly, with an unmistakable glance at the clock, bringing him to his feet at once. 'Helen, will you ring for Bessie, if Mr Bethune really must be going.'

'Oh, I won't trouble her; I can show Mr Bethune out,' Helen said quickly, already moving to the door before her aunt could struggle to her feet. Her heart beating so swiftly that she felt almost light-headed, she led him from the room.

The passage was cold after her aunt's overheated parlour, and very dim. As she helped him on with his greatcoat, heavy with the rain, her hands shook with the cold, and with that half-pleasurable sense of tension which overcame her once more, now that they were alone.

'I wanted to come sooner,' he murmured, 'I waited until I was sure . . .'

From the half-open door of the parlour Miss Anderson's cough was heard, short and disapproving.

'Your umbrella is in the stand by the door, I suppose,' Helen said loudly, with a warning glance. She took him through the inner door to the front entrance, where his dripping umbrella stood beside the abandoned ivory-handled cane. She lifted it for him, leaving a train of raindrops on the tiles. The cold was glacial.

She looked up at him. 'Your collar . . . it's twisted,'

she said, and raised her hand to straighten it for him, stroking the damp nap of the velvet a second in an involuntary caress. His hand closed over hers where it lay on his shoulder, and held it tight. A great warmth spread through her body as he raised her hand to his lips. She heard his umbrella clatter unheeded to the floor as he gathered her in his arms.

The roughness of his coat was against her cheek; silver drops of moisture hung on the hairs of the tweed, like dew on moss. She closed her eyes as his hands moved over her back, straining her close. His breath was warm on her neck as he pressed his lips fiercely against her skin, grazing its delicacy by the roughness of his cheeks.

She did not hear her aunt's bell jangling in the kitchen below, nor the clatter of Bessie's shoes on the stair. Every sense failed her but the one of whose very existence she seemed to have been ignorant until now, the sense of touch. Outstripping thought, her body came into its own at last; her neck arched beneath his kisses, offering her throat to him, bringing her face from its concealment.

'Helen!' It was his voice as she had never heard it, urgent, almost anguished. He buried his face against her hair as though he were breathing its scent, fixing it for ever in his memory.

And suddenly, his arms flew from her; he looked at her in desperate longing as she heard, too late, the rustle of Bessie's approaching skirts.

He stooped quickly for his umbrella. 'Tomorrow? May I come?' he whispered as she handed him his hat and gloves from the stand. Scarlet with humiliation beneath Bessie's disapproving eyes, she nodded. He hurriedly pressed her hand, and was gone.

Trying to keep her face averted from Bessie she turned from the door, hoping to slip unobserved to her room; in vain.

'Miss Anderson would like to have a word with you, Miss Lambert,' Bessie said, condemnation in every syllable, in the very sway of her squab hips, in the flounce of her decent black skirts as she preceded her into the parlour.

Helen would have liked to disobey the summons, but a lifetime of obedience was not easily overthrown. She entered the parlour, hoping soon to escape. As she crossed the floor to her aunt, she caught sight of her own reflection in the oval gilt mirror. A strand of hair had strayed onto her shoulder. The skin of her neck and throat was blotchy and reddened, her cheeks were flushed, her eyes seemed enlarged, their pupils wide. It was a face almost strange to her, heedless, radiant with quickened life.

'Did you want something, Aunt Jeannie?' she asked as lightly as she could, hoping to be able to find some pretext to leave before Bessie turned from mending the fire to what would be her next task, lighting the gas.

Her aunt's only response was an eloquent glance to Helen's chair. Reluctantly she seated herself. Not another word was uttered until Bessie had, with a precision which seemed to Helen's overstretched nerves exaggeratedly, maliciously slow, built up the fire, lit the gas, closed the shutters and drawn the curtains.

'Thank you, Bessie. I'll ring for my tea presently.'

'Very good, Miss Anderson.'

As the door clicked shut behind her broad back, the bombardment began. 'Well, a fine tale she'll have for the kitchen! It'll be all over the street before supper!'

'I'm sure I can't think what you mean, Aunt Jeannie,' she said, wavering between innocence and lofty dignity, achieving neither.

'Look at you! Your hair hanging about your shoulders' – Helen belatedly attempted to put back the errant lock – 'your neck red as fire! I've never seen such a shameless display! A High Street whore could not look more wanton!'

'Aunt Jeannie!'

'Aye, you're too mealie-mouthed for plain speaking, but you're not ashamed of carryings-on that no self-respecting servant would entertain! Worse than a scullery maid at the area gate!'

She stopped, gasping for breath, her hand clawing at her breast, her lips bluish, contorted by her fight for air.

'Aunt Jeannie, please! You musn't excite yourself!'

'And what must I do? Sit here and say nothing, while you give your hand to that red-headed advocate to paw and paddle? Pretend I'm blind while you make sheep's eyes at him? Do you think I'm so doted that I never noticed you rush out after him, grudging Bessie the handling of his coat, and then stand in the biting cold ten minutes letting him slaver over you?' Pain as well as anger was twisting her features now, but still the onslaught continued. 'My own niece, beneath my own roof . . . not a shred of common decency . . .' The words ended in a groan which, indomitable as she was, she could not repress. In utter terror Helen turned the bell handle, and flew to release the collar about her aunt's swollen throat.

With Bessie's help she got Miss Anderson to bed while the kitchen-maid, Phemie, was sent for Doctor Cairns. It was some while before he could be found. By the time he arrived the pain had long since left her, although she remained short of breath and somewhat confused, taking little apparent interest in her surroundings. He wrote a line for some remedy to ease her breathing, made a few practical suggestions concerning her management, and moved quietly to the door.

'Can you spare a moment, Helen?' he asked, as she nodded to Bessie to show him out. 'Bessie will do very well here, you know.

Helen glanced doubtfully at her aunt; sunk in a waking dream, she seemed to care nothing for Helen's absence or presence. She accompanied him from the room, into the parlour.

'It's warmer here,' she murmured. 'We will be to hand if we are needed.'

He motioned her to be seated, watching her intently. 'It has come as a great shock to you, and yet it was scarcely unexpected, was it? She will very probably survive.'

She twisted her hands together in her lap and turned to him a face of utter wretchedness.

'What is it, Helen?' he asked, with a gentleness which brought her close to tears.

'I blame myself, that's all. We were quarrelling before her seizure. I should not have allowed her to grow so heated.'

'What power on earth could keep Jeannie Anderson cool when she'd taken a notion to speak her mind? Another attack was always to be expected; it could have struck her at any moment, quarrelling or no.'

She sighed, unconvinced. 'And now? What will her state be?'

'I think it likely that she will recover, but in a weakened condition. She will tire more easily, be able for less – be still more of an invalid, in short. She will need you more, Helen.'

The words rang in her ears like the clang of hammer on anvil, forging the last link of a heavy, dragging chain.

She was silent, then asked abruptly, 'How long? Is another attack likely soon?'

He shrugged. 'The last seizure was in September, six months or so? That doesn't give any great cause for optimism, but you can never say . . . with careful management and a quantity of luck it might be years. She's a fighter.'

'Years.'

He looked at her seriously. 'Was the quarrel important?'

'Oh, at the time,' she said wearily, 'but we shan't quarrel again. I've learned my lesson.'

'Well . . .' He rose. 'I shall look in again tomorrow. Call me sooner if there is any cause.' He hesitated, as though he would have said more, had there been any consolation he could give to the abstracted, unhappy

222

woman before him. But, wrapped in thought, she hardly noticed his departure.

That night Bessie slept in Miss Anderson's room, with instructions to call Helen if she were needed. Through the dreary night Helen lay wakeful, listening for the call which never came, her body rigid, her mind all too active, desperately twisting and turning in the search for escape from the future she saw inexorably closing in on her.

And always, seductive, shameful, in the shadows lurked the memory of those few snatched moments in the dim, freezing doorway. She did not dare to allow herself to dwell on what had happened. The hope that she was loved, and the sudden understanding of the joy her awakening senses would find in that love, should have been a secret treasure, to examine with growing wonder and delight. But what pleasure dare she take in a treasure already guilty of causing her aunt's illness, and likely to do worse, if not renounced?

After such a night it was a relief to rise early, as soon as the murmur of Mrs Blair's voice reached her, enquiring after Miss Anderson from Bessie, no doubt.

She entered her aunt's room with some little nervousness. Propped up into almost a sitting position in bed, Miss Anderson looked weary and ill, but more alert than the previous day. Helen bent to kiss her.

'I'm glad you're looking so much better, Aunt Jeannie.'

The old woman's hand reached out to clutch hers; Helen felt an absurd, childish desire to pull it away, but let it lie still in her aunt's swollen, slightly trembling fingers. Miss Anderson waited until Bessie had left the room to bring tea before she spoke.

'We won't think any more of what happened yesterday, Helen. I'm sure you meant no harm, however foolish you were. I've told Bessie that we'll have no visitors at present. You'll not quarrel with me over that, will you?'

'I . . . I . . . Whatever you wish, Aunt Jeannie.'

'I knew that you wouldn't vex me,' Miss Anderson said,

223

still detaining her. 'I will recover all the more quickly if my peace of mind is not disturbed.'

'I wouldn't see you disturbed for worlds,' Helen said, making an effort to smile. 'But would it not be courteous at least to explain the situation to anyone who might call? I shall just see any visitors for a moment, I suppose, to tell them about your sudden indisposition and need for perfect rest?'

'Helen! What would you be at?' Her aunt moved her head fretfully on the pillows, as if seeking a yielding spot. 'How can I rest easily here, knowing that you are next door, alone with that . . . that person? It will be the same story over again, and worse. How can you dare to propose it?'

'No, Aunt Jeannie, I see now that I was quite wrong,' she said hurriedly, watching in mounting panic her aunt begin to struggle for breath. 'Let Bessie see all our callers, if you wish. I'm sure she will explain the matter quite adequately.'

Satisfied, Miss Anderson relapsed into silence against her pillows, her agitation gradually subsiding. Helen was scarcely away from her side all day. In the afternoon she fell into a doze. Helen, exhausted by her tormented night, was herself on the verge of sleep by her sickbed, when the bell rang. At once, her heart began to pound. It was at about this time that he had called the previous day; she could almost have fancied that she recognised his ring.

Miss Anderson did not stir. Helen rose stealthily to her feet, spread her hands on her skirts as though to silence their rustle, and with an apprehensive look towards the bed tiptoed to the door. Only a moment, to assure him that it was none of her wish that he should be denied! Bessie would be bound to know of it; then let Bessie take on herself the responsibility for telling Miss Anderson.

Her hand was already on the door when her aunt's voice reached her, drowsy but anxious. 'Helen? Where are you going? Was that the bell?'

Why not slip away with a murmured excuse, a hurried

lie? For a fraction of a second her hand froze on the door-knob, as she willed herself to utter that lie, surely a justifiable one. It was impossible. Everything in her upbringing, everything in her nature conspired against it. Shoulders drooping in hopeless submission she turned back into the room.

'You're awake, Aunt Jeannie? Yes, I believe it was the bell; Bessie will have seen to it. Can I get you anything?'

Within a few minutes she heard the front door click firmly shut behind the caller.

Sheer exhaustion ensured that Helen fell rapidly asleep that night, only to waken with a start before dawn. The house was profoundly silent; the ticking of the long-case clock in the hall echoed up the stairwell like a muffled, funereal drumbeat.

In the cruel, slow-passing hours of early morning even the most sanguine hopes may lose their cheerful complexion; Helen's thoughts were sombre indeed. Her past declarations, confident as they were ignorant, rose up in mockery. How often had she not said that she was happy to sacrifice herself for her family? That she asked only to be useful, wished for nothing more? Sacrifice! How grand the word had sounded, and how little it had conveyed to her! But in the sacrifice which was now demanded of her there was nothing noble. Now, unwilling, inwardly protesting, she was being dragged by the thick-twisted ropes of family duty and female training towards the blunt knife, the reeking altar: a reluctant offering to an indifferent god.

And yet what could she do? She might be morally certain that her aunt was likely to suffer another attack, whatever her actions. She might know that the restrictions she exacted were excessive, unreasonable. But could she exercise her rights, however justifiable, at the risk of bringing about another seizure, and that quite possibly fatal?

And what must Francis Bethune be thinking? They

had parted in the guilty consciousness of a servant's disapproving stare; on his next visit, he was refused admission through the medium of that same servant, with Heaven only knew what of coldness, scorn or insolence. What must he, so slow to trust his own heart, to rely on anyone, be feeling now? Would he assume that she was responsible for his rebuff?

The doctor had said that her aunt might live for years. Was she not to see him again for so long? And even a few months, weeks, even, might see his removal to some distant region as Sheriff.

In sudden decision she got up, put on her wrapper, lit the gas, brought through her writing case from the adjoining room. Shivering, she carried it back to her bed, and muffled in shawls against the cold, she opened the case, rested it awkwardly on her knees, and began to write.

It was not an easy letter. Before she had completed it she heard the first stirrings of the day's work in the kitchen; a sudden fear of detection by Bessie, bringing her water, at least enabled her to bring it to a close.

She barely reread the letter, once finished, for fear lest dissatisfaction might cause her to tear it up. The explanation of her aunt's indisposition was not in itself difficult, nor even the fact that Miss Anderson wished her not to receive him. It was the whole tone of the letter which caused her to agonise over each word. She wanted to open her heart to him, to tell him, simply, that she loved him and longed to see him again. Not only the caution which was instilled into every girl held her back from such an open declaration. There was that in his nature which did not invite such confidence. She trusted him, if he would only continue to trust himself. She knew him well enough to be aware that the possibility of a retreat within himself always existed. She accepted the possibility without rancour, but inevitably it gave a guarded quality to what she wrote.

She concealed the letter in the pocket of the dress she

would wear that day. While waiting for her water, still muffled in one of the heavy shawls which had been her mother's, she drew the curtains, folded back a leaf of the shutter and looked down into the gardens.

It was still dark, but dawn could not be far away. Here and there in the back windows of Great King Street, whose gardens and greens adjoined those of Northumberland Street, a glimmer of light showed from imperfectly drawn curtains. An invalid? A poor soul sleepless with grief or anxiety? An eager student, grudging every moment away from his books? A woman groaning in the unimaginable pain of childbed?

Motionless, dreaming, she hugged her arms more closely about her breast as she looked down into the gardens, while the stars paled in the grey dawn.

14

If Helen had hoped for peace of mind from the letter she posted, she was deceived. The fear that her enforced seclusion might be misunderstood was replaced by a preoccupation almost as obsessive: when, and what, would the reply be?

A correspondence would displease her aunt no less than Francis Bethune's calls, even more, perhaps, as being less open to her control. Helen knew that in not forbidding him to reply to her letter, in making no reference to the impossibility of a correspondence while she remained in her aunt's household, she was tacitly consenting to a course which would outrage Miss Anderson and gravely endanger her health. By all that was rational, and by the standards by which in the past she had accepted without question, her actions were headstrong, foolish, immodest even.

But all that was reasonable and sanctioned by custom seemed of little moment, struggling as she was in a turbulent, capricious sea. And if she could have stood placid and unmoved in her former security, and looked on with incomprehending disapproval at love's sufferings, she would have refused both the ignorance and the safety.

On the day following the despatch of her letter, Helen's existence was dominated by the hours of the post. Her letter ought to have reached him in the evening delivery; any post might bring a reply, although it might more reasonably be looked for in the last delivery, or even the following morning. She told herself that he was likely to make a considered rather than a hasty reply; her aching disappointment each time the postman passed along the street without checking his pace before the parlour window told her how fragile her philosophy was.

On the second day after posting the letter, Miss Anderson urged her to take a little exercise. Helen knew that it was a kind thought on her part, and took in Drummond Place at the end of her stroll.

Kitty was already home from school. She insisted on accompanying Helen home, a walk of less than five minutes. She hung heavily on Helen's arm, pouring out a stream of anecdotes and breathless confidences, of rivalries and injustices and triumphs. Helen listened with what patience she could muster; Kitty's enthusiasms had never communicated themselves easily to her.

Now, turning into Northumberland Street, where the lamplighter was already beginning his round, Helen stopped as if in sudden pain. At the end of the street, walking quickly, a tall, straight figure was about to turn the corner into Howe Street. Even in the uncertain light she knew him at once, as he vanished from sight.

'What is it, Helen? Have you forgotten something? Have you got a stitch?'

She murmured some scarcely coherent excuse to Kitty and forced her limbs into motion. Had Francis Bethune called during her absence, despite Miss Anderson's prohibition? Or had some other business happened to bring him this way?

Kitty gladly stayed to share her aunt's tea, happy in the complacent belief that her unbroken chatter enlivened the sick-room. Helen contributed nothing. Her aunt bore Kitty's hearty presence more patiently than she would have expected; she seemed subdued, and at times cast a look at Helen which vaguely surprised her, so uncharacteristically timid was it.

At last Bessie was called to remove the tea things and escort Kitty home. Helen got up to adjust the curtains, and lingered by her aunt's bed.

'Are you quite comfortable, Aunt Jeannie? Shall I leave you to rest?'

'In a wee while.'

'You are looking a little weary. I hope Kitty didn't tire you?' She paused, and added as though it were an idle after-thought, 'Did you manage to sleep this afternoon? Were you disturbed by many callers?'

'Miss Johnson just. I had her in for a minute or so.'

'No one else?'

There was the slightest of pauses before Miss Anderson replied. 'No. I think Bessie mentioned seeing that advocate going by when she was drawing the parlour curtains. As she said, you might have thought he would have enquired after my health, but he walked by without a glance.' She looked swiftly, almost furtively at her niece, but Helen was standing by the fire, trifling with the faded screen, and said nothing.

'Everything will go to you when I die, you know,' she said suddenly. 'The house and all its contents, and an income of three hundred a year from sound investments. It will all be yours. You'll want for nothing.'

'Aunt Jeannie . . . I'm sorry, you're very kind . . . let us not speak of it, please,' she whispered, her face still averted.

'But I wanted to tell you,' the old woman insisted, more as though she were seeking than conferring a favour. 'You will be independent. I could have left everything between the nine of you, or even the six girls, but I wanted to let you have the power to make your own life, Helen, without needing to look to any man — your father, or Jack, or anyone else. Rosemary and Sophie have made their choice; no doubt Julia and Phoebe will go the same way. Even Kitty will probably marry some muscular Christian or other. But you've never looked to a man for the purpose of existence. You'll have your freedom, although I shan't see it.' She paused, and added deliberately, 'I couldn't bear to see you going the same way as your poor mother.'

Helen turned sharply.

'My Margaret. She was more than even a sister to me,

Helen. With twenty years between us, it was as though she were my own child. Oh, you can't know what she was! How do you remember her? Pale and weak, stretched on her sofa, fatigued by the slightest effort?'

Helen nodded.

'You never knew her as I did, wearing out two pairs of slippers in a night at a ball, and still laughing and bright, and ready for more. None of you girls came near her for looks, or spirits, or the joy she took in everything she did . . .'

'Aunt Jeannie, don't distress yourself . . . it isn't good for you to become so agitated.'

'If I don't tell you, who will? Who else remembers her now?'

'Papa.'

'Your father! No, he'd not be the man could tell you what she was, before he blessed her with nine bairns, and a tenth that killed her, as he knew it could.' She spoke the last words almost defiantly, looking at Helen as though she were afraid of what she had said.

'What do you mean?' she asked fiercely.

'Doctor Cairns told her after Kitty that another child might cost her her life. She lost such a lot of blood, you see.'

Helen caught her breath.

'But it did no good. After Kitty came Philip, and after Philip Andrew, and so on, until he killed her.'

'It wasn't Papa's fault . . .' she whispered.

'Then whose fault was it? Show me the woman can equal the selfishness of even the best of men! Your vigorous, clever, handsome father killed her as surely as if he'd cut her throat.'

The old, sick voice was trembling, burdened by years of grieving love, years of tormenting hatred.

'But did Mama think that? She loved him,' Helen said, raising her blurred eyes to her aunt's face.

'Love! Don't talk to me about love! I loved her too, but my love wouldn't have killed her! If she'd stayed

231

here with me, my sweet Margaret would be alive to this day. From the moment she was born she had only the finest, most delicate of things about her . . .' Her aunt's voice softened, sad and proud. 'I made every stitch of her clothing until her marriage. I worked through the night to finish her gown for one ball; I wouldn't let another hand touch it. It was the palest of pale blues, fit for a princess. You never saw her equal, in that gown, so fresh and full of life. It was that night, wearing that gown, that she met your father. Seventeen years old, and doomed from that moment. If I'd known, I'd have torn the gown from her back and flung it on the fire before I'd have let her cross the threshold that night!'

'And if she'd known? Perhaps, after all, she would still have gone,' Helen said, frowning, trying to understand.

'She's dead, and she could have been living still, here with me!' Stubbornly the old voice repeated the lesson learned years before and never forgotten.

'It's all in the past, Aunt Jeannie,' Helen said, knowing that for the other woman her plea was meaningless. 'We can't know the whole truth . . . I can't fight my mother's battles for her now.'

'Oh, you'll not go the same way, Helen, not if I . . . not if you're wise. You've everything you could need already, haven't you? I've heard you say so often, when you were looking after your father and the children. You're happy here, aren't you?'

'Of course I am, Aunt Jeannie,' she said, trying to throw conviction into her words.

'I knew it . . . that other nonsense was forced on you. You'll be glad, one day, that I acted as I did, in your own best interests . . .' She looked at Helen, in her triumph mingled uncertainty, even guilt.

'I believe I hear Bessie; I'll send for her, if you don't mind,' Helen said, moving to the bell. 'I feel a headache beginning, this room is a little warm, you know. It seems airless . . . if I'm not needed, I'll rest before dinner, if you have no objection.'

'Of course, dear. Bessie will rub your temples with my eau de cologne, if you like. I always find it soothing.'

'No! There's no need, Aunt Jeannie. I'm overtired, that's all.'

As Bessie entered, Helen went quickly from the room.

In February Tam Crearie's sentence was served, and he returned home, paler than Lizzie remembered, his hair in an ugly crop, but her brother none the less. She laid out the last of the pound she had borrowed through Gillanders on a meal of some magnificence by the reduced standards of recent months.

Tam was in good spirits. He ate alarmingly well, praising the food, relishing the dram she had provided, joking with Joseph, cutting up choice morsels for May, dandling the baby on his knee. But for all his incessant banter he missed nothing. When the children were finally asleep he beckoned Lizzie over to the fire. She sat on the sole remaining chair while he squatted on his heels by the hearth. He looked up at her, serious now.

'So, Lizzie, no so good?'

'No.'

He nodded to the denuded room. 'The wee pawn?'

'Aye.'

'I'll need to look about for more.'

'Ye'll no!' She stopped, and checked her vehement tone as Danny murmured indistinctly in his sleep. 'I'll not see ye going yon gate, and be taken up again. I'd rather have neither a stick nor a rag in the house than see ye lifting, and back in the Penitentiary. If ye canna come by it all fair and proper, I'll have none of it.'

'Now, Lizzie!' he protested, eyes wide with innocence. 'Who said anything about lifting?'

'I ken ye, Tam.'

'So ye should. I'll no be took up again, dinna fash. I'll be douce as a minister at a preach-in, ye'll see.'

Despite herself, she smiled. 'Elgin, then? Father can get ye work up there, in the joinery shop maybe. It's no bad money.'

'Joinery? Elgin? I'd as well still be in the jail! It's no my trade, Lizzie.'

'And what is your trade? Thieving! And where has it got ye? See our Joseph: eight year old, and out all hours for bawbees to buy us bread! May's stick thin, but she sews sarks until her wee fingers bleed. And Tam? The oldest of us all? Our braw Tam? What will ye do to put bread in the weans' bellies?'

'Dinna start, Lizzie! I'll need to look about, ken, see the boys . . . I'll come up with something, only give me a week or two . . .'

'A week or two? I'm two pounds in debt! I canna keep a pair of idle hands, another muckle mouth to fill!' She raised her hand to her mouth to conceal, even from him, the helpless working of her lips.

'I didna jalouse things had been so bad,' he said, in an altered tone.

'Ye ken the now,' she muttered, drawing the back of her hand over her eyes.

'Ye owe two pounds? Who to?'

'Nicholas Gillanders. He's awf'y good. We'd have been starved long since without him.'

'Gillanders? What like is he?'

'An old man, runs Cooper's menage. To let ye understand, it's no his two pounds, he got it from a friend of his to give me.'

'What friend?' He was frowning; for the first time the oddity of the arrangement struck her.

'I dinna rightly ken . . . I pay interest, it's an investment, Mr Gillanders says,' she ended, as though that explained all.

'I dinna like the sound of it over much. Ye'll need to watch yourself,' he said, standing up. 'I'll be away up north, soon as we can find the fare.'

She nodded, and drew a shuddering sigh of relief and

satisfaction. He knew her better than to look for any other thanks.

The following morning Tam was out before even Lizzie was up, and did not return until gone midnight. A sixpence for holding a horse, a few coppers from sweeping a crossing while the regular sweeper warmed himself in the congenial fug of a dramshop, a coin or two earned by hanging about the railway stations, helping laden travellers with their luggage; he gave every penny to Lizzie, that day and every day until the fare to Elgin was scraped together. Even then he refused to leave before establishing her with another few shillings as a reserve, after the purchase of work clothes from a second-hand shop in the Cowgate.

She knew that he didn't want to leave Edinburgh, but the money on the railway, once spring brought longer days and full pay, would be better than anything he could get in the town, legally. She didn't tell him how much she appreciated his willingness to put his own wishes last; sympathy, as much as self-pity, was a luxury she could not allow herself. But the night before his departure she kept the fire in even after the children were in their beds, and silently brought out for him a teacup half-full of whisky. She could ill afford the tuppence, but the need to make a celebration is a human urge which only starvation will erase.

'Thank God ye're no a right drinker, Tam,' she said, swinging the kettle over the fire for the extra pot of tea which was her own treat.

'Oh, I'm no all bad,' he said, half seriously.

'Ye'll do.'

He smiled up at her. 'Ye'll get every penny I can spare.'

'Ken.'

There was a silence as she made her tea, and settled back in the chair with a sigh of pleasure. She looked into the glowing coals, their flickering casting a softening glow on her severe young features.

'The weans'll miss ye, Tam,' she said suddenly. 'It'll no be the same.'

'I'll maybe be back sooner than ye look for me,' he replied, sipping his dram.

She gazed down at him, squatting easily on the floor, and sighed, the light seeming to die away from her face. 'What can we do with ye? What would ye settle to? If ye had the chance?'

'A packman,' he said without hesitating. 'A good crack, sell a wheen needles and handkerchiefs and on to the next house – please yourself, free and easy. That would do me fine, Lizzie.'

'Ye'd make a braw packman, at that. Ye're that gabbie, ye could sell a pair of boots to a man with no legs.'

He regarded her over the rim of his cracked, handleless cup. His eyes were the same nondescript grey as hers, but lively and humorous where hers were guarded. He took life easily; she could not, dared not.

'Still and all, ye'll give the railway a try?' she asked, anxiety tightening her thin face again.

He drained his cup. 'I'll give it a birl,' he said lightly, rising to his feet. 'I'll just take a daunder down to the close, while ye sort yourself . . .' He went out into the forbidding cold of a February night, to allow his sister a few moments of privacy to prepare for bed. By the time he returned, she was huddled beside May and Danny beneath the rags which had replaced the blankets, pawned long since. Next to Joseph, on the mattress, his place awaited him.

Lizzie urged Tam to impress on their father the need for the family to join him in Elgin. The reply, with the next money order, was as discouraging as ever: there was no suitable accommodation, he might try his luck on the Inverness line soon, better to wait until he was settled . . . She could have predicted it.

Tam was taken on, but only as a labourer. Her father assured her that this was simply a temporary measure, that he would soon be found a place in the carpentry shop. Lizzie felt far from convinced. Tam had never followed his father's trade. He had no skill with his hands, and no interest in acquiring any. But even so, she hoped that her father did manage to have him taken on in the carpentry shop; she could not see Tam surviving for long as a navvy. Small and slight, he had never undertaken heavy labour. She thought of him pushing a laden wheelbarrow along a treacherous muddy plank, up a steep cutting; handling a pick; shovelling tons of earth. She doubted whether he would last a week.

Winter wore into spring and they survived, after a fashion. Bad weather kept the earnings low on the railway. During one stoppage, more prolonged than usual, even the indoor work of the carpentry shop was halted. Still, with what the children brought in there was enough food and coal, the rent was paid and the menage kept up to date. There were no more trips to the pawnshop, even if the pledged goods were not redeemed.

The debt to Gillanders did not diminish. Each week she hoped that the money order might be big enough to enable her to pay off a substantial sum, five shillings or so. But each week there was nothing to spare. The debt was a gnawing anxiety to her, but Gillanders never pressed her. Indeed, when she did feel able to scrape together a shilling for him, he often refused it.

'Keep yourself straight with Cooper's,' he would advise. 'My friend can wait. He's a patient man, he can bide his time.'

The respite was welcome, and yet she felt far from easy in her mind. Things would improve, certainly. Better weather would come, Tam might be moved in beside his father, they would need less coal in the spring, May would grow stronger, able to sew for longer. But in the meantime there was the harsh rasping wind, and May's listless face and poor appetite for the coarse food which was all she could provide. Danny was struggling to walk, requiring constant attention, hindering Lizzie in the sewing of which she had long done the better half.

What was worse, Joseph's teacher had been complaining of his inattention, even of his falling asleep at the Industrial School.

'He's a promising boy,' he had told her, bringing him home early one afternoon, clearly dropping with exhaustion, 'but if he is to be kept out at night when he needs his sleep . . . why, I think we must consider whether his place could not be used to more advantage by another child, less gifted but more regular in attendance.'

He was friendly enough, but Lizzie was quick to sense the criticism beneath his kindness. She promised to see about it, and kept Joseph at home after dark. Tenaciously she clung to the belief that in Joseph, at least, there would be the hope of something better.

So she sacrificed the few pence a day which had tipped the scales in favour of a slender security, and Joseph regained his former quickness. The teacher had the satisfaction of seeing it, and remarking to his fellows that, 'These people need to be handled firmly, that's all. It keeps them to regular habits. They have no self-discipline, you see . . .'

And so Lizzie struggled on, sharper in feature, shorter in temper, harsher in manner. She lived, she endured. They were one and the same.

Helen could not point to the exact moment at which she recognised the fact that Francis Bethune would not reply to her letter. As the days of waiting turned into weeks, ardent hope became the recognition, more painful than she would have believed possible, that his silence was to be unbroken, that he wanted no more from her.

Over and over again she asked herself why, if he cared so little for her, he had shown such warmth at their last meeting. Why had he taken her in his arms, murmured her name as though it were dear to him? Had it been a momentary impulse, regretted as soon as indulged? Had there been no intention more serious than the fancy for a snatched kiss? She could not believe that of him.

Everything she knew of his character led her to quite the opposite conclusion, that with him only the most compelling of emotions could break through the barriers of his self-command. Surely in those moments he must have been in earnest?

But there, perhaps, lay the cause of his silence. Finding himself on the verge of dependence upon her, had he recoiled? She remembered his cold greeting outside the church in Melrose, only hours after he had told her more of his heart than he could have revealed to anyone since childhood. Certain in her understanding of him, she was sure that a single meeting would be enough to dispel his indifference. But no meeting, it seemed, was to be given to her.

Now that Miss Anderson was confined to her bed Doctor Cairns's visits were more frequent. Helen suspected that he came to lighten the tedium of her aunt's day by a few minutes of news and gossip as much as for any medical aid that could possibly be rendered.

Some four weeks after Miss Andersons's attack he called during one of Helen's increasingly rare respites from attendance on her aunt. Miss Johnson, a crony of forty years' standing, was paying her regular Wednesday visit, and Helen had been able to leave them to their reminiscences. She was in her sitting-room, writing to Sophie, or trying to. In half an hour she had achieved barely more than three lines of apology for her long delay in replying to her sister's last dazzling recital of visits to parties, balls, exhibitions, concerts.

'Doctor Cairns! What an unexpected pleasure!' she said, gladly laying aside her pen and rising as Bessie showed him in.

His face grew lighter at her greeting as he reached for her hand, offered to him in an unthinking impulse of pleasure at the interruption. To her surprise he detained it and scanned her face with a frown.

'Is there a black on my cheek? Some ink smudged on my nose?' she asked with an effort at playfulness.

'You are scowling at me as though I were a perfect fright.'

'No,' he said absently, shifting his clasp on her hand so that his fingers felt the pulse at her wrist. 'You don't mind?' He reached for his watch, and was silent for a moment. She stood, half amused, half alarmed, submitting to the unexpected examination.

He gently laid her hand by her side, and clicked shut his watch case, then reached out to draw down the lid of her eye. He uttered a grunt of apparent approval at what he saw.

'Are you eating well?'

'Oh, I suppose so. I don't have the appetite I used, but then I am often about the house all day without exercise, so it is not to be expected.'

'Hmm. And sleeping?'

She dropped her gaze, and trifled with the sheets of Sophie's letter. 'I can't seem to sleep quite so well as once,' she admitted.

'Any disorder in your monthly cycle?'

'No,' she murmured, colouring.

'Any coughing, at night especially?'

'No . . . really, before you go through every bodily system I may as well tell you that I am in my usual good health, with no symptoms or complaints of any description.'

'You don't seem it.'

'Thank you!' she said, trying for their old teasing relation, but the effort was beyond her. She turned quickly away and walked over to the window, looking down into the garden as though its newly budding trees presented a spectacle of absorbing interest.

'I don't compliment, you know. You have not been looking yourself for the past three or four weeks. It sets my mind at rest that there is no organic cause.' He paused, and added with a studied carelessness which caught her distracted attention, 'We can discuss it tomorrow, if you like.'

240

'Tomorrow?'

'I'm driving out to East Lothian to visit a patient. It's the first child and the husband is insisting that I should give my opinion, despite all the local man can say . . . in any case, it's a pleasant drive, if you care to come. It will put some colour back in your cheeks.'

'But Aunt Jeannie? I don't think I should.'

'If I can absent myself from my other patients for a good part of the day, you can leave your aunt, surely? She'll do very well with Bessie. I'll call for you about ten.'

'I shall be ready.'

'I'll just have a word with Miss Anderson and prepare her for your absence,' he said, his hand on the door. 'Until tomorrow, then?'

'Oh, yes,' she said, and turned back, with a sigh, to the greening garden.

15

Punctually at ten the next morning the doctor's brougham, neat and workmanlike, drew up outside Miss Anderson's house. Helen was on the steps before he had opened the door.

Within minutes Donald had set the horse in motion, and Northumberland Street was behind them.

'Shall I let down the glass?'

'If you don't mind. It's mild enough.'

He leaned across her to adjust the strap. In the confined space, his arm necessarily brushed against her breast. She noted the accidental intimacy as little as if he had been another woman, turning her face to the soft spring air drifting into the close, leather-smelling interior of the carriage.

'You must make a point of taking some exercise every day. Not even your constitution can stand long confinement, Helen. Is it any wonder you're pale and out of sorts?'

She sighed. 'No doubt you're right. I try to be of use to Aunt Jeannie, that's all.'

'What use will you be to her or to anyone if you ruin your nerves and your health?'

She raised her brows in surprise at his vehemence.

'I'm sorry, I was too warm. I saw too much of perpetual invalidism in my own home to be cool.'

'In your own home?' She was not sure she understood.

'My wife.'

'I never knew her,' she said, her dress rustling as she turned in her seat towards him, the breeze setting the drooping feather at the side of her bonnet fluttering.

'She was already in confinement when I first knew your family. I was twenty-eight then. We had been married seven years.'

'Were they happy years, at least?'

'No.'

Her heart sank. She did not want to hear such brutal honesty. And yet he had, over years, given her support, advice, consolation. He had never asked anything in return, until now.

'You must have been a student still when you married. I suppose you were very much in love.'

'I never loved her. It was all a terrible mistake. I paid for it dearly – and so did she, poor creature.'

'How did you meet?'

'She was the daughter of my landlady. Her mother was a sour, narrow-minded woman, an extreme Calvinist and bigoted anti-Papist.'

'I am surprised that you lodged there, or that she would have you.'

'Her rooms were kept scrupulously clean, and they were cheap. I didn't make a parade of my religion; to be honest, I rarely went to Mass in those days. Medicine was my religion. What was I not going to achieve by its means! Oh, what a benefactor to mankind I was going to be!'

'Don't! It's unbearable . . . you mustn't mock your own ideals.'

'You're probably right. In those days they were all I had. I was chronically short of money, often cold and hungry, never well dressed – and I've never been so happy. I loved my studies, I asked nothing better from life. I had few friends, but that didn't trouble me. The usual student dissipations would have been beyond my pocket in any case. When I needed a respite from work I would walk, through the streets, across the Meadows, around Arthur's Seat, it was all one to me, all a golden glory,' he said ironically. But his wistful smile belied his self-ridicule.

'And your wife?'

'Hannah? I scarcely noticed her. She was a thin, timid creature, looking even younger than she was. Her mother never gave her a moment's peace. She was worked harder than a charity girl. I would talk to her if we met on the stair, purely out of politeness – no, that's not true. It was pity, too. What do you think of pity as the basis for a marriage, Helen?' he asked, in the same tone of brittle derision so painful to her.

'Perhaps there are worse,' she said, in gentle reproof.

'Perhaps. Sometimes Hannah would bring me up some little treat when I was working in my room. She would make some excuse: too much bread had been baked, it was going stale; there was a chop left from dinner; could I use a dish of broth, before it was thrown out? I accepted it all, and thought no more about it. Only when I got to know Mrs Edwards' style of housekeeping better did I realise how unlikely these stories were. I had been eating Hannah's own food, smuggled away from the table or the kitchen as and when she could. She got little enough, Heaven knows . . .'

His voice faltered. Helen began to understand why he tried by self-mockery to distance himself from that other Patrick Cairns.

'I gradually noticed that she would often make some excuse to come up to my room on a Tuesday evening. It became the accepted thing between us. Perhaps that's stating it too strongly: she came, and I didn't object.'

'What did her mother think of your Tuesday evenings?'

'She was always out. It was the night of some prayer meeting or other at their chapel. She left Hannah at home to watch the house. She would bring her sewing up, and sit in a corner, working away, so quiet that I would forget she was there. I would be surprised when I looked up from my book to see her, eyes fixed on me. Her eyes always looked too big for her face. They always seemed to be begging the world not to hurt her.'

'Was she beautiful?' Helen asked softly, her own sorrow quite forgotten in his old sad story.

'She was too cowed to be beautiful; if she had been happy, perhaps. Her hair was lovely, very thick, of a light brown, with a marvellous sheen. Another girl might have been vain about such hair; Hannah had been brought up to regard the things of the flesh with such loathing that I believe she could scarcely look in a mirror without guilt.'

'Her mother must have been very strict.'

'She watched over every minute of her daughter's day, and criticised most of it. If the poor girl lay five minutes after the kitchenmaid called her, she was slothful. It was carnal indulgence if she spread butter too thick on her bread. If she trimmed her bonnet with a bit of bright ribbon, she was as good as a wanton. She bore it all. Her little thin fingers would pluck at her apron, and her head would sink . . . I pitied her, but it maddened me to see her so lacking in spirit. But the more I saw of her life, the more terrible it was to me that perhaps the happiest hours she knew were on a Tuesday evening, sitting in my freezing room, totally ignored, watching me at my books! Can you imagine?'

She shook her head. 'Did you stay there for the whole of your studies?'

'I did, more's the pity. I should have left in my last year. By then I had seen enough of her life to know that I was important to her; it made me uneasy.'

'Then why did you stay?'

'I pitied her. I knew she would miss me. I knew that sometimes my presence saved her a scolding. I did try to leave, at the beginning of that year. A fellow medical student offered me the room adjoining his in a house nearer the Infirmary. I accepted, but at the last minute his brother decided to come to Edinburgh and wanted the room.' He shrugged. 'If only that unknown young man had stayed in Perth! He ruined my life, without even meeting me!'

'You can't really mean that, Doctor Cairns,' she said slowly. 'Whether you stayed or not, you were still free, surely?'

'Oh, I suppose so, master of my fate and so forth. But looking back, that was my only chance. After that I never seemed quite in control of events. I could have asserted myself, if I had been willing to hurt her . . .'

'And you weren't?' she asked, knowing the answer, honouring him for his fatal tenderness of heart, her soul going out to him in pity.

'No. That last year, things came to a crisis. I was beginning to look forward to going out into the world; my books weren't as satisfying as before. I found myself taking more of an interest in Hannah. I drew her out, we talked, of my hopes, her position in the house, her mother's strict religious beliefs. The poor child was tormented by doubts as to her eternal future, her worthiness to be saved and so on. Without intending it I was led to point out what seemed to me to be the errors in the Calvinist notions of election, predestination . . . I meant only to comfort her, but I soon began, quite naturally, to talk about my own religion.'

'I don't suppose Hannah told her mother that you had been discussing religion?'

'Hardly! It had to be kept a secret. That added to the vague unease I was starting to feel. I didn't like to be linked by a bond of secrecy, harmless as it was. Certainly, everything else which passed between us could as well have been spoken before her mother. We were together, quite alone, almost every Tuesday evening, and yet nothing could have been more innocent. She might have been my sister; I thought of her in just that way.'

'But how did she think of you?' Helen asked, smiling in rueful sympathy.

'There you have it. As a brother, I would have said. I believed it, because it suited me to believe it. So I treated her with brotherly freedom, and never thought how my actions might appear to her. I was a fool.'

246

'No! You're judging yourself too harshly! Many a man must make the same mistake, from the best of motives!'

'And many a woman, perhaps?' he said, in a tone so low that she scarcely caught it.

'Oh, possibly,' she said, considering. 'But we are early taught to weigh every word, every glance . . . a woman can rarely allow herself the freedom you describe, she knows how easily it may be misinterpreted. It is no common blessing, to be able to lay aside that constraint,' she ended, smiling.

He was silent for a long moment, his head sagging back against the hard, shiny leather upholstery, his eyes shut, in an attitude of defeat. She turned quickly away, to stare out at the rich, pleasant farmland through which they were now passing. It seemed almost indecent to witness his misery. For a long time, the brougham rolled on without a word spoken.

Slowly, his voice took up the thread of his story again, more sombre now.

'It was heartless to offer her the sympathy I did, meaning so little by it. She was lonely, starved of affection; I should have realised . . . but life has a way of punishing our stupidity, sooner or later . . .' His voice trailed into silence, then grew stronger, as though he had got the better of some weakness. He continued more firmly.

'At the end of that year I had what seemed a stroke of good luck. I obtained a position with a country physician whose sight was failing. There was no apothecary in the district; the doctor dispensed his own drugs and needed a skilled assistant to make up the remedies. I was to see to it, keep records for him, attend to the simplest cases, and receive a small fee. The money, and the experience, were a great object with me.'

'But you would be leaving Edinburgh?'

'Permanently, perhaps. The post in the country I intended to keep until I had the means to go down to Liverpool. There was a celebrated surgeon there; I planned to study with him. I might never have returned.'

'Did you tell Hannah all this?'

'Of course, as soon as I heard from the old doctor; I could talk of nothing else. It was a Tuesday evening, as luck would have it. We were in my room. I was talking incessantly of my schemes, my future, my sense of trying my strength at last, my hopes of doing real good; I scarcely saw her at all, in my enthusiasm. It was a summer evening. I remember standing at the window, looking down into the back green, four storeys below. The curtains were stirring in the breeze. The entire world seemed to lie before me, fresh and green and beautiful as what I saw at that moment. I turned away from the window, and she was crying.'

'Oh, the poor girl!' Helen said softly, her own eyes filling with tears.

'It all came out then. She was heartbroken at the thought of my leaving. She had allowed herself to hope, when I stayed with them year after year, that I endured the gloom of the house for her sake. She remembered idle remarks which I had long since forgotten, remarks which could easily be brought to bear a warmer construction than I had ever intended, God help me!'

'Who could blame her for hoping?' Helen said wistfully, her own cheated hopes painfully vivid in her mind.

'No, she was not to blame . . . but what could I do? I put my arms around her, as a brother might. She rested her head on my breast, I stroked her hair, her one beauty . . .' He fell silent, and shrugged. 'It was all up with me from that moment, although I didn't know it. I still thought I was free. I made no promises, not in words, at least, but I kissed her tears away. I couldn't pretend that they were brotherly kisses.'

'And did you go away, to the country practice?'

'To Bankfoot? Yes. I tried to lose myself in my work, to tell myself that Hannah would soon recover from her distress at my departure. I hoped she would forget me.'

In her ears the words rang with unintended significance. 'I hoped she would forget me.' Did Francis Bethune

248

feel just such an embarrassed wish to disclaim any connection with her? Did he, too, regret that far from brotherly embrace? With an effort, she recalled her attention to what the doctor was saying.

'I had not been a fortnight away before her mother wrote to me . . . and such a letter!'

'Hannah had told her?' she asked absently.

'I suppose any mother would have noted something amiss in a similar situation. She had not rested until she knew everything, including our Tuesday evening talks. She accused me of trying to corrupt her daughter's mind, of being an agent of the Antichrist, an evil Popish seducer, an instrument of perdition and I know not what else besides. I was strictly barred from her house, and from ever communicating again with her unhappy child.'

'Forgive me, but was that not rather a relief than not?'

He stretched out his legs as well as the cramped carriage allowed and smiled wryly. 'No man relishes such apocalyptic abuse, but I would have done no more than write back explaining how innocent my motives had been. That would have ended the matter, as far as I was concerned. But Hannah wrote, too.'

'Secretly? She was very unhappy, I suppose?'

'She was scarcely rational. Her wretchedness showed in every smudged letter, every rambling sentence. Her mother was persecuting her, she said, for no longer accepting her church's severe view of Catholicism. She would bear it all rather than condemn the religion to which I belonged. She would sooner put an end to an existence which held only sorrow and suffering. The words lodged in my mind; to feel that, and not yet twenty! I knew she was sincere, that was the worst of it. I won't try to describe my feelings. The desire to protect her had always been the strongest emotion she roused in me. Now she was suffering because of what I had done. I had defended my faith; Hannah was being punished for it. How could I wash my hands of her?'

'You couldn't,' Helen said, with an emphasis which brought her a grateful glance.

'I wrote back, directing the letter to a sympathetic neighbour, as Hannah had suggested. I offered marriage, with the warning that we would be very poor at first, and that she would see little of me while I struggled to earn a living. We would have to marry in secret, I told her, as it was inconceivable that her mother would consent.'

'She accepted?'

'Without hesitation. Her reply was as deliriously happy as her first letter had been the reverse.'

'And you? Did you have fears for the future?' she asked, wondering for the first time what he had been, twenty years or more ago. It struck her that he could have been a good-looking youth, with his black, curling hair then untouched by grey, his shoulders not yet stooping, his face unlined, his figure still elastic. Beneath his heavy brows his eyes were, even in middle age, unusually compelling, but then their expression must have been full of life and ardour, without the resignation which she was beginning to understand all too well. Seeing those eyes, of a very dark blue, fixed on her now, she felt a sudden self-consciousness, as though he could have read her thoughts. 'Surely you must have found some grounds for optimism?' she added hurriedly, to dispel the unusual awkwardness between them.

'Yes. Strangely enough, when the die was cast I had few regrets. I was fond of her, she seemed content with her choice, I saw no reason why we should not be as happy together as the next, if it must be so.' He hesitated, and went on less confidently. 'There was something else, too. It's not easy to talk about, perhaps I shouldn't try. Simply, when I comforted her, that summer evening, holding her close . . . oh, marriage didn't seem such a terrible prospect, little though I'd intended it.'

She could understand, although she did not choose to say so. Again, treacherous memory summoned the disconcerting pleasure of Francis Bethune's body close to hers. The recollection quickened to longing; she bit her lip, hard. 'And Mrs Edwards?' she asked, struggling towards safer ground.

'She knew nothing of it until Hannah wrote to inform her that she was my wife. When she was sure that nothing could be done to change matters, she cast off her daughter completely. Hannah's intention to convert to Catholicism, and marry me a second time according to the rites of the Church seemed to unhinge her mother's mind. We had one or two letters, sheer raving; she died not long afterwards.' He raised his brows, and added drily, 'She left what money she had to a Protestant society, committed to supporting missions in Catholic countries.'

'How did the news of her death affect your wife?'

'As badly as possible. She blamed herself, and I suppose there may have been a connection. In her way Mrs Edwards was deeply attached to her, though it never showed itself in tenderness. The news came at a bad time. Hannah had just lost a child. She miscarried at six months, and nearly died. She knew how much I wanted a child. She blamed herself for disappointing my hopes, she blamed herself for her mother's death, she blamed herself for the poverty and lack of comfort caused by our precipitate marriage. She believed herself a failure as daughter, as mother, as wife.'

'But surely you were able to persuade her otherwise?' she asked, as though it seemed to her the very simplest of tasks.

'Oh, Helen, I did try. Perhaps I could have tried harder. Imagine: I would come home, weary and jaded after a day spent walking from one sick-room to the next, in all weathers, and find what? No dinner, nor even the preparations for one; the maid sitting in the kitchen, feet on the fender, deep in some tale of horror and sensation; the breakfast dishes not yet washed, not a fire in the house, and Hannah, weak and pale, weeping on the sofa without so much as a spark in the grate. At her worst she might be still in her bed, as I had left her twelve hours before. Can you wonder if I was not always as sympathetic as I should have been?'

'Was it always so bad?' she asked, more horrified by his description of domestic disorder than by any possible account of mania or melancholy: it lay within the range of her own understanding, as hysterics did not.

'Sometimes I could bring her to a more cheerful frame of mind, by the expenditure of endless patience and reassurance. Even then, I might fail, and I didn't always have the strength to try. Then she would weep even more bitterly, and say that I didn't love her, had only married her out of pity.'

'She said that? Oh, how terrible for you – for you both!' she exclaimed, her face radiant with compassion, self-forgetful. 'What answer did you make? What could you say?'

'I told her, very gravely, how much it pained me to hear her doubt my love. Was I a hypocrite? Perhaps I should have admitted the truth in what she said, though it hurt her. By denying it I hoped to set her fears to rest. It only added to her burden of guilt: her doubting me became further proof of her wickedness, her unworthiness . . . it went on, and on. Nothing I could say or do changed her. Even now, I would be at a loss how best to treat such an unhappy creature. Then, a young, hard-pressed doctor with little experience of life, I was utterly defeated.'

There was nothing to be said. She laid her hand on his sleeve, and pressed his arm. His hand moved quickly from his knee, as though to remove her hand, or cover it with his own, but fell back again, the movement incomplete. Tightly clenched, it lay rigid by his side, on the scuffed leather seat.

'I tried to believe that her moods were no more than natural grief for her mother's death and the loss of her baby. I hoped that everything might improve when she had another child. It was over a year before she conceived again. She miscarried once more. It was disastrous. She became convinced that God was punishing her for her sins. Nothing I could say could convince her otherwise.'

'So there was never a child?' she asked softly. He shook his head.

'There was something else, too. You may as well know it all,' he said, his voice muffled. A peculiar, indistinct fear seized her, gone before she could have said what it was she feared. 'Any attempt at . . . at marital relations made things worse. I tried to deny it, but the evidence became too strong. If she were in low spirits, they intensified. If she were relatively tranquil, it was enough to plunge her into agonies of self-loathing. It was a terrible realisation; I was young, after all. But I was forced to accept that our marriage could not continue as before, after she tried to kill us.'

The last words were pronounced in so matter-of-fact a tone that at first she did not grasp what he had said. 'To kill you?' she cried, incredulous.

'It was five years after we married. I had made one of my rare demands on her. She never refused me, but I tried not to ask her often. That night some desperate husband rang my bell in the small hours. Thank God it was their first child and he was persistent. He rang fit to waken the dead, almost literally. The maid heard it at last, although the night-bell rang only in our room. When she did not hear me stirring to answer it, she came down to rouse me. As soon as she neared our room she smelled the gas.'

'Surely not!'

'I was fortunate. It was a close summer night, so I had left the top sash open a little. Hannah had either forgotten that, or else she had not dared to risk wakening me by closing it. Even so, she nearly succeeded in accounting for us both. The maid was a quick-witted, sensible girl. She doused her candle as soon as she smelled the gas on the landing, and ran in to throw up the window. It was a near thing, all the same.'

'You're quite sure it was deliberate?'

'At the time, I couldn't believe it either. It was usually I who extinguished the gas. I assumed that I had done so that night, although I couldn't specifically remember. I set it down to a freak accident or a momentary lapse of attention on my part.'

'But did your wife say nothing?'

'Very little. She professed herself as baffled as I was. So it rested, until the following week. I was roused from my first sleep by the creak of the bed as Hannah got up. I was in that drowsy state, between sleep and wakefulness. I lay without stirring. I watched her approach the gaslight, stretch up to reach it – on tiptoe, she was tiny – and heard the hiss as she turned it on. She crept back to bed and slipped in beside me, perfectly calm.

'Do you know, for a moment I lay still, and wondered whether it would be as well to remain where I was, and die? All that was necessary was to do nothing. Sleep would come and the whole wretched business would be over.'

'But you didn't, thank God!' she said fervently, shaking his arm gently, as though to rouse him from such thoughts. 'What persuaded you to act?'

'The simplest thing, the thought of the maid. I suddenly realised that she might suffer from the gas, or cause an explosion on lighting her candle in the early morning. She might even have been suspected of some involvement in our deaths. I got up, and switched off the gas.'

'And your wife? Did she try to deny what you had seen?'

'No. I think it was a relief to her to tell the truth at last. She admitted that over the past year a dreadful longing had possessed her, a longing to die, with me. Once, she said, she had stood over me as I slept, a carving-knife in her hands, judging where to strike. All that had held her back was the fear of causing me some suffering by a clumsy stroke. She was quite prepared to kill me, you see, but not to hurt me; she loved me too much.'

She could not begin to imagine how he had managed to

attain the detachment which allowed him to describe such things so calmly, without rancour. More than anything else, it convinced her that he had told her the truth in saying that he had never loved his wife, unless as a brother.

'At first I insisted that we could no longer continue to live beneath the same roof. I wasn't willing to risk our lives, and those of our servants. I suggested that if we lived apart she might lose her urge to self-destruction. It was useless: she wept as if her heart would break, clung to me, promised never to entertain such thoughts again.'

He shrugged. 'It was the same story, pity. I made some conditions, though. We were to have separate rooms, and she agreed to be locked into hers at night. I abandoned any thought of physical love between us. It was not a satisfactory way to live, in a state of siege, my bedroom door locked as if against murderous house-breakers, but it was the least bad alternative.'

'And did it last?'

'For six months or so. Then one night I returned late from a difficult delivery. Bridget had come to work for us by then. She'd gone to bed without locking my wife's door, as Hannah was still up and said that she wanted to see me when I came in. I knew nothing of it, and assumed that the door was safe as usual. I was so tired that I must have forgotten to lock my own door. I was soon asleep, but not for long. I awakened fighting for breath, choking and retching. Hannah was pressing a handkerchief soaked in chloroform over my face. She confessed later that she'd abstracted it from my medical bag, and had carried it about for weeks awaiting her chance. Fortunately she was ignorant of the dosage to employ, and the technique. If she had applied the cloth more gradually I would have drifted from sleep to insensibility. She then planned to turn on the gas and die by my side.'

'But how could she entertain such a plan for weeks?' Helen exclaimed in horror. 'An impulse of madness is bad enough, but at least it's . . . it's still human!'

'I know. It was that thought which finally brought me to the inevitable. I committed her to an institution near Perth. It was run on humane lines, but it was an asylum for the criminally lunatic all the same.'

'Did she go willingly?'

'No. She understood that it must be so, with one part of her mind, but at the same time she clung to me, begging me not to punish her by sending her away. But this time I held firm.'

'And she remained there? She never came home again? I remember very vividly hearing of her death,' Helen went on, without waiting for a response. 'It was the day after Rosemary's wedding, wasn't it?'

He did not answer at once. Then he said, stiffly, 'She died on the day of the wedding.'

'Of course . . . it was the following morning before you learned of it. I had forgotten.'

He said nothing.

The breeze on her cheek was cooler now; she settled the fur tippet more snugly at her neck, burying her chin gratefully in its softness. She glanced out of the window. To the left, the steel-grey expanse of the sea, with here a steamer, heading for Leith, its trail of vapour a child's clumsy erasure on the sky, there a fishing smack, leaving only a fleeting furrow in the waves.

'We turn off the road shortly. We are not far away now.'

She turned quickly from the window, smiling, but not as she would once have smiled at him.

'Do you think the less of me, Helen?' he asked abruptly.

'No . . .' she said awkwardly. 'Few men would have borne what you did.'

'But it's an unsatisfying, untidy tale, isn't it? A marriage not based on undying passion, madness without a tint of the romantic? But domestic horrors are more crushing than the Gothic variety, believe me.'

'It seems so unfair. You acted from the best of motives;

so did she, I suppose.' She sighed, her breath stirring the dense fur about her throat. 'One could almost say that her mother's grimmest notions were right, and all human efforts to goodness can achieve nothing.'

'Thank God, I have never been reduced to quite such despair, despite everything,' he said, bracing himself against the side of the carriage as it turned sharply off the road to pass between imposing gates. 'I have always been blessed with work I love, and friends, such as your mother.'

'Why have you told me all this, Doctor Cairns?' she asked suddenly.

'I wanted you to know.'

It was not a satisfactory answer, but she did not choose to pursue it. The brougham drew up before a pleasant, irregular building with the crow-stepped gables and external stair of the old Scots style. As the doctor got out and let down the step for her, Helen emerged thankfully into the sparkling spring sunlight.

While the doctor was engaged with his patient, Helen passed her time agreeably enough. The housekeeper showed her over the house, and the mistress's young brother escorted her over the grounds and gardens, solemnly pointing out their beauties.

Doctor Cairns rejoined her for luncheon, seeming satisfied with his consultation. They began their return journey by chatting of indifferent topics, Helen taking comfort from the old teasing relations. She could almost forget what had scored on his face the lines of sadness and resignation into which it so naturally fell in repose.

Before they had travelled half their way, however, she became aware that he was no longer attending to her attempts at light conversation. She fell silent, thinking that he might welcome a respite from unbroken chatter. It was not long before he renewed the conversation, with unusual hesitancy.

'Have you enjoyed your airing, Helen?'

'Yes, I have.'

'You look all the better for it. Don't take it amiss, but I must ask you: are you happy with Miss Anderson? I feel some responsibility for your position, you know, since I suggested the move, and even urged it on you. Do you regret it?'

She answered slowly, choosing her words with care. 'I won't pretend that it's the perfect arrangement. I would like a more sociable existence, but of course it's impossible, with Aunt Jeannie's present state of health.'

'But in other respects? Are you content?'

'In every other way she is kindness itself to me,' she said loyally. 'Ever since our . . . since her attack, she has been lavishing gifts on me. I should think she sends out Bessie two or three times a week to buy me some unexpected treat or other, books, bon-bons, gloves, music. I am quite pampered.'

'It is her way of thanking you for all your attention.'

'Perhaps. I wish she wouldn't, though.'

'All the same, Helen, the way you're living isn't conducive to health, continued over a long period.'

'But what else can I do?' she asked, spreading her hands apart helplessly.

'However indisposed Miss Anderson may be, you must take some exercise every day. I shall tell her so myself, if you like. Are you still keeping up your French lessons?'

'I haven't been a very faithful attender recently. Aunt Jeannie often seemed to feel her condition worsen at about the time I prepared to go. More than once I've been afraid to leave her.'

'But you must keep up your own life! Next time, harden your heart, and go!'

'Perhaps I would, if my lessons were of any use, beyond mere amusement. But what good do they do? There is no purpose in them, or in anything I do. All I am doing is watching an old woman die,' she said with a bitterness she had not intended, but could not restrain.

'Help me, then.'

She looked at him questioningly.

'You could be of great service. I have wanted to raise the question with you before, but I was afraid I might be asking too much. But perhaps the benefits would be more equal than I feared.'

'You're being very mysterious, Doctor Cairns,' she said lightly. 'What service do you require of me?'

'Visit some of my patients.'

'What, a penny lady?' she cried impatiently. 'Handing out tracts and red flannel?'

'No! Nothing of the sort! It's difficult to explain in general terms, each case is different. I'm not thinking of nursing, either. You must simply believe me when I tell you that I know of any number of families to whom I wish that I could give a hundred times the attention that is possible.'

'But how could I supply your place? What could I do?'

'As a woman, you could do much that I cannot. You could help with sewing and mending, I suppose? Sit with an ailing child and let the mother out for a few messages and some fresh air? You could help to write letters, and read to a bedridden old woman or a seamstress who spends every waking minute over her needle?'

'I'm sorry, Doctor Cairns. You know I would be happy to help you – I am in your debt for so much – but I'm not suited to that sort of thing. I'm sure any minister would be able to recommend half a dozen experienced lady-visitors who would . . .'

'I tell you I'm not looking for some worthy female in black mittens to distribute tracts! I want someone who won't insult those whose homes they enter with condescending platitudes, when they themselves are ignorant of every area of the daily existence of the poor.'

'Precisely as I am! I would be more likely to do harm than good.'

'All I have in mind is plain, practical help. A sensible

servant would be of more use, of course, but they have enough to do to keep themselves.'

'But I know nothing!' she burst out in protest. 'I know less of the inhabitants of the Old Town than I do of the Hottentots!'

'I am offering you a chance to remedy your ignorance.'

'You would think the worse of me for refusing, wouldn't you?'

'Perhaps, and yet most people would share your reluctance. It's too uncomfortable to see what lies behind the picturesque fronts of the High Street. I wish they could be lifted up, like the front of a doll's house, to show what they conceal. Perhaps the front of a beehive or a wasp's nest would be a better example,' he concluded, with a bitterness he had never displayed in talking of his own tragedy. 'People are crammed together about as tightly as insects, though not so neatly.'

She sighed. 'You have a way of getting what you want which is little short of miraculous, Doctor Cairns.'

'Oh, not always, believe me.'

'You have my surrender, at least. But don't expect too much of me. The role of ministering angel is a new one for me.'

'It will give you some object, and occupy your thoughts . . . how are the children, by the bye? It is some months since I have been summoned professionally to Drummond Place.'

'They seem well, and happy enough with the new regime, except Jack, perhaps.'

'Is he still unsettled?'

'Less than I feared. His coaching seemed to steady him wonderfully. It has lapsed, though. The boy he tutored went down to London for a medical consultation, and from there on to the south coast. Winter in our harsh climate was not thought advisable. Perhaps he may return with the sun, like the swallows.'

'And your father?'

'Oh, he seems very happy,' she said indifferently. 'It is difficult to believe that he has not been married above six months. He is the most domesticated of husbands. He should have remarried years ago.'

'You really think so?' he asked, barely concealing his surprise.

'Certainly. It would have been better for us all.'

'And your step-mother?'

'I shall never like her. I find her artificial and contriving, but she seems to please my father, and that is what signifies.'

'It doesn't appear to interest you very greatly.'

She considered a moment, then answered frankly, 'It's not my entire world any longer. For better or worse my home is elsewhere. I enter Drummond Place as a guest. It's better so.'

He looked at her with a nod of approval. 'I'm glad to hear you say so.'

'I lost my paradise when my father formed his attachment to Susan Raymond,' she said, her candour touched with irony, 'but after all, it was a fool's paradise . . . can that really be Piershill already?'

16

For Lizzie, the coming of spring at first brought some relief. May's cough improved somewhat; she was able to work at her sewing for longer, so that Lizzie was not so often obliged to sit up, shivering and sore-eyed, by the long-dead fire to finish a shirt for her.

Freed from the need to scramble for coppers, Joseph was making good progress at the Industrial School. Learning seemed to come easily to him. Coming back from getting messages, she had more than once found him poring over battered books outside one of the dealers. Sometimes she called him in vain, so deeply was he engrossed. Secretly she resolved that when times were easier, she would give him sixpence for himself to spend on his precious books, useless lumber though they might be.

But all thoughts of spare pence for such luxuries were turned to bitter mockery by the arrival of a brief letter from her father. Tam had quarrelled with the ganger and been dismissed from the site. He was making his way back to Edinburgh on the tramp, hoping to pick up what work he could on the way. That was a sore blow, but worse followed. Several of her father's essential tools had been stolen, his chisels and a good saw. Until he had paid for their replacement he would be able to send Lizzie only three or four shillings a week, enough to cover the rent, barely more.

As Lizzie laboriously spelled her way through the letter, the bad news was revealed with agonising slowness. Twice she read the short letter, as though she might in her ignorance have made some error, mistaken a word which had altered the import of the whole. But her reading had been all too accurate.

With a wordless exclamation of anger and disgust she thrust the paper into the pocket of her skirt, resentment rising in her, sour and burning. Could Tam not have held his job, made his peace with the ganger? How in Heaven's name did her father expect her to manage?

As she looked savagely around the bare, comfortless room which bounded her life as surely as any prison cell, temptation beckoned: walk out, leave the children, get a place in service, have money of your own, enough food, company, a warm kitchen. Let the children be taken care of – there were orphanages, homes, weren't there? The teachers at the Industrial School could see to it. Why should she fight on any more?

'Lizzie?'

'What?' She spun round fiercely, ready to discharge her misery by some vicious retort, but at May's pale, anxious face her anger checked itself. 'Aye?' she asked, more gently.

'Shall I put the kettle on for tea? Ye've taken the cold, Lizzie, your teeth are chittering.'

'It isna the cold, hen,' Lizzie said, although her sister was right, she was shivering. 'Aye, go on, put the kettle to boil. What for no?' Already her mind was setting itself to the restless searching of ways and means, any other escape silently dismissed. It might be long enough before she allowed herself the luxury of another extra cup of tea.

As May busied herself with the preparations for tea, casting more than one swift, troubled glance at Lizzie, who walked absently to and fro, Danny straddled at her hip, footsteps approached down the passage. Suddenly their significance struck Lizzie, and she stopped dead. It was Monday. The rent had been paid, but what about Nicholas Gillanders? He was early, but what difference would that make?

As she knew they would, the steps halted at their door. The familiar knock: Gillanders. She admitted him, uncomfortably aware of his sharp, calculating glance despite his smiles.

'Well, Lizzie, and how are we today?' he asked, rubbing his hands together.

'Here. See for yourself.' She handed him her father's letter.

As he read she watched his face, expecting to see there a dawning sympathy. But instead, to her alarm, there was unmistakable satisfaction, as though this was the very news he had long looked for, and desired.

'Oh, Lizzie,' he said, folding the letter neatly to return it to her, 'I'm sorry for you, dear, I truly am.'

'No doubt, no doubt,' she said impatiently, 'but ye see how I'm placed? I canna give ye the menage money this week, ken. Ye canna get what I dinna have.'

He shook his head gravely. 'I'll need to see Cooper's,' he said, eyeing her with a suppressed excitement which frightened her even more than his sudden want of sympathy for her plight. 'But as for my friend, I can tell you now that his patience is at an end. This very morning he told me that you must start regular repayments. He's in need of the money himself, you see. "If she can't keep up the payments, she'll need to let me have the whole sum at once," those were his very words.'

'The whole sum? No far off two pound? I canna do it!' she exclaimed, incredulous that he could so much as mention the possibility. 'Every stick in the house wouldna fetch the half of that!' She recovered herself, and said more calmly, 'Your friend's been awf'y good, can he no just wait another wee while, it'll no be long . . .'

She trailed into silence, seeing him purse his lips as though in assessment. Clinging to her trust in his basic goodwill towards her, she feared to say anything to vex him.

'No, Lizzie, he'll need to have it,' he said calmly, 'one way or another.'

'What do you mean?'

'There's ways . . .' he said. 'May, would you be a good girl and just step down to the wee paper shop along the High Street and buy me a pencil? I've laid mine down somewhere . . . here, keep the change for sweeties.'

May looked doubtfully at her sister, who nodded consent. As the door closed behind her, Lizzie faced him. 'Now, Mr Gillanders, what way am I to give your friend what I owe him?'

He licked his lips, and told her.

Doctor Cairns allowed Helen no time for backsliding after her reluctant promise. Before they parted it was arranged that he would call for her the following Tuesday, to visit a family living in Paisley Close.

Helen felt no enthusiasm for the task. She provided herself with a supply of brown sugar candy, and wearing what she hoped was a suitably subdued grey morning dress was ready at the appointed time.

'Did you think I would cry off at the last?' she asked, as she settled herself into the brougham.

'I never doubted you for a moment.'

'I have doubted myself, I assure you . . . is there anything I should know before we arrive? How many children?'

'Six surviving, but only four at home. The oldest is up north with the father, working on the Elgin line, if he hasn't absconded by now.'

'Oh? Is he unsteady?'

'He's not a bad character, and he thinks the world of his sister, but Tam Crearie will never make a navvy.'

'Does he have no trade but that?'

'He's an accomplished thief, if you count that a trade.'

Helen's eyes widened in alarm. 'Did you say he's away from home?'

'I think so. You would like him, Helen, believe me.'

She looked her scepticism. 'There's another child away?'

'Yes, the second daughter, Nettie. She's in service near the Robertsons'. You may see her from time to time on her free afternoon. She's doing well now that she's away from home.'

'How has that improved her?'

'Her sister has consumption, I'm afraid. I always think it wiser to keep children from too close contact with a sufferer, although the disease is so unpredictable. It can claim several victims in one family, yet in another there may be a single child succumb and the rest escape. Where there is overcrowding, though, and poor ventilation I would always err on the side of caution. It seems in general to spread more rapidly in such conditions.'

'And the other children are healthy?'

'So far. There's Joseph, a very bright boy, nine or so. I got him a place at the Industrial School. His mother was desperately eager to see him get some kind of education, poor woman. I think she died the happier for seeing his future at least so far assured. She dreaded seeing him go the way of his brother.'

'When did she die?'

'More than a year ago. It was pneumonia, compounded by sheer exhaustion. Pulmonary infections are one of the great killers in the Old Town since the cholera has kept away. She left a baby only weeks old. I never thought it would survive, but we found a wet-nurse, and Danny surprised us all. Mrs Rutherford – his foster-mother – would have kept him, but Lizzie would have none of it. As soon as he could be weaned, she had him home.'

'Lizzie? She cares for the family, then?'

'While her father's away, and very largely even when he's at home, to be honest. Rab Crearie is a fine craftsman, but he rarely stays in work six months together.'

'Drink?'

'No, he's one of Father Matthew's men, a total

abstainer. He's an intelligent, independent man, and what his employers tend to call a troublemaker. He's always watching for any infringement on the usual rights of the workplace, such as they are, always ready to stand up to the foreman on any petty imposition, more often on behalf of a fellow workman than himself.'

'I can image that giving rise to difficulties.'

'There's not an employer in Edinburgh would take him on. I don't know how he'll fare in Elgin.' He laughed. 'I may as well warn you that Lizzie is very much her father's daughter. She's a prickly, uncomfortable little body. You may not like her, but bear in mind that she's had a deal to thole.'

The brougham had turned down the High Street towards the Palace. Now, almost opposite Blackfriars' Wynd, it drew to a halt. Doctor Cairns helped her to alight and led her through a narrow, tunnel-like passage between two shops.

'This is Paisley Close,' he said, 'watch your skirts. The scavenger hasn't been particularly brisk with his broom this morning.'

The warning was unnecessary. Already, Helen had become all too aware of the sickly smell filling the long, sunless passage, the smell of decaying matter, both animal and vegetable. She felt her stomach protest.

Her companion cast a swift glance at her. 'Don't worry, you'll grow accustomed to it. This is worse than usual, being a still day. Usually the breeze dissipates the foul air. But believe me, this close is a sanitary paradise beside many.'

'Thank Heavens!' she murmured, as they emerged into a small open space, surrounded on every side by tenements. It was untouched by sunlight, but even its chill shadow was a relief after the long tunnel through which, absurdly, she had wanted to run, conscious of the vast weight of masonry towering above the roof of the close.

From the far right-hand corner of the court a stair led upwards into the tenement. Doctor Cairns stopped for a word, joking or sympathetic, with more than one of the idlers who hung about the foot of the stair. Helen noted with a stirring of disapproval that several children were playing about the sunless court, often lugging in their arms a shawl-wrapped infant, presumably some younger brother or sister.

'What can their mothers be thinking of?' she exclaimed, as they began to mount the stair. 'Did you see that little red-headed girl? She could scarcely carry that baby – it was almost as big as she was! And what a place to play! They would be better in the house, surely?'

She heard his sharp intake of breath, then he stopped abruptly on the winding, uneven stair. 'Wait until you've seen the living quarters in which our fellow citizens are stalled, Helen, before you reach such conclusions.'

Ashamed, she said nothing, but lifted her skirts from the damp, dirty stones, and continued their laborious progress. On each level, a passage ran off in two different directions. It was an arrangement new to her, accustomed to the stairs of the New Town, with often only one flat on each level, and rarely more than three.

'What a quantity of doors!' she said, as they paused for breath on the third or fourth floor; she had lost count. 'I hadn't realised from the outside that the tenement was so large. Each door is a separate dwelling, I suppose?'

'Each door is a separate room, it comes to the same thing, more or less.'

'A separate room?' she asked, bewildered.

'Most families live in a single room.'

'But their bedrooms?'

'Bedrooms?' He laughed grimly. 'You will see for yourself, Helen.'

They continued their upward progress. A decent-looking woman, barefoot, passed them as she came down, a large pail in her hand. The plaid which she held wrapped about her instead of a coat or mantle did nothing to conceal her advanced pregnancy.

The doctor pressed himself against the newel to allow her to pass. 'Keeping well, Mrs Harris?'

'I'll be worse afore I'm better,' she said, her hand patting her swollen belly. Helen lowered her gaze, glad of the dimness of the stair.

'Take care how you carry the water up,' he called after her. 'You shouldn't be doing such work, so near your time.'

'Ken, but what can ye do? I canna sit on my hands and look at a clarty house.'

'Well, take it slowly, at least,' he said, as she moved heavily on.

On the next landing, a slovenly, sullen-looking girl was hanging about, twiddling a dirty ribbon between her fingers.

'Well, Bridie, are you coming or going?' Doctor Cairns asked.

For answer she nodded her frowsy head towards a door a short way along the passage. Although it was shut, voices could be heard, a woman's laugh, a man's abrupt command.

'My ma's got a friend with her,' the girl said. The silence which had succeeded the man's voice was broken, not by words, but by muffled sounds which even to Helen were unmistakable. The doctor hurriedly handed the girl a few coppers.

'Here, Bridie, on you go down the Canongate, get yourself a few buckies. It's a fine sunny day, the air'll be better for you than hanging about here.'

Doctor Cairns drew his arm through Helen's and led her quickly, almost roughly, on up the stair. 'I'm sorry. I shouldn't have brought you.'

'Her mother . . . she's a prostitute?' she asked quietly, forcing herself to pronounce the word.

He nodded.

'And the girl hangs about on the stair while her

mother entertains her visitors? She hears what we have just heard? How can a mother expose her daughter to such vileness?'

'I know, I know,' he said heavily. 'But bad as she is, at least her mother is doing something to keep her daughter from following the same trade. She's better on the stair than in the same room.'

'The same trade? But she's only a girl!'

'She must be eleven or twelve. It's old enough.'

Helen stopped where she stood, struck immobile by her horror and disgust. Only the clear signs of compunction in the doctor's face for introducing her to such scenes gave her the self-command to continue.

They came to a halt before one of the doors in a dark passage. At the doctor's knock it was opened by a girl so slight and small that Helen took her for the consumptive child of whom he had spoken, until a weary dragging cough from within the room convinced her of her mistake.

'Lizzie, is it convenient for Miss Lambert to come in for a moment just now?'

'Aye.' She stood back and opened the door more widely, with no great enthusiasm, it seemed to Helen. Her expression was not by any standard welcoming; Helen thought that she had never seen so forbidding a face, nor one so unhappy.

Lizzie gestured Helen to the only chair in the room, recently vacated by the younger sister, as she suspected from the stray threads of cotton which lay on its arm.

'Please, don't let me disturb you,' she said in some confusion, seeing the younger girl, her arms full of some linen stuff, slipping away towards the window, where a piece of wood stretched across the recess formed a rough seat.

The girl smiled, shy but friendly, and retained her seat at the window. She bent her head to her stitching, but whenever she thought herself unobserved, raised wondering eyes to Helen, timidly examining her clothes, her hair, her fine kid gloves, her neat boots, her face.

'Where's Danny?' asked Doctor Cairns, looking about him in surprise, although the sparse furnishings offered little scope for concealment.

'One o' Mrs Shannon's lassies has taken him out. He's aye under my feet, I canna sew a stitch but he's greeting for something or other.'

To Helen the girl's voice was unpleasantly harsh, her frank impatience shocking. Doctor Cairns had spoken of her devotion to the baby; Helen wondered how he could be so mistaken.

'Any news of Tam?' he was asking.

'Left off his work, nobody kens where he is. Away with Auld Clootie, no doubt.'

Her tone appeared to discourage even Doctor Cairns from further comment. He glanced uncertainly at Helen, and moved to the door.

'I shall see you again soon, Helen. Miss Anderson is due a visit from me before the week's out . . .'

Lizzie saw him to the door, her expression as set and strained as when she had greeted them. She closed the door, and walked over to the fire. The silence was painful. A kettle over the fire began to boil; it had been overfilled, and spurted steam and water onto the coals with sudden vehemence. Lizzie deftly removed it from the heat.

'Did I interrupt you?' Helen asked, ill at ease. 'Please carry on with whatever you were intending to do. I don't want to hold you back.'

'I was just going to do a washing,' she said ungraciously. Her eyes, of a nondescript blue-grey, hard and uncompromising, were fixed on Helen as though willing her to leave. Bared to the elbow, her thin arms were placed akimbo in a posture of defiance.

Helen was on the point of standing. She had her hands on the arms of her chair, and was only debating whether or not to offer to return. She could see little point in forcing herself upon a girl who clearly wanted none of her. But suddenly Lizzie turned and began

271

with a great dragging of the wash tub and clattering of jugs to set herself to her task. It should have been the final signal for her departure, but Helen did not leave, because in the second before Lizzie had turned to pull out the tub she had seen what excused all her brusqueness: the girl's lips were trembling, threatening to crumple into uncontrollable misery. Even as she bent with ostentatious concentration over her washing, she had to pause to rub the back of her hand over her eyes. The girl was fighting against some intolerable distress.

Helen was reluctant to leave her in such a condition, and yet she had no wish to intrude. She decided to remain a little longer, but to allow Lizzie to recover before speaking to her.

'I'm sorry, I don't know your name?' she said, turning to the patiently sewing girl by the window.

'May, miss.'

'And what's that you're sewing? Shirts?'

'Aye.'

'Do you get much money by it?'

'Fourpence a shirt, miss.'

'Does it take you a long time to make a shirt?'

'Aye. Whiles Lizzie gives me a hand, but we canna get more than one a day done. I get awf'y weary, miss.'

'I'm sure you must . . . can I not help?' Seeing the girl hesitate, she added quickly, 'I am quite used to plain sewing. My father's shirts were all made by my needle while I remained at home. My mother always believed that every woman should be her own sempstress, in the matter of linen, at least.'

May looked over to Lizzie for guidance, but her back was resolutely turned from them. Even over the splashing and slapping from the clothes tub, Helen thought she could detect a suspicious sniffing.

'Here, I'll move the chair nearer to you, May,' she said, rising. 'We can work together, and you can keep an eye on my stitching. Be sure to put me right if I work differently from the way the merchant requires.'

Helen's deft seams soon put May's doubts to rest. She could not equal the little girl's speed, but her neatness was impeccable. As they worked they chatted, Helen trying to draw the child on to speak of herself. It was no easy task, for at every confidence, however trivial, May would glance anxiously towards her older sister, as if in dread of disapproval. It was an effort to persist in so uncomfortable an atmosphere, but by degrees the girl grew less diffident, and Helen's interest in her remarks, though arising from little more than politeness, soon took on an unforced warmth.

While the conversation centred on herself, May remained shy, but at the mention of her younger brother's name her face was transformed. Joseph's excellences were eagerly set forth: his quickness in learning, his readiness to do all he could to lighten Lizzie's burden, his sweet, willing temper, his patience with the baby.

'So he's fond of reading?' Helen said thoughtfully, pausing to rethread her needle. 'I have a few books from my young days, some of them might be of interest to him. I recall some stories of fireside philosophy which I first read at about his age. They explain such things as thunder and the changing seasons in a way which is suited to young children. Do you think he would like them?'

'Oh, miss!' May began, but at the same moment Lizzie's voice broke in, cold and hostile.

'No. He wouldna.'

Helen's temper began to stir. The girl's rudeness was past all bearing. An angry retort was on her lips, but at the sight of May's white, pleading face she controlled her irritation, not without difficulty.

'May I not bring the books in any case, Lizzie? There's no harm done if he doesn't care for them, it will only be the carrying of them home again. They are no use to me

273

now, and I would be delighted to think that they were being enjoyed again as I enjoyed them myself.'

'What for should we have rich folk's leavings? Joseph'll have all the books he can read once I've got straight.'

Flaming with rage and misery and pride, the girl stood at her wash tub, her arms still immersed in the water, her hair, damp with steam, escaping here and there in straggling wisps from the unflattering knot into which it was pulled back from her face. She was, Helen sensed, being as offensive as she could. Why, Helen was unable to imagine, but some instinct warned her not to notice the insult. She answered calmly.

'I don't think books are like food, or clothes or shoes, which one person uses and passes on in an inferior condition. A book is intended to be read and appreciated more than once. I was a careful child, they are still in good condition. I wouldn't insult your brother by offering him anything which I would not have liked to receive myself.'

'Can ye no give them to your own folk?' Lizzie asked, still challenging, but less fiercely.

'My brothers are too old, my two youngest sisters don't care for books. If your brother would find them of interest, it would please me to see them appreciated.'

No answer, beyond the vicious slapping of the clothes in the water. Helen finished her seam, handed the completed sleeve to May with a smile, put on the hat and jacket she had laid aside in working, and rose.

'I shall bring the books the next time,' she said, moving to the door with a rustle of silk. At the door she paused, drawing on her gloves. 'I may, may I not, Lizzie?' she added, more softly.

'I canna stop ye.'

Helen thought that she would have to let herself out. Her hand was all but on the door before Lizzie straightened from the wash tub and crossed towards her, wiping her arms on her sacking apron.

'I'm sorry that I called at such an inconvenient time,' Helen said, reluctant to leave without some gesture of friendship. 'Would the afternoon suit you better?'

The girl shrugged. With that, Helen had to be content.

In one respect at least, Doctor Cairns's remedy for Helen's low spirits was effective beyond all her expectations. She had gone with him to Paisley Close unwillingly, had found Lizzie hostile, far from likeable, had seen no good in the visit beyond advancing May's tedious needlework by a seam or two, and yet her brief call occupied her thoughts to the exclusion of almost all else. Even her mute grief at Francis Bethune's silence was to some extent pushed into the background by the lively interest she began to take in the young family.

Away from Lizzie's acerbic presence, however, it was the impression of her unhappiness which remained most forcibly on Helen's mind. It was clear to her that Doctor Cairns had known nothing of any particular distress which the girl had suffered, and that he had not, in his hasty call, observed her misery. The thought of Lizzie's tears gave her no rest; she felt a responsibility which she could not evade.

Only two days following her first visit, therefore, Helen found herself once more outside the Crearies' door, clutching the books which were the pretext for her call. Timidly, resigned to rebuff, she raised her hand to knock, and dropped it once more. From within the room she heard a stifled, agonised sobbing.

She hesitated, at a loss. How dare she intrude at such a moment? And yet to turn her back on obvious distress was unthinkable. She took courage, and rapped at the door. Instantly the crying stopped. A tense silence. She knocked again more loudly. No response.

It would have been an undoubted relief to abandon the attempt and go. Who was she, after all, to thrust herself into another woman's misery? Did the poor have no right to privacy? What permitted her to insist upon entry but the reliance on her own superior status?

She raised her hand to knock for a third, a final time, more tentatively than before. As she turned away, troubled and irresolute, Lizzie opened the door, her pale face blotched with tears.

'Lizzie, I'm so sorry to disturb you . . . I brought the books, it was such a fine afternoon, it gave me an object in my walk . . .' She awkwardly proffered the books, speaking almost at random.

Lizzie made no move to relieve her of the books, she gave neither a sign nor a word of welcome. But she stood aside, opening the door more widely. Helen entered, crossed to the table, put down the books, and looked about her for May. The room was empty.

'You're on your own?' she asked in surprise.

'Aye. May's taken the bairn out.'

There was a silence. Helen still stood; she had not been invited to sit. Lizzie had remained near the door, eyes downcast, her narrow shoulders drooping, her arms wrapped tightly across her breast as though she were very cold. Her dress was of thin cotton, of an uncertain, patchy shade of lilac, as though it had lost much of its colour in the wash, as cheap fabrics will. The dress fitted her thin figure too closely. Cut too neat, to save fabric, it must have shrunk. Her breasts were still scarcely developed, her chest almost as flat as a boy's.

'Do you want me to leave you alone?' Helen asked, not knowing what she would say next, but aware that it must be the right thing. 'You've been crying. I don't think you would cry without good reason. I came back today because I was worried about you. Don't try to pretend that nothing's wrong. I'll go away if you want me to, but if there's anything I can do to help, please, please tell me.'

Lizzie seemed to pay no attention to her, but she moved

away from the door, to the bed. She sat there, her arms still clasped about her body, and began to rock slightly, to and fro, her eyes fixed on the floor.

'Is it your brother, Tam?' Helen asked gently. 'Or are you concerned about May? Shall I get Doctor Cairns to call?' She paused. No response. 'Is it money? Are you finding it difficult to manage?'

At that, Lizzie raised her eyes, dull and beaten, the eyes of a creature hunted beyond exhaustion, capable no longer of resistance or flight, only of suffering.

'Oh, Lizzie, what is it?' Helen asked, moving over to sit beside her on the bed.

'I couldna help it, I swear I couldna! May had to get shoes for the winter, and Nettie hadna a decent stitch to put on her back, and he never sent me the full money order . . .' Scarcely coherent, struggling for breath, sobbing beyond all control, the girl poured out her despairing tale, bent double over her tightly clasped arms, as though in physical pain.

Although she did not understand more than a fraction of the outburst, Helen did not dare to interrupt. The end result, in any case, was horribly clear.

'I canna pay him! I canna! But he said I canna owe him another day . . . I was to see his friend Friday night but I didna go . . . I said the wean wasna well and I couldna leave him, but I'm to go the morn's night whether or no . . . what'll I do? Oh, what'll I do?'

Helen had never seen such an agony of grief and despair; she was appalled by the intensity of suffering revealed in the broken, confused phrases. She sensed that Lizzie had not told anyone else; having encouraged her confidence, she prayed that she would be able to resolve her difficulties, still far from clear in all their details.

She waited until the girl's worst abandonment of anguish, almost of terror, seemed to be exhausted, then as gently as she could, tried to draw from her the exact cause of her fears. 'Who is the friend you are to see, Lizzie? Why don't you want to go?'

'I dinna ken his right name, he aye cries him Mr D.'

'And why are you to see this Mr D?'

'I owe him near two pound, and I canna pay, and he kens a man who'll give me five shillings if I do what he wants . . . I'm to see him at Mr D's house, and that's the way I'm to get the money for him . . .'

Curiously, having told the worst, Lizzie grew calmer; not so Helen.

'You can't! He daren't propose such a thing! You're only a child!'

'Seemingly Mr D's aye looking out for young lassies for this man, he's an old man, he said, and he likes green apples the best.'

Helen cried out in anger and disgust, a passionate revulsion against all that contributed its mite towards such a scene as Lizzie suggested. This, after all, was the grim meaning of poverty: the ultimate helplessness, the want of any defence against inhuman treatment.

'And the debt is a little under two pounds?' she asked, preparing to rise. 'Are there any others?'

'Aye, I owe Gillanders' – at the name some vague memory stirred in Helen's mind, only to be at once thrust back by the press of more urgent concerns – 'about a pound for Cooper's menage, but that's only a shilling a week, I can find it most weeks . . .'

'What, and have that man coming here week after week? No! I'm afraid I don't have such a sum about me, but I will be back here within the hour, and you shall have it, every penny.'

'Ye canna do that!'

'Do you think I could possibly see you sell yourself for the want of two pounds?'

For the first time, the girl looked at Helen, as though to convince herself that she was in earnest. Not relief, not gratitude, disbelief seemed to be her chief emotion.

'Ye'll no be the loser,' she said, with returning spirit. 'Ye'll get it all back, I promise ye.'

It was to Helen such a paltry sum that she began to protest, but she checked herself. 'Pay me back as and when you choose,' she said hurriedly. She was beginning to have some understanding of Lizzie's pride.

With the aid of a hackney cab, Helen was back at Paisley Close well within the appointed time. She insisted on leaving with Lizzie rather above the stated amount of the debt, fearing that Gillanders or his principal might try to exact some additional interest, purely in order to keep her within their power. Hearing the details of the transactions in calmer circumstances, she was sure that from the start the desire to set the girl up as a profitable concern had been their chief goal.

Although Helen did not doubt the sincerity of Lizzie's horror at the prospect which had faced her, secretly she could not understand her readiness, however reluctant, to prostitute herself. She told herself that she would have starved to death before agreeing to such a scheme, and really believed it. She did not consider that Lizzie had the responsibility for three other dependent children, nor that she herself had never known even hunger, save as a pleasant appetiser. Secure in her own modesty, she could not imagine any circumstances which might lead her to compromise, or sacrifice it.

With the settlement of Lizzie's debt, came a greater ease in her manner to Helen, although never anything approaching warmth. At first Helen was surprised and a little hurt by her reserve, but she was fair-minded enough to respect her for her independence. Despite the inequality between them by every material standard, Lizzie maintained a fierce dignity which prevented their relation from sinking to that of client and patron.

As her father resumed the payment of substantial money orders with the settling of his outlay on new tools, Lizzie faithfully repaid Helen's loan, a shilling or two at a time. Helen did not insult her by telling her how trifling the sum was to her. She hated to accept the coins so proudly offered, yet refusal would have taken from the girl more than it gave her.

Helen's visits became fixed as a weekly occurrence, more frequent, if circumstances demanded it. She would gladly have called more often, but Lizzie had a way of keeping her at the distance which suited her.

They talked more freely now, Lizzie at times displaying a childlike curiosity as to the details of Helen's life. Often, Helen found herself embarrassed in answering the questions Lizzie asked; to speak of a house in which she had at her sole disposal two entire rooms to a girl whose whole family lived in one not very large room seemed offensive. The mention of a new evening gown, the cost of which would have kept the Crearies in comfort for several months, made Helen uneasy, almost guilty, although Lizzie never commented on such disparities.

Helen soon came to realise that Lizzie cherished an interest in clothes which, in more favourable circumstances, would have led her to dress as fashionably as any of Helen's sisters. It appeared, however, that her clothes were bought ready-made, either from a cheap shop which held out the lure of a clothing club, or from a second-hand shop.

When Helen tentatively suggested that it would be more economical to make her own clothes, she was surprised to discover that Lizzie had no expertise in dressmaking. Like her sister, she could sew well enough to make shirts, already prepared, but the niceties of cutting out, placing darts, gathering and basting were beyond her. Helen's surprise lessened when she remembered how little time Lizzie's mother must have had for teaching her.

Helen was glad to seize on the opportunity of doing some practical good without any damage to Lizzie's pride. An unexpected money order from her brother Tam, now in Dundee, it seemed, was laid out on a fine merino cloth of a pleasant russet shade, enough for a warm winter dress each for May and Lizzie.

Step by step, Helen explained the processes involved. She herself had been taught by her mother, who had insisted that she should help to make her own clothes until she put up her hair, and even after that should make her own linen.

Now skills of which she had thought little won her Lizzie's respect to a remarkable degree. She enjoyed their Wednesday afternoon spent sewing together, although as spring wore into summer the room became almost unbearably stuffy. She and Lizzie would work on the merino gowns, and later, on a few little dresses for Danny, or more adventurous, a jacket for Joseph. May usually continued with her shirts, or on a fine day took Danny down to the close. It was better when he was kept out of mischief, but Helen always missed May. She was easier to talk to than Lizzie, gentler and more winning. With the better weather she was able to go out more, and her health improved, but she remained in Helen's eyes alarmingly fragile in appearance.

Helen constantly looked for means of helping the Crearies without running foul of Lizzie's pride. The dressmaking was one, the loan of books to Joseph was another. Lizzie flatly refused to accept any more books, but consented to the borrowing of any which she produced from her own or the nursery book-shelves.

Helen rarely met Joseph, who seemed to spend any spare time away from the Industrial School in an assortment of odd jobs. From May, however, she learned of his taste in reading. Stories seemed to interest him less than works of natural history, geology and animal life in every form.

On the few occasions on which she met him she asked him about such interests, and was favourably impressed by his retentive memory and ready grasp of the subjects which attracted his attention. He was an open-faced boy, small for his age, wiry but not sickly in appearance. She could not but compare his enthusiasm for knowledge with her own brothers' disinclination for study. Secretly, she began to frequent bookshops, searching for works which might appeal to Joseph. Many a new book found its way to Paisley Close, on the pretext that it issued from her brothers' shelves.

17

With such preoccupations, Helen found time hanging less heavily on her hands. She followed Doctor Cairns's advice and took some exercise every day. Her French classes were no longer neglected, and although she necessarily still spent a considerable part of each day by her aunt's side, she was able to maintain her spirits better than she had once feared.

Indeed, only one thing prevented Helen from considering herself happy: Francis Bethune's scornful indifference. Although with the passage of time and the new interests it brought she no longer thought of him constantly, at times she longed for him with scarcely diminished ardour. She tried to recall his voice, his face, the self-contained grace of his bearing, but she had a poor capacity for summoning even the most familiar of images, and he eluded her. All that she retained was a useless sense of kinship with him, and the dull pain of rejection.

As if to compensate for the restrictions her illness imposed upon Helen, her aunt lavished gifts and treats upon her. Only one thing did she deny her: she seemed reluctant that Helen should accept any evening engagements. In any case, she received few invitations, and in the weeks immediately following Miss Anderson's attack Helen was quite content to decline any which arose, pleading the need to attend her aunt. But as Miss Anderson's condition showed no signs of worsening, Helen gradually began to feel that it would be possible for her to resume a normal social life, insofar as the opportunity arose.

Miss Anderson, however, proved refractory. She was unpredictable. She actively encouraged Helen to invite her fellow students from her French class for dinner, and even urged her to accept such engagements as they offered in return. But if her father and step-mother included her in an invitation to what Mrs Lambert termed as her soirées, at which she assiduously gathered together as much as she could of the cream of Edinburgh society, or at least its literary and academic manifestations with an admixture of legal men, Helen was left in no doubt that her presence was particularly necessary at her aunt's side that evening.

To have to refuse was particularly vexing as she knew that such invitations represented an attempt at reconciliation by Susan Lambert. Helen herself was quite prepared to respond favourably, but still she found herself obliged to consult her aunt's wishes and decline, with greater reluctance each time.

Her increasing frustration at her seclusion from wider society came to a head in June, with an invitation from Harry and Rosemary to an evening party to mark the return of Rosemary to society following the birth of a daughter the previous month. As soon as she received the invitation, the hope, the certainty filled Helen's mind: Francis Bethune would be there.

She did not accept at once. To meet him again in the artificial constraints of the Robertsons' dining-room would be a severe test of her composure. Yet common sense indicated that, so long as he remained in Edinburgh, they were likely to meet again at some time or another. The awkwardness of the encounter would be no greater at her sister's table than anywhere else.

So she reasoned, but equally potent, if unavowed, was the hope that, if they could but once meet, his reserve, his distrust of his own affection, would surely be dispelled, as it had been in the past. And at the thought, her heart seemed to turn over.

She accepted the Robertsons' invitation, but she delayed telling her aunt of it. So important was the occasion to her that she even entertained the idea, alien to her every instinct, of misleading her aunt as to the nature of the engagement. What harm would there be in alleging that she was going to one of the quiet suppers with Miss MacNiven to which her aunt never raised any objection? If she were not to be available to read to Miss Anderson for an evening, was it of any consequence whether she were at the Robertsons' or Miss MacNiven's?

But while she had not yet committed herself on that point it was decided for her. Rosemary called to show her daughter, now some six weeks old, to Miss Anderson. The visit passed agreeably, the infant sleeping throughout her first morning call, and Miss Anderson not unmoved by the sight of her sister's first grandchild.

Helen had not dared, however, to warn Rosemary of the need for caution concerning the forthcoming engagement. The idea had flitted through her mind, but to have spoken to Rosemary on the subject would have been to commit herself to a course of which she was ashamed, and to give rise to speculations in the Robertsons' minds from which she shrank. So, relying on the all-engrossing charms of young Fanny Robertson to exclude all other topics, she said nothing.

All went well, until the last seconds of the call. Rosemary got to her feet, her new sky-blue silk straining at every seam, and kissed Miss Anderson goodbye. Helen, holding her niece, followed her to the door. At the very threshold of their aunt's room, Rosemary turned to Helen.

'We see you on Thursday for dinner, then? We have had no refusals, I don't think, although Francis has yet to reply.'

Helen bundled her sister from the room before she could say any more.

'Really, Helen!' she said peevishly. 'Need you be so abrupt? You might have hurt baby . . . here, I'll take her, you'll be dropping her next,' and with ostentatious care she took the child from her arms.

Helen's hope that Rosemary's blunder might have

passed unnoticed was short-lived. No sooner had the Robertsons' clarence rolled away than Bessie was sent to summon Helen to her aunt.

She saw at once the warning signals of mounting agitation in her aunt's breathing, rapid and noisy as if she had been running uphill. Her hand was plucking at the neck of her nightgown as though it oppressed her. The veins on her forehead were engorged, and she moved her head fretfully on her pillows, seeming to seek an elusive ease.

'Are you not comfortable, Aunt Jeannie? Do you want an extra pillow? Shall I ring for Bessie?'

'No, no . . . don't fuss me, Helen,' her aunt said pettishly. 'What did Rosemary say? You dine there on Thursday? Was that it?'

'Yes.'

'And why is this the first I've heard of it?'

The silence which followed was broken by the wheezing of her aunt's struggle for breath. Seeing that congested face, Helen kept back the bitter retort which rose to her lips.

'A dinner at my sister's is no very great event, Aunt Jeannie. It slipped my mind, that's all.'

'Don't go, Helen, stay here with me.' The sick old voice pleaded, coaxed, selfish and pitiable. Helen wavered. She had been determined to go, but it was just such a scene she had dreaded.

'I need you, Helen.' The swollen hand, mottled with brown, slithered across the coverlet to grasp her wrist. 'Don't go. We'll be quite happy here, won't we? I can't rest when you're out . . . I'll have another attack if I'm worried, you know Doctor Cairns said so . . .'

Indeed, her condition was worsening before Helen's very eyes as her agitation increased. Now she was raising her free hand to her breast, though whether in discomfort or in nervous fear of pain, Helen could not know. Still, stubbornly, Helen held out, impelled by some deep-buried instinct towards life and freedom.

'Aunt Jeannie, Rosemary and Harry are expecting me.

I needn't be late, you know, and you could ask Miss Johnson over to sit with you and have her supper. I'm sure Harry would be happy to let his carriage take her home, when I am brought back. Please, Aunt Jeannie . . . is it too much to ask, a single dinner at my sister's?'

At her continued opposition, her aunt's state became truly alarming. She clutched her breast in apparent agony, her eyes clouding as though she were about to faint. But still her hand maintained its grip on Helen's wrist.

'I'll ring for Bessie – we'll get Doctor Cairns.' She tried to release herself in order to reach the bell, but the clutching fingers did not slacken their hold.

'Promise . . . won't go . . .'

'I promise, whatever you wish, Aunt Jeannie, only let me ring for help!'

Then, at last, the bloated hand dropped heavily off hers, and Helen flew to the bell.

Helen could see that this attack was far more severe than the last. Even when the pain appeared to have subsided Miss Anderson remained in a state of extreme weakness and lethargy which seemed to alarm Doctor Cairns no less than it did her.

'She's exhausted by the pain of the seizure,' he told her, having withdrawn with her to the parlour after examining the patient. 'A condition of deep shock such as hers offers no very great hopes of recovery, to be blunt. One chance in five, perhaps, putting it at its most sanguine.'

Helen turned away, concealing from him not her emotion, but her lack of it. Deadened to feeling by the scene which had preceded her aunt's attack, she was obsessed by the single thought, too shameful to utter, 'How long will this last?'

She carried out with scrupulous fidelity all the instructions which Doctor Cairns left for the nursing of her aunt. That night neither she nor Bessie went to bed. Helen tried to persuade her to take some rest, but the maid, thirty years in Miss Anderson's service, refused to leave her. The most she would do was to doze in a chair by the bed whenever the invalid slept or drifted into unconsciousness.

The night seemed endless, and yet it was, Helen realised dully, Midsummer Night, the shortest night of the year. The early dawn brought no relief, only an intensification of Helen's weariness, with the thought that another day was beginning, and she still unrefreshed from the last.

At about six Helen sent Bessie down to the kitchen to make tea. Miss Anderson was quiet, and Helen urged the maid to take the opportunity to wash and change, in preparation for the day ahead.

Bessie had not been long gone when Miss Anderson began to stir. Helen went over to her. Her aunt's eyes fixed on her face, dully, and then with hazy recognition.

'Can I get you anything, Aunt Jeannie? Water? Bessie will bring tea presently.'

'Water.'

Helen held the glass to her lips as she sipped a few drops. She settled her back on the pillows once more, and sponged her face, cold but clammy. Nothing seemed able to bring any warmth to her body, although the room was stifling.

The sick woman's eyes lingered on Helen's face with vague bewilderment, as though something just beyond her recall was troubling her, something which she could not remember, or else remembering, could not express.

Helen seated herself by the bed, hoping that her nearness would give her some comfort. Her aunt's eyes, their lower lids sagging with age and ill-health, would swim and close, as though the effort of keeping them open was beyond her, but it was no profound sleep. A minute or two, and they would slowly open again, and seeing Helen would regard her with the same puzzled helplessness. She began to wish that she had not encouraged Bessie to make such a lengthy toilet; she was finding her aunt's gaze unsettling, uncanny.

A glimmer of understanding lightened the old face;

with infinite effort, she raised her hand, and gestured towards a table by the door.

Helen turned, to see what her aunt could be wanting. The table, small and semi-circular, stood against the wall. It held a few books and a porcelain container of dried rose leaves. She went over to examine the books. As she had suspected, one was a Bible.

'Do you want me to read to you, Aunt Jeannie?' she asked gently, her hand on the Bible.

Barely perceptibly, the head moved on the pillow in weary negative. Again her hand, scarcely able to lift itself from the quilt, indicated the table. Helen moved the books uncertainly, thinking that they might perhaps contain something precious to her aunt, a photograph or letter. She found nothing, and turned back to the bed.

'I'm sorry, Aunt Jeannie,' she murmured.

'Drawer.' It was scarcely more than a sigh, but it seemed to demand every ounce of her strength.

In the centre of the table, beautifully constructed after the manner of Regency furniture, was a small drawer, shallow, for the table was only a few inches deep. Helen opened it, and looked to her aunt for further instructions, but she was already asleep once more.

What could she have wanted? She examined the contents of the drawer. They seemed to consist for the most part of letters. At the front of the drawer lay a bundle of what appeared to be legal documents. Other bundles, extending to the back of the drawer, still unrevealed, seemed to be more personal correspondence.

A small, satin-wrapped object at the front of the drawer looked promising. Helen uncovered it: a miniature of a young girl with the abundant ringlets of an earlier day. The painting was of no very high order, but Helen fancied that she could trace a faint resemblance to her mother. Satisfied that she had found what her aunt had wanted, she shut the drawer without examining its clutter of papers any further, and took the portrait over to the bed, so that her aunt's eyes would rest on it when she awoke.

When Miss Anderson next regained consciousness she had drifted so far from life that she hardly knew either Bessie or Helen. Nevertheless, Helen held up before her the little picture, hoping that it might give her some satisfaction. But it seemed that her sight was failing, for she gazed at it without recognition, and even tried to fix her eyes on the table once more, as though not realising that Helen had already found the miniature.

The end was not long in coming. Bessie, a devout adherent of the Free Church, occupied the last moments of their vigil in reading such portions of Scripture as she felt might be of comfort. Helen did not prevent her, fruitless though she considered the reading in view of her aunt's insensibility. But for one last sobbing breath it would have been difficult to say the exact moment at which she suffered the great change, in her case reduced to its smallest possible dimensions.

The consequences of Miss Anderson's death were not immediately felt by Helen. The first necessities, the funeral arrangements, the ordering of mourning, the legal processes concerning the will, might be melancholy, but they at least occupied her time and thoughts. But with the conclusion of these formalities came the time for other decisions, and the full realisation of her situation.

A week after the funeral Helen dined at Drummond Place, a strictly family affair to which her mourning was no bar. Over the meal, which Philip now attended as a matter of course, conversation remained general, but at its conclusion the party broke up.

'You'll not mind, Nell, if I go out?' Jack asked. 'Grant was due back from Torquay this afternoon, so I must do the civil and call . . . it's a bore, and all that, but there you are . . .'

'I should have thought tomorrow would have been time enough?' his father asked, frowning.

'Oh, I may as well get it over with,' he replied, already opening the door.

'I wish he carried out every duty so promptly,' Susan Lambert said, with unusual sharpness.

'Are you coming up, Philip?' Helen asked. It was still an effort to consider him as one of the adults, although he was almost taller than she now.

'No, I've some swotting to get through.'

'I'll sit with you for a while in the library,' his father said, rising. 'There's an article I must look through . . . I'll join you upstairs shortly.'

Entering the drawing-room with her step-mother, Helen felt as ever the curious mixture of familiarity and estrangement at seeing the changes in the room where she had once reigned, undisputed sovereign. Was it only a year ago?

'So, Helen, Miss A. left you well provided for,' her step-mother began, with her unfailing gift for setting Helen's nerves on edge. 'You made quite a coup, nearly four hundred a year, and that's forbye the proceeds from the house, isn't it?'

'The house?'

'Yes, have you made up your mind yet whether you'll sell or rent? You'd better take advice from your poor aunt's legal man, if you're keeping your affairs in his hands. Your papa favours a sale. He thinks you would get a better return on your money if you invested it in older property. For a small outlay you get remarkable profits . . .'

'But I have no intention of selling! Or renting, for that matter; I shall continue to live there. It's too big for me, I grant you, but in every other respect it's ideal. I shall have room in plenty, for example, when Sophie and Tom come up during the summer – why ever should I sell?'

'You can't remain there alone, Helen dear. You'll be coming home when you've settled your aunt's affairs and disposed of her things; we took it quite for granted. You won't mind sharing with Kitty, will you?'

'My home is Northumberland Street now.'

'But what will people say? It was all well and good while you were helping with Miss Anderson, but now? It would almost seem as though there were some dissension in the family if you were to stay away!'

Helen tactfully ignored the suggestion. 'I have become accustomed to lead my own life. It will be better for us all if I continue where I am.'

'But Helen, a woman on her own! And consider how awkwardly you would be placed, if . . .' She dropped her eyes, with the coyness which still contrived to irritate Helen, for all her newfound tolerance.

'If what?' she asked, more patiently than she felt.

'If you should form an attachment. How difficult it would be for you, unchaperoned as you are! Your reputation!'

'Aunt Jeannie lived alone for almost twenty-five years. Her reputation survived intact.'

'You know that this is a different case entirely!' Susan Lambert stopped short, biting her lip, as though to prevent a further outburst of vexation. 'At least look out for a companion, a respectable widow would be ideal!'

'No.'

'But think, Helen! Even suppose that Doctor Cairns were to call as frequently as before, what stories might . . .'

'That is simply nonsense!' Helen cried eagerly, fastening on a feature of the problem which seemed to her absurd, uneasily aware that other aspects were less tractable. 'Doctor Cairns is exempt from any such slurs by virtue of his profession, quite irrespective of the idiocy of any hint that such old friends as we are . . .'

'And what makes you think that long friendships can never become something even dearer?'

At the arch smile, the finger wagged in playful reproof, Helen made a sound of disgust. 'It may not be possible for everyone to appreciate the nature of our friendship, but all those whose opinions I value will be in no doubt as to its innocence.'

'Then we'll say no more about it. I wouldn't offend your delicacy for worlds.' It was all Helen could do to bear the soft clasp of her step-mother's little hands about her arm. 'Do think again, Helen, about a respectable lady companion!'

'The implication is that a single woman cannot be relied upon to lead a virtuous life. I refuse to hire a custodian for my good name.'

'You will make life very difficult for yourself.'

'Perhaps,' she answered, tilting her chin upwards a little, in an arrogant gesture which her step-mother knew better than most.

'Helen, Helen, what a wilful creature you are!' she cried, exasperated. It struck Helen as one of the most honest statements she had ever heard her utter. She smiled.

'Oh, perhaps you're right.'

'Believe me, it's safer to give way to the normal prejudices of society. A companion — where would the harm be?'

Helen considered a moment, not even herself sure of the reasons which impelled her to reject the suggestion, sure only that they arose from whatever in her could not be denied without crippling her whole nature. She shrugged, unable to express that sense of vital struggle. 'I want to lead my own life, that's all. To take on some respectable widow would be to remain a child, or at least not to be absolutely an adult.'

She stopped. It was impossible to convey the exhilaration, the fears even, of her new life. Freedom. The chance to leave childhood behind her at last, with its security, its illusions, its dependence. She would be her own woman. She would not take a companion.

Her step-mother was regarding her with a frown. It spoilt the pretty smoothness of her brow. Unlike so many of her winning gestures, it struck Helen as utterly sincere.

'Do be careful, Helen. Don't forget, I am always here. Not even your father need know anything of what you say to me.'

Curiously, Helen believed her, even though the implications of the offer vexed her. For a second the two women regarded each other with understanding and some approach to respect, as equals.

Edward Lambert's step was heard on the stair. A simper sprang up on his wife's face even before the door handle turned. For once Helen was amused rather than contemptuous.

'So, Nell?' he asked, rubbing his hands together in a bonhomie which was the merest shade too hearty to be natural. As he spoke he looked to his wife, an unspoken question. She shook her head slightly. It struck Helen that their little interview had been far from accidental.

'We have been discussing my plans, Papa,' she said calmly. 'I was just about to make a suggestion which I hope will meet with your approval. Would Jack care to make his home with me, do you think?'

'Jack?'

'Yes. I should like to see more of him, and I have room enough to offer him his own sitting-room, if he wishes to entertain his friends.'

'I don't know, Nell,' her father said, glancing to his wife for support. 'Any riotous living on his part would do him little harm in the eyes of the world, but be disastrous to you. It doesn't do to shut your mind to it, unpleasant as the subject may be.'

'Jack has not repeated his lapses of last year, has he?'

'No,' he admitted. 'He's been steady enough recently.'

'Oh, why not let Helen ask him?' Susan Lambert said unexpectedly. 'He's restless here, we've often said as much, Edward. It might do him good, and it will be an extra room here . . .' She dropped her gaze, seeming genuinely embarrassed.

Helen looked at her in surprise, and then at her father, who was smiling in a remarkably foolish manner.

'Well, you may as well be the first to know it, Nell. You can expect a new sister or brother in the New Year.'

'A half-brother . . .' The correction rose in her mind,

cold and carping. She put it from her, the last echo of an old, tired quarrel. She rose, and kissed her step-mother and her father.

Jack's consent to her proposal was quickly gained, although not without demur. She called to see him the following morning, a Saturday. He had not yet heard of her suggestion, having returned home after her departure the previous evening. Eagerly, she outlined her plan.

'I don't know,' he said slowly, his fingers combing his drooping whiskers. 'I would like to get away, of course . . .'

'Well? What is the difficulty?' she asked lightly.

'For one thing, the money. I wouldn't be able to pay my way.'

'That doesn't signify. Aunt Jeannie's legacy leaves me with enough for both of us, and you will still have your allowance from Papa for your own expenses.'

He hesitated, seeming ill at ease.

'It isn't really the money, is it? Tell me honestly, do you think we should quarrel? Are you afraid I will interfere?'

'No, I think we might agree quite well now.' He was silent, tugging at his whiskers, as if debating how much to say. 'I tell you what, Nell,' he said suddenly, 'I don't care to pull you into my scrapes. Women have to watch out for scandal and all that.'

'Scandal?' She laughed. 'I'll run that risk, if you will. Even you lords of creation have your good name to consider, don't you?'

'Yes . . . Oh, I don't know; I would like it above anything, but really . . .'

'Not another word!' she said gaily. 'Will you come over now and see the rooms I have in mind for you?'

'No, later perhaps. I promised James Grant that I'd go over as soon as I could. He's mislaid some papers somehow or other in the course of his travels. I said I'd help him to search for them today. He's probably found them already, though.'

'Oh, most likely,' she said absently, too full of her plans for their life together to pay much heed to the trivial matter of a few lost papers.

Jack's rooms, Helen had decided, were to be the bedroom and parlour which Miss Anderson had latterly occupied on the ground floor. She would have liked to have them redecorated for him, but Jack seemed as eager to make the move quickly as she was to have him. She put off the scheme, satisfying herself by the purchase of several nice pieces of furniture more suited to his taste than Miss Anderson's things would have been. She kept a few pieces of the latter for her own use; the semi-circular table she put into her own sitting-room. It stood between the windows as though designed for that very spot.

She had still not found the time, or the spirit, to face the task of clearing Miss Anderson's letters from its drawer. The bundle of official papers she had given to William Ramsay, who had charge of her affairs. The rest, some tied neatly into packages, others lying in confusion at the back of the drawer, she left untouched and unexamined until she should feel disposed for the melancholy work.

Jack was soon installed, to her great contentment. Far from any riotous excesses, his life was even more secluded than her own. He was much at home although he went to the Grants' often, in the first few weeks almost daily. From such visits he would return subdued, even anxious, but his only response to any query on the subject was that James Grant was still fretting over his lost papers. Helen assumed that they constituted some academic work, or even a literary endeavour, some juvenile verse, perhaps. She did not press Jack. Even over so trifling a question she was resolved to give no appearance of prying.

Although she scarcely avowed it even to herself, her aunt's death had given a brief spurt of renewed life to her hope that Francis Bethune might contact her. It had occurred to her that a scrupulous sense of honour or pride might have held him back from engaging in a clandestine correspondence. But now that circumstances had changed, might he not make some sign?

There was nothing. She could not even rely on the excuse that he might be unaware of Miss Anderson's death. Rosemary, not without grumbling, had cancelled her proposed dinner as a mark of respect. As a guest, he must have known of it. It was no longer possible to cherish the slightest illusion. Not even a letter of sympathy or condolence came from him. He had broken off all habits of friendship, and even of common acquaintance with her. Nothing could be clearer.

There were diversions from such thoughts. There was Jack to consider now in her household plans, a longed-for visit from Sophie and Tom to arrange, Rosemary's daughter to admire and pet, in addition to her continuing visits to the Crearies and her French lessons, with the quietly enjoyable social engagements to which the latter gave rise.

So the loss of Francis Bethune, of what might have been, faded into a dull pain, never quite forgotten, not incapacitating, but subduing every pleasure. She accepted it, and merely wondered how many other women, self-possessed and gracious, had each their own wistful might-have-been, a pride and a grief.

One curious incident troubled her, although she tried to conceal as much from Jack. It was only two or three weeks after his move to Northumberland Street. Not long before dinner, the bell rang. As it was much about the time of his usual return, she assumed that it was he. But instead of her brother, Bessie came into her sitting-room, disapproval in every feature.

'There's a person to see Mr Lambert. I said Mr Jack wasn't at home, and he asked to see you.'

'Oh? One of my brother's student friends?'

'I'm sure I couldn't say,' the maid said, with a sniff which spoke volumes.

'It may be important. I'll come down to the parlour, I think.'

In the hall, wandering idly about, eyeing his surroundings as though estimating what they would fetch, was the man whose appearance had so aroused Bessie's distaste. He was undersized, considerably smaller than Helen, but not otherwise ill-favoured. Yet there was something in his manner which repelled her, some boldness in his glance, some easiness in his bearing as he stared at her with the same speculation with which he had been evaluating the furnishings.

Helen waited until Bessie had left them alone in the parlour before she began to speak.

'Now, may I know whom I am addressing?'

'My name is neither here nor there, Miss Lambert.' His tone was not discourteous, but the curious answer increased her disquiet. He was not ill-spoken, his accent English, with a trace of Irish. He seemed very sure of himself.

She knew at once that he was not of her own class, and yet his clothes were of a quality as fine, a cut as fashionable as her brother's. He wore a heavy watch-chain across his waistcoat: from the affluence of his costume, it might well have been gold. She would have put his age at thirty or so; he had a head of glossy black hair, a little too obviously pomaded. The scent, pleasant enough in itself, so tainted the air that she seemed to taste it.

'My brother is not at home. Can I be of assistance?' She felt some urge to deal with him politely, despite the insolence of his too-familiar gaze, part calculating, part admiring.

'You would oblige me by giving him this.' He handed her an envelope bearing Jack's name. She took it from him with some reluctance. 'It's confidential, you see, I didn't want to trust it to a servant. Nasty, low creatures they are, for ever prying into their betters' business.'

'You need have no fears on that score,' she said coldly. 'I would trust Bessie as I trust a member of my own family.'

Her answer seemed to amuse him. 'Ah, but the likes of you, Miss Lambert, never knows what servants get up to when they're not watched. You wouldn't sleep easy in your bed if you did, believe me.'

'Is there anything further?' she asked, not deigning to notice his odious freedom.

He looked her coolly in the face, and allowed his gaze unhurriedly to follow the line of her shoulders and bust. She coloured angrily beneath his scrutiny; she had never before been aware of herself as constituting what she did to this man: a piece of sexual merchandise, so much flesh, without personality. He was not ugly, although his features were thin, his cheeks hollow, but she had never met a man who affected her so unpleasantly.

'Anything further?' he said, considering. 'Not this time. Say that to your brother. Tell him that will be all, for now.'

Helen rang for Bessie, who answered the summons with suspicious speed.

He took his leave with an exaggerated bow, a parody of courtesy. He strolled from the room as though he owned it. Helen crossed to the window, and opened it, trying to clear the room of the scent of his hair oil. She saw him descend the steps from the front door, and whistle to a small terrier which was sitting by the railings. The dog ran to him, and followed him down the street. The sight puzzled her, as though it should have aroused some memory.

She gave the letter to Jack at dinner, not seeing him before. 'I didn't care much for your correspondent,' she said with attempted lightness. 'I hope he won't be calling here again for any reason.'

'And he didn't give his name? What did he look like?' he asked, turning the letter irresolutely in his hands.

'Small, slightly built, dark, well dressed but rather forward. He had a little dog with him, I think.'

He shook his head doubtfully at the description, and opened the letter. She watched him read it, and saw him turn white to the very lips. As he hastily refolded the paper and thrust it back into its envelope, his hands were trembling. He fumbled so badly that he dropped it; she bent to see whether it lay within her reach, but he snatched it up at once, looking at her in fear, it seemed.

'Jack, what is it? Are you unwell?'

'No. It's . . . it's a joke. The letter's a joke, and for a moment I fell for it. I don't know how I could be such a flat. It was cleverly done.' He laughed, unconvincingly.

'If it is such a clever production may I see it?'

'No!' he cried, then, recovering himself, added, 'You wouldn't understand the humour of it, Nell. It all depends on knowing the characters involved . . . James would see the joke. I must take it over to him after dinner.'

'I almost forgot, there was a message too. I was to tell you, "That will be all, for the present." Does that make sense?'

'Oh yes, it's quite clear,' he said, his face ghastly. 'The room is a little warm, don't you think? If you'll excuse me, Nell, I believe I won't wait for dessert. I may as well go over to the Grants' directly; the air will do me good.'

Before she could protest, he was gone. The whole incident struck her so unpleasantly that she slept poorly, and paid for it the next morning with a heavy head and a lethargy unusual in her. Doctor Cairns, who called in for a moment, was quick to notice the change in her spirits.

'You are looking remarkably heavy-eyed this morning, Helen. Were you at some scene of dissipation last night?'

'No, I was at home.' She hesitated.

'You may as well confess whatever's on your mind,' he said briskly. 'Don't try to protest that it's nothing. I won't believe you, I warn you.'

'How you bully me! Well then, if you will have it

so . . .' She told him as simply as she could about the visit which had alarmed her, and Jack's response. She half expected that he would laugh away her fears. Instead, his expression grew grave.

'Well? What do you think?' she asked anxiously, as he remained silent.

'I don't think there's anything to be drawn from it, so far,' he said slowly. 'Leave him to tell you in his own time . . . but let me know at once if anything else happens which alarms you.'

'Of course,' she said, feeling as a patient might who had brought symptoms to him, expecting reassurance, and found them taken all too seriously.

'But you've nothing else on your mind?' he asked, as he prepared to leave.

'Since you mention it, there is something, but it's not urgent. I would like your advice, but I know you're not at leisure just now. It can wait.'

'No need; walk up to York Place with me and tell me as we go. You'll be all the better for the exercise.'

'And you won't, I suppose?' she said, with a nod towards his comfortable figure.

'Oh, Bridget will spoil me,' he said, patting his expansive waistcoat.

'You should look for a wife, she would be far less indulgent,' she said, laughing, as she turned to the door on her way to get shawl and hat.

They strolled slowly up the hill towards York Place. The day was bright and cloudless as July can be, but rarely is, in Edinburgh. Only a breeze kept the sun from becoming oppressively warm, although its brilliance was dazzling; Helen was glad to screen her face with her parasol.

'So, Helen, what's on your mind?'

'Oh . . . it's the Crearies.'

'You're still seeing them?'

'Every week. We sew together.'

'You're enjoying it?'

301

'Lizzie is as prickly as a hedgehog still, but we get on well enough.'

'How are they managing? I haven't seen them for a while.'

'I gather that things are improving. Her father seems to be able to send them a more regular wage now that the good weather has come. But in the long term, I suppose that things remain unchanged, and that's what I've been turning over in my mind. I'd like to do something of real use. I inherited so much from Aunt Jeannie, more than I need, to be honest. I'd like to put at least some part of it to some purpose which will benefit others. I think it would have pleased her.'

'And have you any particular notion of what?'

'Joseph.'

'Joseph?' Recovering from his momentary surprise, he nodded his approval. 'He's a quick, intelligent boy, certainly, but he's well established at the Industrial School. In a year or two he'll be equipped for some trade.'

'But he's capable of more! He reads anything he can get his hands on! I've questioned him; he reads with real interest and understanding. He has a passion for science, or at least for all the science he can pick up from such books as I've been able to put in his way.'

'Hmm. So what do you have in mind for him?'

'Send him to the High School. If he succeeds, to the University, as a medical student, if his interests remain as they are at present.'

He drew in his breath. 'Well, that's a bold scheme, certainly. It might be fifteen years before he could support himself; are you prepared for so long a commitment?'

'Yes. I would be willing to make a legal settlement to that effect, to safeguard his future in the event of my death.'

'And what if he changes his mind? Wants to abandon his studies?'

She hesitated, then said firmly, 'He would be free to do so, at any time.'

'And have you thought of the earnings he would have brought in, during his years of study? Would you expect Lizzie to forgo them?'

'No. His family would be paid an allowance, increasing with time, to compensate for his earnings. I don't wish or expect them to be the losers by it. Well,' she added eagerly, as he still hesitated, 'what do you think of it?'

'The scheme does you every credit, Helen, but it has its dangers. In many cases I would think it might be a false kindness. With Joseph Crearie . . . I think it would be worth the risk.'

'What risk?' she asked, surprised and a little nettled at his cautious reception of her plan.

'The risk of spoiling a first-rate artisan to make a third-rate doctor, ill at ease in every class, at home in none, ashamed of his family, despising yet envying his new equals.'

'But you don't think Joseph would find himself in such a position?' she asked, dismayed. In all her enthusiasm, all her practical consideration of the question she had never looked at it in this light.

'No. Joseph is no common child, and what's almost more to the point, Lizzie is no common girl. I think it could be done.'

'Then would you sound her out? As soon as possible? I think if we are to begin it must be now. With some tuition over the summer months he might be able to enter a class at the High School in October not much below his age, if at all.'

'You've devoted a good deal of thought to it, haven't you?'

She nodded. 'I think it may be best to set up a trust of some sort, so that the money comes to Lizzie through some impersonal channel. It would make it more palatable for her, as well as securing the plan should I die, as I said.'

'You've experienced Lizzie's pride by now, no doubt.'

'But you'll raise the idea with her?'

'Certainly, if you wish it.'

'Oh, what would I do without you?' she said, half teasing, half serious, shaking his arm playfully as they paused for a breathing space, having gained Queen Street.

'Torment the life out of some other poor soul,' he replied gruffly, as they resumed their walk east towards York Place. 'I suppose you've taken into account the need for clothes and boots for Joseph if he . . . Helen?'

She did not see the alarm in his face. She had stopped, clutching his arm, with a sudden gasp, as at a stabbing pain. Her face drained of colour, she was staring down Queen Street, helpless, dazed, and yet there was nothing in the least remarkable to see. The usual scattering of pedestrians, going quietly about their concerns, and a hackney cab, a box strapped on behind, no doubt bound for the station on Waverley Bridge: what was there in such a scene to alarm?

'Helen! What is it? Are you unwell?' His words, spoken in a tone she scarcely recognised, roused her. She resumed her pace, though leaning more heavily on his arm, and he was able to see the colour suffuse her cheeks before she shifted her parasol so that her face was concealed from his view, by chance or design.

'I am quite well, thank you,' she said, her very voice trembling. 'It was nothing.'

'Do you take me for a fool?' he asked savagely. 'Young women in a healthy state do not halt in their tracks without any cause, cry out, and turn pale as death . . . Was it a sudden spasm of pain? Cramp? Some faintness?'

'No, no!' she cried miserably. 'Please, I'm quite well, I assure you . . .'

'You are not being honest with me. As your medical adviser, to say nothing of anything else, haven't I some right to your confidence?'

Silence. A sigh. 'It was a momentary foolishness. I caught sight of someone who was once . . . once very dear to me. He was in that cab, going away.' She pointed to the laden vehicle, just toiling up the hill into St Andrew's Square.

'Who?'

The concentrated vehemence in the syllable compelled an answer. Reluctantly, she whispered, 'Francis Bethune.'

'He doesn't deserve you,' he said fiercely.

She shrugged. 'Perhaps he thought so, too. He broke off all acquaintance between us, after giving every appearance . . . for a time I thought . . .' Despite herself, her voice wavered, and trailed into silence.

'So it is all in the past?'

A choked murmur of assent.

'He's not worth a thought, far less a tear! What is he but a commonplace Edinburgh advocate, wrapped in complacency, as dense as his ignorance? He sees nothing, knows nothing, feels nothing. Why should you care for him? A straight back, the good looks of a superior shopman, nothing besides! Empty!'

'Don't!' It was a warning, angry as much as distressed. He said nothing; when he spoke again, it was more coolly.

'And what is so affecting in the sight of Francis Bethune in a hackney cab?'

She coloured, realising for the first time that she had made an unwarrantable exhibition of herself. 'I know that he thought it likely that he would soon be leaving Edinburgh if he received an appointment to a sheriffdom. I suppose that we may have seen his final departure from here.'

'Bound for Sutherland or Cromarty?' He laughed. 'Oh, he's going much further than that. Norway.'

'Norway?'

'Salmon-fishing.'

Absurdly, the news delighted her. 'How do you know?'

'We met at the Lindsays' one evening last week. He looked far from well. I told him that I hoped he had not been neglecting his health for his profession. He shrugged, and told me that he would have a month to recover, in Norway.'

'He looked unwell?' she asked anxiously, unable to help herself. 'Was there any serious indisposition? Has he been confined to the house? Is there any danger?'

'Oh, Helen! No, no serious indisposition. Perhaps I was wrong even to speak of ill-health. He appeared to be under an intolerable burden, that's all. His work can't be the most restful of occupations, particularly to a man of his temperament. He would break before he'd bend.'

They had drawn to a halt before the house at which the doctor was to call. 'I need not say,' she murmured, dropping her gaze, and paying close attention to the clasp on her parasol, 'that no one knows anything of what I have told you . . .'

'Oh, trust me for that!' he interrupted her. 'I am well practised in the art of keeping secrets, believe me.'

She smiled, and left him to his work. As she stepped lightly along the street, it was he who seemed more oppressed by care.

The mission which Doctor Cairns undertook was a success, in so far, at least, as Lizzie could give her consent to Helen's proposals without her father's approval. Within a week it was granted, and Helen was free to consult her lawyer as to the most effective way to provide for the support of Joseph Crearie until the completion of his education.

It was with some trepidation that Helen approached Lizzie for the first time following Doctor Cairns's explanations. She knew Lizzie well enough to realise that the opportunity which was being offered to her brother had its shadow side, in the dependence which it brought, and that for years.

She received Lizzie's stiff expressions of gratitude almost as awkwardly as they were made, and quickly turned the conversation to practical details, coaching, admission to the High School, the provision of clothes, boots, writing equipment and similar necessities. Such ground was safer for them both.

Helen was much away from the house at this time. The arrangements for Joseph Crearie's future involved her in a great deal of time-consuming business. The Lamberts, in view of Susan Lambert's pregnancy, had ventured no further from the city this year than Portobello, and Helen was often asked there to dine. Jack was always included in the invitation, but he rarely accepted, preferring, it seemed, to dine alone in Northumberland Street.

To Helen's surprise he now rarely visited the Grants, although he denied that there had been any quarrel. Helen did not press the question, but it puzzled her a little. On the whole she believed that his entry into her household had been a success, and yet she felt some disquiet at his behaviour.

He was not, as she might have feared, using his greater freedom to indulge in riotous living. He had few engagements, and had even found employment in the counting house of a Leith timber-importing business. He was to remain there until the opening of the new term in the autumn. He had never before passed his vacation in this way, and she expressed her surprise when first he told her of it.

'Oh, it will bring in some extra cash,' he said, with an attempt at indifference which at once roused her suspicions.

'Jack, are you in debt?'

'No . . . my allowance hasn't gone very far this quarter, that's all. I shall be clear presently.'

'I can let you have something if you need it.'

'I didn't want to tap you . . . but if you're sure?'

'Would five pounds help?'

'Considerably. You really are a brick, Nell!'

Helen laughed at the unorthodox praise, drew the five pounds for him, and put the matter from her thoughts, apart from a niggling concern that, having received his quarterly allowance at the beginning of July, he was already in such straits by early August.

But her smouldering unease flared into life with the most unexpected of incidents: a visit from the police.

When Bessie announced the identity of the callers, Helen stared at her in disbelief. 'Detective Constable McIvor? Sergeant Rennie? There must be some mistake! They've come to the wrong address, surely?'

'No such thing, Miss Lambert. They asked for Mr Jack by name.' Bessie was showing a scandalised relish which vexed Helen considerably.

'Show them into the back parlour, then. I'll be down directly.'

The interview proved less of an ordeal than she had feared. Detective Constable McIvor was surprisingly affable, with a countryman's ruddy complexion and a fine set of sandy whiskers which all but met beneath his chin. In his rough pepper-and-salt tweeds he might have been a Selkirk farmer up in Edinburgh for a cattle fair.

Sergeant Rennie, who remained in the background throughout, was even less of a policeman in her eyes. Slight, young, with a bashful air, he more nearly resembled a probationary minister than a hound of the law.

'Miss Lambert? I'm much obliged to you, ma'am, for giving us your time,' McIvor began, with a reassuring smile. He waited for her to seat herself before continuing. 'It's a very slight matter, but these things can often be worth following up . . . has your brother suffered the loss of any of his possessions, do you know?'

'Jack? Why, no. I'm sure he would have mentioned it to me. There's been nothing.'

'A gold watch and chain? A silver hip flask? A morocco dressing case?' he asked, reading off the catalogue from a list in his pocket-book, pausing after each item for any response. 'A pearl tie-pin? A set of cufflinks, set with agate?'

'No. I recognise some of those items, but Jack has

certainly not lost them. May I ask why you wish to know, and how you came by such a list?'

'Oh, there's no mystery there, Miss Lambert,' he said easily, replacing his pocket-book. 'We've had our eyes on a pawnbroker and dealer in the Grassmarket for some time. We were checking his books the other day, and came upon these items, pledged by a Mr Jack Lambert, of this address, and never redeemed. It seemed to me more likely to be a case of reset of theft. Young men of a good address don't commonly resort to depositing such things in the Grassmarket.'

'I can only repeat that my brother has not been robbed, to my knowledge. The dressing case at least could only have been taken from the house, and we have certainly not been burgled.'

'Well, we won't detain you any further,' said the Detective Constable, catching his colleague's eye and rising. 'Perhaps you would be good enough to ask your brother to contact me at the Police Office if he has by any chance missed any of his things.'

That evening, Helen could barely wait for Bessie to bring the dessert and leave them alone. As soon as the door closed behind her she entered on the subject which had never been far from her thoughts all day.

'Jack, the police were here this morning.' She realised, too late, how abruptly she had spoken. His mouth dropped open. Ashen-faced, he stared at her, fear in his eyes, unmistakable, agonised. He was holding a fruit knife; it shook in his hand. With what seemed a conscious effort he placed it on his plate, very gently.

'That's a facer, Nell, quite out of the blue,' he said with an attempt at insouciance which struck her as pitiable. 'What did they want? Nothing serious, I don't suppose?'

She dropped her eyes and sipped her wine. It seemed cruel to observe the naked terror in his face, and his desperate efforts to conceal it. 'It was rather strange. They had a list of things which may have been yours.

They'd been pawned in the Grassmarket. They wanted to know if they'd been stolen, that's all. I told them they hadn't.'

'That was all?' he asked eagerly, his relief almost palpable.

'Yes.' She waited for him to reply, but he said nothing. He moved the wineglass on the table in tight little circles, frowning, as though he were planning his response as carefully as a chess move at a critical stage of the game.

'Did you pawn your watch, and tie-pin, and all the rest?' she asked gently.

Her tone seemed to move him. He looked up, and for a moment she thought he would unburden himself without reserve. But the second passed. He answered in a careless manner which she knew was contrived.

'As it happens, I did. I was a bit strapped for ready cash, and as I didn't choose to borrow, I popped a few things.'

'But a good many things were on the list, and many of them precious! How can you be in such need of money? Why didn't you come to me, or to Papa, for that matter?'

'Don't make such a fuss, Nell! You'd think I was the only fellow ever to overspend his allowance! You should be glad I didn't come sponging on you.'

'But where is the money going? Not on clothes, I can see so much!'

'Oh, you know how it is,' he said irritably. 'Money just vanishes, there's nothing in particular.'

It was an unsatisfactory answer, as they both knew. She sighed. 'If you find yourself in need of money again, tell me. I suppose the watch was the one Mama gave you, her father's?'

He nodded.

'Will you still be able to redeem it? How much would you need? I'll give it to you gladly. Go tomorrow, will you? Promise, Jack!'

There the matter rested. He accepted enough money

from her to enable him to buy back the watch, and half agreed that in future he would come to her, and not the pawnbroker.

Helen spoke to her father the next time she dined out at Portobello. Without revealing the extremities to which Jack had been reduced by want of money, she hinted that his allowance was not meeting all his needs. Her father grumbled, as she had known he would, but seeing his wife inclined to favour the proposal, he promised that as from October Jack's allowance would be raised.

And so the summer wore on, the first that Helen could recall spending in town. Some of her acquaintances were away, but those who remained valued each other all the more, in the relative poverty of social life. Sophie and Tom Hewitt came up for a month, spending a week with Helen, the remainder being claimed by the Hewitts, once more spending their summer in Elie.

Helen had been eagerly awaiting Sophie's visit, and it passed off pleasantly enough, without any disagreement. But it was impossible not to feel that Sophie had changed. London seemed to have given her a superficial gaiety, a brittle manner which made any deep confidence between them out of the question. She wore fashionable clothes, teased Helen about her bonnet, and was shocked that she had not yet replaced every stick of Miss Anderson's furniture with new.

'After all, Helen, what are you going to spend your money on?' she asked, fingering the old rose silk curtains, and tossing them dismissively from her. Helen did not see fit to mention Joseph Crearie's education. She doubted whether the project would meet with Sophie's approval.

All in all Helen was glad when Sophie and Tom left for Fife, having given her the benefit of London wisdom on every aspect of her life, from Jack's whiskers to the manner of serving dessert. More than anything else, Sophie's visit brought home to her the reality of that splitting of the family circle which had begun with Rosemary's wedding. And yet, although she felt a sort of nostalgia for those uncomplicated, unreflecting days, had she the chance, she would not have returned to them.

To Lizzie, the summer brought an easing of the anxieties which had so nearly broken her earlier in the year. Her father was sending her good money regularly. Taught a terrible lesson, she put something by every week, if only a few pence.

Tam, having held down his job in Dundee for a few months, was writing of his wish to return to Edinburgh. Through Joseph she replied, urging him to remain where he was, if he had work. From the tone of his letter, she feared that she would soon see him again. She would have welcomed him indeed, but for the dread that his old haunts, his old companions, would lead him to drift into the habits which had always ended in disaster.

Nettie, in her quiet situation, gave her no anxiety, unless it were that, at almost fourteen, she was revealing a disconcerting taste for silk gowns and richly trimmed bonnets. More sturdily built than Lizzie, she already prided herself on a swelling bosom, and was beginning to grumble at the roughness and redness of her hands from kitchen work. To be a lady's maid, that was the object of her ambition. Lizzie could still, by the sheer force of her personality, keep her in her position, but soon she would be overridden, she knew. Nettie would go her own way, and her heart misgave her at where that way would lead.

At times she wondered whether it would have been better to have kept Nettie at home, under her own eye, despite the doctor's advice. Certainly, May's cough continued to trouble her. She had benefited from the better, more plentiful food which Lizzie could now provide and from the easing of the family's financial straits. Lizzie no longer had to harden her heart, and remain silent when she saw May wearily lay down a half-finished seam, as though even one more stitch was beyond her. Now, as soon as she saw signs of fatigue, she took away May's work, and ordered her to rest. A few more pence in the week no longer justified the dangers to her health.

Danny, a forward child, was already beginning to speak a few words. Ruddy and mischievous, he was happiest outdoors, when May was well enough, or Joseph could be spared, to watch him.

On Joseph's good fortune Lizzie's mind was divided. On the one hand, it almost passed understanding that her brother should be so lucky. It seemed at times little short of a miracle. It had always been her mother's strongest wish that Joseph should be educated. In the chance he was being offered she could believe there was the result of some intercession from beyond the grave.

And at times only this superstitious fancy ensured that she did not step in and put a stop to Helen's plans. She feared, with a deep, unreflecting instinct, the slackening of the family bond which would result from Joseph's elevation beyond his origins. How could he belong to them when he became a great man? That he would be a great man, once educated, she never doubted. Would he be ashamed of them? Would he still obey his father, or her, when he knew so much more than they?

Yet, seeing Joseph's delight at the prospect of attending a school at which he would no longer spend his time in learning skills which, however useful, did not feed or stimulate his appetite for knowledge, she had to silence her doubts.

Joseph passed the months which separated the news of Miss Lambert's offer and the opening of the High School in October in a daze of happiness. He began lessons with a student, a friend of Miss Lambert's oldest brother, in order to bring him up to the standard for his age, including some Latin. Greek he could begin at school, but Miss Lambert herself promised to give him help in that language, should it become necessary.

Lizzie watched Joseph for any sign of pride or affectation. She found none. Happy himself, he redoubled his efforts to help her. She never needed to ask him to amuse

Danny, to read to May and so lighten her weary hours of drudgery, to go for water or messages. It was as if with quick sensitivity he had understood her fears, and sought by his actions to prove how groundless they were.

He spoke little of the future, beyond the longed-for day of his entry to the High School, but once, long after the room was in darkness, Lizzie heard his voice, from the mattress he now shared with Danny.

'Lizzie?'

'Aye.'

'See when I'm a man, I'll work for us all, and get us a braw house, with a garden for May, and a wee canary, and a cuddy for Danny, and a silk gown for Nettie, and no just for Sundays, either . . . ye'll see . . . ' His voice was thickening in approaching sleep, as he spun his dreams to her.

'Aye, we'll see,' she said, softly, sadly, wishing that life was as simple, hope as easy, as it was to him.

With Miss Lambert, as she invariably thought of her, her relations remained formal. Lizzie insisted on repaying her the money she had received for Gillanders, although she was perfectly aware of Helen's reluctance to take it. It was a point of honour with her, however great the new obligation since conferred on her.

With mingled envy and distaste Lizzie watched May's uncomplicated admiration of their visitor, and the ease with which they chatted together. She herself could never drop her guard; wary, ever alert for any slight, she never for a moment forgot the gulf fixed between them.

When Helen was involved in some conversation with May, neatly stitching as they spoke and laughed, Lizzie would secretly observe her. Despite herself she was fascinated by the older woman's appearance and manner. Everything about her proclaimed her alien to the house in which she sat.

It was not only a question of her expensive clothes, perfectly fitting, chosen for other qualities than wear, cheapness and not showing the dirt. Her bearing; her smooth, healthy face; her skin, flawless, delicately suffused with colour, like some unblemished fruit from a tree favoured by soil and situation; her voice, even, all spoke of a different world. Clear, never harsh, to Lizzie English-seeming, it hinted at an existence without anger or ugliness, where suffering was unknown; of order and comfort. Her white, soft hands, her slim feet in their dainty, pretty boots, the rich lace edging her petticoats, the gold chain on the little watch she kept in a neat pocket in her waistband, the faint smell of lavender from her handkerchief, the swift grace of her walk, made her in Lizzie's eyes a wonder, an exotic, beautiful animal, such as those which, unfit to struggle for life in a harsh climate, require to be cosseted, and fed on only the finest and rarest of foods.

Lizzie would have died rather than reveal her admiration, allow it, like May's, to shine in her eyes, a willing tribute. For Lizzie could never accept, as May did so readily, as even Joseph did, that the differences between them were natural and inevitable.

Lizzie told herself that she did not blame Miss Lambert because she lived in a house which would have provided homes for four families from Paisley Close of a comfort beyond anything they could even imagine. She told herself that Miss Lambert could not help being lovely, and healthy, and untouched by grief, when she already, at just sixteen, knew herself to be hard-featured, dressed in drab, ugly clothes, pinched and crabbit from endless worry. She told herself that it was no fault of Miss Lambert's that Doctor Cairns's face lit with sudden pleasure whenever he saw her, that his eyes rested on her with an expression which Lizzie had never seen before, kind and patient though he had always been to her, May and the others.

She told herself, and really believed, that Miss Lambert had no obligation to trouble herself with the problems of Lizzie's family, that her generosity to Joseph, her gentle ways with May, were proof of a rare and true goodness. And yet, for all that, she could not believe that a world which gave so much, so lavishly, to one and so little to a multitude of others, was as it should be.

18

And so, far from disagreeably on the whole, the summer passed. Helen made the most of her reduced circle of acquaintance, worried over the effect of his unaccustomed confinement at the counting-house on Jack, who seemed every day to grow paler and shabbier, and herself faithfully took daily exercise.

Often her walk would take her along Heriot Row, past Francis Bethune's house. It was a secret indulgence she allowed herself, although she would have been hard put to it to explain what benefit she drew from it. The housekeeper must have been left in residence on board wages. Helen saw her sometimes, polishing the brasses, shaking a mat down in the area, or even, on a warm afternoon, sitting with another servant outside the kitchen, in the shade cast by the steps to the front door.

During the master's absence some redecoration appeared to be in progress. The long windows of what she took to be the drawing-room were whitewashed and curtainless. Their blank stare was disturbing, like sightless eyes. It was a relief, early in September, to see them cleaned and the curtains replaced, ready for his return, she supposed. She liked to think of the housekeeper removing the dustcovers from the furniture, taking the lustres from their extinguishing brown holland bags, lifting the drugget, replenishing the larder.

Rosemary and Harry Robertson were amongst the first to return to Edinburgh, at the beginning of the third week in September. Helen had missed them. She had expected to be invited down to Melrose to see them, at least for a weekend, but to her slight surprise it had never been suggested.

She called on them on the very day following their return. Her niece was brought down from the nursery, and Helen's appreciation of her beauty and precocious skills satisfied even Rosemary's notions of what was proper. Helen stayed for longer than she had intended, and finally rose to go with real reluctance.

'I'd hoped Harry might be back, it's an age since I saw him,' she said, pulling on her gloves.

'Oh, he'll not be home before dinner. He can scarcely tear himself away from his beastly plans and elevations,' Rosemary replied, pouting.

'You and he must dine with us in Northumberland Street. After cooking for Sophie with all her finicky London ways, Bessie and Mrs Blair won't baulk at a dinner for you.'

'It would be one less meal for me to plan,' Rosemary said plaintively, 'and at least Harry would be obliged to spend the evening away from his schedules and specifications for once. Really, I hardly see him.'

'Rosie, how can you grumble?' Helen asked, glancing quickly into the mirror as she settled her bonnet. 'You know quite well that Harry is the best-tempered man in Edinburgh. At least when you do see him you're sure of a pleasant face and an agreeable manner! Shall we say Friday, then? I may see if Doctor Cairns is free. Mrs Blair always excels herself when she is cooking for him!'

Doctor Cairns was happy to accept, subject to the usual unpredictable demands upon his time, and, after a little thought, she also included Philip in the party. He was to enter on his studies at the University that autumn, and could, she supposed, be regarded as an appropriate guest. He would also be company for Jack, who had never been close to Rosemary.

Helen looked forward to the engagement, without any anxiety on the score of reconciling uncongenial characters. Harry could be relied upon to create an easy atmosphere.

But Harry Robertson had not long been beneath her

roof before she recognised, with a surprise which soon ceased to be amused, that he was out of humour. She hurried eagerly forward to greet him; he barely touched her hand, scarcely met her eye. Cold, distant, his bluff face aloof, he was utterly changed from the Harry Robertson she remembered.

At first, she assumed some domestic disagreement, and looked in alarm to Rosemary, expecting anger or sulking in her plump, all too expressive features. Neither was to be found. Rosemary was as much at ease as her husband was the reverse.

The meal had scarcely progressed as far as the fish before Helen reached the conclusion that Harry's displeasure was not general. He addressed his wife with perfect naturalness, showed interest in Jack's work for the timber merchants, joked with Doctor Cairns, offered Philip advice on the course he proposed to follow. To every other member of the little company, in other words, even to the servants handing the dishes, he was his usual genial self. But to Helen?

If she made some general remark, he ignored it. If she addressed him specifically, he replied as curtly as he well could, never raising his eyes to her face. The conclusion was painfully clear. He was nursing some grievance in regard to her and her alone.

The instinctive wish to preserve the appearance of harmony made Helen ignore as best she could her brother-in-law's scarcely veiled hostility. But for all her smiles and ready attention to her guests, she was inwardly enraged by his manner. Had she been less sensitive, had she liked him less, she might have shrugged it off. But to be snubbed at her own table, in total ignorance of any crime? It was an insult which she had no intention of bearing meekly.

Helen awaited her moment. As she and Rosemary rose from the table, she turned to her sister with a smile, as though she had just remembered something.

'Would you mind going up alone, Rosie? You can amuse yourself for five minutes with the ladies' magazines

Sophie brought with her, I suppose? I want to consult Harry about the best way to improve the drains here. I'm sure he will spare me a few minutes to explain the steps I should take, won't you, Harry?'

He murmured something inaudible, but did not refuse point blank, as she had known he would not.

'Would you just come up to my sitting-room?' she continued, ignoring his reluctance. 'I should like to take down the names of any tradesmen you feel able to recommend. I want to make a start before the winter sets in, Aunt Jeannie let it go too long . . .' Talking easily, she waited at the door for him. He could do nothing but comply with her request.

Once the door had closed behind them, she gestured Harry to a seat, herself remaining standing. He cast a sullen, uneasy glance at her, like a truculent child before a scolding.

'I believe I owe it to you to give you an opportunity to explain yourself,' she began, as pleasantly as she could. 'You obviously feel some resentment against me, Harry, though I can't conceive why. If I'm at fault I would sooner know of it than have you insult me for the remainder of the evening as you have so far.'

He looked at her with marked distaste. 'Believe me, if it had lain in my hands I would not have been here this evening. It gives me no pleasure to sit at your table.'

'Harry!' she exclaimed, even her anger eclipsed by shock at his brusqueness, and the sense that some serious misunderstanding underlay his attitude. 'We parted as friends, did we not? How can you think I have offended you?'

'Not me,' he said, looking at her as though he expected her to understand the reference.

'Who then? Rosemary? She has given me no sign of it, I'm sure.'

'You know perfectly well what you've done — or not done.'

'I don't know!' she cried, exasperated. 'I only know

320

that your behaviour to me this evening has been so uncivil that in anyone else I would never have stooped to request an explanation. Were it not for the affection I have always felt for you, I . . .'

'Affection?' He laughed contemptuously. 'Pity help the man who relies on that! It's a transient state, isn't it, Helen?'

'Harry, will you tell me in plain language what it is you are accusing me of! There's some mistake, that's clear.'

'Mistake? You've broken Frank's heart, there's no mistake about that.'

'Frank?'

'Francis Bethune . . . you may recall the name?'

She ignored his sarcasm. It didn't matter, he didn't matter beside the startling reality which lay behind his anger, his contempt.

'I broke his heart?' she asked wonderingly. 'But how?'

'Oh, cleverly, by inches, with the most exquisite refinement of cruelty: by silence. You encouraged him. You drew him out of himself. Even in Melrose, last summer, I could see how attached to you he was growing. In my stupidity I was glad of it. I admired you, Helen. I trusted that you would understand Frank. You know he's been a brother to me . . . but what's the good of talking about it? Why should you care? Clearly, you don't!'

'You could not be more mistaken, Harry.'

For the first time, his anger faltered, at the evident sincerity of her tone. He replied less certainly, with some return to his usual manner.

'Frank is not the sort of man to be generally pleasing. Many find him cold, formal. With women in particular . . . he has no real ease of manner, he never relaxes. But with you I could see from the first that he was different. He was drawn to you, carried out of his usual reserve. He told you about his mother, didn't he?'

'Yes.'

'Not even Rosie knows that. And his father? You know

how he rejected him? Did he tell you how hurt he was when his father did not even reply to the letter he wrote at the end of his school-days?'

'I certainly remember him telling me of it. His father's silence seemed to me a piece of most unnatural cruelty.'

'Then how, how in the name of Heaven could you do the same – worse?' he cried, with all his earlier vehemence. 'A refusal would have been bad, in all conscience, but even that would have been nothing, compared to silence!'

'Silence? It was he who was silent! He left my letter unanswered!'

'*Your* letter?' he asked, incredulous.

'I wrote to explain that in view of Miss Anderson's indisposition I could no longer receive calls, even his.' She stopped, colouring as she recalled the guarded tenderness she had allowed herself. 'The contents can be of no significance to anyone but Mr Bethune, and perhaps not even to him. He did not reply, in any case. I have not received a word from him since. His silence was surprising . . .' She hesitated, and added, 'It hurt me, Harry, I will say so much.'

'But he did write!'

'He didn't! He couldn't . . . I received no letter, I've told you!'

'He delivered it here, to your aunt's own woman. He could not bear to trust to the delay and uncertainty of the post.'

Helen gazed at him, bewildered, still not believing. She moved to the hearth, and rang. 'How do you know all this?' she asked, as they waited.

'I met Frank by chance, shortly before he went off to Norway. He was so changed that I thought he must have been ill. He tried to put me off with excuses about the pressure of work and so on, but in the end I got the truth out of him. Helen, he worshipped you. People think him unfeeling, but . . .'

She made a warning gesture; Bessie was approaching.

'Shall I light the gas, Miss Lambert?' she asked, on entering the twilit room.

'No. We will be going into the drawing-room directly. I simply wanted to ask you one or two questions, Bessie. Do you recall a Mr Bethune, who visited the house on the day of Miss Anderson's seizure earlier this year?'

'That red-headed man? Oh aye, I mind him,' she said, with no very complimentary emphasis.

'And did he ever call again, when I was out?'

'Well now, I think he may have,' Bessie replied, with the prudent caution of one who cannot see how she could possibly be incriminating herself, but is sure a trap lurks close by.

'Did he ever leave a note for me? A letter?'

'A letter? Oh, I'm sure I couldn't rightly say, Miss Lambert. If he'd brought a letter, you'd know better than me.'

With an effort, Helen restrained her impatience. 'I am wondering if it was mislaid, that's all, Bessie. It would have been no one's fault, for example, if it had been left where it could have fallen into the fire, or dropped down behind some furniture . . .'

Bessie eyed her speculatively for a second, and then, apparently struck by a lightning flash of memory, exclaimed, 'Now, wait a minute! You're right, Miss Lambert. A letter was brought for you, one afternoon when you were out. Miss Anderson was in her bed, poor soul, and she asked who'd been at the door. She had me bring her the letter, so that she could give it to you herself. I laid it down on the wee table by the door, as she bid me.'

'And what happened to it then?'

'Oh, I couldn't say, Miss Lambert. I never saw it again, nor gave it a thought, it not being any of my business,' she concluded, with a self-righteous sniff.

'Thank you, Bessie. I'm much obliged to you for your excellent memory. Will you bring us up tea whenever you hear the gentlemen joining us?'

'Very good, Miss Lambert,' she said, with an air of martyred innocence. Her bustling steps receding down the stair were alive with the interesting communications she would shortly be making to those in the kitchen.

Harry Robertson broke the silence. 'Helen, I owe you an apology.'

'You do, but I'm glad your cousin has so loyal a champion.'

'Even so, I'm sorry.'

Impulsively, she hurried over to him, hand outstretched. 'Not another word, Harry! I'm in your debt. If you had been better able to control your resentment, I should never have heard of all this. Does anyone else know, by the bye? Rosemary?'

'No, no one.'

'Is he back in Edinburgh?'

'I'm not sure. He goes on circuit some time about now. He may well have left already.'

'No matter. If you should see him, say nothing of our conversation, please.'

'If you wish,' he said doubtfully. 'You won't leave him long in ignorance, will you? He has taken all this very much to heart.' They walked together towards the door. As they left the room, he added in a sudden rush of confidence, 'I'm very fond of Frank, for all his High Tory notions. Don't be deceived by his manner. He's more easily hurt than most men.'

She smiled at him, but she had scarcely taken in the meaning of what he said. Her thoughts were elsewhere.

Rosemary received them with some impatience. Doctor Cairns was not long in following, with Jack and Philip. Helen, abstracted, presided over the tea, leaving the management of the conversation to Harry. The letter! What had happened to it?

Obsessed by that single question, she paid no more attention to the talk amongst her guests than if it had been birdsong. She did not see Doctor Cairns's expression as he watched her averted, abstracted face, nor did she mark how his anxious concern gave way to a look of resolution.

The pealing of the front door bell broke in upon even Helen's thoughts. Bessie entered.

'A person to see Mr Jack Lambert,' she said ungraciously. 'A Mr Donoghue, or some such name.'

'One of your friends, Jack?' Helen began, with a sudden guilty recognition of her poor showing as hostess. 'Bring him up to join us, if you wish . . .' She stopped, at the sight of her brother's face. Terror: there was no other word for it. The abject fear seemed almost ludicrous on the features of a healthy, well-educated young man, sitting at his ease in a comfortable drawing-room in an eminently civilised district of Edinburgh.

He made no reply. His hands scrabbled at the sides of his chair, as though he lacked the strength to rise, then, murmuring an apology, he followed Bessie from the room.

A surprised, awkward silence succeeded his departure. Harry exchanged a glance with his wife, then looked in enquiry to Helen.

'Oh, Jack has his own concerns, like any young man,' she said lightly.

Harry smiled, and did not pursue the question. The conversation resumed its placid flow, the incident ignored, if not forgotten. Jack did not return. Even by the time the Robertsons' clarence was brought round, there was no sign of him, to Helen's vague disquiet.

'Can we give you a cast, Doctor Cairns?' Harry asked as he rose to go. 'You don't have the brougham with you, I think you said?'

'No, I told Donald I'd make my own way home,' he said, glancing at Helen with uncharacteristic indecision. 'I believe I may inflict my company on Helen for a little while longer, if she has no objection. There was something I wanted to ask Jack.'

'Oh, he might not be back for a long time!' Helen

said quickly, alarm patent in her face at being denied the solitude she craved.

'I see,' he said, his voice suddenly sounding very weary. 'Harry, I'll trouble you for that cast, if I may . . .'

'By all means,' Harry replied, ushering him to the door where Rosemary was already waiting. Helen saw her guests to the carriage. Philip had already left, refusing any offer of a lift for the short journey to Drummond Place. At the last moment, as Doctor Cairns was in the act of mounting into the carriage, he turned back, colliding with Harry who was politely giving him precedence.

'Tomorrow morning, Helen? May I call?' he asked hurriedly.

'What? Oh, yes, do,' she answered vaguely, already going back into the house. 'I'll ask Jack to stay at home to see you.' By the time the door had closed behind her, she had already forgotten his confusion, his hesitancy, and the unusual formality of his request to call.

Helen did not return to the drawing-room, but to her own sitting-room, more intimate, more a part of her life. She wandered about the room, unable to settle, knowing that sleep would be impossible. Everywhere she found a memory: in the chair where she still seemed to see Harry, angry and reproachful; in the writing case on which she had slowly, timidly, composed her letter to Francis Bethune, sitting up in bed, swathed in her shawl against the cold; in the elegant little table on which Bessie had put his reply, his lost reply.

She passed her hand lovingly over its glossy surface. There his letter had lain; and afterwards? Had Miss Anderson destroyed it? Dragged herself from her bed, and furtive, fumbling, thrown on the back of the fire the letter which she feared would take from her the niece for whom she had designed a different life?

It must have been so, and yet Helen could not believe it of her aunt. Her hand dropped to the handle of the drawer, that drawer which had held something that had troubled the dying woman's last conscious moments. She opened it.

The drawer stuck. She exerted her full strength, willing if necessary to tear the delicate piece apart. With a sudden jerk, it was released. She reached in, pulled out the bundles of letters she had always intended one day to sift through, but had never examined. One after another she leafed quickly through their dry pages, traced with the fading lines of long-dead scandal and gossip, and threw them to the floor, useless.

The bundles were soon disposed of. The single letters remained, of a more recent date. Now she moved more slowly, examining each cover carefully. The drawer was almost empty now; she had to reach far into it for the last letters, her nails scrabbling against the wood. And there, crumpled but still unopened, she found it. A letter in an unknown hand, a regular, pleasing script, addressed to her.

She had to sit down before she opened it. '*My dearest Helen.*' The first words gave her a pleasure so intense that it outweighed all the doubt and sadness of the past months. She could scarcely bring herself to read on, and leave those opening words.

At the first reading she could not absorb the full sense of the letter, it was too unexpected, too much desired. Here and there a phrase startled her with sudden joy, '. . . I never believed I could know such happiness . . . my only fear is that I will be unable to make you as happy as I am . . . is it possible that you love me? Am I wrong in daring to think it? . . . Holding you in my arms for even a few seconds was a joy such as I never thought to know on this earth . . . does this letter seem foolish to you? With you, with you alone, I can dare to be myself, foolish or not . . . only tell me that you will be my wife, and I will be content to wait until your aunt's health allows me to call once more, or to hope to see you in society . . . I will not rest, will not know a moment of peace, until I hear from you . . . I need you . . . write soon, my darling, my dearest, dearest love . . .'

She put down the letter, no longer able to see. And with her joy mingled anguish, equally piercing, that for so long such a letter, from such a man, had gone unanswered. She remained a moment longer, given up to her thoughts, then suddenly rose, and hurried through to her bedroom, searching hastily for a shawl in the semi-darkness. She snatched up a wrap, ran downstairs, after ringing for Bessie.

She had reached the front door before Bessie toiled up the kitchen stair.

'I shall be out for a short while – I forgot to give Philip a message to my father,' she said, with a placatory smile. 'I shan't be long, I'll try not to keep you up . . .' She spoke the last words from the steps as, beneath Bessie's curious gaze, she hurried down to the street, and turned, not to the left, towards Drummond Place, but right.

Bareheaded, shivering in the cool September night, she flew along the streets. 'Let him be there! Oh, please, let him be there!' The words filled her mind, setting themselves to the rhythm of her hurrying feet. Mesmeric, they kept other, more anxious thoughts at bay.

Outside his house she halted, breathless. The fanlight was illumined, chinks of light showed from the curtains in a room to the right of the door. It seemed that he might be at home, her wish – her prayer – had been granted, and her heart misgave her. Was she not, after all, making a fool of herself? Would a letter not serve just as well?

She hesitated, looking up at the steady glow of the fanlight. A letter would be more discreet, it was true. But when would it reach him? He might be leaving on circuit the next morning at first light; would his letters be forwarded? Could she leave him for a week or more still thinking that she had treated him so shabbily? What if he should meet with some accident in travelling, and die believing her cold, himself unloved?

She lifted her skirts and skimmed up the steps, and

without allowing herself space for further reflection, rang the bell. She heard it peal with startling abruptness within the sedate facade, and could almost have run away, appalled by her own boldness.

She had ample time for uncomfortable thoughts during the long pause which ensued before the door was opened by an elderly man, a few crumbs caught in his flourishing whiskers the evidence of an interrupted supper. Seeing her, his dignified demeanour remained unchanged, but she noted the faintest shade of surprise widen his eyes.

'Is Mr Bethune at home?' she asked, with little of the composure for which she had hoped.

'If you will excuse me, ma'am, I'll enquire. The name . . . ?'

She hesitated. Would he even admit her, thinking of her as he must? 'It is of the utmost importance that I should see Mr Bethune at once. I assure you that he will wish to see me, when he knows the message I am bringing. I am a relation by marriage of Mr Harry Robertson. You will know him, I'm sure?'

'Well, ma'am, I hardly like . . . if I could just announce your name, now, there would be no difficulty.'

'Please!' Unconsciously she employed all the power of her wide, clear eyes as she fixed them desperately on his face.

He pursed his lips doubtfully, and stepped back, conceding her victory. 'Mr Bethune is in his study. If you'll come this way . . .'

He led her through a dark, quiet hall to a door at the back of the house. He opened it, pressing himself against the door as she squeezed past him, even before the door was fully open. She hurried into the room.

A fire was burning, the gas was lit, books and papers lay in businesslike disorder on a leather-topped table. There was a sense of recent occupation, but the room was empty. She turned back in dismay to her guide, who was hovering at the threshold for a glimpse of an interesting encounter, unprecedented in the history of the household.

'He isn't here!' she said, childlike in her disappointment.

'He'll not have gone up yet,' he said, conspiratorial now. 'He's maybe gone down into the garden. I've seen him do that when he can't just settle to his books. It must clear his head.' He walked over to the window, where one curtain was partly open. He pulled it back, revealing a French window.

'You'll need to mind the stairs, miss,' he said, as she paused on the little landing at the top of the steps, to allow herself to adjust to the darkness. As soon as she dared, she picked her way down the narrow, wooden flight, away from the light, into the dim stillness of the garden.

Built on a slope, the north side of the house was lower than the south, the ground floor of the front being the first floor at the back. It was a calm night, the moon a silver paring in the soaring vastness of the sky. She walked slowly away from the steps, making out nothing, only the pale blur of flowers at the edge of the grass, and the flickering flight of a moth blundering past. She looked back to the house. The manservant was outlined against the oblong radiance of the French window. In the adjoining houses here and there stamps of light showed at random.

She continued down the garden, the grass damp beneath her satin slippers, the scent of some late-blossoming flower sweet and frail in the motionless air. Two or three trees stood at the end of the garden, apple trees, she thought. Beneath one of them was a bench. On it, head bowed, shoulders drooping, hands supporting his head as he bent forward, was Francis Bethune.

'Francis.' She was at his side before he could look up, crouching beside him, kneeling on the damp grass, heedless of her pale, fragile silk, her hands clasped about his arm.

'I never received your letter, not until tonight. My aunt kept it from me, I think she tried to tell me at the very

330

last, but it was too late. I didn't know! Oh, Francis, I'm so sorry! What must you have thought, my love?'

There was a moment of silence, and then she heard, not a word, not an exclamation, but a sigh, of contentment, of relief, like that of an awakened dreamer, returning to reality after some distorting nightmare. Her head sank onto his breast; she felt his chest rise and fall in a long, shuddering breath as his fingers tightened over hers, his cheek pressed against her hair. For a long moment they clung together, as though not daring to move and break the enchantment.

'Helen. Come here.' At the sound of his voice, low and tender, her heart seemed to lurch, that indescribable surge of excitement and panic which she never thought to feel again. He pulled her up onto the bench, close to him.

She glanced quickly back to the house. The screening branches of the trees hid them from view. They were alone.

Warm and live, his arm encircled her shoulders, naked in the low-bodiced evening gown she wore. His hand swept slowly along her arm, as though marvelling at its smooth roundness. She luxuriated in the caress, as his fingers passed over the delicate skin at the inner fold of her elbow.

'You're cold,' he said, his voice in the darkness curiously intimate, unfamiliar.

'No, not at all,' she murmured hastily, fearing that they must return to the house.

'Did you have a shawl?'

She looked about, bemused. A little way off, forgotten, her shawl was a dark stain spilled on the grass.

'It will be damp from the grass. Here . . .' He drew away, struggled free of his coat, and draped it, with anxious clumsiness, about her shoulders. The warmth from his body soaked into her chilled flesh, animal comfort.

Emboldened, she nestled close to him, holding him to her, running her hands over his back, neat and lean in its silk-backed waistcoat. His shirt-sleeves a ghostly blur in the dark, he bent his face to hers. A moment of confusion; his lips grazed against her cheek. She, not knowing whether by accident or design, gazed up at him questioningly, and then there was no more doubt, as his lips pressed soft and fierce against her mouth. In the first strangeness she saw his face, so close, his eyes shut in rapt concentration, beyond thought, beyond self. She felt sudden shame at watching him; her own eyes closed as she strained him to her, in the kindly, moth-haunted darkness.

Lizzie Crearie greeted the return of her brother with no show of enthusiasm. She had received no warning of his coming but it was not unexpected. She knew Tam. So when one evening, as she sat up after the children were in bed to finish May's shirt, she heard the familiar jaunty chapping at the door, she knew the truth. Her face relaxed into one of her rare smiles, although by the time she had crossed to the front door her expression was as usual wary and taut but for a lingering warmth in her eyes.

'A bad penny, eh no, Lizzie?' he said, throwing his arm easily about her thin, rigid shoulders, and looking appreciatively round the room, its semi-darkness heavy with the sleeping breath of the children.

Lizzie moved away, shrugging off his affection like a cat which will not endure petting. She busied herself at the fire, stirring up the coals, adding fresh, setting the kettle to boil.

'So, Tam?' she asked, reaching up for the tea-caddy.

'I've no come empty-handed,' he said quickly, as if defending himself against some unspoken complaint.

She stopped in the act of measuring the tea, looking at him sharply.

'Dinna fash your head, it's all came by honest.' He pushed a purse across the table to her, small but well filled.

She opened it, glanced at the sovereigns it contained,

and put it away from her, as though fearing contamination. 'Ye've no earned all that honest,' she said scornfully. 'Do ye think I'm buttoned up the back, Tam?'

'Aweel, I maybe had a wee bit luck with the horses,' he admitted with a smile, 'but all won fair and square, Lizzie, I swear it on my mother's grave.'

She looked at him searchingly, but made no further protest.

'Ken what I'll do with it?' he asked, stretching out his hands to the reviving embers, as he squatted down by the fire.

She seemed to ignore the question, as she set the tea to mask on the hob and cut two thick slices off the remains of a loaf, but a nod told him of her interest.

'I'm going to set up for a packman,' he said triumphantly. 'Another two-three pound, and I'll put thegether the brawest pack in the Lowlands. Only the best, Lizzie! Ye'll need to give me a hand with buying the ribbons and trimmings, and all they things. Ye'll see, I'll no gang the wrong gate.'

He reached up and took from her the battered toasting fork, holding it out to the fire. She poured his tea, and seated herself once more to her sewing. He examined one side of the toast, and turned it.

'I'll get on the road by October,' he went on, the fireglow lighting up his eager face, his wide-set, undaunted eyes. 'The whole pack'll be sellt before the Year. I'll be back home for the worst of the winter, put thegether a new pack, and away again by March. Oh, Lizzie, what rare it'll be!'

He jumped up, and spread the toast while it was still hot with the scrap of dripping she had set out for him. He sprinkled it plentifully with salt, and resumed his place by the fire, with a sigh of satisfaction.

'Ye wanting one?' he said, holding out a slice.

'No.'

He frowned. 'Money short again?'

'No the now.' She hesitated, and added, 'If ye're needing it, there's a wee bit I've put by . . .'

Over the edge of his chipped teacup his eyes looked up at her, widening in surprise. 'Ye dinna mean it!'

'Anything, to keep ye out from under my feet.'

He laughed, understanding her, for all her harsh tone. 'Ye're awf'y good, hen. I can maybe make the pack up on what I've got. I ken a boy down the Cowgate can get me . . .'

'Tam! Ye'll no put a pin in that pack that's no bought all square!'

'Neither I would; do ye think I'll throw away the chance of my life?'

She looked at him, and believed him.

19

That night, when Francis Bethune had walked her home through streets of which every stone seemed to reflect the golden glow of her happiness, Helen's first thought was to share with Jack the news of her engagement. He had returned long since, as Bessie pointedly informed her, and had gone to his bed.

'And what is to be done with that gown is more than I know, Miss Lambert,' she added, settling her shoulders with a little wriggle of distaste.

Helen gazed down at the grass stains on the skirts of her gown, at the knee and the hem. 'Oh, it'll wash, I suppose,' she said vaguely. 'You're sure my brother is in bed?'

'Like all sensible folk.'

Helen understood the hint, and with an apology for having kept Bessie up so long, made her way to bed. Sleep, she knew, would be impossible. Instead she set herself to write to Sophie. She did not explain Miss Anderson's interference, but spoke of a misunderstanding, now resolved, and of Francis's and her wish, subject to Edward Lambert's approval, for an early marriage at the beginning of November. This would allow a week's marriage trip before the opening of the new legal session on the twelfth.

She could exclude her aunt's actions from a letter, but not from her thoughts. When at last she went to bed, mingled with her happiness was the struggle to understand her deceit.

Was it only selfishness, the fear of a sick old woman that she would lose her companion? Did she grudge her the love she herself had never known, or wanted? Or had she, sincerely, persuaded herself that she was acting in Helen's best interests in saving her from a fate such as had overtaken her adored sister?

It was impossible now to be certain what had influenced Miss Anderson, if indeed even she herself had ever known. In her joy, Helen felt no resentment. She dwelt instead on her aunt's kindness and generosity, and her final wish to make amends.

But as she at last drifted asleep, her thoughts were not of her aunt, but of a mouth moving urgently on hers, the lithe strong sweep of his back beneath her hands, the faint, pleasant smell of his clothes, his body, his breath, subtly exciting, the sudden realisation of the power she possessed over a man so self-contained, so urbane and, with her, so vulnerable. It would be a week before they met again; he was to leave on the Western Circuit early on Saturday morning. Already she longed to feel his arms about her again, and eagerly to offer her lips to him.

Despite her difficulty in falling asleep, Helen awoke at the first sounds of life in the household. She rang at once for her hot water. A long delay ensued before it was brought.

'The range was scarcely lit when you rang, Miss Lambert,' Bessie offered as reproachful excuse.

'I'm sorry, I didn't realise how early it was . . . is Mr Lambert up yet?'

'He hasn't rung, but I thought I heard him moving about his room as I came by.'

Helen thanked her, and began to wash. Dressed, she went out onto the landing. She listened outside her brother's door. Certainly he was awake and up; she could hear his steps within the room. She raised her hand to knock and then, smiling, lowered it, and hurried lightly down the stair and, more carefully, on down the uncarpeted stone flight to the kitchen.

'Bessie, is Jack's water ready? Good, I'll take it up for him. I have something to tell him.'

She waited, fidgeting with impatience, while Bessie filled the canister with boiling water. Refusing aid, she

336

carried it gingerly up the narrow stair. Light-hearted, she tapped on Jack's door and entered at once without waiting for a reply.

Jack was over by the window, his back to the door. At her entry he spun round, white-faced. He was in his shirt-sleeves, his collar open at the neck, and in his hand was a razor.

'What, shaving? You won't get very far without hot water, surely?' she said, laughing, and lifting the canister. She moved towards his washstand, and only then, meeting with no answering smile, did she begin to realise that something was wrong. She looked at him more closely, at the streaks of blood on the blade he carried, at the scratches on his neck, fresh and angry.

She put down the water. 'Jack?' She took a step towards him, hand outstretched. 'Give me the razor, Jack.'

His eyes flickered about the room, hunted and desperate. Suddenly the blade was at his throat, pressing against the skin. She dared not move, nor speak. Hours seemed to pass in that moment of frozen anguish. Then he flung the razor on the floor. Spinning, it skimmed over the polished boards surrounding the carpet, clattered against the skirting board, recoiled, and was still.

As she scrabbled to retrieve it, she heard his voice, savage in its self-disgust. 'A coward! Oh, God! I couldn't even do that right!'

She opened the door and put the razor out on the landing, hastily stuffing it under the carpet out of sight. When she turned back into the room Jack was lying on his bed, his face buried in the pillow, his fists, tight-clenched, pressed one on each side of his head. It was a curiously infantile posture, or at least the parody of a child's repose, and it moved her unbearably. Not knowing what to do, not daring to leave him, she sat by the bed, and stroked his hair timidly.

She waited, glad of the respite. The sun was falling across his pillow, catching his hair. As a boy he had been so fair. Now he had darkened almost to brown.

337

She had always suspected, without begrudging it, that he had been their mother's favourite, not indulged, but protected. Had she sensed in him even as a child the capacity for suffering which Helen, aghast, now saw?

At last, she felt some relaxation in his rigid attitude. She heard him sniff, and saw him furtively rub the back of his hand across his eyes. Silently, she put her handkerchief into his hand.

'Now, what is it?'

Low, muffled, his voice barely reached her. 'I can't tell you.'

'After what's happened? Jack, you must tell me! Take your time, but let me know everything. This can't go on, you must see that.'

There was a long silence. She wondered whether he had fallen asleep, exhausted by his violent emotion. She couldn't see, without moving, whether his eyes were closed. So she sat and waited, dreading by some single act of clumsiness to precipitate unimaginable catastrophe.

'I'm in trouble, Nell.' He still kept his face turned from her, but his voice was stronger.

'Money?'

'Yes, but that's not the real heart of it. I'm being blackmailed.'

She suddenly remembered his hurried departure from the drawingroom the night before, overlooked until now in all that had happened since. 'Donachie, was that the name?'

'Donoghue,' he said dully.

Donoghue. Suddenly she remembered the name, and Francis's encounter with the man. Her heart sank.

'And why is he able to blackmail you?' she asked, steadily. This was what had to be faced, the central truth.

'He got hold of some letters. He deals in them. Some men make a living by buying their masters' cast-off clothes from servants. Donoghue buys letters.'

'But whose?'

'A servant of the Grants must have taken them with him when he was dismissed. I suppose he knew where to dispose of them to advantage. Donoghue has been milking me dry ever since.'

He stopped. Did he hope she would not press him further? Did he think he had said enough to explain? But still she did not understand.

'So these were . . . what? Letters you had written to James Grant?'

'Yes.'

'And in these letters you referred to something which made you vulnerable to blackmail?'

'Yes.' It was scarcely more than a whisper, as though his mouth was dry with fear.

'A crime? Some indiscretion?' There was no answer. 'What did you tell James Grant?'

The silence was so profound that she heard the distant creak of the dining-room door. Bessie would be preparing the breakfast table, in that other world from which they were so remote. Then, slowly, defiantly, he answered.

'I told him that I loved him.'

Relief flooded Helen, sweeping away her fears; relief, that she was not to hear some tale of debt or debauchery, of violence, even, in the heat of a drunken quarrel.

'Why, Jack, is that all?' she exclaimed. 'Where's the harm in that? I thought you had done something wrong . . .' She faltered into silence. Money cannot be extorted for nothing. Men do not attempt suicide without some terrible cause. She resumed, more soberly, 'I'm sorry. I am very ignorant, I don't understand.'

'I loved him – I love him still – as a man loves a woman.'

'No!' The cry escaped her before she could gather her thoughts; she would have given worlds to recall it.

'I have disgusted you.'

'Don't expect too much of me, Jack. I will try to understand, but you must give me time.'

'You think I am corrupt? Defiled?'

'You are my brother. Nothing changes that.' Even as she spoke the words, she realised how true they were; whatever was to come, that was solid ground beneath her feet. 'Will you tell me about it?' she asked gently.

She thought he spoke with some reluctance. 'It began at school. I always noticed James, although we weren't in the same class, of course.'

'He is younger . . . two years, isn't it?'

'Yes. I would see him in the yard, and I was aware of him, that's all. I don't believe we ever spoke, but sometimes he would smile at me, shyly, as though he thought it might annoy me. I can't explain it, but a kind of consciousness grew up between us.'

'I think I can imagine,' she said softly.

'I liked to look at him, somehow, and after a while I would watch for him in the yard. If he weren't there – he was often absent – the day seemed to lose something. That was all. I don't think anyone else noticed anything. I was never ragged about it, anyway. I didn't even think about it very much. It didn't worry me, certainly. It was just as though we were secretly friends, without the need to speak a word.'

'What is he like?' she asked, as though it were the most natural topic in the world. He was speaking more easily now, more easily than for months, she suddenly realised. At last, he was completely himself again.

'He's small for his age, dark, like his mother – she's Italian. Perhaps it was some look of being foreign, different, which first drew my attention, I don't know now. He is slight in build, frail even. Something in him made me want to protect him. One winter, at play, a bigger boy in his class was trying to stuff ice down his collar; I served him the same way, and then helped James to clear the ice away. His bones were so close to the skin, so fragile . . .' There was a sense of wonder in his voice; she recognised it. It would have sounded in her own voice if she had been able to tell him of her love for Francis.

'And when you left the Academy?'

'James remained there, of course. For most of the first year at University I saw nothing of him. I didn't forget him, but I would never have sought him out either. If I thought of it at all, it was as some ideal bond, Nisus and Euryalus and so on . . . I suppose things would never have gone further, if I hadn't met old Moncrieff.'

'Moncrieff? Wasn't that one of the masters at the Academy?'

'He took the higher classes for mathematics. I met him quite by chance that Easter, on Princes Street. I had always rather liked him. I used to enjoy his classes, and always worked hard for him. We chatted for a while, and had actually said goodbye when he called me back, as an after-thought, to ask if I knew of anyone who might care to earn a small sum by coaching. It was a boy who had fallen behind through illness, and needed help to make up the lost ground in mathematics.

'I would have made some vague promise to bear it in mind, and have forgotten it within seconds, I suppose, if I hadn't asked him, largely for want of something to say, who the boy was.'

'James Grant.'

'I can remember Moncrieff's exact words. "Oh, you won't know him, Lambert. He missed the greater part of the winter term through an inflammation of the lungs. Grant, James Grant . . ." I didn't hesitate. I told him that I was low in funds, as it happened, and would take on the coaching myself, if he thought me equal to it. He seemed to think I would do as well as another, and gave me the Grants' address. He told me to mention his name, and said he would give Mr Grant a formal recommendation should he require one of me. Poor old Moncrieff! He was so pleased with his afternoon's work!'

'Oh, Jack! Didn't you realise the dangers of the situation?'

'No! Believe me, I didn't! I never imagined for a second that James returned my feelings – and after all, what had they amounted to? I had liked to see him, I had felt some

341

urge to protect him. I didn't think I was in any way different from others. I assumed, in a vague sort of way, that I would marry when I was in a position to support a family.'

'Had you never felt a fondness for any girl?' Helen asked, a little awkwardly.

'No.' He paused, and added, 'You won't remember, I don't suppose, towards the end of the summer term, not long before Rosemary's wedding, I dined with Robert Field and some of his set. After dinner – we were all pretty much the worse for drink by then – Field suggested ending the night in style, at a house of assignation. A brothel. He said he could recommend it. I'm sorry. It's not a fit subject for you to . . .'

'For Heaven's sake, Jack! Don't treat me as though I were feeble-minded!' she said, although her cheeks were aflame. 'How can I help if I don't understand? Go on, please.'

'Well then. Field took us down the Canongate. I wasn't reluctant. I didn't want to seem a muff and cry off, although some of the others did, to their credit. Besides, there was curiosity, and Field vouched for the girls, said there would be no risk of disease . . . I went along. Some girl took me up to her room. She was not unattractive, I suppose.'

'What happened?'

'Nothing. Nothing at all. I paid her anyway. She was very decent about it, said it was the drink, that it often affected men that way, I should come back sober the next time. I didn't tell Field, of course. I thought the girl was probably right, but it worried me, all the same.'

'And did you go back?'

'No. The whole thing sickened me, to be honest. The next time Field invited me I made some excuse. By then I knew that it hadn't only been the drink.'

'So you had started the coaching?'

'I went over to see Mr Grant the day after meeting Moncrieff. Moncrieff's name was good enough for him;

he rang for James to be called down. The look on his face when he came into the library and saw me with his father! He hadn't forgotten me; I had meant something to him. I walked over to him, and shook hands. I remember saying something absurd about believing that we should get on famously with our studies. And all the time, I could feel his hand trembling. His eyes never left my face, as though he couldn't believe that I was really there.

'At first we saw each other once a week. Then James asked his father if we could have a second lesson, as he felt he was benefiting so much.'

'And was it true – did he make progress?'

'Oh yes, we were most conscientious. It was weeks before we spoke of anything but calculus and the binomial theorem. I earned my money fairly, I promise. I looked forward to our lessons, quite unthinkingly at first. I enjoyed them, I liked visiting the house, I was happy to be asked to dine, to be accepted by the Grants as a welcome visitor.'

'But something changed?' Helen prompted, as he hesitated.

'Yes. There was nothing dramatic. I simply realised the truth. If there was any one moment of revelation, I suppose it was an evening at the end of the summer term, just before Rosemary's wedding. We were in the library as usual, sitting together at the table, his shoulder just touching my arm, very lightly. It would have needed the merest movement on my part, or his, to shift a fraction and break off the contact. With anyone else, I suppose the movement would have been automatic, it would have been natural to keep some distance between us. But with him, it was different. With him, it seemed natural to be touching. I'm not explaining very well, am I?'

'Just carry on, tell me everything,' she urged. What he was saying was so strange to her, so unexpected; and yet strangest of all, perhaps, was the degree to which she could enter into his feelings now.

'After that evening, I began to dream about him. I was

343

horrified, disgusted with myself. I wanted to get away, go where I was not known. I couldn't have stayed in Edinburgh and not have seen him, but I felt I couldn't trust myself any longer in his company.'

'Was that when you began to think of Canada? And I stopped you!'

'I hated you for it, and yet at heart I didn't want to go. I accepted it, in the end, almost with relief. Fate seemed to have made the decision for me. I took it as a sort of sign. It was stupid of me, of course. You can't really shirk your responsibilities like that.'

'There was that reading party,' she said, frowning as she tried to recall details which had never seemed significant before. 'You were away from Edinburgh for a while, weren't you?'

'Yes. I began to write to James, at his request. He said it would help him in his studies if he could report to me on his efforts.'

'That must have pleased you.'

'No! It was a torment. It made me loathe myself all the more, to think of the innocent friendship he was offering me, me, a beast, a monster . . .'

'Jack, don't! You mustn't!'

He looked up at her, quickly, shyly thanking her for her loyalty.

'Was there anything in the letters . . . ?'

'To incriminate me? No. They could have been read by anyone. I told him much what I would have told Philip or Andrew, descriptions of our walks and fishing, the weather, the food. I told him that I missed him and our lessons, nothing more than that.'

'And when the lesson resumed in the autumn? You seemed reconciled to staying then.'

'Things had changed, over the summer. James had worked hard during the vacation, to please me, although I didn't know that. In fact, he had made such progress that I really didn't feel able to teach him much more. I forced myself to be honest with him, and tell him that as far as I could see there was no need for any more lessons. He didn't reply. I looked at him more closely. His head was bowed, he seemed to be on the verge of tears. I didn't dare to speak. Finally I asked if he wanted our lessons to continue. He nodded. I didn't remain long after that, I came away half mad with joy and doubt.

'I wrote to him that night – looking back, I still don't know how I dared. Perhaps I knew in my heart how he would receive what I said.'

'You told him that . . . that you loved him?' she said, stumbling a little over the words.

'Loved him, and trusted him. I told him that if he wished not to see me again, he had only to give his father a letter which I enclosed, explaining that our lessons had reached such a point that further coaching was unnecessary. If he still chose to see me after my confession, I asked him to return to me the note to his father. The next day he brought it to me himself. His face told me everything.

'We walked together about the city all that afternoon, until he had to go back home for dinner. All the time we were talking, going back over all the stages we had passed through, each thinking himself alone. He had struggled against his feelings far less than I had, perhaps because I was older and felt more responsible. I saw him home, and went back to Drummond Place. I wrote to him again, telling him how happy I was. There was no one else to tell; I had to do something.'

'Oh, Jack! How could you be so foolish? Didn't you realise what a terrible risk you were running by writing such letters?'

'I asked him to burn them – I always assumed that he had.'

'So there were more?' she cried, dismayed. 'How many?'

'I don't know, exactly. When he went down to Torquay with his mother for the winter I wrote often, once a week at least. They weren't all dangerous. I knew how much

345

my letters meant to him – I honestly don't think he would have consented to spend the winter away but for that.'

'And these are the letters which Donoghue is now using against you?'

'Five or six of them, yes. As I said, he must have come by them from a servant in the Grants' household, a valet who was dismissed for some dishonesty. He hadn't been long gone before James realised what he had taken with him.'

'Did he tell you at once?'

'James? He didn't need to; I knew as soon as I saw him that something had happened. I was inclined to take the matter less seriously at first. I hoped that he might have lost them in all the confusion of his return from the south, and that they might turn up safely; and even if the valet had taken them, I thought it might have been a pure act of spite, and that he might have destroyed them, not knowing their significance, or not daring to use them. A week passed, then two. I had almost convinced James that there was no cause for alarm. Then, Donoghue came here.'

'I remember,' she said, with a shudder.

'I think he came here deliberately, to give me a taste of what exposure would mean.'

'You met him later, then?'

'On Calton Hill, as he appointed.'

'On Calton Hill,' she repeated dully. Again, the echo of Francis's story reached her, reinforcing her dread.

'He was very clever. He asked for only five pounds, and he did give me a letter in return, one of the least harmful. I tried not to show it, but he must have seen how frightened I was. I offered him twenty pounds for the lot, trying to appeal to his greed. It was a mistake. It proved how much harm they could do me. I should have refused to pay a penny, defied him to do his worst. Perhaps I might have dared to stand up to him if it had been only my name at risk, but James . . .'

'You soon heard from him again, no doubt?'

'Two weeks later. It was twenty pounds then. I told him to go to the Devil. He didn't argue, just said that in that case he would see if old Grant, as he called him, set much value on his son's good name. I paid; he gave me another letter. I was frantic, but at least there was an end in sight. I knew that he could only have six letters at the most, and already I had two of them back. The third cost me fifty pounds. That was when I had to start pawning my things.'

'Why didn't you tell me?' she cried impulsively, although the answer was all too obvious.

'It was after my third letter was redeemed that I really despaired. He must have realised that with every transaction his hold on me weakened. The next time he approached me there was no more talk of returning letters. Since June I've been paying thirty pounds a month simply for silence. If I default he threatens to send the three letters where they'll do most harm, to James's father, I suppose, or to the police, or the Dean. I don't know what he intends.'

'He might be bluffing, his own position is vulnerable. You could charge him with unlawful extortion, surely?'

'Oh, Nell, how can I?' He turned abruptly on the bed to face her for the first time, his face flushed, almost feverish, wretched, but open. She realised with mingled pride and helplessness that he was looking to her not only for sympathy, but for assistance.

'The threat alone might frighten him away,' she ventured. 'He has done well out of you, perhaps he would be satisfied . . .'

'And if he wasn't? Think, Nell! Our name would be a by-word. Think of the effect on Philip and the rest, and you, for the matter of it . . .'

'You needn't fear for me,' she said, but even as she spoke, the words were falsified by the realisation of what was at stake. She could vouch for herself, for her own loyalty to her brother. But Francis? Would he accept as

347

brother-in-law a man known to have written criminally immoral letters? She was silenced.

He looked at her sharply, as though he sensed her confusion. 'It's not a pleasant thought, is it?' he said bitterly. 'Look at Field. He boasts openly of the servant girls he has ruined. If he can't debauch a woman with drink or money, he'll deceive her with lies and promises, even force her if she remains obdurate. He's a libertine, without compunction or restraint. And will any of it be held against him when he comes to marry? Don't believe it for a moment! He's sowing his wild oats, that's all; a man isn't expected to live like a monk, is he? He's made a dozen decent girls wretched, reduced to prostitution, no doubt – no maidservant is safe near him – but do you think he'll ever undergo the fear that has tortured me this year? Have I inflicted a hundredth part of the suffering he metes out almost daily?'

No answer was possible. She put aside the thought of Francis, steeling herself to do what was necessary to help her brother, whatever it might prove to be.

'You know that Donoghue came here last night. He wanted forty pounds.'

'Was that what drove you to despair?' she asked, her eyes glancing in horrified fascination at the livid scratches on his neck.

'He's swallowed up everything, my allowance, my wages from Raeburn's, everything I could raise by selling or pawning, down to my very clothes, everything James could give me. Last night I realised that this would be my life for ever, living in fear, scraping about for money to buy off that parasite, that bloodsucker. I can't face a future like that, Nell,' he said, quite calmly.

'No,' she said, getting up, and moving over to the window, away from the consciousness of his eyes resting on her so trustingly. 'No, I can see that. Something has to be done. Things can't go on as they have.'

He waited, as though she were still the older sister who could intercede for him with their father to gain a treat or deprecate a punishment. 'I think we must seek advice, Jack,' she said reluctantly, fearing clamorous protest. To her surprise, he said nothing. Who were they to tell? That was the question.

Francis? He was a man with a legal training, an acute, competent mind; he was the man whom she was to marry, whom she should trust in all things. To whom was she to turn, if not to him?

She bit her lip, irresolute. He would already have left Edinburgh; it would be a week before his return. The thought came as a relief, not a disappointment.

'Papa?' she said doubtfully.

He laughed. 'He should understand, if anyone, I suppose. The Greeks rather favoured such friendships, didn't they? Or perhaps he didn't choose to enlarge on that particular aspect of Hellenic culture?'

'Oh, Jack, don't! Papa wouldn't be harsh, I'm sure.' As a new thought struck her, she crossed the room quickly towards him. 'Jack, he could help you to go to Canada, as you always wanted! You could make a fresh start there, be free . . .'

'And leave James to bear it all alone?' he cried angrily. 'It would kill him. The rheumatic fever affected his heart, you know. Do you think he could stand the persecution I've suffered over the past six months?'

'How is he bearing the ordeal?'

'That's the worst thing of all, Nell; I scarcely know. He is too afraid to see me. He sends me what money he can, that's all. Whatever happens, I don't suppose we can ever be what we were to each other. Ironic, don't you think?'

The front door bell pealed; Helen started in alarm, exchanging a panic-stricken glance with her brother, although she could scarcely have said what it was she feared.

'Early for a call, isn't it?' he said, with a show of insouciance which only emphasised the anxiety in his eyes.

'Barely nine . . . Jack! Of course! Doctor Cairns! He said last night that he would call today, though I can't think why he couldn't have said whatever was on his mind yesterday. You could tell him, surely? He can be trusted. Shall I ask him to come up?'

'Would you . . . would you tell him, Nell?' he murmured, as though ashamed of his request.

'Of course I will! Shall it be here, though?' she asked doubtfully. 'We could see him more comfortably in my sitting-room, don't you think?'

'Just as you like,' he replied, swinging his legs over the side of the bed, and sitting up. He fumbled with his collar, looking in alarm to the door, as Bessie's footsteps approached. Understanding, Helen hurried over to the door, shielding him from view as Bessie knocked and bustled in.

'Doctor Cairns, Miss Lambert.'

'Good . . . show him into my sitting-room, will you? Tell him we will be with him directly.'

When Helen turned from the door, Jack was already at the mirror, nervously adjusting his cravat, pulling his collar as high as he could.

'Don't worry about that,' she said, picking up his jacket and holding it out for him. 'He's coming up already; we mustn't keep him waiting.' She smoothed down his lapels for him. 'Will you give me your arm?' she asked lightly. And on his arm, she entered the sitting-room.

For all her preoccupation, Helen stopped in surprise at the sight of her visitor. 'Why, Doctor Cairns!' she exclaimed in near dismay, then, recovering herself, added, 'How very nice you look this morning!'

Certainly his appearance warranted surprise. In place of his usual baggy coat, nondescript and dusty, he wore a frockcoat of evident glossy newness, a rose at his buttonhole. The remainder of his costume was in keeping, well cut, still in the first uncreased sleekness of clothes fresh from the tailor. Nothing could conceal the heaviness of his figure, nor the stoop of his shoulders, but none the less there was something impressive even in that massive quality so closely linked in her mind with reliability, unchanging and predictable. She hardly liked even to see him in unfamiliar clothes.

'Not at the counting house this morning?' he asked, a little gruffly, nodding to Jack.

'Oh, Jack!' Until that moment Helen had not given a thought to his neglected duties.

'I'll make the time up.'

'I see.' He looked at Jack with an impatience which verged on hostility. 'Was there anything very particular?' he asked pointedly.

It was an uncharacteristic sally, and an unfortunate one. Helen felt Jack's arm beneath her hand stiffen.

'Yes, there was,' she said quickly, before her brother could pull away from her. 'Jack and I need your advice; you are the very person we wanted to see — it's quite providential that you should call just now.'

She spoke eagerly, with obvious warmth, yet a look of pain passed over his face as she spoke, as at some wounding blow. He glanced more searchingly at Jack, and shrugged.

'Shall we sit down?' he suggested, once more the kindly old family friend. 'Now, what's all this about?'

Slowly, often at a loss for words, trying to spare Jack and yet to tell the doctor everything that was significant, Helen put the case before him. He listened intently, interrupting only to clarify some point here and there.

One fact alone Helen sought to conceal: Jack's attempt at suicide. She had found him that morning in a state of despair, she said, and hoped that he would not seek to know more. In vain; he rose to his feet with an agility which belied his bulk, and strolled over to Jack. His stubby, sensitive fingers reached out, and delicately moved aside his high collar.

'I thought so,' he said, resuming his seat. 'So, Jack, what's to be done, eh? The most obvious course would be to leave Edinburgh. From the sound of it this blackguard

351

has had a good dividend on his investment. The chances are that he would let it go at that.'

There was a moment of agonised silence. 'No!' Jack burst out, his vehemence showing how tempting the suggestion was. 'I can't leave my friend to face what I've undergone. He isn't strong – it could kill him. It's out of the question.'

'You know best. Consult some legal man, then. Put the whole story before him; tell him as precisely as you can recall what was in the letters, down to the very wording . . . it's essential, believe me,' he added, not unkindly, as Jack made some angry movement of protest and humiliation. 'You need to know whether you are open to legal action. Is your friend a minor, for example?'

'Yes. He's two years younger than I am.'

'Then his father might put the matter in the hands of the law officers, I suppose, if the letters did come into his possession. Everything depends on the character of your friend's family . . . and your friend. Would he defend himself by blaming you? If he were under pressure, would he claim that you pestered him against his will with these attentions? As the older party you might be open to such an interpretation, I have to say. Do you think he might be induced to act against you?'

'I don't know. He . . . he might.'

And Helen knew, as surely as if he had told her, that he would understand and forgive even that betrayal.

'Francis Bethune could give you an opinion, although it would be irregular,' Doctor Cairns went on, glancing quickly to Helen, as though begging pardon for introducing his name. 'He's discreet, and a family connection of sorts. No one would know better than he whether any sort of prosecution could be mounted on what you wrote. If he judged it unlikely, as I suspect, then you could offer Donoghue a final payment in exchange for the remaining letters, and tell him to go to the Devil if he refuses.'

It was clearly a sensible suggestion, and one which

had already suggested itself to Helen. Now, as then, she rejected it. Because she did not want the man she was engaged to marry to learn of his future brother-in-law's disgrace? Because she feared to put him, as public accuser, into a position in which private interest would conflict with his duty? Both considerations had their influence, no doubt, but more insidious, more fraught with danger for the future, was the reluctance she felt to raise such a subject with him. To Doctor Cairns she had been able to speak, not indeed without embarrassment, but openly. But to Francis? His reserve summoned up her own. She loved him, wanted him, yet the distance with which he always surrounded himself had its effect. It was natural, she told herself hurriedly, as Jack gave his answer.

'No. It wouldn't do. I couldn't bear Bethune to know. Besides, I couldn't carry it off. Donoghue would be quite likely to send the letters to William Grant out of spite. It's no use, is it?'

Doctor Cairns bent forward a little in his chair, his fingers, interlaced, thoughtfully rubbing his chin. 'There is one other possibility,' he said, frowning.

Lizzie Crearie threw herself into the preparations for Tam's new venture with unusual enthusiasm. She and Tam visited warehouses, haberdashers, milliners, comparing qualities and prices, talking to any well-disposed shopman of the coming fashions, of what appealed to servant girls, and what to the country wives who would be his chief market. Gradually they laid in a store of goods, weighing each purchase gravely; Tam could not afford to carry dead stock.

When she heard the timid knock at her door that Saturday afternoon, Lizzie was engaged in making up papers of needles. They had bought a job lot at a dealer's in the Grassmarket; they would bring Tam a healthy profit, once she had sorted out any rejects, and divided the rest into tens.

'Carry on with it, May . . . mind, check them all, now!'

she said, hurrying over to the door. 'Why, Miss Lambert!' she exclaimed, in undisguised surprise. 'Come ben, come ben!' she added, more warmly than usual. She had seen Helen's expression. 'Sit down, miss . . . Here . . .' She pulled the chair nearer to the fire, and swung the kettle over the coals. 'Ye've caught us at our darg; we've all they needles to put in papers before the day's out.'

At the table May silently sorted out the needles, discarding one here and there, laying others in their papers, folding them with thin, nervous fingers. But whenever she could spare her attention her eyes strayed to their visitor's face, not in her habitual admiration, but in concern.

Lizzie made tea, busying herself in between times by proudly bringing out all the purchases made for Tam since Helen's last visit. As she displayed the magenta ribbons and blonde lace, the combs and buttons, patting, stroking, touching each item with proprietorial fondness, she appeared unaware of her guest's unusually muted response. Not until the last length of taffeta had been put away did she look up from her low stool and ask, 'Eh, Miss Lambert, is there anything ailing ye? Ye're no just yourself the day.'

Helen made no reply, but looked quickly over to where May sat at her work.

'Never worry, she'll no mind what ye say,' Lizzie said, in an undertone, as she followed the direction of her gaze. 'I'd send her out for messages, only it's so wet, and she's hoasting sore the now, with the nights coming in colder.'

'Oh, don't think of it!' Helen said in alarm. 'The truth is, Lizzie, I'm in very great trouble.'

'I'm fair sorry to hear it.'

'Yes.' Helen stopped again, seeming to find difficulty in raising her eyes from the glove in her lap at which her fingers were incessantly plucking. Pale, shamefaced, she seemed a mere wraith of her usual serene self.

'Is it Joseph, maybe?' Lizzie prompted, her thoughts naturally turning to her own greatest reason for distress:

money. 'If ye canna see your way, now it comes to it, and ye've need of the money, ye've only to say so. The bairn'll feel it, no doubt, but he'll . . .'

'No! It's nothing to do with Joseph. That's all in order, never fear.'

'Do ye find ye've no just the same time to spare, is that it? Dinna be shy, Miss Lambert. If ye canna come to see us now that ye've the house to manage for your brother, I ken what like it is . . .'

Helen looked up. 'It's Jack,' she said hesitantly. 'He is in a terrible situation.'

'Oh?'

'He's being threatened, some letters are being held over him. For months now money has been extorted from him. I only found out this morning when I came upon him trying to cut his throat.'

'Eh, miss!'

Helen said nothing more, and yet it was apparent from her manner that there still remained something unsaid, and that perhaps the worst of all. Lizzie got up to mend the fire. 'What will he do?'

'What can he do?'

Lizzie looked up quickly, catching some tone in Helen's voice, some peculiar emphasis. She carefully placed a last lump of coal on the fire, and wiped her fingers on her sacking apron.

'I dinna follow your meaning, Miss Lambert,' she said sternly.

Helen dropped her gaze once more. 'Nothing,' she whispered, 'I meant nothing.'

A taut silence. Lizzie waited, grimly. Suddenly, under the goad of desperation, Helen added the shameful truth. 'Your brother. He's the only one who can help Jack to recover his letters. I would pay any sum you care to mention . . .'

'Pay! Recover his letters!' Lizzie cried, mocking Helen's words, aping her accent, turning it into something false and affected. 'Steal them, ye mean? Why no cry it the right name? He's only a common thief, is he no? He'll do to save your brother's skin! If he's took up, what's the harm? It's only the Penitentiary . . . the likes of Tam will be none the worse of seven year behind bars, eh no?'

With every lashing word Helen's head sank lower. She put up her hands in their pretty, lavender kid gloves to hide her face.

'Ye come here, with your silk gown and your sovereigns, and ye smile, and act the friend, but when it comes to the bit, what then? Ye use us. Ye'd make Tam your cat's paw, as ye'd make him your scavenger, as your brothers would make me their skivvy or their whore. Who'll pay, if Tam gets lifted? Who'll stand in the court, afore the sneers of the lawyers? Will ye come and tell they sleekit advocates whose idea it was? No. Ye'll hold up your head, high as ever. There'll be none to point the finger at ye, will there? And my brother, who's set his hand to honest work at last, he's to pay for all, is that it? Oh, no, I'll no stand for that!'

'I'm sorry. Truly, Lizzie . . . please, don't . . . I shouldn't have asked.'

'Ye shouldna! Do ye think your sovereigns will buy ye anything ye need? They'll no buy ye my brother!'

'I was desperate. Jack's *my* brother.' Shamed, humiliated as she was, she at last faced Lizzie with essential dignity; it was for him that she had asked, not for herself. Face ablaze, anger staining her pale cheeks, Lizzie stared back at her, conscious of victory. For a second, perhaps, there was a gloating sweetness in the triumph, before the girl's sense of justice asserted itself.

'Ye're fighting for your own, the same as me,' she said. It was the offer of a truce, in its way.

'Could you not ask him for me if he knows anyone who might be able to help?'

'No. I ken him. He'd do it himself out of pure devilment. Yon was aye his way. But I tell ye, Miss Lambert, if he lets this chance pass him by, he'll no get another.'

Helen rose to her feet, humbled as never in her life before.

'Will you forget that I ever asked?'

'No. I canna forget, any more than I can ever forget all your kindness to me and Joseph.'

Defiant, inflexible, the stuff of martyrs, Lizzie saw her to the door. The last thing Helen saw was the timid sympathy in May's face as she sat at the table, forgotten.

20

Helen told Jack of the failure of her visit on her return, just before dinner. He said little. They sat together over an appetising meal, the linen spotless, an excellent wine in their glasses, Bessie, neat-handed and quick, attending to their every want, and neither of them could force down more than a mouthful or two, and that only for form's sake. But for the need to maintain some facade of normality before Bessie they would not even have spoken; compelling themselves to speak, they could not rise above stilted exchanges.

'By the bye, Nell,' Jack said, rousing himself as Bessie refilled his glass, 'you never told me, I don't believe, what it was you wanted to tell me this morning. Doctor Cairns's arrival seemed to put it out of your head.'

'This morning?' She actually had to think before she could recall the news which had kept her sleepless from sheer happiness. Now, like so much else, it seemed uncertain. 'It was of no real importance,' she murmured.

The bell rang; they exchanged a glance of frightened complicity, as Bessie rustled away to answer. She returned after an absence which seemed longer than usual.

'A person to see you, Miss Lambert. He wouldn't give his name. He had the impudence to say that you'd be glad to see him.' Despite her scornful manner, Helen suspected that the unknown's impudence had not been absolutely displeasing.

'Show him into the drawing-room, please. Jack, would you . . .'

'Of course.' He drained his glass, and rose.

They entered the drawing-room to find their visitor staring with apparent interest at a worked fire-screen.

'Are these things still all the go?' he asked, as Helen approached. 'I'll need to mind and put a few hanks of wool in my pack . . . Tam Crearie, I should have said. I didna give my name, ye never ken . . . and this'll be your brother? Pleased to meet ye, Mr Lambert.'

He, at least, seemed totally at his ease. Helen had scarcely the self-possession to gesture him to a chair.

'Can we offer you any refreshment?' Jack asked awkwardly.

'A dram, now? I'm no great hand at drinking, but I dinna see the harm in the odd nip.'

Jack murmured an apology and went in search of the whisky; further interruptions from Bessie were far from desirable.

'Ye'll be speering, "What's he doing here?" eh no?' Tam said, smiling.

'Yes, I am,' Helen replied, with equal frankness.

He laughed. 'Lizzie dished it hot and strong?'

'She was quite right.'

'Aye, so she was.'

'But she told you after all?'

'No, never a word.' He waited, to see if she could solve the puzzle. 'Our May.'

'Ah!'

'She was heart-sorry for ye, and so she tellt me.'

Jack re-entered, bearing a tray. He helped Tam Crearie to a generous measure of whisky, and took a glass himself. Tam raised his glass to him, and sipped the contents with evident pleasure.

Studying him, Helen could see the resemblance to Lizzie. Slight, narrow-faced, pale, he made an unremarkable figure such as could be seen on any street in Edinburgh. But what distinguished his face from his sister's, what would have marked him out from any knot of loafers at a close mouth, was the irrepressible good humour and optimism it expressed. It was impossible to believe that life would ever totally defeat Tam Crearie; clearly, Tam himself had no fears on the subject.

'Now, this wee job ye're needing done?' he asked, looking with mild interest from Helen to Jack. He might have been a gardener, she thought, come to discuss the laying of a lawn. The everyday normality of it was the most bizarre aspect of the whole day.

'Lizzie was quite correct to point out the terrible risk you would run,' she said, hardly daring to look at her brother. 'I . . . I don't believe it is right to put you in that position.'

'Our Lizzie aye sees the black side,' he remarked easily. 'Dinna fash, if it canna be done I'll tell ye so soon enough, but we'll give it a birl, eh?'

Helen made no further protest, uneasy though she felt.

'Now, Mr Lambert, if ye'd just tell me all ye ken about the de'il who's on your back?'

'His name's Donoghue.'

'Dark-headed, about my size, has a wee dog, a terrier?'

'Yes, he often has a dog with him, he calls it Dandie. You know him then?' Jack asked eagerly.

'Aye, he's the biggest whoremaster in the town, begging your pardon, miss. He's got a hizzie on our stair. We'll need to keep all our wits about us, to best Barney Donoghue.'

He sat back in his chair and sipped his whisky, seemingly oblivious to his surroundings. Now and then he threw out a question to Jack concerning his next meeting, its time and place, and how long such transactions generally lasted. To judge by his deepening frown, the answers were far from satisfactory.

'Aweel, it'll no be just so easy as I'd jaloused, but we'll see . . .' He set down his glass with a smart click and bent forward, his lean, alert face alive with excitement. 'I need to ken where he keeps the letters. When do you see him next?'

'Monday, on Calton Hill, nine at night.'

'And ye're to give him . . . ?'

'Forty pounds.'

Tam's eyes widened at the sum, but he made no comment on it. 'Dinna take a penny. Say ye'll give him no more until he gives ye proof that he still has the letters. Say ye dinna believe he has them, ye'll need to see at least a page, afore ye'll pay. Fix a time to meet him again, as soon as ye can. Do ye follow me?'

'Yes . . . but what good will it do?'

'I'll be at his back from Calton Hill, to see where he gangs. He'll most likely keep your letters in his house, but I'll need to be sure. If ye canna gar him fetch ye a page of them, I can do no more for ye. Can ye do it?'

'I'll try.'

'And dinna press him to give ye the page he brings, mind. If I lose him, it'll give me another chance, if he's to put it back.'

'And shall I give him the forty pounds then?'

'No. Give him twenty, and say ye canna find the rest afore Friday. Promise him what ye like for Friday, but no a day sooner.'

'Why?' Jack asked, his fingers tangling nervously in his whiskers. Helen could see how uneasy he was at being asked to stand up to his persecutor.

'Why? To give me time to provide myself with tools, ken, and look about,' Tam said, standing. 'It'll depend on where the letters are. I'll come over again Tuesday morning, as early as I can, if ye dinna mind, miss.'

'No, of course . . . if Jack's at his work you can leave instructions with me.'

'That's all we can do the now . . . thank ye for the dram.'

'Can I . . . do you need any money just now?' she said, with some embarrassment. 'Will you not be put to some expense?'

'I'll let ye ken,' he said, shrugging. 'I'll see ye the morn's night, Mr Lambert, though ye'll maybe no see me . . .' At the door he paused, and turned to Helen with the first signs of hesitation in his manner. 'Dinna come round to see Lizzie until all this is settled, miss. She'd ken ye were holding something back from her – Lizzie's awf'y sharp yon way. I'd never hear the last of it.'

Helen promised, knowing that he was right. She would make a wretched liar. She felt, yet again, relief that Francis was away. By his return the whole business should be over. If successfully, he need never know anything about it. And if not? She did not dare to pursue that thought.

Sunday was an agonising day for Helen; what Jack's sufferings must be, she could only surmise. They lunched at Drummond Place, Helen forcing herself to carry the chief burden of the conversation to cover Jack's strained silence. Susan Lambert glanced sharply at him more than once, but made no comment.

It was early evening when they returned to Northumberland Street. Helen had at least the resource of sewing – she was no strict Sabbatarian – but Jack seemed to find even reading beyond him.

'What will you do when all this is over?' she asked softly, pausing in her work.

'If Crearie gets me the letters, you mean? Get away, I think. I couldn't bear to stay in Edinburgh, and not able to see James.'

'Perhaps if the letters were recovered he might be happy to renew the friendship?'

'No. He's been too badly frightened, Nell. He'll never dare to see me again. I know him; I don't expect it. He shrinks from anything brutal or ugly, it's in his nature.' He shrugged, with a detachment which she knew was feigned. 'You can't pick and choose. He's got the weaknesses which go with his virtues. It was for his sensitivity that I loved him; how else could he feel, after all this?'

She didn't answer. Let him preserve the picture he had so loyally built up. Perhaps, after all, there was some truth in it.

'So you will go away? Canada?'

'I've scarcely dared to think so far ahead . . . I have

been giving satisfaction at Raeburn's, you know, despite everything.'

'The timber merchants?'

'Yes. I only took the position in desperation, as a temporary measure, but the firm is a good one, with go-ahead notions. Young William Raeburn has just been taken into partnership with his father. He's eager to open up a permanent bureau in St Petersburg – they import a good deal of Baltic timber, and young Raeburn wants to expand that side of things. He's talked to me once or twice about his plans, as we've walked up from Leith after the business closes. I think he'd be willing to give me a place in the new venture, a very junior one, of course, but I wouldn't object to that.'

'St Petersburg! Oh, Jack!'

'It would be something to occupy my thoughts, and it would get me away from this place – Edinburgh, I mean. I hate it. Hypocrisy, complacency, faces buttoned against every feeling but smugness . . . it's a city of Pharisees, Nell.'

'You would give up your studies, then?'

'Oh, yes,' he said carelessly. A year ago, she had used all her influence to prevent it. Now she was silent.

Sunday night seemed interminable, but the worst of the ordeal was still to come for them both. Monday evening demanded of Helen a passive courage; almost, she envied Jack his more active role. Now that matters had reached a crisis, he displayed a coolness of nerve which surprised her. He did not return until well past eleven. She hurried over to him as soon as he entered the sitting-room.

'Are you all right? Did everything go well?'

'Yes!' he cried, elated. 'I told him I wouldn't give him any more until I had absolute proof that he still had the letters. I asked why he hadn't returned any for so long, whether he really expected me to pay him for ever on his word alone. He didn't like it, of course, but I wouldn't move . . . in the end he told me he'd be back within the hour with evidence.'

'Did you see Tam Crearie?'

'No. I hope he knows his business, Nell.'

'And Donoghue brought you the letter?'

'A page from each of the remaining three. I said I was satisfied, and gave him twenty. That provoked another storm, of course. He was all for sending me back here to beg or steal the other twenty from you, but I begged for time. It's to be Friday, at eight o'clock.'

'On Calton Hill?'

'No. I don't know whether he's getting suspicious at my proving so refractory, but he fixed on the Tron this time.'

'I wonder if that will make any difference to Tam?' Helen asked, frowning. 'If Donoghue lives near the High Street, it wouldn't allow him very long, if he intends to make the attempt on Friday.'

'I didn't dare to object after pressing him so hard already.'

'It may not signify. Eight o'clock on Friday at the Tron; I'll tell Tam Crearie tomorrow.'

'Nell, where would I be without you?' he asked, half joking. She smiled, recognising the affection, but in her stomach was still a hard knot of anxiety. Their difficulties were far from over.

As she feared, Tam Crearie was dismayed at the news of Jack's arrangement.

'The Tron?' He pursed his lips doubtfully. 'Donoghue stays in the Lawnmarket, in a close up by Milne's Court. I followed him to his very door, on the top flat. The letters are in there, but I'll need time . . . it's only a step from there to the Tron. If he comes straight back, I'll no get more than fifteen minutes clear. It's no lang enough.'

'Could it not be done before Friday?'

'I'll need to get a key made, that takes time. I could maybe be ready sooner, but I couldna be sure how lang he'd be out, ken. I need an hour, no five minutes while he's away on a message. To let ye understand, it's no just a case of lifting anything to hand; I'll maybe need to check the bed, the floor, the wall, the lum, the window.'

'What if he's left his dog?' Helen asked, her spirits sinking at the new difficulty.

He winked. 'A bitch in heat, miss.'

'What? Oh, I see . . .' she said, somewhat taken aback. 'I'm afraid the problem of the meeting place remains, though. Jack has no means of contacting Donoghue to change it. It has to be the Tron.'

'Could he no keep Donoghue back? Get him to a dramshop?'

'He could try, but Donoghue might find it suspicious. My brother told me last night that he thought that was why he fixed on the Tron this time.'

'He's nobody's fool,' Tam agreed. 'I dinna ken the boy myself, but ye hear the crack . . . he's the very de'il with the lassies.'

'He seemed to fancy himself rather a lady-killer, certainly.'

'Ye've met him?'

'Oh yes. He came here once, when Jack was out. I didn't realise what his business was, of course.' She stopped, seeing his expression change. 'What is it?'

'That depends.'

'Upon what?'

'On yourself, Miss Lambert.'

'Me? If it's money, you know that I won't quarrel with any expense you find necessary; you have only to tell . . .'

'No, no, money's no use here.'

'Then what? Tell me plainly, please,' she said, some undefined fear giving a touch of hauteur to her manner.

'Entertain Donoghue here, then,' he said boldly. 'Your brother tells him at the Tron that ye're aye asking after him, speering for him to bring him to the house again . . . I ken, it'd no be what ye'd chose, a lady such as yoursel . . .'

'I couldn't! It's impossible! I couldn't even address a civil word to the monster!'

He shrugged. 'It's all down to your brother, then. He'll need to hold Donoghue back what way he can. Tell him I'll be glad of every second. I'll maybe be lucky and find the letters straight off, or maybe Donoghue'll take a dander and no be back for hours.'

'But if he does come straight back, and catches you?'

He pulled a face, and was silent.

She turned abruptly, and busied herself with making some minute adjustment to the folds of the curtains, scarcely knowing what she was doing.

'He would never believe that I could wish to see him again. It's months ago . . . he was here for only a few minutes. I disliked him, he must have realised as much.'

'He fancies himself, miss, ye saw that. A boy like that expects women to hing after him. He'd believe it.'

Her fingers plucked at the thick velvet. She forced herself to speak. 'I'll tell Jack to invite him here from the Tron,' she said heavily. 'I can't allow you to run any risk which might be avoided. If my brother can induce him to come back with him, I'll detain him for as long as I can.'

'Ah! We'll do it yet!' he exclaimed. She wondered wryly whether he had ever really doubted her co-operation.

'It'll maybe no come to that,' he went on, reassuring her now that he had her promise. 'If I can, I'll get in afore Friday. If no, if ye dinna hear from me . . .'

'You can rely on me,' she said, with a proud tilt of her chin. There was little more to be done. She gave him the sum he requested, to provide himself with the means of having a key made, she supposed. She did not ask for details. They agreed that, if there seemed any likelihood of detection, he would destroy the letters as best he could, but that otherwise he would bring them to Jack intact. She sensed that actually to see them safe would help Jack to accept that he was free at last.

At the door, Tam Crearie paused. 'Dinna fash, miss.

Your brother will be with ye. It'll be no more than a wee blether and a smiling face. It's no for lang.'

She murmured her agreement and he left her. And when she had closed the door, she leaned against it a long moment in silent horror, praying that she would see him again before Friday, triumphant, and be spared.

But no word came from Tam. Even on Friday, she hoped desperately that he might find means to achieve his purpose without her aid, but the day passed with no news.

She and Jack made a pitiful pretence of dining. Helen could not eat, but she took a glass or two of wine. It might lend her a gaiety she was far from feeling. At last, reluctantly, Jack rose to keep his appointment.

'He might not come, you know,' he said, with a clumsy attempt at comfort.

'Do your best to persuade him. Tell him . . . tell him that I have never forgotten him, that I have often spoken of him as personable . . . and gentlemanlike, if you think he'd swallow that.'

'Oh, very probably. He has an excellent conceit of himself, certainly.'

'Say that no other friend of yours has ever been so noticed by me – say anything, but bring him here.'

Jack left. She went up to her room. There was no point in half-measures. She examined her gowns. Which was best suited to the part she was preparing to play? She was not long in making her choice: a low-bodiced evening gown in bright sea-green silk. She had worn it once or twice at large gatherings. To display so much of her shoulders and bust at a ball, a formal dinner, had cost her never a qualm; now, seeing her flesh rising, unprotected, from the shimmering fabric of the corsage, her hands rose instinctively to her throat, to shield herself. Almost, she resumed the sober, high-necked merino she had put aside.

But there was no time for further changes. Even as she hesitated, a cab drew up before the house. She snatched up a shawl, and flinging it about her naked shoulders, hurried to the drawing-room. It was barely twenty minutes past eight. Tam Crearie needed at least an hour. Come what might, she would ensure that he was given it.

She positioned herself by the hearth, forcing herself to release her tight grip on the shawl so that it fell a little open. Footsteps drew closer. As the door opened, she composed her features into a smile.

'Jack, what a pleasant surprise!' she exclaimed, moving forward. 'You should have warned me that you would bring your friend home! It's Mr Donoghue, isn't it?' she added, offering him her hand. 'You were shy the last time you visited us, and wouldn't leave your name, but I learned it from my brother . . . I have urged him to invite his friends to dinner so often you can't conceive, but I think he's determined to keep them all to himself, aren't you, Jack?' she said, squeezing his arm, as though in play. The contact gave her courage, steadied her.

'I'm sure I'm pleased to meet you again, Miss Lambert,' Donoghue said, his gaze flickering down to her half-exposed breasts. 'You're quite a sight for sore eyes, as they say.'

Jack took a sudden step towards them, angry disgust plain in his face. She glanced at him, warning him of what he must know only too well, the need for restraint. He recovered himself. 'Take a seat, Donoghue. Do you want a drink?'

Helen deliberately seated herself on a long couch. As she had expected, Donoghue joined her. He whistled his little pepper-and-salt terrier to him, and bent to pat its rough fur.

'You don't mind Dandie, I don't suppose? He's quite used to ladies' boudoirs, eh, Dandie?'

She heard Jack's sharp intake of breath and said hurriedly, 'Oh, I have no objection to dogs. He's a delightful little animal.'

'You can trust a dog where you can't trust a friend,'

he said, and turned insolently to Jack. 'I'll take a whisky, Lambert.'

Jack went over to the chiffonier, where Helen had taken care that glasses and decanters were standing ready. Only now, hearing how he addressed her brother, did she realise how confident Donoghue must be of the mastery he exerted over him. He seemed to exult in his own brutality to his victim; Helen marvelled that Jack had borne it so long. As he handed his tormentor a glass, she stole a glance at the clock. Barely five minutes had passed since she first entered the room.

'Would your little dog like a drink?' she asked. 'Shall I ring for milk for him, or water?'

'Oh, don't put your woman to the trouble,' he replied, glancing at Jack with careless contempt. 'Lambert, just go down and fetch my dog a saucer of milk, will you?'

She saw Jack hesitate, looking to her, unwilling to leave them alone.

'If you wouldn't mind, Jack,' she said steadily. He nodded, and went quickly about his errand.

'How fond Jack is of you, Mr Donoghue,' she said, smiling at him. 'You have the most wonderful ascendancy over him, I can see so much.'

'Few men care to defy me, Miss Lambert, and still fewer women.' He leaned carelessly back in his seat, his eyes straying with undisguised interest over her throat and bust. She twitched the shawl closer over her bosom. So long as she could keep him idling by her side, she had no intention of compromising her modesty if it could be avoided.

'What is your profession, Mr Donoghue?' she asked innocently. 'Are you a student, such as my brother?'

He laughed, accepting the flattering assumption at face value. 'A student? A whey-faced, out-at-elbow, half-starved student?'

'Well, not many students dress so well as you do, I should have realised as much. What a beautiful tie-pin that is!'

'Diamond,' he answered complacently. 'The gift of a fair friend of mine.'

'Oh? But I'm sure you're too discreet to say more. No doubt you have many fair friends?'

'You wouldn't be wrong there,' he said, lounging back now, thumb stuck in his waistcoat pocket, his chest thrust out as though to show off his rich waistcoat, his heavy gold watch-chain and dangling seals. Everything was of the very best, but worn with a self-conscious striving for effect which made them look tawdry.

'Oh, Lambert, back already?' he said irritably, as Jack entered with a bowl. 'Couldn't you have had the sense to keep out of the way? Two's company, three's none.'

Crimson with anger and humiliation, Jack stood before him. 'Put the milk down there.' He obeyed.

'What a nice little creature, isn't he, Jack?' she said, fearful of some outburst. 'We must set up a dog. Can you recommend the breed, Mr Donoghue?'

'Oh, a terrier's a loyal little beggar. I always have a dog. They're a grand excuse for being where you've no business to be. A man walking his dog, what could be more innocent?'

'Oh, Mr Donoghue, I'm sure you would never put yourself in such a position – of being where you shouldn't, I mean.'

'You'd be surprised. Wee Dandie has been worth his weight in gold before now.' He picked up the empty dish, which the dog was pushing about the carpet, snuffling noisily, as it attempted to clear it of the last drops of milk. 'Here, Lambert. Take this down, and don't hurry back. We're getting on famously without you, ain't we?'

She dared not answer, but managed a nervous smile. As her brother turned reluctantly to the door, she felt a surge of panic at the prospect of another *tête-à-tête*. 'Jack!' she called desperately, looking for any pretext for keeping him in the room even a few more seconds, 'won't you refill your friend's glass?'

Donoghue put his hand over his glass. 'No, thank you.

I always keep my head clear, whatever I'm about. That's how I've got where I am today, a clear, cool head. Many a man has missed his place in life for the want of it.'

Jack had no choice but to leave, but she noted with some relief that he had not closed the door. Unfortunately, it did not escape her companion's eyes either. He rose, with a suppressed mutter of annoyance, and pushed it sharply to. Even worse, when he resumed his seat, it was perceptibly closer to her. Her heart began to thump in real alarm.

'You still haven't told me what your profession is?' she ventured.

'My profession?' His chin sank forward into the carefully ordered folds of his neck-tie, as he considered the question. 'Let me see now. You could say that I have more than one iron in the fire. In general though, I deal in the pleasures of life, as some men deal in the necessities, such as corn and potatoes.' He looked at her, as though calculating the depths of her gullibility, and the ease with which she could be duped.

'The pleasures of life? A wine merchant? Do you have investment in a theatre, or some other place of amusement?'

'You could say so. Place of amusement describes it pretty well. I'm a capitalist, let's say. I invest in going concerns wherever I find them.'

'And is that how you know my brother?'

'No,' he said contemptuously. 'Your brother's pleasures are quite a different question. I told you, I've got more than one iron in the fire. We have a shared interest. It benefits us both.'

'You are prospering, at any rate,' she said, almost at random. She had caught the welcome sound of Jack's steps drawing close, the same sound which brought a scowl to Donoghue's thin, dark face, as Jack re-entered the room.

'Will you take some tea, Mr Donoghue?' she asked, almost light-headed with relief. 'My brother and I often have a little supper at about this time. You would be most welcome to join us.'

'No, no,' he said impatiently, looking at the clock. Barely twenty-five minutes to nine. He was surely not planning to go? Desperately, she laid her hand on his.

'Must you rush away? And I have been looking forward for so long to renewing our acquaintance . . .'

He hesitated, and sat back. She kept her hand on his for another second, negligently, as though she had forgotten where it lay. As she moved it away, she allowed her shawl to fall open a fraction. She loathed herself for it.

'Are you a married man, Mr Donoghue?' she asked.

'No, not such a fool.'

'How very ungallant!' she cried, with an affectation of coyness. 'You must have broken many a poor girl's heart, I'm sure.'

'If they play with fire . . .' he said, shrugging.

'Oh, but fire is so very tempting, is it not? Who can resist stretching out their hands to a warm blaze? I never can, for one!'

'Nor you neither, Lambert?' he replied, with his customary sneer. 'You've been burned pretty bad in your time, eh? A burnt child dreads the fire, they say. I meant to ask you, by the bye, do you still see our young friend? What was his name . . . you must know who I mean . . . the pretty boy?'

'Grant.' It was barely audible. Jack's misery might have moved a stone to pity; it seemed to rouse Donoghue to fresh cruelty.

'And are you still in favour? Or has he found another friend, a very particular friend, that is?'

Jack had poured himself a glass of brandy at the chiffonier. He held the glass close to his chest, in both hands. 'My coaching of James Grant is at an end,' he muttered.

'Oh! He's passed beyond your teaching, has he? You'll need to look out for another pupil. Old Grant would give you a corker of a character, if he realised all that your lessons covered.'

To see her brother so humiliated and to make no protest made Helen feel almost an accomplice; she felt defiled. Twenty to nine. Another twenty minutes of torture; she had long since abandoned any hopes of detaining him past nine.

'You aren't Scottish, I don't believe?' she put in, trying to start a new subject and deflect the conversation from her brother. 'I can't quite distinguish your accent. Irish, perhaps?'

'I left Ireland at an early age. My family fled in the Great Hunger. We got to Liverpool, and the typhus struck. I was the only one to escape. We might as well have starved at home.'

'But you survived.'

'By scrabbling for dirty bread, by lying and cheating, and working and never letting the chance of earning a penny slip by me. I dragged myself out of the stink and filth of a Liverpool cellar. Believe me, if I'd been nice about how I got my money, I'd have died there with the rest.'

He looked about him, at the light, high-ceilinged room, the rich drapes, the marble fireplace and elaborate cornice. In his sharp, hard face she saw hatred, and triumph, and an insatiable hunger.

'Lambert,' he said, savouring his power, 'get out, will you? Go for a walk. Don't come back for an hour or so. And you can mend the fire before you go, and tell your woman we'll not want to be disturbed.'

'No!'

'What did you say, Lambert?'

'I said no! You can't expect to stay here alone with my sister. It's . . . it's quite improper!'

'Improper, is it? Well now, you should know all about that, at any rate.' The sneer was intended for Jack's benefit alone, as a threat. At least his confession robbed it of much of its venom, but still she feared for what might be his next attack on his victim.

'Jack, I am quite happy to entertain your friend for a

while if you wish to go out. It's only a quarter to nine,' she added, with a warning emphasis.

Jack lingered as long as he dared over the task of raking and replenishing the fire, but all too soon it was done. As the door closed behind him, she began to regret her courage, or her folly.

'Good riddance, eh?' he said, and to her horror stretched out his arm along the back of the couch, so that his hand just rested on her shoulder. She felt his fingers brush aside the shawl, as though they were acting quite independently. She shifted her position, out of his reach, but made no reference to his boldness.

'Your early days must have been extremely unhappy . . .' she began, trying to guide the conversation to a safe topic.

'So they were, but what of it?' he said impatiently. 'They taught me one thing, to look out for myself. I get pleasure wherever I can, and money too, and I don't much care how.'

Again, she felt his hand on her shoulder, but this time his grip was determined.

'Mr Donoghue, you're forgetting yourself,' she said, still trying to maintain some lightness in her tone.

'No, I'm not. Why beat about the bush? You're a fine-looking woman. Lady or not, you're all the same under the skirts. Do you think I don't know why you sent Lambert away when he would have stayed? I don't mind giving you what you want . . . why waste any more time?' Even as he spoke, he made a lunge towards her along the couch, trapping her in a corner. She was unable to move; he was sitting on her spreading skirts. As one hand encircled her shoulder, the other dragged aside her shawl, and grabbed her breast.

'How dare you! Leave me alone! You must be out of your mind!'

'You'll be singing a different tune in a minute, Miss Prim!' he muttered, pulling at her bodice, using the weight

374

of his body to pin her immobile. Sweet, cloying, the smell of his hair oil rose in her nostrils.

She no longer gave a thought to the clock, to Tam Crearie or her brother: they must take their chance. With all her strength she began to fight him off, pulling at his slick hair, wriggling away from the hateful weight of him crushing her, fending him off with blows and kicks.

Some of her efforts must have struck home, but he was not deterred; if anything, he became rougher. As he wrenched once more at her gown, she heard the silk giving way; with a grunt of satisfaction, he tore down her linen, exposing the whole of her left breast.

'You've put up your struggle, now you may as well give over,' he said, his voice thick and blurred. 'You won't stop me, and it'll be worse for you.' He squeezed, pressed her flesh, weighing her full breast in her hand as though estimating its value. His arm left her shoulders as he shifted his position, but only to pull her skirt up above her knees.

Sobbing with rage and terror, scarcely able to believe what he was doing, she redoubled her struggles. He did remove his hand from her breast, but her triumph was brief; instead, he began to fumble with his own clothing. In utter panic, she rained blows upon his lowered head, wriggling frantically to free herself. With the strength of sheer desperation she managed to roll off the couch, falling clumsily onto the floor, unable to rise, for her skirts were still caught. His little dog, excited by the stir, skirmished about her, yapping and prancing.

'You damned bitch!' he hissed, and threw himself down on top of her. And at that moment, the bell rang.

For a second, they froze.

'Get off me.'

He hesitated, and obeyed, hurriedly readjusting his clothing. She stumbled to her feet, gathered her ripped bodice about her breast as well as she could, and snatched up her shawl.

'Go away, and never come back.'

He rapidly smoothed down his hair, glancing in the mantel-glass. 'It'll be Lambert. I'll soon get rid of him.'

'Jack has his key. Bessie will be here directly to announce the visitor. If you don't go I will tell her to send for the police.'

She managed to maintain her composure until he had left, his little dog trotting at his heels. Then, as though that effort had used the last ounce of her strength, she tottered to the nearest chair, her legs as weak as though she had just risen from a sickbed. Even now she did not truly believe that her ordeal was over. Despite what she had told Donoghue, she assumed that it was in fact Jack who had rung, that meeting him, her tormentor might return. Hearing rapid steps mounting the stair, assuredly not Bessie's, she looked fearfully at the clock. It was just before nine. She turned her frightened gaze to the door, as it burst open, to admit Francis Bethune.

'Helen!' He almost ran across to her, his face glowing. She had never seen him so lover-like, so boyish. She clutched nervously at her shawl, as he stooped over her, looking for a kiss.

She had longed for the moment of their reunion, but now she turned away her face, presenting only her cheek to him. She was possessed by the fear that the taint of the other man's hair oil would cling to her. She felt polluted, she wanted to wash her skin, her hair, to burn the gown he had pawed and defiled. Holding her shawl with one hand, she gave him the other, still trembling uncontrollably.

'I've distressed you,' he said, kissing her hand, and holding it against his cheek, a little, loving gesture which brought the ready tears to her eyes. 'I was thoughtless, forgive me. I came straight from the station – I got away early. I couldn't stay away from you a minute longer.'

'I . . .I thought it would be tomorrow.'

'We got through the cases quickly, thank Heavens. I don't know how I've conducted them, to be honest. You've been in my thoughts night and day . . . oh, Helen!' Clumsily, laughing at the awkwardness of his

376

posture, he knelt before her, and gathered her in his arms. She longed to cling to him for comfort, but the fear that in doing so she might release her shawl kept her stiff and unyielding.

'What is it, my love?' he asked, his breath warm on her ear.

'I . . . I'm so happy to see you . . . I've missed you so much,' she whispered, her throat aching with urgent, unshed tears.

'There . . . it was selfish of me to come unexpectedly.'

'No, no!' she sobbed, crying helplessly against his shoulder.

'You are glad, then?' he asked, gently putting back a stray wisp of hair which hung down on her neck.

'Yes . . . I'm sorry . . . I'll be better soon, now you're here.'

He said no more, seeming content to hold her in their awkward embrace, his lips just touching her skin, so lightly that she scarcely felt it. Suddenly, he drew away from her.

'That will be your brother, no doubt?' he said, rising.

Her head muffled against his shoulder, she had heard nothing, but the thunder of steps, apparently mounting the stairs two at a time, announced that he was right.

'Nell! It's all right! I've got them! I met Tam –' He was calling out his news almost before he had well opened the door; seeing Francis Bethune, he stopped abruptly. 'I'm sorry . . . I didn't realise . . .' He hovered, a little way into the room, as though uncertain whether to advance or retreat.

Quite suddenly, it was all too much for her. She rose unsteadily to her feet. 'I'm sorry, I'm not myself tonight, you must excuse me . . .' and lowering her head to conceal her tears she ran from the room.

The next morning, Jack came to see her while she was still in bed. The change in him was total. He seemed like a man cured of an insidious disease which had for months been sapping his strength, destroying all joy, all colour in life. Seeing him, she could not believe that the terrible price she had paid for his redemption had been too high.

He seated himself on her bed. 'How are you today, Nell?'

'I shall be quite well now. I needed a little rest, that's all.'

'Was Donoghue a beast, after I left?'

'Yes.'

'He didn't . . . he didn't hurt you?'

'No, but I'm glad that Francis came when he did . . . I don't like to think of it.'

'Francis?'

She turned her head away, feeling her cheeks burn.

'Nell?'

'Oh, you may as well be the first to know . . .' she murmured.

'Nell! How long have you known?'

'Last Friday.'

'That was what you came to tell me, wasn't it? And all week you've never given a sign – you've thought only of my concerns! Oh, Nell!'

'Don't think of it now; wish me joy, that's all.'

'With all my heart! I had no idea . . . Bethune has never called here before, surely?'

'Not since before Aunt Jeannie died.'

'A quarrel?'

'A misunderstanding.' She hesitated, longing to hear him praise the man she loved, yet dreading his coolness. 'You spoke to Francis last night?'

'A little. He . . . he seems a decent sort.'

'It takes some time to know him,' she put in quickly.

'Yes . . .' he murmured, as though doubtful. 'He doesn't deserve you, Nell, that's certain.' He stood, and suddenly stooped to kiss her. 'I can't ever repay you, you know that. When I think of the last months . . . I can't believe it's all over, thanks to you . . .'

'Not another word!' she cried. 'It's all in the past; Donoghue can't hurt us now.'

He smiled, and left her to dress. But when she saw the green silk, lying crumpled in a heap as she had flung it the night before, and marked the ugly tear in its bodice, she felt a chilling shadow on her contentment. Handling it with loathing, as though it were contaminated with the plague, she rolled it roughly into a bundle, and thrust it into the wall-press. It was a beautiful gown, of costly fabric, but she would see to it that it was burned. With it, she hoped, the last traces of the whole painful business would be destroyed. And Francis Bethune need never know anything of it. If a dissentient voice murmured unease, she easily stifled it. After all, she told herself, what he didn't know could not possibly hurt him, could it?

21

Helen's wedding day was fixed at the very beginning of November, some six weeks ahead. It barely left time for the preparation of the trousseau, but they would at least have time for a wedding trip of a week, before the Court of Session resumed on the twelfth. The alternative would have been to wait until the brief interval at Christmas, or until March.

Under normal circumstances, one of the later dates might have been preferable. But Jack was to leave Edinburgh even sooner. Raeburn's had decided to proceed with the opening of the foreign branch in St Petersburg; Jack and William Raeburn were to leave Scotland midway through October, in order to reach Russia before the worst of the winter set in. Edward Lambert made no protest; it was, Helen saw, a relief to him to have another child settled, as he began his second family.

Jack's departure at least simplified her own decision. She had no desire to remain alone in Northumberland Street, and even less to return to Drummond Place.

To prepare her own things in time was difficult enough, but much of the arrangements for Jack's move also fell on her. In some ways she was glad to be kept so incessantly occupied. Of necessity, her visits to the Crearies were during these weeks less frequent than before, and briefer. Lizzie had never discovered her brother's involvement in the recovery of Jack's letters. Neither she nor Helen ever reverted to the subject again.

Her manner to Helen, when she resumed her visits to Paisley Close, was rather gentler than before. In rejecting Helen's request she seemed to have discharged some long accumulation of resentment. She made no protest when Helen asked to be allowed to present May with a canary and cage, as a companion during the winter months to come, when she would be all but imprisoned in their room.

As winter approached Lizzie was growing restless. Tam, his pack filled to bursting, had launched himself on his hopeful new career; Joseph began his new school in October, amid the teasing of his former companions at the Industrial School. He bore it with good nature; he was too well liked for there to be any real malice in the baiting.

Occasionally, the mother of one of his former school companions would remark to Lizzie on Joseph's altered future, with few signs of envy. The Industrial School offered solid benefits: three substantial meals a day, training as tailors, shoemakers, boxmakers, carpenters. Some mothers, indeed, seemed almost to pity Lizzie at the prospect of Joseph's lengthy dependence. She herself was far from certain that she would sooner see Joseph a doctor than a well-doing tradesman, but Joseph himself had no doubts. He took to his new schooling with enthusiasm. He seemed to have a natural craving for knowledge, a joy in learning. Lizzie could only wonder at it, and acquiesce.

As usual, May's health was worsening with the colder weather. Each year, Lizzie hoped that she might have outgrown her weakness, but each winter saw the same cough, the same exhaustion. Now, her condition, having improved over the summer, seemed to be more alarming than ever. At night she would often awake drenched in sweat, and an ominous new symptom had developed: she had begun to cough blood.

It was this which spurred Lizzie into action. She got Joseph to write to their father, dictating to him, during May's brief absence from the room, a forceful account of the girl's illness and her own fears. She clung with an increasingly desperate tenacity to the belief that May's health would improve away from the smoke and dirt of the Old Town. And although she did not say it to Joseph, she had never forgotten Doctor Cairns's warning of the dangers of overcrowding in such cases.

Her father replied, vague as ever. The railway line was almost complete, his plans were uncertain, it would be folly to move the family from where it was so well settled, and at the beginning of winter. She could almost have written the letter for him. As always, he was quite content to support his family, at a distance.

Helen saw Francis Bethune almost daily, although rarely alone. They were frequently asked to dine together at Drummond Place, or at Rosemary's. Harry, it seemed, could not do enough to compensate for his former brusqueness. As the engagement became widely known, Helen was usually included in dinner parties in Francis Bethune's circle.

They were often together in a wider group, therefore, but he seemed to avoid calling on her when she was likely to be alone, particularly after Jack's departure. Her unchaperoned liberty put her in a paradoxical position; she suspected that, had she been still living at home, she would have been discreetly allowed far more solitary interviews with him than he, with scrupulous delicacy, sought of her.

At first, while the memory of Donoghue's violence was still fresh in her mind, she was glad of his restraint, to which she suspected her distressed reception of him that night had contributed. But as the marriage approached, she found herself awaiting ever more eagerly the few moments of intimacy which they tacitly allowed themselves, the brief farewell kisses in the draughty passage, the silent, self-conscious embraces which left her restless and unsettled.

The discovery of her pleasure in such contacts was nothing less than a revelation to her. The sensual delight she found in their kisses, their caresses, was unexpected, almost alarming. She sensed that, for her, physical love would be, not an ordeal, but a glory.

Amidst all the bustle of her preparations, and the half-conscious discoveries of her own sensuality, she was happy as never before. Only two things marred her pleasure.

The first was the report that a man had been hanging about the street, and had engaged the kitchenmaid in conversation, showing particular curiosity on the subject of her mistress's forthcoming wedding. The girl, who was far from quick, had spoken readily, and thought no more of it. When she happened to mention the incident to Bessie, however, Helen was at once told of it, Bessie having imbibed from long years with Miss Anderson a proper dread of strange men trying to insinuate their way into a household, with Heaven knew what of burglary or mischief in their minds.

Helen received the news calmly, reassuring Bessie, and dismissing the stranger as no doubt a tradesman's tout, trying to whip up business by ingratiating himself with the servants' hall. But secretly, the trifling affair left her with a vague unease. His questions, it seemed, had centred about the date of her wedding, the name and address of her future husband. Neither were in any sense secret, and yet such enquiries disturbed her, particularly from a man whom Phemie declared to be good-looking and well-dressed, with a little dog at his heels.

The second cloud on her happiness was just as unexpected; Doctor Cairns appeared to have broken off their longstanding friendship. There had been no quarrel, but on telling him of her projected marriage, she had met with not a word of congratulation. She had prefaced her announcement with the news of Jack's escape from his long ordeal; the pleasure which still lingered on his face was not redoubled, as she had expected. Instead, it slowly faded, leaving him heavy, tired, old.

'Well?' she said at last, when the silence grew oppressive. 'I didn't expect my news to be so surprising that it would take away the power of speech!'

Still he held aloof, not relaxing into their old teasing. 'It is, as you said, a surprise. Now, if you will excuse me, I only called to ask after Jack's concerns. Tell him to be more cautious for the future, will you?'

His coldness wounded her, as did his subsequent failure to call. She assumed that he might be unusually busy, although never in the past had so long elapsed between his visits, however many the demands on his time.

But even such concerns, troublesome as they were, could not mar for long her essential happiness. Even the parting from Jack was less painful than she would have expected. It was best for him, she knew, that he should leave Edinburgh, where so many memories lay in wait for him. He seemed genuinely interested in the commercial enterprise he was undertaking; of his more distant future, it was perhaps better not to think.

As the last week before the wedding approached, she paid her final visit to the Crearies before the ceremony and wedding trip. To her surprise, she noted workmen busy on the third floor, setting the whole building ringing with the sound of their hammering.

'What's going on, Lizzie?' she asked. 'Are there repairs to be made? I saw one workman measuring the walls of Paisley Close as I came through it – I had to wait for him to move his barrow before I could get through. Then as I came up the stair I heard nothing but sawing and banging – there, you can even hear it up here!'

'It's the joiners, doing repairs on the third flat. I've had them up here sorting the door, it's been sticking awf'y bad. I ken one of them, he used to work beside my father, Gavin Greenshields. My father aye said he was a rare craftsman . . . I'll need to ask him about Paisley Close next time I see him.'

She stirred the fire, a curious look of irresolution on her face. Suddenly she added, as though ashamed of the

384

admission, 'Ken, Miss Lambert, I hate that close. I never walk down it but I want to run out, as if the whole land is about to fall on me. Is that no daft?' she concluded, with a forced laugh, as she swung the kettle over the coals. 'I've clean taken a scunner to this house, I tell ye.'

Helen looked about her. 'You've got everything very homelike, although I can imagine that you feel the need of more space.'

'Aye, we're more comfortable than a while back,' Lizzie admitted grudgingly, as though reluctant to see any good in the room.

'Your father is able to send you more regular sums now?' The girl nodded. 'Have you not considered looking for a bigger flat?'

'A room and kitchen? Aye, I could have taken the Shannons'. They flitted to they new houses down at Pilrig.'

'Why didn't you?'

'I hate this whole land, and that's the truth. It's rotten. They beams – Gavin Greenshields tellt me ye could drive in a nail with your bunnet! And see yon door? He sorted it no a week since, and there it's sticking same as ever. And the window?' Helen followed her pointing finger. The curtains were stirring in the draught. The frame was badly fitting, gaps plugged with scraps of paper and rags.

'Another flat might be better. And you could always look elsewhere, beyond Paisley Close.'

'Houses are no just so easy come by, Miss Lambert. There's many far worse, and forbye that, Father'll surely send for us . . .'

She fell silent, glancing over to the bed where May was dozing. And as she brooded over her, Helen saw on her thin features a look of such gnawing anxiety that she realised for the first time the depth of Lizzie's wordless love for her sister.

'She'll never mend while we stay here, Miss Lambert. I'm heart-sure of it. If I could just get her into the country, with better air and good milk, and a wee bit garden . . . My ma used to tell me about it, ken. She was from the country. In her day, there wasna all this consumption.'

It was the first time Helen had ever heard her utter the word. She wished she could dismiss her fears as groundless. Her silence spoke for her. With a sigh, Lizzie picked up the shirt which May had been too weary to complete.

'It's a sair fecht, ye canna weaken,' she said wryly, quoting the old saying almost to mock her own, all too real, struggle.

'Pass me the sleeve, will you? There's no sense in my sitting idle when I could just as well be sewing.'

'Aye, we may as well get the good of ye the now,' Lizzie said briskly. 'We'll no be seeing ye for a week or more, and ye'll no be our Miss Lambert when we do . . .'

Helen coloured, as much with pleasure at her dry affection as at the reference to her change of condition. 'Mrs Bethune . . .' she murmured, the title sounding strange to her still.

And the two women sat together at their endless stitching, silent for the most part, wandering in their separate worlds of dreams and anxieties, of fears and sweet, insubstantial hopes.

The days before the wedding passed in a dizzy whirl of fittings and farewells, sudden panic at forgotten details, hurried changes of plan, trivial decisions so important at the time.

Many decisions, of course, were taken after discussion with Francis. She found him eager to put her wishes first, generous, level-headed, with a knack of going to the crux of any problem and considering it dispassionately.

She enjoyed their discussions, centring on such practical questions as the future of Northumberland Street, the desirability of his moving from Edinburgh if he should be offered promotion elsewhere, the composition of their household, the servants who were to accompany them on their wedding trip. But although they could speak freely of such matters, and of all that flowed from their joint life together, of the central factor in that life they never spoke. If anything, his reserve seemed to increase as the wedding approached.

With the growing closeness arising from their talks and plans, Helen longed increasingly to be alone with him. Only in his arms did she feel complete. At times she even wondered whether he did not avoid such contacts, and whether what she took for self-restraint was in fact a want of enthusiasm.

The night before the wedding she dined at Drummond Place without Francis, who had excused himself on the grounds that one or two matters of business had still to be settled before they went away. Her father and step-mother had pressed her to stay there overnight, but she refused. The last night of her independence was precious.

At about ten, she was preparing to leave for Northumberland Street, when to her surprise Francis Bethune was announced.

'Francis! Is anything wrong?' she cried, springing to her feet as he entered the drawing-room.

'No; what could be wrong?' he answered, taking her hand for a second, and pressing it with secret warmth. It was unusual for him to show such affection before others, even her parents. The little tenderness gave her a surge of happiness. 'I finished my papers earlier than I anticipated, and thought I might as well walk over and see you safe home.'

'The delightful evening tempted you, no doubt?' her father put in drily. It had been raining steadily since dusk.

He had brought an umbrella and went out onto the step before her, and put it up. She ran to its outstretched shelter, and clinging to his arm, shivering at the sudden cold after the warmth of her father's house, set off down the gleaming, rain-dark street.

'Did I hurry you away?' he asked. His voice was given a particular resonance by the silken screen of the umbrella, protecting them in a little world of their own.

'Not at all. I didn't want to be late.'

'Before tomorrow,' he said, his arm pressing hers closer to his side.

They were passing by a golden pool of light from a gas-lamp. She looked up into his face. He was smiling down at her, boy-like in his happiness.

'I'm so glad you came for me.'

'I couldn't settle to work.' He laughed. 'The papers still aren't finished, you know.'

'Francis, for shame! I hope you won't be obliged to work while we're away?'

'I may take a few books, in case of wet weather. If it's dry, we needn't stay in . . . unless we choose,' he added, his voice a little unsteady.

They were already within sight of her home.

'Will you come in, for tea or a night-cap?' she asked.

'If I may.'

It was the first time he had accepted such an invitation. They went up to her sitting-room, where a fire still burned. Bessie brought tea, but before Helen could pour it she felt his arms about her waist, as she lifted the lid of the teapot to stir its contents.

'Leave it another minute, Helen!' he murmured, drawing her to the couch. She made no protest, her heart already beating more quickly at the unexpected embrace. They half fell, laughing, on to the couch, his lips moving eagerly to hers before she had well recovered her balance. If she had ever thought him cold, she knew her mistake. As her hands strayed helplessly through his hair, still damp from the rain, he pressed against her, as though longing for a closeness he had never before allowed himself. His kisses aroused her in a passion which left her light-headed, as his hand rose to her breast, and lingered there.

Suddenly her clothes seemed to her a carapace, an unnatural barrier of buckram and linen and whalebone

388

and silk, confining her soft flesh, stifling and denying the first, the most powerful of senses, the sense of touch. A wordless murmur broke from her, a moan almost, in a voice she scarcely recognised as her own, as he pressed urgently against her, covering her body with his. Without her conscious volition her hands held him close, feeling the taut muscles of his thighs and hips even through their muffling cloth.

A sound in the next room; they started apart. 'Bessie . . . she'll be turning down my bed,' she said, her heart still pounding.

'Tomorrow. Oh, Helen, if only this were tomorrow!' he said, taking her hand in his as he sat back. She noted with fond amusement that his hand was hot, his chest rising and falling rapidly, his hair disordered. It was still a sort of wonder to her that she could affect him so, he who was in public so imperturbable, so calm and self-controlled.

'What are you smiling at?' he asked, smiling himself.

'Oh, just at how different you look now,' she said, reaching out to put back a lock of his hair from his brow. His temples always struck her with a curious sense of vunerability; the skin was so white, the fine structure of cheekbone and forehead so close to the surface.

'Look? I *am* different.'

'You musn't change too much,' she said, reaching over with new boldness to kiss him.

'Don't! How will I ever leave, if you kiss me?'

'Do you know, I wondered at times if you were indifferent to such things.'

'Indifferent? Helen, it would have been a torment to have allowed ourselves this freedom before now.'

'I can see that.' At last, they were acknowledging the reality which they had until now ignored. Her fingers closed more tightly over his. 'You will be patient with me? I do so want to learn to please you.'

He brought her hand to his lips, kissed it again and again with passionate tenderness. 'What do you have to learn? It is I who must be taught, taught to be fearless in trusting you as I have never trusted anyone else. I have to learn to be as open with you as you are with me. It is one of the things I have always loved in you, your complete candour, your calm blue eyes that cannot lie . . .'

'Don't!' she cried, in a sort of superstitious fear, hiding her face against her shoulder.

'Why should I not praise you? It is no more than the truth; from my earliest days, I have valued the truth as the great, the essential virtue, without which all the rest must fall, like a house without a foundation. Truth, without pretence or fear, it radiates from your eyes. We will have no secrets, will we? I shall try to be as open with you as you deserve . . . you, I know, would never stoop to concealment.'

It was not a question, it required no answer, but it flashed through her mind that now, if ever, she should tell him of Jack's misery and her own nightmare.

She had never felt closer to him; would it be so difficult, after all? She drew a deep breath, seeking the right words, but already he was starting a new train of thought, smiling.

'Do you remember my first visit here? Miss Anderson was scarcely welcoming, was she? . . . That conversation was uphill work . . . I talked about Donoghue, I think.'

'Yes, I remember,' she said, heart beating faster. Now, now was the moment.

'That man humiliated me, you know,' he went on in a sudden burst of confidence. 'I was all but a laughing stock. I went home from court that night and for the only time in my life I seriously considered abandoning my profession. To be made a fool of by a man whose very glance seemed to defile what it rested on . . . I'm sorry I spoke of him again to you, he's not a fit subject even for your thoughts.'

She hid her face against his shoulder, all thought of confession destroyed. It was a relief to be spared the ordeal, and yet when he had gone, not long afterwards, she wished that she had been braver.

*

Like her sisters, Helen was married from the drawing-room of Drummond Place. It was a brief ceremony, but although she tried to maintain her concentration on the solemn vows she was making, a growing disquiet hindered her.

She had not seen Francis before the ceremony. He had been shown up to the drawing-room while she was still with her step-mother and her attendants, making final adjustments to hair and dress in a flurry of activity and excited laughter. When she moved slowly on her father's reassuring arm, more nervous than she had expected, to kneel beside him, she kept her gaze fixed steadily on his long straight back, on his thick red-brown hair, just curling onto his collar; he managed to maintain, even in that uncomfortable posture, the unstudied grace of bearing which had always marked him out in her eyes.

Her father helped her to kneel, on one of the same pale-blue silk cushions which had been used at Rosemary's and at Sophie's weddings. Her attendants fussed about her, settling her skirts, as though she were their creation, a favourite doll whom they had dressed, and would allow no one to spoil. She let them work, fluffing out frills, spreading lace, smoothing creases in her gown, their finicky, jealous fingers striving restlessly for perfection. What was it to her? She stole a sidelong glance at the man who knelt beside her, for whom alone she wished to be pleasing. She expected to meet a glance as joyous and loving as her own, but on seeing his face, her smile faltered.

He did not turn towards her; she saw only his profile as he stared straight ahead, at the windows. They looked onto the gardens, where the stripped branches tossed in the wild abandon of ecstasy or despair. His face was white and taut. She could see from the tight set of his mouth how rigidly his jaws were clenched; the whole curve of his lips was altered, pulled into a severe line. He seemed like a man in pain, to which only the constant exercise of will refused utterance. When he gave his responses his voice was muted, as though it reached her from a great distance. He took her hand, on the clergyman's instructions, but without any token of secret understanding, any hidden pressure to reassure her of the love which underlay the formality of the rite.

At the conclusion of the ceremony he helped her to rise. Then, at least, she expected that he might relax, the most solemn part of the proceedings being at an end. But if anything his aloof manner seemed to intensify. He seemed a different being from the passionate lover who had scarcely been able to tear himself from her embrace only the previous night. Yet what, during the few intervening hours, could have caused such a change?

Helen had little leisure for speculation. The newly married couple were to remain for the wedding breakfast, before setting off on their wedding trip. They were returning to the Borders, to the cottage near Newtown St Boswells which the Robertsons had occupied the previous year. It was big enough, and they had no wish to go far in November.

As she received the congratulations and good wishes of her guests, Helen largely succeeded in throwing off the anxiety which had arisen during the wedding ceremony. More than one, it was true, commented with a smile on the new husband's manner: 'More nervous than the bride?' 'Thinking better of it already, Bethune?' Although she saw him colour with annoyance at such remarks, they were of some comfort to her in showing how commonplace was some sign of nervousness on such occasions. Once they were alone, no doubt his manner would become more natural.

At the last, they caught the train with only seconds to spare. The carriage was empty. Helen took the window seat; he seated himself opposite her, but in the centre, not directly across from her. As she looked at his remote expression, she had the curious illusion that they were absolute strangers, whom chance had brought together.

'Francis?' she began, with a timidity she could not avoid, 'Are you unwell? Have you received some bad news?'

'What bad news could I have received?'

She raised her brows, taken aback by his abrupt challenge. 'I have no idea. I merely asked because you don't seem . . . you don't seem yourself.'

'Not myself?'

'Not as you were yesterday.'

At that, he looked at her, for almost the first time that day, she realised. Bleak, reproachful, his brown eyes rested on her, moving her to a quick pity. The train was well out into the country; she moved, on sudden impulse, to sit beside him. She took his hand. It lay in hers, cold and inert. She raised it to her lips, and then chafed it gently in both her hands.

'You're so cold, Francis! See, I'll warm you as I used my little sisters, when they came in half-frozen from their walks in winter.'

She lifted his hand, and breathed on the fingers, with a little sigh, as though she were trying to melt the icy ferns on a window-pane. 'I never noticed before . . . you have beautiful fingers, so long and fine. I believe mine are scarcely more slender – look!'

She measured her hand against his, laughing to see how much his fingers overlapped hers, although as she had said, they were not much thicker.

'Do you know, you haven't kissed me once since we were married,' she said, untying her bonnet, and laying it aside, and lifting her hand to his cheek. She caressed him, and drew his face down towards her own. At first, she thought he would resist, but with a sigh he gave way, not to her urging, she believed, but to his own. His lips fastened on hers, but with an intensity which disturbed, almost frightened her, as it had never done before. It was a joyless embrace, of desperation rather than sensuality. But gradually his tight grip on her arms slackened, relaxed into a more natural embrace. She looked up at him.

'What is it, Francis? Only last night you said we would have no secrets. You're unhappy; won't you tell me why?'

He waited a moment before replying, and then did not answer her directly. 'A curious thing came to my mind this morning. Do you recall the Friday evening when I returned unexpectedly from circuit? I never mentioned it to you, I don't believe, but as I entered your house I met a man on the staircase. He seemed to be coming down from the drawing-room, or at least, from that floor. I didn't get a distinct impression of his face. The stair was dim, and you know how short-sighted I am. I had the feeling that there was something familiar about him, though. Can you tell me who it was? He had a small dog with him, I think.'

His eyes watched her, steady, almost dispassionate. She had an obscure sense that the question was a test of some sort, that much depended upon her reply. She had to drop her gaze before she could answer. 'It was an acquaintance of Jack's. Jack was out. He left a message. I don't think I recall his name. I haven't seen him since.'

'I see.' He sounded suddenly very weary. 'We are approaching a station. Perhaps you should resume your seat.'

No longer did she think to pursue the subject of his altered mood. Now, preoccupied, she sat in troubled silence.

Her evasive reply – she shied away from the brutal word 'lie' – clouded her happiness as a dank, chilling fog will hide the sun. Why could she not have answered his direct question with equal directness? It could not, now, hurt Jack, except in her husband's estimation. The previous night she had been on the point of trusting him with the whole sad story: even now, she might have done so, despite his distant, strained mood, but for those ill-timed comments of his concerning Donoghue.

How could she tell him the truth, knowing that he would feel that she had been contaminated by her contact

394

with the man he so loathed? She feared the strength of his reaction, feared some revulsion of feeling on his part. He was a man of sensitive pride; Donoghue's provoking sneers, the judge's reprimands, had almost led him to give up the profession he loved. How might the knowledge that Donoghue had embraced her, pawed her, all but raped her, affect his feelings for her?

With the quick imagination of love she put herself in his place. He would be humiliated. She had suffered already, but she could spare him, by silence. Fear, and embarrassment, and the desire to shield him from a crushing blow, all combined to suppress the confession which would always have been painful, but now would be all but impossible.

And so she sat silent, as self-absorbed as he, as the train crawled southwards through the stark landscape of skeletal trees and stripped fields, and the brief November afternoon declined into an early dusk.

22

Tait, Francis Bethune's manservant, had travelled down by an earlier train, together with his cook and Bessie. They had ordered an early dinner. When the fly from the station deposited them at Bowden Cottage, there was barely time for them to change before the meal.

They went up together to the room they were to share. As she surveyed her evening dress, laid out on the bed, the strangeness of her position struck her afresh. She glanced nervously at her husband.

He crossed to where a dressing-room gave off the main room. 'Good. Tait has laid my things out here. I shan't disturb you,' he said, with a half-bow, and closed the door behind him.

It was an undoubted relief to be left alone. She rang for Bessie. The maid worked silently. She was no admirer of matrimony, Helen knew. Her grim face was scarcely cheering, but at least she spared her mistress the tiresome babble with which a more sentimental lady's maid might have seen fit to accompany the task.

Helen's toilette was complete before the dining bell. She dismissed Bessie and tapped hesitantly at the door of the dressing-room. It was a small room, but it contained a fire. Helen noted with surprise that a bed was made up, occupying the whole of one wall. She looked hurriedly away.

'You're ready?' she asked, self-conscious in her new gown.

At her entrance, he had stood. When the door opened she had caught a momentary glimpse of him in a chair by the fire, staring absently into the flames. Evening dress became him, the close-fitting jacket emphasising his straight shoulders and neat waist, but in its austere black and white, for even his waistcoat was sombre, his tall figure seemed unapproachable. Her heart misgave her. Even his straight bearing, his head held high and a little back, seemed to add to his aloofness. She could hardly believe that there was any bond between her and this immaculate, remote figure.

'Shall we go down?' he asked, with the grave courtesy of a stranger, newly introduced.

'Francis!' she said, appalled. She crossed to him, her new gown softly rustling. She twined her naked arms confidingly about his waist, and laid her head on his shoulder.

'You will be kind to me?' she asked. It was all the appeal her pride would allow. She felt his hand move to her back, half exposed. Stiff, reluctant as the action was, it was a caress none the less. She found some reassurance even in so much contact. The bell rang, and they went down.

Tait waited at table. His presence seemed to rouse Francis from his preoccupations. Although his manner remained painfully formal, he chatted politely with her. She was happy to second his efforts, and the meal passed with less strain than she had feared. He ate little, she saw, although he drank rather more than was his custom; he was naturally abstemious. As her spirits rose, she began to believe that her forebodings had been exaggerated, that nervousness alone was causing his apparent coldness, that all would be well once their first night together was past.

When Tait had removed the cloth and retired, Francis gave up any pretence of eating. He rose from the table with a murmured apology, and went to the window. He parted the curtains and stared out into the darkness. The rattle of gusty rain could be heard against the glass.

'A good night for the fireside,' Helen remarked.

'No doubt . . . I think I may take a stroll, all the same,' he said, dropping the curtain back into place.

'Tonight?'

'It is still barely eight. I often take a walk after dinner if I have no work to attend to, it helps me to sleep, particularly if I have taken no exercise all day.'

'But . . . oh, just as you choose, Francis,' she said, trying to conceal her surprise, her alarm, almost. 'You will dress warmly, won't you? It seems a wild night.'

'Of course . . . have you quite finished your dessert?'

He offered her his arm, saw her established in the little parlour: he could not have been kinder, yet her heart ached at the impersonal attentions, and at the smooth mask which seemed to be covering the fresh, ardent face he had begun to show her.

At the last moment, as he was leaving her, she thought of begging him to remain: her pride revolted. If he preferred his own company, she would not coax him to stay. But when she heard the front door close behind him, minutes later, she felt more completely alone than ever in her life.

It proved no easy matter to occupy herself during his absence. She brought down a novel. It was one she had long wanted to read, and she had saved it for her wedding trip, as a special treat. She read a few pages, without pleasure or understanding, and put it impatiently aside; she thought she had never read anything so stupid. There was a bookcase in the room. She roamed over to it and examined its contents, behind their Gothic doors, glass and dark oak. Scott, and a few devotional works. She did not break in upon their cloistered repose.

She set herself to sew. It was plain work, a shirt for Joseph Crearie. She had brought it without expecting to make any great progress. She had visualised a homely scene, she stitching while her husband read to her, or talked eagerly, opening his heart, or debated with her on those questions, at once abstract and painfully practical, on which they increasingly differed. Since she had begun to know the Crearies, she had found that such subjects as the housing, education and health of the labouring classes had taken on for her a more immediate significance, and a grimmer.

But other daydreams rose to mock her, fond imaginings of how he would come and disturb her at her work by his impatient caresses, would take her in his arms, ignoring her laughing pleas to be allowed to finish just one last seam . . . at the memory, she threw aside the shirt in tearful disgust.

She roamed about the room, her arms tightly clasped about her breast. An album of views of the Borders lay on the table, next to it a commonplace book. She leafed through it. Hackneyed extracts from Scott and Romantic poets, copied in a careful, girlish hand. Love! It was the subject of almost every passage. She scarcely knew whether to laugh or cry.

She did neither: she rang for tea. No doubt her husband would appreciate a hot drink on his return. He could scarcely have happened on a worse night for his exercise. The rain was spattering against the windows like handfuls of fine gravel flung by a petulant child.

Sure that he must return at any moment, she delayed pouring the tea. She consulted her watch. Well past nine. He had been gone above an hour. She poured her own tea, and in mounting anger rang for Bessie to remove it.

'I shall be going up directly,' she said. 'Is the bed . . . is the room ready? Then I shan't need you any further tonight, thank you. I can manage myself, and Tait can wait up for his master, I suppose.'

But despite her declared intention, Helen lingered by the fire long after the tea was finished. It was ten before she went up. At the landing, half way up the stair, she paused, and drew aside the curtain. She could see nothing, beyond the brave patch of light thrown onto the grass by the window at which she stood. The absolute blackness was to her, city-bred, a thing uncanny, unknown. And somewhere in that foul night her husband was wandering.

Once in her bedroom she prepared for bed with nervous rapidity, fearful of being disturbed half-clad. She need not have worried. She had been in bed a full hour before she heard the bell ring, and a few moments later his weary steps on the stair.

He entered the room softly, as though not to awaken her. The cottage did not have gas in the bedroom; he had brought up a chamber candle. Hers had all but guttered; by the renewed light she saw his face, gaunt with fatigue, his soaked hair plastered against his temples. And at the sight, her resentment melted. She raised herself on one elbow in the bed.

'Francis!' she said, tenderly chiding. 'Where have you been all this while? You're soaked – bring a towel and I'll rub your hair.'

He put the candle down on the washstand and brought her a towel, stumbling against a chair as he came, stupid with exhaustion. He sat, docile, on the bed beside her, as she threw the towel over his head and began to dry his hair.

'You must be so tired . . . whatever made you stay out so long? I've been waiting for you . . . I thought you might have fallen, or missed your way . . . how cold your cheeks are, and your poor hands . . . there, at least your hair is drier.' She laid aside the towel and smoothed down his ruffled hair. 'How thick your hair is! I didn't realise . . .' She ran her fingers through it, with childlike wonder.

'Oh, Helen,' he said, and rested his face against her shoulder.

'Come to bed,' she whispered. 'It's warm. You'll soon feel better.'

'In a moment.' He got up, and moved with sudden resolution to fetch the candle, putting it on the cabinet close beside the bed.

'May I?' he asked, with the curious formality which had distinguished his manner all day. His fingers, stiff with the cold, began clumsily to unfasten the buttons at the neck of her nightgown.

She could scarcely believe what he was doing. There seemed no link between his actions and his emotions – nothing further removed from ardour could well be imagined. There was no sensuality in his face, lit by the unsteady candle-light, no pleasure even. He seemed rather to be impelled by some compulsion, towards a revelation which he dreaded. As he fumbled with agonising slowness about his joyless task she felt herself totally apart from him, a mere object laid out beneath his loveless scrutiny.

Button by button, he exposed her tender white skin. His head was lowered, the better to examine her breast. His finger delicately put back the fabric, where it impeded his short-sighted vision, and moved dispassionately over the beautiful, generous curve of her flesh. And suddenly, his finger stopped.

'What's that mark?'

Her face burning with humiliation, she turned to see where his finger pointed. It was a red blotch, low down on her left breast, almost beneath it.

'That? Oh, a birthmark, a strawberry mark, I think they call it.'

'It isn't visible when you're dressed?'

'No, not even in a low-bodiced gown. I'm fortunate, I suppose. I think it would embarrass me if it showed. But it is always well hidden . . . I never give it a thought.'

'I see.' He hurriedly replaced the gown over her breast. 'I'm sorry – will you see to the buttons yourself . . .' He got up, and almost ran into the dressing-room, banging the door shut behind him. But even through the door, she could hear the muffled sounds of retching, painful and prolonged.

Her first instinct was to go to him. She threw back the covers and was in the act of rising, when it struck her that he might not wish to be seen at such a moment. She lay back, and covered herself once more, mechanically fastening her nightgown. From the dressing-room, silence.

He must be in darkness; the candle still burned where he had left it, beside the bed. She was about to rise, when a discreet tap sounded at the outer door. Tait entered.

There was a moment of mutual embarrassment, from which the manservant was the first to recover.

'The bell rang belowstairs,' he said, clearing his throat.

'My husband was taken ill; perhaps you would go through to the dressing-room to see if he needs your assistance?'

He went with his candle to the door. Helen heard the murmur of her husband's voice, although his words were indistinguishable. Tait reappeared, bearing the bowl from the washstand.

'Don't worry, Mrs Bethune, nothing serious. He'll be well in no time,' he said, with the avuncular tone which occasionally made itself heard when he addressed her.

As soon as the man's steps had retreated down the stairs, she slipped out of bed and went to the dressing-room, timidly pushing open the door.

'Francis?' The candle was still lit, but at first she could not see him; he was in bed. She went over to him, and knelt by his side.

'How are you? Can I get anything for you?'

'Nothing, thank you. I must apologise; it must be unpleasant for you.'

'I'm blaming myself for not realising sooner that you were unwell . . . why did you not tell me?' she said, smoothing his hair from his forehead. He did not seem fevered.

'It's nothing, I assure you.'

'Won't you . . . won't you come into the other room?' she asked awkwardly. 'I would be with you then, if you should feel worse during the night. Please, it would set my mind at rest.'

'I am better here. I should hate to disturb you.'

There was a polite finality in his voice which told her that further protest or persuasion would be useless. She

402

sighed. 'If you feel worse, you will call me? Promise me that, at least!'

'If it proves necessary.'

There was nothing else for her to do. He did not return the kiss she placed on his cheek. When she looked back from the door, his eyes were closed, but within seconds of her leaving him, the door which she had purposely left ajar was pushed shut. The tiny gesture cut her to the heart.

The following day, her first waking thoughts were of him. She forced herself to wait until she heard movement from the dressing-room before going in to him. Even then, the room was in darkness, she was unsure whether he was awake.

'Francis?' she whispered.

A long pause. A sigh. 'Yes?'

'May I draw the curtains?'

'If you wish.'

She did so. The rain had stopped. The Eildons showed, bare and bleak in the first light.

'How are you?'

'As well as I'll ever be.'

'Will you be getting up for breakfast?'

'I shall get up, but I won't want anything to eat.'

'You know best.' She sat on the bed beside him. 'Was there ever such a start to married life?'

'It is not auspicious.'

'Oh, no doubt we will look back and laugh over it,' she said, with an attempt at lightness. He made no response. She shivered. 'This room is cold. Would you like your fire laid before you get up?'

'There's no need. You might ask Tait to bring my shaving water, though.'

'Certainly. I would have thought Bessie might have brought up the water before now.'

'Oh, the servants will not disturb us before we ring,' he said stiffly.

'No . . . I suppose not.' There was an awkward silence.

The room was so cold that she could see her breath. She wondered if she dare ask to creep in beside him, as Phoebe and Julia used, when they came down to see her and Rosemary early, on a birthday or after a ball. It would have been a comfort to lie close to him, cuddling into his back, in the delicious warmth of the bed.

She looked down at him. Pale, perfect in shape and structure, his face was turned blankly to the ceiling, impassive and remote as a carved knight's upon a tomb. She left the room, as cowed as if she had been rebuffed.

Although cold, the day remained dry. Francis joined her for luncheon, and afterwards suggested that they might walk over to Dryburgh. She readily agreed. It had been a favourite walk the previous year.

They were together, at least, but Francis remained silent. Things must, would improve, she told herself, but a doubt remained. His father had maintained to the end of his life a resentment which was scarcely sane. Was there, after all, something of the same gloomy tenacity in his son? She clung to the memory of the eager love he had shown on the eve of their wedding. If she were patient, surely that must return.

She tried to respect his apparent wish for silence, but from time to time she essayed a remark. Occasionally a discussion ensued, if the subject were impersonal. But too often, a courteous, monosyllabic assent was all her answer.

How different he was from her brothers and sisters! Quick to anger, quarrelsome, opinionated, they were equally ready to be reconciled or to engage in noisy recriminations. She wished he would shout, complain, storm, anything but the impassive, impeccable courtesy which excluded her from any true contact.

They walked through the dead landscape, they crossed the cold, deep waters of the Tweed, they dutifully admired the ancient ruins and modern tombs of the Abbey, they returned through the gathering gloom, they exchanged bland, civil conversation, they dined, amid all the decencies of correct society. And Helen's misery grew with every lifeless second.

Lizzie Crearie had been glad to see Gavin Greenshields among the workmen engaged to repair the third flat. Her father had always spoken of him with approval as a steady, conscientious workman. Early in November, as she went to pass through Paisley Close, she stopped, seeing him at the mouth of the close, frowning over a measure.

'Ye're awf'y busy-looking, Mr Greenshields!'

'Aye.' He looked up and nodded a greeting, but his frown lingered.

'Take your twelve-hours with us the day, what for no?' she said, on sudden impulse. 'Bring your piece, I can give ye a dish of tea. Ye ken your way?'

'I'll be up,' he said hastily, with a warning glance.

'Greenshields! Blethering again? If your hands went as fast as your tongue ye'd do no bad! Where's the hurley-barrow?'

A short, stout man was coming down Paisley Close, shouting as he approached. Lizzie shot Greenshields a look of understanding and turned towards Baillie Fyffe's Close, to avoid passing the foreman, as she took him to be. As she left the court she could hear him still berating the workman.

'If the hurley is sticking in Paisley Close bring it by Baillie Fyffe's! And mind what ye were tellt, and keep your daft notions to yourself!'

Although she hardly expected him, Gavin Greenshields presented himself at twelve, with his piece box.

'I'm glad to see ye, Mr Greenshields! Come ben — ye ken our May, eh no? And wee Danny? Tea'll no be a minute; or would ye take a drop of broth? Ye're welcome, ken.'

'Tea'll do me fine, Lizzie.'

'Set yourself down at the fire, get a warm!' she urged.

'Yon wee man was giving ye the rough side of his tongue when I seen ye . . . Is he the heidsman?'

'Samuel? Aye, I work for him.'

His manner was abrupt, unlike his usual easy crack. Perhaps he didn't like to be reminded of the tongue-lashing he had received. She gave him his tea and left him to make his meal in peace while she helped Danny.

She was still spooning up the last of the broth for him when she heard Greenshields setting his cup down on the table with a decisive tap. She looked up.

'It's no use, Lizzie. I canna keep it to myself, for all it'll maybe lose me my place. I tell ye, hen, ye'd be well advised to look about for another house, the day if ye can. I wouldna leave my bag of tools here overnight, and that's the truth.'

'What's all this?' she asked, half alarmed, half puzzled.

'This land canna stand much longer,' he said bluntly. 'The wall of Paisley Close is near two inches from the true; the hurley-barrow wouldna gang through it the day – it used to, ken. I've seen some old buildings in my day, but never in such a state as this one. Every door sticks, there's cracks in the ceiling up in the attic, the windows'll no shut . . . I tell ye, there's something far wrong with this land.'

Bemused, Danny looked at the man's vehement face and began to whimper, his cheeks beslobbered with the broth he had tried to feed himself while Lizzie's attention was elsewhere. Silently, May came and comforted him, and took over Lizzie's task.

'A whole land canna fall, Mr Greenshields!'

'It can so, if it's rotten! Do ye no mind Leith Wynd, six, seven year ago? It was pull they tenements down or they'd have fallen. I wouldna stay here, no if ye paid me.'

'And Mr Samuel? Does he say the same?'

'Samuel?' He laughed. 'All he cares about is getting his money off Mr Redford, for doing the repairs on the

406

third flat. Redford bought it no long since, ken. The day Samuel gets his pay, the whole land can gang to glory for all he cares. He's tellt me, if I bring the matter to him again, or talk about it to any of ye, that's me out. Ye'll ken from your father, it'd no be easy to find another place, with the character I'd bear from Samuel. I was going to keep my mouth shut, but I canna see Rab Crearie's bairns staying here, and no give a word of warning.'

'And ye really think it'll fall? It's stood for hundreds of years! But still and all . . . I'll get our Joseph to write to Father . . .'

'I wouldna leave my toolbag here overnight, hen,' he repeated solemnly. 'Dinna give my name, but ye can tell anyone who'll listen that this whole land's just as rotten as soft cheese. Paisley Close is bulging out the way; it canna hold, and when it gives, what's to stop all the floors abune it from falling?'

She had no reply.

'I'm sorry to gar the wean greet,' he said, as he picked up his hat to go. 'I had to speak out, hen.'

'I'm sure we're obliged to ye, Mr Greenshields,' she said, going with him to the door, and opening it with some difficulty.

'See that, Lizzie? What is it, ten days since I sorted it? The whole land is leaning to the west, I tell ye. The beams'll no hold – they'll snap like match sticks. Get out while ye can.'

'I'll mind,' she said, moving the door, testing its resistance, frowning at the undeniable evidence of her own senses. She forced it shut, and turned back into the room to see May's frightened eyes looking at her. Danny held up his arms; she picked him up, absently.

'Oh, Lizzie,' May said fearfully. 'What can we do?'

The next evening, Francis Bethune did not repeat his solitary ramble. Pleading the need to work on the review of a legal publication for Edward Lambert's magazine, he returned to the dining-room after the table had been cleared. Left in the parlour, Helen managed to occupy herself more usefully than the previous night. She would have been glad of his company but it was reasonable that, needing to concentrate, he should wish to be alone.

At about nine she rang for tea, and went to ask if he would like to join her in the parlour for it. He was sitting by the fire, a book on his knee. As she entered she saw him hurriedly remove the spectacles he had been wearing.

'Francis! I didn't know you were so vain!' she said, smiling. 'Won't you put them on for me? Let me see you at your worst . . . it can't do any harm now, you know, we're married, I've taken you for better or worse, spectacles and all!'

He returned them to their case, shaking his head a little.

'You should trust me, Francis. I'm sure you look quite delightful in them.'

'Trust?' he repeated, with a bleak, almost hostile intonation. She lowered her eyes and trifled with his bookmark, lying on the arm of his chair.

'I quite forgot the purpose of interrupting you . . . tea is ready. Won't you join me in the parlour?'

'I think not, thank you. I may as well retire at once, for all the sense I'm making of this book. I didn't sleep well last night.'

'I won't be long, then.' She hesitated, then slipped her hand into his, and bent to kiss his cheek. 'You won't sleep in the dressing-room tonight? I know you are very tired, dear . . . I was so lonely last night, without you.'

'I think I would prefer to remain where I was. If my indisposition should return, I would know that you at least would not be disturbed.'

'But you've been quite well today, haven't you?' she asked, her heart sinking.

'It may return suddenly, as it did last night.'

She said no more, too proud to insist. She kissed his averted cheek; he offered her no embrace. As she went to drink her solitary tea, she heard him going up to the bedroom.

Helen slept no better that night, but in the long, lonely hours of darkness she reached a decision: she would not allow the estrangement to continue for a third night. Tomorrow she would seek either a full explanation of his coldness, or his presence beside her. She felt an inner certainty that once that barrier were surmounted, there would be a return to the happiness which had once been so close.

Alas, her decision was futile, thwarted by the simplest, most inexorable of events. Several days before she looked for it, her period began. At the best of times, she would have found it difficult to give any notice of the fact to her husband. Now, remote, aloof as he was, it would have been impossible. She was glad to avoid the necessity, glad of the privacy which his absence won her.

The cold weather intensified her misery. Wretched, aching, she was glad that he was content to take his walks alone, never pressing her beyond a first refusal. And so the remainder of the week passed, with no further attempt on her part towards an understanding. He walked, whatever the weather, he worked on his review, he slept in the dressing-room, and at mealtimes, beneath the servants' eyes, he spoke to her politely.

They returned to Edinburgh on the Saturday, to Heriot Row. Helen had still reached no firm decision as to the future of the establishment in Northumberland Street. She had intended to sell it after their marriage, but now she wavered. It was her home, after all. The thought gave her a sense of security which she had not expected to need.

As they neared Edinburgh her spirits rose. Her period was over; in the more natural setting of his own house she hoped that her husband might regain something of his former manner.

The evening passed pleasantly. Helen settled down to the numerous small concerns of a newly married wife. There were letters to answer, wedding cake to send, their first dinner to begin to plan. She was kept happily absorbed in the small sitting-room which was to be particularly her own. Francis was engaged in the library. He joined her for tea, but returned immediately to his work. He had warned her that it would keep him occupied until well past midnight. When she went in to bid him good night, at eleven, he was still deeply involved.

She intended to remain awake until he came up, but she drifted asleep. She awoke with a start, from some disturbing dream. The light was still burning. She looked at her watch, which she had hung at the head of the bed. Two o'clock. She was still alone. The dressing-room, she knew, did not contain a bed. Where was he? Why was he treating her in this way? The servants must be aware of it; it must be the talk of the kitchen: the virgin bride. Heaven knew how long it would be before every kitchen in the New Town heard the salty rumour.

Angry, hurt, confused, she resolved once more to bring matters to an explanation.

The following day was Sunday. Helen went alone to the Episcopal service. She had asked whether he would care to accompany her; he declined, with his invariable courtesy. She would have gone with him to his church, had he asked; he did not. She bore herself proudly in her wedding finery, receiving compliments and congratulations with her usual grace, inwardly as desolate as though she were in mourning.

After luncheon, he retired to the library. She took her courage in both hands, and went in to him.

'May I sit with you a while, Francis?'

'If you wish.'

She closed the door behind her, and went towards him. She had no idea how best to proceed, but no confrontation, however unpleasant, could equal the ordeal of dragging through a dreary November Sabbath alone.

He had stood at her entry, and remained politely standing by his chair until she should be seated. She had intended to sit opposite to him, but instead she approached him, her heart beating fast at her boldness.

'Francis, we've been married for more than a week and I don't believe we've embraced once. The servants won't need to disturb us, will they? Then may I . . . may I sit on your knee? There can be no impropriety now, can there?'

'I . . . I . . . really, it's not quite . . .'

'Please!' she said, more confidently. He was clearly taken aback by her request, but not absolutely hostile.

He made no further protest, but resumed his seat.

'Is that comfortable for you? I'm not too heavy?'

He shook his head. With a sigh of contentment she laid her cheek against his, as his arms stole close about her. Her hand, resting over his heart, rose and fell with his chest as his breathing quickened.

'How long it seems since we were comfortable together like this,' she murmured. 'Why were we such strangers last week? Something was wrong between us . . . oh, Francis, I do love you so, I do want us to be happy . . .' Tears welled in her eyes, she could not go on. She raised her face, and slowly, timidly pressed her lips to his. He remained passive, but she saw his eyes close. She held his face between her hands, covered it with light, tender kisses, murmuring endearments. Forgetful of herself, of his coldness, his neglect, she saw only his unhappiness in his self-exile.

Suddenly he opened his eyes, brown and once more trusting. For a few moments at least the distance he had set between them was gone. Slowly, his voice low and halting, as though it was of infinite importance that he should find the right words, he began to speak.

'Helen . . . tell me, now that we're quiet together, is there anything . . . anything that you have kept from me? Perhaps you were afraid of hurting me . . . perhaps you thought I would be angry . . . is there anything, anything at all? If there is even the least thing on your mind, tell me now. I will try to understand, I promise you.'

Tears rose in her eyes at the loving warmth in his voice, his gaze. It was, surely, the first sign of his former tenderness returning. But how fragile might it be? Dare she risk plunging him once more into coldness and rejection? After the experience of the past week, she shied away from the prospect; only let him continue as he now was for a few days, only let their loving relations be firmly re-established, and then, then it would be easy to trust him with the whole sordid tale.

'Oh, Francis,' she murmured, blinking back her tears. 'You are almost your old self again, I am so glad . . .'

'But tell me, is there anything you wish me to know?' he persisted.

She hid her face against his shoulder. 'I love you. That's all I want to tell you, all that's of the slightest importance.'

'I see,' he said dully.

'Last night I was expecting you. Did you fall asleep over your work?'

'No. I worked very late, and didn't want to disturb you. I have a bed always made up in the little study off the library. I often slept there when I had worked far into the night, in my bachelor days.'

'But you won't live like a bachelor any more?'

He smiled, but said nothing. The light seemed to have died from his face again. Troubled, but still hoping that all would now be well, she left him to his reading, more certain than ever that she had made the right decision in not risking the extinction of the first glimmer of returning affection.

But that night she waited in vain for his step on the stair. He had already left the house when she went down to breakfast. Tait handed her a note, a single sentence: 'I shall not be dining at home this week.'

23

As the week progressed, she realised how little of his life he intended to share with her. She literally did not see him for days on end. He seemed to leave home long before breakfast, and to return past midnight. She sat up for him, ill at ease in her sitting-room which still lacked any feeling of home for her. He never sought her out; she assumed that he must go straight to the library. To hunt him out there was more than her pride would allow.

The strain of living such a life was great. She found herself constantly restless, unable to concentrate, she slept badly and scarcely ate. Her solitary meals were a torment to her, for all Tait's kindness. He appeared to take a fatherly interest in her welfare, urging her to eat more, recommending this dish or that, telling her what her husband's favourite soup or pudding was. She recognised the goodwill underlying his remarks, and was glad of some diversion from the thoughts which were always particularly painful at mealtimes, but she writhed at the thought of the speculation to which her husband's clear neglect must be giving rise.

Even Tait's sympathy roused her pride, which seemed to be growing more touchy with each day.

'Don't worry, Mrs Bethune,' he said, as she rose from the dinner table on Thursday evening, her plate hardly touched. 'The start of the session is always a bad time. He's not always as busy as this.'

'Thank you, Tait,' she said, forcing a smile. 'My husband has so many responsibilities; I would not have him neglect his duties for me.'

'Of course not, Mrs Bethune,' he agreed, a little too readily.

'I will have tea in the library tonight, I think,' she said, on sudden impulse. 'You may ask Bessie to bring it in an hour or so.'

It had been the last thing she had intended, but Tait's sympathy had stung her. As she endured the slow hours before her husband's return, her anger grew.

It was after midnight when she heard his key in the door. Her heart began to pound, as his steps came closer, slow and heavy. As he entered she stood. He stopped, seeing her, his hand still on the door, then turned to close it, and faced her.

'You look tired, Francis.' It was true. His eyes seemed weary, and beaten. She had wondered where he had been dining all week. Seeing him, she wondered if he had dined at all. His face was haggard, his cheekbones more prominent.

He shrugged. 'Was there some particular reason . . . is there anything of importance, anything which cannot wait? I am, as you said, tired.'

'Then come to bed. This has gone on long enough; I shan't ask you again for your reasons for choosing to build a wall about yourself as you have . . .'

'Please . . . !'

'. . . but I will no longer be humiliated in this way. I am tired of seeing pity in the servants' faces, and of wondering what gossip is circulating amongst the kitchenmaids and butchers' boys of Heriot Row. If you wish to spend every waking minute away from your home and me, you are free to do so. I shan't protest, although you are quite plainly making yourself ill. But in order to preserve some show of a normal married life, is it too much to ask that you spend the night upstairs from time to time?'

All the resentment of the past two weeks flamed in her voice, her eyes, her proud, defiant bearing. There was nothing of the suppliant about her now. Sensing her advantage, she moved to the door.

'I am going to bed now. Don't be long; you must be exhausted.'

She had not long been in bed before he came up. Her anger gave way to pity as she saw how wearily he moved to the dressing-room.

'Good night, Francis,' she said, as he extinguished the light and joined her, bumping into the washstand as he picked his way across the darkened room, lit only by the uncertain glow of the embers in the grate.

The bed creaked as he climbed in. He lay without touching her.

'Cuddle up to my back, won't you?' she asked, wriggling towards him a little. 'Rosemary and Sophie always used to snuggle up close; we'll be asleep in minutes.'

She had no conscious motive in making the suggestion, beyond what she avowed, the wish to re-create the cosy warmth of those innocent, maiden days. But perhaps her body knew better than she did what it was about, as it pressed close against him.

'That's better, isn't it?' she murmured, as she felt the warmth of his body against her back, fitting snugly. She closed her eyes, really believing that she was composing herself for sleep.

In the darkness, the last coals settled into the ash, the tiny sound loud in the stillness. Only one other sound broke the silence: his breathing. His hand was at her waist, lying loosely at first, then gripping her more tightly. As his breathing grew more laboured, she felt his standing flesh, proud and taut, nudging her thigh. Through the fine linen of their nightclothes, she was aware of him heavy against her; no longer confined, or protected, by the cage of a crinoline, by petticoats and stays, she was unprepared for the effect of their closeness. Her own breathing began to quicken, as he pulled her round, onto her back.

Not a word was spoken. He did not kiss her, nor caress her. His hand tugged irritably at her nightgown, pulling it up above her knees. And the movement recalled, quite suddenly, that other night, the frightening, undignified struggle. Where was the difference? Where was the gentleness of a lover, the sensual delight in their bodies' play?

He was joyless. He might have been a man compelled by his appetite to an act of which he was ashamed; he would, she supposed, have behaved exactly so if he were having a connection with a prostitute.

Was this to be the beginning of their married love, this feverish, furtive coupling? Was she to allow herself to be used by him as a mere thing, without personality? If she acquiesced, it would be silent complicity in the loveless act.

She raised her hand gently to his face, the merest blur in the darkness. 'Won't you kiss me, love?' she murmured. 'Would you like me to take off my nightgown?'

At once, his hand abandoned its struggle with her clothing. He froze into immobility. Then, abruptly, he pulled down the linen again, and moved to the far side of the bed.

'You needn't trouble,' he said, his formality at incongruous odds with his still uneven breathing.

'I have wondered at times if my person is distasteful to you,' she said, in cold fury, 'but it isn't that, is it? It isn't my person, it's me, my whole being. You only wanted me when you could forget who I was. As soon as I spoke, it was over. What have I done?'

'You have lied to me, over and over again. You have lied in words, and in silence. You have refused to tell me what I know you owe it to me to reveal. You have deceived me even when I have begged you to be open with me. I thought you were candour itself; you have dissembled without conscience or remorse.'

Bitter, tormented, his words poured out in the darkness, appalling her, not by their anger, but their pain.

'I loved you! I would have staked my life on your honesty – perhaps I have! I would have forgiven you anything; why couldn't you have trusted me?'

'I have done nothing for which I need to ask your forgiveness,' she put in quickly.

'Except to lie.'

'Yes. For that I am truly sorry. But it was not easy for me to explain to you . . .'

'You needn't try. Whatever you may have to say can't alter the cold-blooded lies you told me – even on Sunday, when you came to me, oh, so beautiful, so loving, so true!'

He was almost choking, fighting to express with his usual control the headlong torrent of emotions which pressed forward for utterance.

'How could you do it to me? Smile, and put your arms about me, and rouse every sense with your kisses and all the time lying and laughing at me for my stupidity . . .'

'No! No! It wasn't like that!'

'I thought I could trust you! I wanted there to be not a thought between us which we could not share! You don't know what you were to me!'

'Were'. The word struck a chill note for her. Again, she remembered the grim spectre of his father, unforgiving to the very last. 'Francis, if you would let me explain . . .'

'There's no point. I don't care what Donoghue was doing here that night when I met him on the stairway; I have no interest in knowing, that's not what has been tormenting me since the wedding. It's the fact that you could deceive me. If there's no trust between us, what is there?'

'Does a single fault on my part have to destroy everything?'

'I didn't believe it was possible that you should deceive me, can't you see?'

'You put me on a pedestal; you were bound to be disappointed, sooner or later,' she said wearily. 'Can't you accept me as I am? If you love me, won't you try to forgive me . . . at least to listen to the full circumstances?'

'They can't alter the case.'

'Francis, you are being absurd,' she said, her temper beginning to stir at his stubbornness. 'You are exactly like Andrew when he was still in short frocks; if he couldn't have a sweetie exactly the same as Philip's, he wouldn't have one at all! Look at it coolly. I have been much in error, I own it. I kept from you facts which I should have confided in you. But is it so terrible? Have you not kept your secrets from me?'

'No! I told you, the evening before we married, there would be nothing hidden between us.'

'So you did. So, Francis, will you answer me plainly: are you a virgin, as I am?'

'I . . . no.'

'I'm sure you will have no objection to describing to me every detail of every encounter?'

'Helen! What purpose would that serve?' he asked uneasily.

'You would find it difficult?'

'Of course I would!'

'And when you spoke of having no secrets between us, you didn't include that?'

'It was all a thing of the past, when I was a student. It didn't concern you; there was never any question of love . . . It was simply a temptation of the flesh, a physical necessity.'

'Ah, I see! These were connections with prostitutes?'

'Yes,' he muttered.

'But you didn't feel obliged to tell me of them because you would have found it embarrassing? Because there was no question of love, although you went with them willingly, I suppose?'

'I always hated myself.'

'And yet you have no spark of understanding for me, when I try to tell you how difficult it would have been to explain the single moment in my life for which I feel shame! I was attacked, do you realise that? If you hadn't rung when you did, if you hadn't come over straight from the station, he might have been successful.'

'He wasn't?'

'No. As I said, I am still a virgin,' she said, with deliberate emphasis. 'And because I shrank from telling you, I am never to be forgiven? And your willing

419

unchastity? Your concealment of it? Have you ever compared the two?'

There was a long silence. 'No,' he said, humbly.

'Perhaps the subject might provide a useful occupation for your thoughts for what remains of the night. You will probably find yourself more comfortable downstairs, after all.'

'You want me to go?'

'I do. For you, Francis, lack of candour may be the unforgivable crime. For me, I rather think it's hypocrisy.'

When he had left her, the cold anger which had carried her on its wave of indignation and scorn began to ebb, stranding her, alone and helpless. For all her brave hauteur, she could have wished that he was beside her still.

The next morning, after her usual solitary breakfast, Helen was possessed by a longing to escape from the house. She had not yet seen the Crearies since her return; the day was cold but dry. She set off at a brisk pace for the Old Town.

Lizzie greeted her with somewhat distracted warmth. For all her own troubles, Helen saw at once that something was causing her anxiety.

'Now, Lizzie,' she said, glad to brush aside the girl's congratulations and enquiries, 'what's wrong?'

'Gavin Greenshields tellt us the land's sure to fall, miss, and I'm just about daft with the worry,' she burst out, without any of the concealment of her old, wary self.

'He said that? Have you written to tell your father?'

'Aye, but he's no wrote back. I've tried, and I've better tried to get us another house, but there's no a room to be had, no unless a sunk flat in Blackfriars' Wynd. The floor was just awash with fulzie. May'd no see the week out, with the cold and the dirt and no even a window . . .'

'You couldn't take her to such a place!'

'It'll be gone by now, anyway.'

420

'But surely this man – Greenshields? – can't be right? Does he have any proof?'

'He kens his business . . . see this door!' Helen watched as she pulled it open. It grated slowly along the floor. Grooves were worn in the boards, where the door would not clear them. 'It's been sorted twice already in a month.'

'But doors often stick in old houses!' Helen exclaimed, uneasy despite her attempt at reassurance. 'The proprietors know of Greenshield's allegations, I suppose? What do they say?'

'He tellt Mr Redford, who's bought the third flat.'

'And what has he done?'

'No a thing. But Samuel has given him warning he'll lose his place if he says another word. He canna do any more.'

'And the other tenants? Do they know?'

'Oh, aye, ye canna keep a secret on a stair, Miss Lam – Mrs Bethune. But the bigger half of them just laughs at him.'

'It certainly does seem a very solid building, Lizzie. The front on the High Street is one of the most handsome I've noticed. There are many with stonework in a far worse state of repair. Don't you think Greenshields may be taking rather too gloomy a view?'

'Maybe,' the girl said, shrugging. 'We'll have to bide here the now, as I tellt ye. I canna get us anywhere else.'

'No doubt your father will soon write back to you.'

'Dinna ken . . . see, Mrs Bethune, it's no me, to take things to heart this way. I've been out of my mind, and that's the truth.'

Helen looked with quickened compassion at the girl's drawn features. 'I can see how worried you've been, but don't you think it's more than just these frightening rumours? You've had a great deal to bear this last year and more. Not many women could endure as you have.'

'What else could I do?'

'I know . . .'

Lizzie looked at her more closely. 'Dinna be angry with me, but ye're no just so well-looking yourself the day. That's no you fallen already?'

'Fallen?'

'Ken . . . a bairn!'

Helen's mouth opened; she gazed at the girl in an agony of embarrassment, crimson flooding her cheeks.

'What ails ye, Mrs Bethune?' she asked in surprise. 'I dinna mean to . . . who's that now?'

As the tap at the door was repeated, Helen hastily lowered the little veil on her hat to conceal her confusion, glad of the interruption to save what remained of her composure.

'So, Lizzie, how's May?' The voice was familiar. She looked up quickly, as Doctor Cairns came into the room.

Seeing her, he stopped. His face changed; for a second she almost expected him to turn on his heel and leave. With a visible effort, he took another step or two towards her, and bowed.

'I didn't realise that you were here, Mrs Bethune.'

His cold formality, the withdrawal of warmth from his voice, his smile, his whole bearing, struck her like a blow. She gazed up from behind the flimsy protection of her veil, her eyes brimming.

'I was only saying she's no herself the day,' Lizzie put in, with some wish to ease what seemed an unexpectedly awkward encounter. 'There's maybe a good reason, eh no? A wean on the way?'

The remark could not have been more unfortunate. As Helen lowered her gaze and felt for her handkerchief, she saw through her welling tears his eyes close, as at some sickening pain, scarcely endurable. She rose hurriedly.

'If you will excuse me, I must go . . .' she murmured.

Curiously, the evident signs of her distress seemed to diminish his.

'Wait a moment, Helen!' he called urgently, as she struggled with the door. 'I only called to see May. If she isn't here, I'll come back tomorrow. I'll give you a cast home, if you like.'

She had no strength to protest. She felt, as never before, the luxury of depending upon his solid, fatherly protection. Even the few moments of coldness in his manner had showed her how much she looked to him for comfort; now that his old friendship seemed to be reasserting itself, there was an irresistible urge to forget the loyalty she knew was owing to her husband, and to confide in him.

He shepherded her down the long, grimy stair. At the foot he drew her hand through his arm as they crossed the court, although they could not pass through the close except in single file. The brougham was waiting on the High Street; he helped her in.

'Shall I take you straight home?' He paused. 'Or would you like to come back to George Square? I've been out and about from first light; I was going home for a plate of soup, to be honest, and to see what messages had come in for me.'

'George Square, then,' she said, with an obscure sense of defiance. His face lit with sudden pleasure, as he gave Donald his instructions, and joined her in the carriage.

'So, Helen?'

'I am quite well, you know,' she answered quickly.

'And happy?'

She lowered her head. Again, her nerves betrayed her, delivering her to the shameful tears which seemed never far away, weakened as she was by so many sleepless nights, so many conflicting emotions. He said nothing more, but in the dimness of the jolting, leather-smelling carriage she felt his hand reach out for hers, and hold it.

They were not long in reaching George Square. Bridget took her hat and mantle; without her veil, Helen felt oddly exposed.

'Will you take some soup? You're sure?'

'A cup of tea, if I may.'

He left her while he gave Bridget her orders. She took the opportunity to examine herself in the glass, fearing for the effects of her half-suppressed tears on her complexion. She saw there none of the blotches she dreaded, but something far worse, the strain of the past weeks, clearly visible in the tightness about her eyes, the nervous, apprehensive set of her mouth. She turned away, almost in guilt, as he re-entered.

'Come through with me to the dining-room, will you? A doctor needs to eat when he can, you know.'

She went in on his arm. Bridget had set a place for her despite her refusal; she needed no very great persuasion to accept a plate of potato soup, thick and comforting, nursery food.

'You look all the better for it,' he said, peeling an orange for her with deft, economical movements of his knife. 'Do you want to tell me what's wrong?'

She received the fruit from him, and began to part it into segments, her fingers working restlessly, seeking occupation. Something held her back from the confidence she wanted to make, and yet she knew how futile it would be to pretend to him that she was as happy as she had expected to be. So she sat with lowered eyes, separating the orange, and saying nothing.

'Things are not going well with Bethune?'

She did not deny it.

'A quarrel?'

She nodded, barely perceptibly.

'But it wouldn't be easy to quarrel with him, would it?' he continued, reflectively. 'There would be no outburst, clearing the air. Quarrels are hateful things, but silence can be even worse.'

She looked at him, grateful for his understanding, still uncertain how far she ought to unburden herself. 'It isn't all his fault. It all stems from Jack's wretched

424

business. If I had trusted him, there would be no difficulty now.'

'He's withdrawn into his shell, I suppose?'

'Yes.' She ate some of the orange, less from appetite than for something to do. Across the table, Doctor Cairns was regarding her intently.

'Helen, forgive me if what I'm about to say appears to you an intrusion. I must speak. I've seen, over and over again, the change in the expression, the manner, the whole bearing of a young girl when she marries. I can't describe it, but it's unmistakable. When we met, I looked for it in you. I don't see it.'

She said nothing. She raised the fruit mechanically to her lips, and put it down untasted.

'Come through to the parlour, Helen,' he said, rising. 'We can talk more easily there.'

The fire in the parlour was newly lit, barely taking the chill from the air. She hugged herself, shivering, and went to the window overlooking the long garden at the rear of the house. There was little to see, beyond a rose bush or two, still bearing buds, buds which the frost had blighted, never to bloom.

He remained at the door, watching her. She was visible to him in profile, cut out against the heavy brown velour curtains and the net which screened the windows. She was wearing a high-necked gown of some clinging woollen stuff, a greyish-blue. Its simple cut, its subdued colour, lent an almost Quakerish self-effacement to her as she stood, lost in thought, her arms tightly clasped about her body, her head a little thrown back, as though dragged by the weight of its thick fair hair, gathered in a club at the nape of her neck. His eyes traced the flowing line of her throat and neck, emphasised by the disturbing abandon of her stance, and the glorious curve of her breast.

'Helen!' he said abruptly, taking a step towards her.

Mutely, she turned to him grave, guileless eyes.

'You know, don't you,' he said, very quietly, 'that an

425

unconsummated marriage is no marriage at all? It can be annulled. You could remarry.' He paused. 'You could marry me, Helen.'

Her eyes did not leave his face. He read his fate there, in their dawning comprehension, and their infinite pity.

'It hasn't been long . . . he may want me still.'

'And if he doesn't?'

'I don't know.'

'Would you have had me?'

There was a long pause. 'No. I never thought of you in that way. I'm sorry. I don't want to hurt you.'

'I'm glad that you've been honest. I always knew. That's why I never asked – at least . . .'

'The morning when Jack made the attempt on his life; that was why you came, wasn't it?'

'Yes. The worst thing since then has been the doubt whether, after all, if I had spoken . . . it will be easier now.'

'I'm sorry! Oh, Doctor Cairns, I'm so sorry!'

'We can't command our affections,' he said, with a wry smile. 'Bethune is a lucky man . . . and a very great fool.'

She coloured. 'I did wonder at first, if it was my fault, if there was something in my appearance . . .'

'Helen!' he cried, half laughing, half in earnest. 'Don't provoke me past all bearing! It's no fault of yours if Bethune has ink in his veins instead of blood!'

The bell rang. He shrugged. 'Some patient, no doubt.'

'Perhaps it's just as well,' she said, offering him her hand.

He took it, made as though to raise it to his lips, and instead, somehow, folded her in his arms. For a second she nestled there, wrapped in the comforting warmth, before he reluctantly released her.

'God bless you, Helen. Don't forget, I'm always here.'

'I won't . . . I don't deserve your . . . your good opinion, you know.'

426

'Of course you don't!' he said briskly. 'I shall need to look out for some sensible widow woman to keep my feet on the ground . . . Yes, Bridget, I'm coming directly; tell Donald to bring the brougham round, if you would.'

Helen refused a cast home. She wanted to walk, to be alone while she tried to see a pattern of some sort in the jumble of events and emotions. To her own surprise, it was a sense of joy which predominated, despite everything. Every shadow had passed from her friendship with Doctor Cairns. To have gained the love of a man whom she so liked and admired was precious to her; not until she felt her spirits rise at the thought did she realise how badly her self-confidence had been shaken by her husband's coldness.

Helen reached Heriot Row just in time to receive a call from her sister. Rosemary was affable, but for all her indolence her eyes were sharp. Helen exerted herself to guide the conversation into safe channels – the Robertsons' new conservatory, Rosemary's latest gown, and above all, the health and precocious talents of her daughter. Time slipped harmlessly by as they discussed Harry's involvement in the building of some model cottages of a novel design, or Rosemary's own difficulties with unreliable nursemaids and drunken cooks.

'Is that the time? I didn't intend to stay so long . . . I'm sure that minx of a nursemaid drinks half Baby's milk herself if I'm not by to see her fed.' Rosemary got to her feet, and smoothed the creases from her skirts, while Helen rang for her bonnet and shawl, congratulating herself on the success of the visit. Suddenly, Rosemary stopped.

'There! With all our gossip I all but forgot; will you and Francis dine with us tomorrow? It's short notice, I know. To be honest, Harry proposed it on Monday. I quite forgot about it until he asked me this morning what I intended to give you. Of course I didn't tell him I hadn't invited you yet . . . you will come, won't you?'

'Really, I hardly know . . .'

'Oh, Helen, you can't let me down! Harry would catch me out in a fib; he'd never be done teasing over it! You must come!'

'But Francis may not be free,' she said helplessly.

'Why, don't you know? Married a fortnight and not know whether your husband is dining out tomorrow? Heavens, you need to train him rather better than that! You should begin as you mean to carry on; if he's made an engagement without telling you, he deserves to be obliged to cancel it. Don't let him away with it, Helen! Tell him you've accepted for you both, and there's an end to it.'

In the face of such self-interest combined with righteous indignation Helen offered no further protest. She dared not even hint at the truth, and undo all the effort of the past hour.

'You may expect us then,' she said, with a timidity which brought a superior smile to her sister's plump face.

'Oh, what a lot you have to learn!' she said, wagging a fat finger at her, and, much to Helen's relief, swept complacently down to the clarence.

Helen debated whether to inform her husband of the engagement by means of a note. If she had been sure that the arranged visit would meet with his approval, she might have done so. But sensing that he might well be displeased by her acceptance, her pride refused her that easy escape: it might appear cowardice. The thought was enough to determine her to speak to him.

She waited for him in the library, as before. He was so late home that she fell asleep in the chair, despite all her efforts. It must have been the opening door which woke her; at least, she awakened to find him already in the room, quite close to her. He must have moved noiselessly across to her, reluctant to wake or disturb her. Still half asleep, she smiled dreamily up at him, moved by the yearning in his eyes, the sense of irrecoverable loss in his gaunt, drawn features. She stretched out her hand to him, and then she remembered all the weary tale of his withdrawal from her, his bitter disillusionment. Her smile faded, her hand dropped to her side, as she saw his undisguised longing replaced by an impassive mask.

'Rosemary called today to ask us to dinner tomorrow. I felt I had no choice but to accept.'

He frowned.

'Was I right? Will you come?'

'You must go if you wish. Present my apologies. Say I am indisposed.'

'Francis! What will they think?'

'They will think I am unwell; why should they doubt it?'

'But we can't continue to live like this! You can't be indisposed every time we are invited to dine!'

'It won't be necessary.'

'What do you mean?' she asked fearfully, struck by some new resolution in his manner.

'The sheriff of Banffshire died two days ago. I will very probably be offered the position. I will choose to be resident.'

'And I?'

'You may remain in Edinburgh.'

'A discreet separation?' she asked, her pride rising to conceal the blow she had suffered. 'That is what you want?'

He made no reply.

'Very well,' she said, stiff-necked as he, and perhaps as unhappy. 'I shan't plead with you. But while we remain beneath the same roof, while we at least pretend to be man and wife . . .' She had to pause a moment, to recover her composure, and resumed all the more coldly, '. . . for so long at least, I believe that I have the right to expect your co-operation in the normal forms of social inter-course. If you choose not to accompany me to Rosemary and Harry's, you must make your own excuses. I shan't lie for you.'

She rose, and left him without another word, her head held high, and in her heart a desolation such as she had never known.

24

It was pride alone which gave Helen the strength to preserve some appearance of normality the following day. Left to herself she would gladly have seized on any excuse to avoid their dinner engagement, but the urge to keep up a facade of happiness and unanimity before her sister's avid curiosity overrode any other consideration.

She dressed for the dinner with the most scrupulous care, even sending to Drummond Place for her stepmother's maid to arrange her hair in an elaborate style far beyond Bessie's art. Good-looking though she was, she rarely strove to create any very particular impression by her appearance. To know that her gown became her and was what Edinburgh considered fashionable had always been enough for her; not tonight. Tonight, she felt a defiance which demanded more.

The gown she chose, after long consultation with Mrs Lambert's knowledgeable maid, was of black velvet, low-cut with a trimming of silver about the neck. Lucille braided thin ribbons of black velvet and silver amongst her hair, which she wore high on her head, pulled up from the nape and twisted in a thick coronet. On the temples and before her ears, she teased out little tendrils of hair, softening the severity of line.

Helen's preferred colours were the various shades of blue and grey; in black she appeared, even to herself, startlingly different. She was doubtful, considered changing, but did not. She added ruby ear-rings; there was a matching necklace, but she laid it aside. Her shoulders and breasts, it seemed to her, were more impressive unadorned. And tonight, rejected and contemned, she wanted to make an impression.

She went down at the last moment, at the arrival of the clarence which the Robertsons had sent. She carried herself with deliberate dignity, her shawl draped loosely over her arms, hanging down from the crook of her elbows. Francis was awaiting her at the foot of the stairs. She glanced at him, unsmiling, and saw what she had wanted to see: the unwilling tribute of admiration, and desire.

To flirt had always been in her eyes a paltry activity, beneath contempt. To flirt with one's own husband she would have considered impossible, a contradiction in terms. Perhaps she would have been correct; whatever there was between them that night was something more serious than flirtation. She wanted from him more than admiration. She wanted, and was conscious of wanting, his recognition of what he had lost, or wilfully rejected. If she could not have his approval, she would have at least his bitter regret at what might have been.

To prove to him the value of what he had thrown away; that was what she believed to underlie her ambition to excel that night. She would have hotly denied any suggestion that she was setting out, not to flirt with her own husband, but to seduce him. And yet, she had never appeared more seductive than that evening, as she slowly descended the stairs towards him, unsmiling, watching every shade of expression on his upturned face.

The atmosphere in the clarence was charged. By tacit agreement they sat as far as possible from each other, but even in a spacious carriage her spreading skirts encroached upon him, the jolting and swerving of the vehicle brought some involuntary contact.

Street lamps, widely spaced, and the flaring gas-jets which illumined the shops of Princes Street and the Bridges, lit the interior of the carriage. Again and again she found her eyes drawn to his face. There was a quality in his good looks which survived the evident strain of the past weeks and the noticeable thinness of his features: if anything, his face was refined by it. Her husband, sitting inches away from her, yet remote and unattainable as a stranger.

The glaring gas-jets were left behind as the clarence neared the Grange. It was in her mind to say something to him of the need to maintain appearances before her sister; she thought better of it. Despite everything, she believed that some bond of loyalty still existed between them, rendering such a warning demeaning.

As she had expected, once the Robertsons' villa was reached, his behaviour to her became that of a model husband, attentive though not demonstrative. They were taken first to a bedroom where Rosemary's maid, after taking their outdoor clothing, disappeared with a murmured excuse to attend to her mistress, unpunctual as ever, it seemed.

'Really!' Helen exclaimed, setting herself to examine her gown as best she could without the girl's aid. 'Am I fit for the drawing-room, Francis? My skirts aren't crumpled at the back?'

He came over to her, scrutinising her with his slight, short-sighted frown. He touched her arm. 'Would you turn round, please?'

For a moment his words made no sense. All her sensibility seemed focused on the touch of his fingers on her skin. Reluctant to break off even so trivial a contact, she slowly turned.

'There is a little dust, I think . . . here, at the hem. Wait a moment.' He stooped, and with his handkerchief brushed at the offending area. She looked down. Her hand could have rested on his head as he crouched beside her, could have passed lovingly over his thick auburn hair. It was a freedom which a young wife should have been able to allow herself, confident of receiving in return a murmured endearment, a sweet, hasty kiss, a glance which recalled past pleasure, and promised future. She could imagine such a glance from him, ardent, impatient, intimate.

He had finished his task, but for a second he remained

in his uncomfortable posture, and reached out to stroke the soft velvet of her gown in a quick, timid gesture.

'You make an excellent lady's maid,' she said, her voice unsteady.

He rose at once, staggering a little as he straightened. Instinctively, she reached out to steady him, and gripped his arm. She raised her troubled eyes to him.

'Francis . . .' she said hopelessly.

The door opened; Rosemary sailed into the room in billowing pale-blue satin.

'What, spooning already?' she said briskly, not without a certain malicious glee. 'You're not still at that stage, are you? Harry's waiting in the drawing-room, when you can tear yourselves apart . . .'

The first moments in the drawing-room were no better. Harry kissed her enthusiastically, and then turned his attention to his cousin.

'Frank! My dear fellow, you're wasting away!' he exclaimed, laughing, as he threw his arm easily about his shoulders. 'You look quite worn out . . . too much bed and not enough sleep, eh?'

'Harry!' his wife protested, scandalised but amused.

'Well, Rosie, there's no need to be so fearfully proper with Helen any more, is there? Married life holds no more secrets now, does it?' Irrepressible, he clapped his cousin on the back, serenely undisturbed by the lack of any response to his teasing.

Despite her own agony of embarrassment, Helen's heart went out to her husband. At the best of times he would have writhed beneath such sly comments, fastidious as he was; now, pale, tense, he was a pitiable spectacle – although not to Harry. Never had Helen heard the dinner bell ring with a greater sense of relief.

The presence of the servants imposed some restraint on Harry's witticisms, and the meal passed off without incident, although Helen was shocked to see how little her husband ate.

After a single glass of dessert wine, Helen and her

sister retired. Helen doubted whether Francis would sit long with his cousin, however good the Sauterne. Heaven only knew what anecdotes he might see fit to offer the novice husband.

'Come over by the fire, Helen!' Rosemary urged, patting the seat beside her on the sofa. 'Let's be cosy and confidential while we have the chance . . . now, tell me truthfully, are you happy?'

'Of course.'

'No need to bite my head off! I'm only showing a sisterly concern, you know.'

'You needn't trouble. There is no need for concern of any description.' Belatedly Helen smiled, attempting to soften the rebuke.

'No? Is he . . . good to you?'

'He is kindness itself.'

'Oh . . . of course,' Rosemary said, sounding cheated, as though no fish had risen to an artfully cast fly. 'I meant . . .'

'Yes?'

'Oh . . . nothing,' Rosemary muttered, cowed. It was possibly a greater relief to her than to Helen when, soon afterwards, the men came upstairs.

Helen was the first to break the silence. 'Harry, I must ask you now, before I forget again: do you know the tenement over Paisley Close?'

'Opposite Skinner's Close? Yes. I've never had any professional dealings with the property, but I know where you mean. Why?'

'Oh, something in your line, that's all. I visit a family in one of the top flats. The oldest girl has been alarmed by a report from one of the joiners engaged on minor repairs there. He's told her that the whole land is about to fall.'

'Fall? For Heaven's sake, Helen!' Rosemary said scornfully. 'She surely doesn't listen to such stuff!'

'Oh, it does happen, Rosie,' her husband put in. 'There's such a quantity of old housing in the town,

435

not all of it well kept up. That tenement looks to be in fairly good repair, though.'

'It is.' Helen looked in surprise at her husband. He had spoken with unexpected authority. 'I rather think I have some interest there,' he added, seeing her surprise.

'In Paisley Close!' she exclaimed.

'I believe so,' he said carelessly. 'I seem to remember the name cropping up in MacGregor's reports.'

'But has he not contacted you with news of faults in the structure?'

'What is it but rumour, the idle gossip of a workman wanting to make himself important to a credulous girl?'

She made an inarticulate murmur of anger at his casual tone, his dismissive words, but strove to answer calmly. 'Even so, does it not require some investigation? Harry, what do you think?'

'On what grounds does the prophetic joiner base his predictions?' Harry asked, stretching.

'Oh, doors sticking, cracks in the ceiling, the walls of Paisley Close bulging a couple of inches from the true.'

He pursed his lips doubtfully. 'It could amount to something seriously amiss, but it's highly unlikely. The bulge in the close would alarm me most. Some settlement is almost inevitable in old property. Every tenement in the High Street could show its sticking doors and cracked ceilings, but bulging walls can be a danger signal. More than likely, though, it's no more than some cladding coming away, a job for a plasterer, nothing worse.'

'So you wouldn't advise the Crearies to move out?'

'Is that what the joiner has been recommending? What a Jeremiah! I'd have to carry out a thorough survey to be sure, of course, but I doubt whether there's any need for such urgent action. As long as there's been no tampering with the foundations these old properties are basically sound. It's the conditions within them which do the harm, rather than structural defects.'

'Certainly the overcrowding is a great evil,' Helen said, glancing at her husband. 'The Crearies have only a single

436

room for the whole family. It's so common that it passes unremarked.'

'It is how they choose to live,' Francis said, to Harry rather than to her. 'Would they be willing to pay double for two rooms? Or even more, if a convenience were added?'

'Willing? If they had the money!' Helen said, leaning forward in her eagerness to explain, to plead the case of those whose voice was never heard.

'Oh? And I suppose the keepers of dramshops and shebeens on the High Street dispense their wares free, from the Castle to the Palace?' He looked quickly at his wife, at her ardent, self-forgetful face, and turned back to his cousin, his sarcasm becoming a sneer. 'I suppose every penny the industrious poor earn is spent on rent and nutritious food? On kindling and coals?'

'Francis, what do you know of how the poor live?' she said passionately. 'The girl I spoke of was almost reduced to prostitution, for want of means to pay a debt of two pounds.'

'And what had the two pounds been spent on?' he said, still appearing to address his cousin.

'On shoes for her delicate sister, and a decent gown for another sister, to enable her to go into service! You don't realise . . . the poor have no chance to accumulate savings; when her father was injured, then put on short time . . .'

'Short time!' exclaimed Rosemary, highly amused. 'Why, Helen, you've become a perfect political economist! I had no idea!'

'I have had excellent teachers!' she said proudly. 'Could you manage on twelve shillings a week, Rosemary?'

'No, and neither could you, Helen dear, so we needn't waste a moment in worrying over it.'

'But look at the result! A girl of fifteen reduced to selling herself, for want of two pounds!'

'Very regrettable, no doubt,' Francis said impatiently, 'but what alternative is there? No sane human being would claim that such an outcome is desirable, but what

437

would result if the poor were assisted in every crisis by unrestricted public funds?'

'Well, Francis, tell us!' she cried, taunting him, claiming his attention, even if it were hostile. 'What would the result be, except to keep fifteen-year-old girls from offering themselves to whoever can buy?'

'The poor would be pauperised,' he said, still avoiding her gaze.

'And that's a worse fate than prostitution in your eyes?' she asked, her face alive with her fierce belief in what she was saying; for her, this was no merely intellectual discussion. She knew the reality of his theories: she had seen. If she had not suffered herself, she had witnessed the sufferings of others. 'Lizzie didn't appear to think so, when I gave her the two pounds.'

'You gave it to her?'

'Of course. What would you have done?'

'Ah, Frank's case might have been a little different!'

'Well?' she persisted, ignoring Harry's sly innuendo. 'Would you have seen a fellow human being reduced to prostitution, if you had the means to prevent it?'

He hesitated. She hoped it was from reluctance to admit the truth, rather than from any doubt. 'No.'

'You would have given her the money?'

'Yes . . . yes, I suppose so.'

'What, and pauperised her?'

'You may choose to belittle the dangers, Helen,' he said, stung into real contact with her at last, 'but I tell you, indiscriminate charity and ill-advised tampering with market forces do incalculable harm. If the poor can get money for nothing why should they work? They would be fools to sweat for what they could get without labour. And if they refuse to work how is wealth to be created, wealth to support the charity which has undertaken to feed and clothe and house the idle? If charity gives free bread how will those who charge its true price sell it, and make the profit which keeps them in business? Philanthropy can't charge itself with the upkeep of more than a tiny proportion of the poor. Once the able-bodied are reduced to dependence by well-meaning interference . . .'

'Well-meaning interference?' Helen repeated, her eyes flashing. 'You would include my actions under that heading, I take it?'

'Not if you value your domestic peace, Frank!' Harry warned, looking at his sister-in-law in mingled awe and amusement.

'Laws can't be broken! The laws of supply and demand aren't some arbitrary human imposition – some eccentric by-laws. They are as invariable as the law of gravity, or as any of the laws which govern the operation of mechanical processes. They cannot be broken with impunity. Meddle with them, and the last state of the poor will be worse than the first.'

They were sitting apart, opposite to each other. He too had abandoned his former detachment, catching fire from her. He no longer looked at Harry when he spoke, instead his eyes were fixed on her, as though they were alone, a vehemence, a desperation in his voice, his gestures, his expression, which might have led an onlooker, not understanding his words, to assume that he was speaking of something very different from mercantile theory. He shifted impatiently in his seat, reached out a hand towards her, as though to touch her, across the emptiness between them.

'Take housing as your example, if you like. It can stand for any number of areas: the principle remains the same. If philanthropy were to intervene in the housing market to any extent, and charged unprofitable rents, how would capitalists be encouraged to build, confident of a good return on their investment? The only houses to be built would be those of charitable bodies. But where does philanthropy gain its funds? From the profits of other investment! Strike a blow against capitalism at any point and you lay an axe to the very philanthropy you hope will supplant it.'

'So there is no need for change? Let capitalists make their profits, pay the lowest wages they can, charge the highest prices, and divert a prudent sum to respectable causes, to take care of a few deserving casualties of the Juggernaut?'

'On the whole, yes,' he said, defiantly. 'There may need to be adjustments made, fine alterations to enable the system to function more smoothly, but generally speaking, improvement in the lot of the poor must come from their own industry.'

'And families living in a single room, without any of the decencies you or I would expect? A child dying of consumption in the same bed as her healthy sister? What fine adjustment would you recommend there, Francis? What is this machine, in any case – an instrument of torture?'

'Really, Helen,' Rosemary broke in with an artificial little laugh, 'I'm not sure that Francis will allow you to continue your visits . . .'

'Allow me?' she asked, her voice dangerous. Harry and his wife exchanged a glance.

'I would be the very last to seek to prevent anyone from visiting the poor,' Francis said quickly. 'I know how to value acts of mercy and pity, even if . . .'

'Even if you don't care for them yourself? What room is there in all your laws, your system, for human frailty? The poor deserve their fate – let them clamber up from the filth by their own efforts, or lie in its corruption! If they err – if anyone errs – let them bear the consequences. They needn't look to you for anything but blind Justice, need they, Francis? One fault and they're damned, cast into outer darkness with no hope of return?'

Even as she spoke, she realised that she was going too far, but still the bitter torrent swept on, beyond her conscious control. Although Harry and Rosemary might not understand the precise significance of her words, the tense silence which succeeded proved that they had heard enough to rouse their suspicions.

'We thrive on differences of opinion,' Francis said, clearing his throat. Through her anger, she still recognised his loyalty. She gazed at him, a silent message of thanks and near apology.

'You should leave these difficult questions to the men, dear, I always do,' Rosemary said, yawning. It was a comment which at any other time would have brought a ready protest from Helen, but now she bit her lip and remained silent. She was afraid of herself.

'Harry and I were hoping to go down to Sophie in the spring,' Rosemary remarked, ringing for tea. 'I've never been to London and it's a chance not to miss; who knows how much longer they may be there? No doubt she'll be glad to catch up with all the Edinburgh gossip.'

'No doubt, dear,' Helen replied, more calmly. 'I can quite picture the scene, I assure you. Ah, the tea things at last . . .'

They did not remain late, but Helen felt the fatigue of the evening more than if they had spent the whole night dancing. Once safely installed in the clarence, she let her head sink back on the cushions, her eyes shut. The vehicle moved smoothly off, its motion soothing. She could almost have been lulled to sleep, had she been alone.

She kept her eyes shut, but not now from exhaustion. She did not want to give any sign of readiness to begin a conversation, because she knew that she ought to apologise to him for speaking as she had before the Robertsons. She had insulted him, had betrayed the bond which she had invoked to ensure his presence there. 'I'm sorry.' The words rang so clearly in her head, but she could not speak them.

Tait was waiting up for them; Francis dismissed him at once. Helen gathered up her heavy velvet skirts, and began to climb the stairs.

'Helen . . .'

She had gone only a few steps when she heard his voice. She turned and looked down to him. He was looking up at her, and she knew suddenly that only a word, a gesture was needed, only a smile, or the stretching of her hand towards him, and he would follow her. And in the same moment she recognised that he would not join her without that sign, whether from pride or diffidence. No matter how great his longing for her, he would not confess it, would not make the first move.

'Yes?'

At the tone, deliberately drained of any emotion, his hand dropped from the banister. She was standing a little above him, perfectly erect, not leaning towards him, as was natural. Her face, with its clear blue eyes and regular features, which had for so long seemed made to express to him all that was open, generous, guileless, was cold and guarded. The shawl had slipped from her shoulders, displaying the tender curve of her breasts, startling in their smooth whiteness against the thick rich black of her gown.

'Oh, good night, that was all,' he said, stepping back. He watched her as she gravely inclined her head, and continued up the stairs; his wife, beautiful as a goddess, and as unattainable.

They spent most of the following day, Sunday, at Drummond Place. In all the bustle of a busy household, their estrangement was easier to conceal. It could not be said to be an enjoyable day, but it was bearable, and Helen was grateful even for that negative comfort after her outburst of the previous evening.

On Monday afternoon, Helen determined to return to the Crearies, to pass on Harry's reassurance, for what it was worth. It was an excuse, at least, to give some sense of purpose to her long, empty day.

Perhaps in keeping with her own mood the long, tortuous stair seemed even more grim and sordid than usual in the chill November afternoon. She climbed slowly, and paused for breath before reaching the top flat. She had been aware of an unusual sense of stir in the court as she crossed it, of a greater animation in the customary little knots of idlers who hung about there, whatever the time or the weather, but as she reached a landing not far from the top, the reason for the excitement became apparent.

Along the passage leading away from the stair a door was open; the hysterical yapping of a dog reached her, and a woman's voice, slurred with drink . . . 'I tellt him no, I tellt him . . . no my Bridie, she's a good wee lassie, I'll no see her yon de'il's whore . . . no my Bridie, I tellt him . . .'

'Aye, we ken all about it, hen.' It was a man speaking, hasty, but with rough kindness. From within the room came sounds of awkward movement, shuffling feet, muttered orders, growing louder as they neared the door. Nearer the stair, another door opened a crack; a grey-headed old woman, supporting herself against the lintel by her twisted, arthritic hand, peered out. Catching sight of Helen, she beckoned to her.

'Come ben – they're fetching him out!' she whispered, her face alive with greedy curiosity and an excitement which baffled and repelled Helen. But as the heavy, stumbling footsteps drew closer, she allowed herself to shelter within the old woman's doorway.

'I doubt she's killt him!' she muttered, looking up at Helen in eager complicity. 'See! She's done for him!'

Two policemen were bearing a sheet-wrapped burden along the passage to the stair. A sodden dark patch on the linen told its tale of seeping blood. As they began the difficult descent, grunting with the effort, one of the men staggered, pulling the sheet from the face of the dead man.

Even in the dimness of the stair she knew him. The pale face was contorted in a grimace, more of disgust than of fear or pain, the thick black hair flopped unheeded down his cheek, but there was no mistake.

'Donoghue.'

'Ye ken him?'

'Slightly.'

The old woman held up her hand, and bent closer to the door again. A blowsy, powerfully built woman was being led past, muttering and at intervals shouting aloud some curse or plea. Helen glimpsed her, coarse-featured as spirit drinkers become, her hair tangled loose about her shoulders, her eyes bold and uncomprehending.

'He'll no get his clarty fingers on my wee lassie!' Blurred but defiant, the cry echoed up the stair-well, as the door was locked, and the last policemen made their ponderous way down to the court, the frenzied barking of the little terrier almost drowning their steps.

With some difficulty, Helen disengaged herself from her companion, who seemed prepared to retail every insult, every threat and taunt which she had heard in the course of the last, fatal quarrel. By the time she reached Lizzie's door, her legs would barely support her.

'Here, Miss Lamb – Mrs Bethune!' the girl exclaimed in alarm, helping her over to the chair.

'I shall be perfectly well in a moment . . . I saw a terrible sight as I came up.'

'No the stramash in the back tenement? Are the polis away?'

'I saw them go.'

'And her? Is she sober yet?'

'I don't think so . . . oh, Lizzie, what will happen to the daughter?'

'Bridie?' Lizzie shrugged. 'Dinna ken. The workhouse down the Canongate, maybe. At least the lassie's out of here.'

Helen looked up quickly, startled by a note in the girl's voice which she had never heard before, a note of barely repressed hysteria.

'You're still worried about what Greenshields said?'

'Would ye no worry yourself? Would ye sleep? Would ye rest a minute by day or night?'

'I told my brother-in-law about it. He's an architect,

you know, and he believes that there is probably nothing seriously amiss, providing that the foundations are sound.'

'And who kens that?' Lizzie bit back. 'Does he?'

'Well, no . . . but he saw no reason why they shouldn't be,' she said lamely.

Lizzie snorted her contempt. 'Aweel, only another week,' she said deliberately, watching for Helen's reaction.

'Another week? What do you mean? Has your father sent for you at last?'

'Aye.' Lizzie's strained expression relaxed into one of her rare smiles. 'He's left the railway, with winter coming on, and he's got a place in a shop in Elgin. Right cabinet-making, ken. He aye likes that best. He's fixed us up with a wee house to ourself, Mrs Bethune – three apartments!'

'And you're to travel up a week from today?'

'Aye, the Monday. He's sent the fare. He's been putting it by, week by week. He's sent word to Nettie. She's to give a week's notice, and come up with us. She's no best pleased, but she'll do as she's tellt.'

'Monday? Lizzie, I can scarcely believe it! I will miss you – but that's selfish. For your sake, I'm glad. It will be easier for you, won't it?'

'Better for the weans,' she said, with a glance to the bed where May's still figure lay, asleep or drowsing. 'We'll aye mind ye, Mrs Bethune.'

'I shall certainly never forget you all . . . Joseph is to go too, I suppose?'

'There's a braw school, Father says . . .' Lizzie replied hesitantly, looking at Helen as though in some doubt as to her reaction.

'Oh, I have no objection!' Helen said quickly. 'I want him to have the chance of as much education as he can benefit from, that's all. I'll see my lawyers to make arrangements for any necessary changes in the fees, and the payments for his upkeep. I hope Joseph will write to me himself, and keep me informed about his progress.'

'He'll write, dinna worry!'

'So . . . only a week!'

'Ken, but I'm more feared with every hour. I canna sleep in my bed at night for listening out for creaks and cracks from the house. Whiles . . . whiles the whole land seems to stir and shuggle, like a string that's stretched too tight and canna hold . . . ye think I'm havering, eh no? Aye, ye do. Weel, I'll tell ye this: there's no a mouse left. They've all went, lang-tails and all. Ye'll no hear any of their wee scartings and scrabblings any more. They aye ken, and they've went.'

'It's really troubling you, isn't it?' Helen asked gently. The girl nodded. Helen hesitated. What would Francis say? Almost she decided not to speak, but a stubborn defiance hurried her on. What right did he have to censure her actions, after all?

'Come to stay at Northumberland Street until next Monday. It's lying empty and there's plenty of room. Mrs Blair – the cook – and Phemie are still there on board wages, to keep the house warm and in good condition until I decide what to do with it. You will be able to sleep peacefully there, if the mice let you, that is! We have plenty, I assure you.'

'I canna!'

'Of course you can!' Helen urged, her own doubts swept away in her growing enthusiasm. 'Think of it as a holiday before you leave Edinburgh. It will do you good. You won't need to cook or shop, Mrs Blair will see to all that. You will only have to make the arrangements necessary for your move, and for the rest of the time you can sew, read, do nothing at all, just as you choose!'

'No, Mrs Bethune! It's . . . it's too much!'

'Lizzie, it's an empty house! Mrs Blair and Phemie have only to make up the beds – you can go today, if you like. Will it take you long to get ready? Do you want to come tonight or tomorrow?'

'The night.'

'If I send a cab for you and your things . . . shall we say eight o'clock?'

'We'll be down by the victual dealer's waiting.'

'I'll try to be at Northumberland Street to meet you. If not, Mrs Blair will have her instructions, and I'll be over first thing. What about your furniture?'

'I'll leave it the now. The morn's morn I'll see the broker down the Cowgate. The rent's paid to next Monday. I dinna need to clear it out afore then.'

'Good,' said Helen, rising. 'I'll go straight to Northumberland Street to see Mrs Blair. I'll very probably see you there this evening, otherwise tomorrow.'

She was glad to escape from the girl's thanks, glad too to avoid any possible enquiry as to her husband's likely thoughts on the question. As she neared home after informing Mrs Blair at Northumberland Street of her new duties, the latter prospect became ever less appealing.

She had thought it probable that Francis might not be dining at home, but nothing had prepared her for the news which awaited her.

'Mr Bethune asked me to give you this, Mrs Bethune,' Tait said, as she gave her outer things to him. She paused in the act of untying her bonnet strings to accept the note. 'He came back early from the High Court,' he added, more confidentially, 'I had to pack a bag for him, and call a hackney cab. He told me that he couldn't give a forwarding address, or say exactly when he might be expected back.'

'Thank you, Tait,' she said, with an effort. She read and reread the few words her note contained. 'I have had to go away, I don't know when I shall be back. A.F.B.' She stared stupidly at the initials, before remembering that the A. stood for Arthur, his father's name; he used it only in his signature. She had not been aware that it formed part of his own name until she saw him sign the documents at the wedding. She looked up at the man, not knowing how much to say.

'I thought Mr Bethune looked far from well, if I may say so,' he said, as though reading her doubts in her face. 'He's been working too hard; that, and all the stir of the wedding . . .'

'Thank you, Tait,' she said hurriedly. He bowed and withdrew, as she slipped the letter into her pocket. She went to her sitting-room. The smell of smoke lingered in the air, joyless and oppressive, negating the comfort of the fire. She would have gone elsewhere, but it was the one room in the house which she felt to be her own.

A stranger in her own home. A letter from her husband, containing not one word of affection. Solitude, neglect. For the first time, she seriously considered what Doctor Cairns had said: an annulment. It would be an unpleasant business. There would have to be a medical examination, she supposed, to prove her still *virgo intacta*. And Francis's reputation? His name would be a by-word, a smoking-room joke, fit subject for sniggers and sly innuendo. And her own good name? Would it escape unscathed? Could she expose him to such an ordeal, or endure it herself?

The air seemed to choke her. She rang for Bessie, intending to dress for dinner, but when the maid answered, she merely asked her to see that the chimney was attended to, and went up alone to her room.

Why, after all, should she trouble to change for yet another solitary dinner? The futile effort was suddenly beyond her. Instead, she seated herself by the fire, and gazed absently into its fiery caverns, its coiling smoke and flickering tongues of flame.

'Do I love my husband?' It was a shocking question to ask herself, but she could not evade it. Why had she married him? In the bleak disenchantment of the moment, the first answer to rise in her mind was shameful, to her who had been educated to ideal conceptions of love, duty, wifely devotion. With ruthless honesty she admitted to herself that the essence of the bond attaching her to him had not been ideal, or intellectual, or spiritual; it had been physical. He exercised some power over her, which Doctor Cairns did not, for all her liking and admiration of him.

She had known before their marriage of their different beliefs concerning social questions, beliefs which sprang from the very sources of their personalities, impossible to reconcile perhaps.

She had known, too, of the coldness inherent in his nature, liable to fix him in a polar desolation of his own making at those inevitable setbacks which would pass unnoticed by more robust characters.

But all this she had overlooked, and willingly, because with all her intelligence, all her education and her independence, she was a slave to bodily sensations which her whole upbringing, like that of every girl, had ignored.

Nature, slighted, had taken her revenge. She had been ruled by the sensual pleasure she discovered in their every contact. Even to think of the few moments of intimacy since their marriage sent the blood to her face, brought disquieting sensations for which she had no words flickering to life.

And was this physical yearning truly all that she had felt for her husband? What else, more elusive, subtler?

Pity. She acknowledged the truth of it. She wished to comfort, to cherish him. For all his self-containment, there was something of the lost child in him which called out to her. She wanted to give herself to him without reservation, but he had, it seemed, no use for the gift.

The dinner bell rang. She rose, tall and graceful, and went with sad dignity down to the empty dining-room.

The evening, at least, was occupied. She stayed until past ten with the Crearies in Northumberland Street, helping them to settle in. Lizzie proudly assumed indifference to the spaciousness of her new surroundings; Helen honoured her for it. She was herself almost ashamed to guide the family over the house, which had never before seemed so large. She saw the younger children put to bed before she left Lizzie, stiff and ill at ease in the parlour, but gamely preserving a show of unconcern.

The following day was taken up with the Crearies, and with a visit to her lawyers in connection with Joseph. In the evening, however, she went back to Heriot Row. It struck her as probable that Francis might return before night. She could not believe that he would stay away long, whatever the business which had called him. But she might as well have remained with the Crearies. He did not come.

25

The week dragged by, day by hollow day. Calls, visits, consultations with the cook, appointments with the dressmaker, walks, books, solitude and meaningless conversations from which her true self was banned. Only her dealings with the Crearies had any real value to her, and they would soon be over.

Lizzie had gradually cleared the room at Paisley Close of all that was to travel with them. The remainder a second-hand dealer had taken. The canary which Helen had given to May had occasioned a good deal of thought. It was unlikely to survive a long train journey in November. May's reluctance to part with her pet was eventually overcome. It was agreed that the bird would be returned to Paisley Close, to another family whose daughter, a year or two younger than May, had often come to admire Jockie.

To soften the pain of the sacrifice, Helen had arranged for a cab to take her and May up to the High Street to deliver the bird and give full instructions for his welfare to his new owners. Helen had already given Lizzie money for a replacement when they were settled, but even so it was a melancholy journey, put off until the Saturday morning at May's request, so that she could have Jockie with her for as long as possible. The girl scarcely showed any enthusiasm even for the unusual treat of a ride in a hackney cab. She had been crying, Helen could see, and her face was so pinched and pale that the shadows beneath her eyes showed purple, like bruises.

Helen made to go through Paisley Close, as usual. The entrance was barred. At the far end she could see a pile of rubble, and timber supports propping up the wall of the close. At the door of one of the shops flanking the passage she saw a shopman standing in his long white apron.

'What's happened in the close?' she asked.

'Oh, a wee bit stone's fell,' he said, without much interest. 'They're waiting on getting it lifted. A builder's to come and sort it, the next again day. Are ye wanting into the court? Ye'll get through Baillie Fyffe's Close.'

Helen thanked him, and delayed no further. Even to stand so briefly seemed to tax May's strength. They found the room which was to be Jockie's new home in the front tenement, looking onto the High Street. A place had already been found for his cage at the window. Instructions were given and carefully repeated; his new owner seemed scarcely to believe her good fortune. She was clearly as devoted to him as May had been.

May was downcast, not far from tears. Helen wanted to take her away quickly, but she lingered a moment, impelled by something more than curiosity.

'Did you notice the fall of masonry in Paisley Close, Mrs Fletcher?' she asked the girl's mother, a neat, brisk woman.

'Oh aye, I seen it. Ye kinda worry, ken, but what can ye do? I've tellt the rent-man, and I've better tellt him, Monday after Monday, but the factor's no came near. They dinna bother. We pay our one and nine a week, and there's an end to it. It isna them as has to stay here, eh no?'

'What factor is that?' she asked, as she nodded to May to go; the cab was waiting.

'MacGregor.'

'I . . . I'll see that he is informed of it on Monday morning. The proprietor too, as soon as he returns to Edinburgh.' She smoothed on her fine gloves, over the wedding ring which might have been bought with that long accumulation of one and ninepences.

The cab set off into the eddying traffic, to the New Town. Helen tried to raise the girl's spirits by talking cheerfully of the train journey north and the reunion with her father. May smiled politely, and answered her questions, but there was a strange apathy in her manner which frightened Helen. She seemed suddenly to have reached the end of her strength.

Helen did not remain long with the Crearies. At the back of her mind was the thought that today, surely, her husband would return. She had not expected him to be absent even for so long. The High Court sat on a Monday, and he would scarcely choose to travel on a Sunday if it could be avoided.

Expecting him at any moment, she could settle to nothing. Afternoon passed into evening, dinner came and went, with the usual silent witness to her solitude in the place set, 'just in case', in the very choice of dishes, planned on the cook's advice to suit his taste.

And as the lonely meal progressed, her anger grew. The eager love which had been her sole, her simple response to him had changed, embittered by resentment, by humiliation, by wounded pride. She scarcely knew any longer how she would greet him when he did return.

It was almost nine when she heard steps in the passage, approaching the little parlour at the back of the house where she sat sewing. Assuming it was Tait, come to inform her of some trifling matter, she laid aside her work with a sigh, and looked up as the door opened. Her husband entered, still in his greatcoat, a scarf loose about his neck.

'I had my key,' he said awkwardly, shutting the door behind him.

She stared up at him, wary. He came over to her, unbuttoning his coat. He placed it neatly on the back of the chair opposite hers. She suddenly realised that he was putting off further conversation: he must have hurried in to her without stopping even to summon Tait to take his things, but now he was delaying, laying his gloves with unnecessary precision on top of his scarf. Unsure of himself, he was hoping that she would make the first move. She lifted her chin in her old stubborn gesture, and said nothing.

He glanced uncertainly at the chair, and then at her. She gave him no sign. He remained standing.

'No doubt you are wondering where I have been?' he asked, with forced geniality.

'Not any longer. I did want to know, at first. Now, after so long, it scarcely interests me.'

'Ah,' he said, raising a hand to adjust his neck-tie. 'In any case, you will wish to know the decision I have . . .'

'I wish to know nothing!' she cried, jumping to her feet. '*You* have reached a decision, have you? Perhaps I have reached a decision of my own, during the hours I've been here alone, an object of pity to the very servants! To go away, without a word!'

'I . . . I left a note . . .'

'A note? It would have been an insult to have given it to your housekeeper, far less to your wife! And now you choose to return, and to inform me of your decisions! Do you think me so lacking in spirit, that I will endure such treatment?'

He put out his hand in mute appeal; she ignored it, overwhelmed by a wave of anger which left her shaking and breathless, frightened by her own violent feeling. She moved hurriedly to the door, afraid of what she might say.

'Helen, wait!'

She paid no attention; her hand was already on the knob.

'Helen, I beg you!' He seized her hand, and drew her forcibly away from the door. One arm about her shoulders, he pulled her round towards him. Defiantly, she kept her face averted, although he held her so close that her breasts were pressed against him.

'Look at me,' he said, and she knew from his voice that he was as aware of their disturbing proximity as she was. 'Will you do me the justice of reading this?'

454

The unexpected request disarmed her. As though he realised as much, he released her, and reaching into his pocket brought out an envelope. With the very briefest hesitation she took it from him, and moved back to resume her seat, examining the cover, frowning as she went. It was addressed to him, but bore no stamp. It must have been delivered by hand, she supposed. She opened the letter. It was a single sheet, in a hand she did not recognise, careful but uneducated.

'So you are tying the knot today Mr Bethune? I will be thinking on you tonight you will have a rare time I know . . .'

'Really, what purpose is it serving for me to read this stuff?' she cried contemptuously. 'I would have put it on the back of the fire as soon as I read the first two lines!'

'Please read a little more, if you can. It will help you to understand.'

Despite herself she was impressed by the gravity of his tone. She raised the letter again.

'Look for the red mark on her left tit when you find it remember me I was there before you. Give it her rough she likes it that way shes a good piece of – '

She threw down the letter, unable to read on. She felt her gorge rise; for a second she feared she would be sick.

'Have you read it all? No? Better not, perhaps.' He picked it up, tore it in half and threw it onto the fire. 'You're right, that's where it belonged. I wish I had never opened it.'

'On the morning of the wedding?'

'It was waiting for me when I came down to breakfast. I would have put it down to the foul ravings of a troublemaker if I hadn't remembered something. That Friday evening, when I came back unexpectedly from the Circuit, I passed someone on the stair, a man coming down from the drawing-room flat, a man with a little dog. At the back of my mind I must have known all along who it was.'

'Donoghue.'

'He would have been well pleased with the results of his letter, don't you think?' he asked grimly. 'He was even with me, and more.'

'He's dead now, did you know? He was stabbed by one of his prostitutes. She lived on the same stair as the Crearies.'

'I hope it doesn't fall to me to conduct that case.'

'But surely, knowing who had written it, you didn't give any credence to such a letter?' she asked. 'Did you believe I could possibly have had any willing contact with such a man?'

'I knew that you were keeping something from me.'

'Lying: why not say it?'

'Very well then,' he said steadily, looking her full in the face, 'I knew that you were lying to me.'

'And you've forgiven me?' she asked bitterly.

'I think . . . I think it would be best to forget the whole wretched business and start afresh,' he said, moving towards her. 'I went away, I allow, because I could no longer live beneath the same roof with you under the terms which had obtained since our marriage – '

'Celibacy, you mean?' she broke in impatiently. 'For Heaven's sake, Francis, you're not arguing a relevancy in the High Court; can't you forget your precious dignity for a minute?' Too late, she saw the hurt in his face, and regretted her unkindness.

'It's not easy to alter the habits of a lifetime,' he said slowly. 'I realise that increasingly. But it must be done, I can see that.'

'Oh?'

'I went up to Banff. The post of sheriff is mine, if I want it.'

'And do you?'

'Yes. I believe we could be happy there. I went with some idea of living there alone. It wouldn't do. I . . . I need you, Helen.'

She knew what the admission must have cost him,

but the recognition was lost in anger at his too-honest explanation of his intentions.

'I see,' she said coldly. 'And if I decline to go?'

Surprise bordering on alarm widened his eyes. He recovered himself. 'It is asking a great deal of you, I am well aware. It will mean leaving your family and birthplace, but a wife has often to . . .'

'A wife? Am I your wife?' she asked deliberately. 'Why am I to trust myself in a strange place to your moods, your coldness, your suspicion? You have graciously decided to take me with you, as a useful domestic? I have been treated with less consideration than a kitchen maid, and now I am to go with you to a small town, far from my friends, where I know no one? You have all but broken my heart. I don't know if I . . .' She stopped, as the bell rang with clamorous urgency. 'Are you expecting anyone?'

'No, and I shan't receive the Lord Advocate himself tonight,' he said, turning irritably to the door, as approaching steps were heard. 'Yes, Tait, what is it?'

The man prudently suppressed any expression of surprise at his master's unannounced return, and proffered a note to Helen.

'A young lad brought this for you, Mrs Bethune. He is waiting for a reply.'

The note was brief. 'Dear Mrs Bethune, Lizzie asks me to tell you that May has been taken very poorly. She may not live the night.'

It was signed by Joseph Crearie; it would be he who was waiting outside.

'Tell the boy I will be with him directly. Have my things brought down, if you would, Tait – my sealskin, I think.'

'Helen, you're not going out at this time!'

Silently she handed him the note. He read it hastily. 'The family from Paisley Close?'

'Yes . . .' she said distractedly, already at the door, looking out for Tait's return. 'I was down there this

457

morning, there has been a fall of stones in the close. I promised to see you about it, I'm sure it can't be safe.'

'Not safe? Then you mustn't go!'

'A week ago you thought Paisley Close perfectly safe,' she pointed out.

'But you can't put yourself in a position of danger! You musn't!'

For all her preoccupation, she could not be unaware of the real alarm in his voice, a striking contrast to the complacency with which he had discussed the tenement only a week before. It was in her mind to reassure him, to tell him that she was going to Northumberland Street, not Paisley Close, but his very anxiety dissuaded her. It was the first sign he had ever given of concern over his property in the Old Town: let his thoughts dwell on it a little longer.

'What is safe enough for your tenants is surely safe enough for your wife?' she asked, as Tait entered with her outdoor clothes. 'Thank you, Tait. Perhaps you will see to providing some supper for Mr Bethune? It may be a considerable time before I come back.' Still tying her bonnet-strings, she hurried from the room.

Helen soon saw that Lizzie had not exaggerated. May had begun to cough blood earlier that evening. At first Lizzie had not been unduly alarmed; this had happened before, and had stopped of its own accord. But this time had been different. Phemie had gone for Doctor Cairns as the girl's condition worsened. He had been out on a call; she left a message with Bridget. He arrived not long after Helen. By then it was clear that no human skill could help the dying girl.

'She has broken a blood vessel,' he said quietly to Helen and Lizzie, putting back with infinite gentleness a damp wisp of hair from May's pale, dazed face.

'But she's no hoasting, it's wore off, she'll be all the better for a wee sleep, eh no?'

'Lizzie, she's lost a great deal of blood. She's been in a

458

weakened condition for so long . . . you must be prepared for the worst.'

She looked up at him as though she hated him, but beneath his gaze, honest and compassionate, her anger died, and with it her hope. She drew her lips tight together and nodded, her shoulders drooping in surrender.

By May's bed sat Nettie, stout and ruddy, her thick hand clutching her sister's as though to keep her from slipping away. Lizzie did not dispute the privilege. She had never been to May what Nettie had. She stood alone, at the foot of the bed. Helen moved closer to her. She pitied her with all her heart, and yet something in Lizzie, her fierce independence, her self-containment, forbade any closer contact. They watched together as the end came, without a struggle, as gently as the girl had lived.

Helen did not remain much longer. There was nothing practical to be done at that hour and she could see that Lizzie had no wish for company. She and Doctor Cairns left together shortly before one in the morning.

Donald had brought round the brougham. It was a clear, frosty night, the stars shining distinct and hard, the first stirrings of wind beginning to disturb the cold stillness.

'I'll give you a cast to Heriot Row.'

'Send Donald on; I'd like to walk, unless you're tired?'

'No. Let's walk, if you like.'

Their footsteps rang on the frosting flagstones. For a long time they walked without speaking. Her mind was full of the scene they had just left. It seemed unreal already, beside the still, austere beauty of the night, the soaring vastness of the silent sky.

'Is Bethune still sulking?'

'What?' she asked, bemused by the sudden question, so remote from her thoughts. 'Oh, no . . . he's been away all week, you know. He came back shortly before Joseph brought the news.'

'And is he more forthcoming?' he asked, with an effort at lightness.

459

She considered a moment. All her anger, her long-pent resentment, had gone. She looked back on her reception of him with a sense that she had been ungenerous. 'I think things will mend,' she said slowly, her heart lifting as she realised that for the first time since her marriage she was returning home without unease.

'I see . . . For your sake, I'm glad to hear it.'

She pressed his arm. 'God bless you, Doctor Cairns.'

They were almost at her door, where Donald waited. The horse was shifting uneasily, its hooves clattering on the cobbles.

'So, Helen? Old friends?' he said gruffly, and bent to kiss her cheek, very gently.

'My very dearest . . .' She stopped, as a sudden muffled roar, distant and reverberating, was carried to them on the still, cold air. 'What was that?'

'A signal gun from a vessel in Leith Roads, perhaps?'

'I would not have said that it came from that direction. You don't think there can have been an explosion at the gas works in the Canongate?'

'It was more from that quarter, certainly, but there was no light in the sky . . . still, I'll get Donald to take me home that way. Now, in you go, you're shivering.'

She did not protest. As she ran up the steps, she saw him speak hurriedly to Donald and jump into the brougham, which set off at once at a smart pace.

Tait, blear-eyed with fatigue, admitted her as the carriage turned up towards the gardens and vanished from her sight.

'I'm sorry to have kept you up so long, Tait,' she said, pulling off her gloves with quick, eager movements. 'Mr Bethune has gone up already, I take it?'

'Oh no, Mrs Bethune, he's still out.'

'Out?'

'You must have missed him. He went out to meet you, at Paisley Close. It's a wonder you didn't see him, he left only half an hour or so ago. I think he was quite concerned that you might not find a hackney cab.'

460

'But I was never at Paisley Close!' she began, and fell silent. She had forgotten; he knew nothing of the Crearies' move.

'You may as well go to bed now, Tait, I'll wait up for my husband. I doubt he'll be much longer, he'll realise that he's missed me.'

'Well . . . if you're quite sure, Mrs Bethune?'

'Of course. Perhaps you wouldn't mind attending to the fire in the parlour before you go? I will sit there, I think.'

The man soon mended the fire and retired. It had been allowed to die down, and had almost gone out, but with fresh coals its warmth soon revived. As she had so often, Helen sat alone beside its flickering light, but now her thoughts had altered.

He wanted to begin afresh. She had treated the suggestion without enthusiasm, had all but refused to share his life up north. But, paradoxically, her doubts, her reluctance, had lost their force with the act of utterance. She had spoken her mind, it had been necessary perhaps, but now she too wanted to make a new start.

She was glad that he had shown her Donoghue's letter in all its vileness. Only through reading it could she begin to understand what had tormented him since the day of their wedding. If only he had shown it to her that very day! And if only, honesty forced her to add, she had found the courage to tell him Jack's unhappy story. That must still be faced, that night perhaps – morning, rather, for it was already not far off two. He could surely not be much longer.

She began to wish that she had not sent Tait away. She would have liked to go out to meet her husband, as a gesture of the reconciliation he had offered and she spurned. It was hardly a sensible idea; she could easily miss him. Quite clearly, the wisest course was to remain by the fire and wait for him. But having once started the notion, inactivity became unbearable. She dared not go out alone, so late, but on a sudden impulse she went out into the passage, and into the front hall. She opened the front door. At least he would see her there, and know so much sooner of her impatience for his return.

She clutched her shawl close about her, shivering. Distinct in the still, frosty night, footsteps rang out, slow and measured. She craned her neck eagerly in their direction, standing at the top of the steps onto the street, ready to fly down them, to break through the deadening wall of coldness and distrust which each day had been building between them.

A bobbing light proclaimed the identity of the tall figure approaching: a night policeman, with his bullseye. She drew back. He halted as he came up to the house.

'Cold enough the night.'

'Yes,' she murmured.

He looked at her sympathetically. 'Have you someone out helping up on the High Street?' he asked, keeping his voice low in the sleeping street. 'I'd be up there myself only I'm feared to leave my beat.'

'On the High Street? I'm sorry, I don't understand . . .'

'I thought you must have heard, seeing you on the lookout . . .' He leant forward confidentially, shaking his head. 'A terrible business it must be; a whole land fallen, not an hour since. Folk crushed and smothered in their very beds as they slept.'

There was a gloomy relish in his horror which sickened her. She interrupted him. 'Where?' But she already knew.

'Paisley Close. I heard it from a boy who was at the Tron when it fell, a mason. He was just running down to Albany Street to pick up his tools, then going back up to give a hand. Seemingly there's bairns greeting, trapped in the rubble . . . it would break your heart to hear it, the boy said . . .'

'An hour ago?' she asked, dry-mouthed with fear.

'Just going off one. I heard the noise myself, right enough, it put me in mind of the time-gun.'

Her mind flew to the sudden reverberation she had

noted on her way home with Doctor Cairns. Just past one; and her husband had left the house half an hour before. Just in time for him to have reached Paisley Close by one.

'Had you not best go in out of the cold?' the policeman asked with rough kindness. 'You're shaking, you'll take a chill out here in the frost.'

He was right, her very teeth were chattering, but not through the cold alone. She stammered a few words of thanks or farewell, scarcely aware of what she did, and turned back into the house. A chair stood in the hall, for the benefit of visitors waiting to be announced. She reached it, not without difficulty, and sat there, her eyes wide with terror, seeing not the dimly lit hall with its few solid furnishings, but some nightmare vision.

Its horror erased all lesser fears. Within minutes, having snatched up bonnet and mantle, she was alone in the silent streets, hurrying up to the Old Town.

Crossing the North Bridge, she saw the first signs of the disaster. The sky to the left, over the High Street, was lit by a lurid, flickering glow. She feared that fire had been added to the torments of the trapped survivors, but on turning the corner into the High Street she saw that they had been spared that, at least. The jets and globes had been removed from the street lamps, to give as much light as possible to the rescuers; that, with the smoky flare of a number of torches, had caused the infernal glow.

From the Tron the street was packed with onlookers, blocking her further progress. A great silence, uncanny in so large an assembly, and the strained anxiety on every face, gave a dreamlike quality to the scene; a sense of unreality assailed her so strongly that for a moment she almost believed that by an effort of the will she should be able to struggle free of the vision, and awaken in the safety of her bed.

But even as she paused in her confusion, a low moan unlike anything she had ever heard spread through the crowd, accompanied by a rippling movement, as it parted to give passage to a struggling group bearing a grim burden.

'A man . . . it's a man,' she heard, whispered, rustling throughout the great concourse. And at that she pressed forward, towards the bearers, the crowd giving way before her, as though recognising her urgency.

'My husband . . . I'm afraid he may have been in Paisley Close . . . please . . .'

The body was being carried on a door or panelling of some sort. One of the men assisting in its removal gently pulled back the rags which, in some effort at decency, had been thrown over the dead man's face.

Thick with plaster, the face was set in a grimace of terror and agony, the eyes staring up, their last sight fixed on some vision of crushing, choking death. Some warning there must have been, denying even the mercy of an unconscious end, of sleep passing unknowing into nothingness. She drew back, shaking her head. With a look of sympathy, the bearers moved on, to be stopped after another few yards by a similar request; late or soon, recognition would come; he was, he had been, someone's husband, or son, or brother, or friend. There seemed to her something shameful in her relief that it was not hers.

She was able to move forward more easily, having been seen to stop the bearers. The fact that she was seeking her husband seemed to be communicated throughout the throng; they made way for her with a respect based on that terrible distinction.

The police were erecting barricades at some distance from the ruined building, barring further approach. She saw at once the need for their action. Not only would the press of people have hampered rescue work, but the crowd would have been themselves in danger. Some walls still stood, unsupported, seeming as though a breath of wind could bring them crashing down to join their fellows.

For all the evident danger, there seemed to be no short-age of workers, toiling to free the trapped, themselves at risk of suffering the same fate if the crazy masonry suspended above them should fall.

Helen moved along the barricade until she stood by a policeman, his plaster-streaked uniform suggesting that he too had taken his turn in the search.

'Have there been many saved?' she asked fearfully. See-ing the destruction it seemed impossible that any should have been brought out alive.

'Oh, aye,' he said, as though sensing her reason for concern. 'They've found some with scarce a scratch on them, bairns mostly . . . There's been fifteen or so brought out alive, and there'll be a few more yet, I should think. Is there someone belonging to you in there, miss?'

'I . . . I don't know. My husband came up, to meet me . . . he hasn't come home . . . I don't think he would have been in the tenement, but waiting at the close, perhaps . . .' She faltered into silence, willing him to assure her that in that case her husband would have been in no danger. But in his pitying gaze there was no comfort.

'If he was right by the close . . .' He shook his head. 'I tell you, miss, I'd have been standing there myself, two minutes earlier. I'd just come up to the victual dealer's, meaning to stand a wee while in Paisley Close, everything being quiet, like, but just as I stopped, a stramash broke out in Skinner's Close, just opposite. It was "Murder! The de'il's half killt me!" and I don't know what else, fit to waken the whole Canongate . . . I ran over, no best pleased, mind, and I think the better half of the loafers hanging about the close mouths came over with me, to see the fun. It was nothing more than a bit argle-bargle between man and wife, drink well to the fore. We were coming back up Skinner's Close, and . . . and . . .' He moved his hands in vague, helpless gestures. 'The whole land just went. It just came down, straight down, like it had been hammered into the earth. There was a kind of

465

sound I'll never get out of my mind, a kind of doughy sound, and then just clouds and clouds of dust . . .'

'You said most of the people standing about the closes ran over to Skinner's Close with you,' she broke in quickly. 'Can you remember . . . did you notice a tall gentleman amongst them, he would have been wearing a greatcoat . . . ?'

'I'm sorry, miss . . . I think I would have noticed. There was no one you'd call a right gentleman came with us down Skinner's Close.'

'Thank you.' It was what she had expected. She could not imagine Francis running across the High Street to investigate a drunken brawl with a gaggle of idle spectators. He would have held aloof, have ignored the stir which had saved the policeman's life.

She leant against the barricade for support. The dust was still so thick in the air that she could taste it, could see it settling on her glossy sealskin mantle. Beneath the lurid glare of the gas, all seemed confusion, but as she watched, she saw that there was order of a sort in the apparent chaos. The workers seemed to be organised into teams, each allotted a distinct area. Many were firemen; the light glinted on their helmets. Now and again a voice would be raised in command or caution – once a team withdrew from its work near the north wall, freestanding now, at a fall of rubble, but the danger passed, and they returned within minutes.

The further, northern area of the ruins was concealed from her view, but the north wall drew her eyes, partly by the constant dread that it would collapse, partly by the traces it bore of the interrupted lives it had sheltered. Several fireplaces remained affixed to the wall, with here and there a fire still burning, particularly in the upper part, least affected by the billowing dust. The clear, calm moonlight silvered pans hanging in a recessed press, touched here a Dutch clock, stopped at a few minutes past one, there a china dog, still keeping its position on a mantelshelf, although its fellow had gone, smashed

466

into a million shards. On one fireplace stood a bottle of porter, set to warm, she supposed; on another, a kettle rested on the hob, ready to be put to boil in the morning which never came. On nails on the wall Sabbath clothing stirred uneasily in the slight breeze, a woman's grey dress, its arms lifting and tossing, a man's decent black jacket, hanging stiffly. And intact amidst the destruction of a window hung a birdcage, the very one, perhaps, which she had that morning brought to Paisley Close.

Her hands clutched the barricade at the sudden pain of the recollection. She had promised to tell her husband of the fall of masonry in Paisley Close that morning. She had mentioned it to him, true, but what action had she urged? Perhaps even at that late hour something could have been done; perhaps they could have taken Harry Robertson to the tenement, have asked him to examine the foundations. How many lives would have been saved if she had insisted, if she had risked being thought a fool for her fears?

And her husband? He would not have been in any danger if she had told him honestly of the Crearies' move to Northumberland Street. Her lack of candour had brought him to Paisley Close, as her inability to be open with him had poisoned their marriage from the start. She remembered the night before the wedding, their last moments of happiness; would it have been so difficult to have trusted him with the sad, sordid tale? And even tonight, when he had struggled towards a reconciliation, what encouragement had she given? She understood him, knew his nature in all its imperfection, but resentment had stopped her ears.

'Stretcher! Over here!'

The call came from the far corner of the ruins; two men started forward, carrying the poles of a stretcher. As they picked their way over the rubble a low murmur rippled through the crowd. They were not long in returning; seeing the anxious faces turned towards them, one of the bearers shook his head, his meaning unmistakable.

'Wait!'

A man straightened from where he had been working, in the very shadow of the tottering north wall. Without a coat or jacket despite the bitter frost, he stumbled over to the bearers. He seemed to ask a question of the man; one briefly answered, and they paused to allow him to come up to them. Helen caught her breath as he emerged from the gloom into the shifting gaslight. He steadied himself a moment, then reached out to lift the covering from the face of the corpse. A glance was enough; he turned away, wiping the back of his hand over his eyes, his shoulders bowed in grief and exhaustion.

He started back towards the work he had left; he never reached it.

'Francis! Francis!'

He turned. Struggling towards him, sobbing, stumbling, almost falling, her arms already reaching out for him, was the woman he had sought amongst the dead, the mutilated, the agonised. And amidst the ruins which he could, in part, have claimed as his own, they clung together. He, the impassive, the aloof, wept with her, the tears smearing the dust and dirt on his face.

'Take him home, Helen.'

She raised her face, and stared at Doctor Cairns, uncomprehending.

'You'll find Donald and the brougham waiting at the top of New Street – he's been taking any of the homeless who are uninjured to relatives, or the workhouse. I don't think he'll be needed again tonight, more's the pity.'

'And you?'

He shrugged. 'There are one or two still trapped; it may come to amputation. I'll stay.'

Francis spoke. 'And I . . . I'll carry on here while there's any hope.'

Doctor Cairns reached out, and gripped his arm; his shirt-sleeve had been torn, and the skin beneath showed, streaked with blood and dirt. 'Frank, you've done all you can, you're not used to work of this sort. Go

468

home; there are fifty men ready and eager to take your place.'

'But I can't go, I can't leave just because I have found my wife . . . my place is here.'

The doctor gently shook his arm. 'God bless you, do you think you'll do half the good of a man trained to it? Your turn will come, never fear.'

'What do you mean?' Helen asked, with a sudden sense of the importance of what he was saying.

'After this, Frank, there'll be a movement for change . . . no, not that, there'll be the chance of such a movement, while well-doing Edinburgh still remembers this night. The moment won't last; people such as you will need to come forward, hold public meetings, put pressure on the city fathers, make sure that some good comes from this terrible waste. You'll have work enough then, believe me.'

'Doctor! Doctor Cairns! Over here!'

At once he went to answer the cry, picking his way swiftly and deftly for all his shambling gait.

'He's right, my love . . . come home. Where's your greatcoat, your jacket?'

He had begun to shiver, now that the strenuous efforts of lifting masonry were over, and perhaps with some nervous reaction. 'I gave them to a man . . . he and his family had escaped in their night clothes . . . I'd forgotten.'

She passed her arm across his back, and led him away unresisting, towards New Street.

In the brougham she unclasped her mantle, and holding him close against her breast, spread it over them both. As warmth flowed from her body into his, his shuddering was stilled.

'I don't understand . . . had you left the Crearies before . . . before I arrived?' he asked. It was the question she dreaded.

'I was never there; I should have told you. They have been staying in Northumberland Street all week . . . oh,

469

Francis, I could have caused your death – I thought I had!'

'I met the Solicitor-General in St Andrew Square . . . he kept me back . . . I was cursing him for it, but I suppose it saved my life. I couldn't think why, believing you were under the ruins . . . why should the innocent die as they slept, and I live?'

'Don't! Oh, don't, my love!'

'But if I'd listened to you, and had that joiner's tales properly investigated . . .'

'Yes, but you weren't the only one. Others knew of them too, and did nothing. And everyone knew that housing was bad in the Old Town, and shrugged their shoulders. We're all to blame.'

He was silent a moment. In the creaking, stuffy brougham the light faded and again grew bright, as they passed the wide-spaced lamps of the New Town.

'So many faces . . . any one of them might have been you . . . how could I rejoice that it was someone else?'

'I know . . . I know.'

Branches were brushing the roof of the brougham; they were passing along the Gardens. In a moment the weary horse would have reached Heriot Row. There was a great stillness in the carriage, a fleeting moment of equilibrium, poised between two worlds. She seemed to foresee in that second something of what their life together would be. He would never find it easy to show her his heart; a retreat into himself would always be instinctive, rather than the open expression of his anger, his fears. She saw it; and accepted it.

'Helen?'

She turned towards him. His features were scarcely discernible in the semi-darkness.

'You are so silent . . . what are you thinking of?'

'Nothing . . .' She stopped, abruptly aware of the evasive reply. 'I was thinking of the future,' she said slowly.

'Yes?'

She caught the strained anxiety in his voice, and

reached gently for his hand. 'I was thinking that . . . that everything will be all right.'

His fingers rose and lightly touched her face, stroking her cheeks and hair, passing blindly over her brow, her lips. With a cry which was almost a sob she pressed his hand to her mouth, kissing it over and over again. She heard his inarticulate murmur as he gathered her in his arms; they clung together as though fearing some stroke of arbitrary cruelty which might at any moment tear them apart for ever. His mouth found hers in a kiss of aching tenderness, absolving all that remained of their doubt and distrust. Only when the brougham swayed to a halt in the pool of light before the house did they draw apart, dazed and trembling.

Their arms about each other, shivering in the cold, they climbed the frosted steps to the house. They were home at last.

AUTHOR'S NOTE

Thirty-five people died in the collapse of the tenement; some twenty were rescued. The death toll would have been higher but for the timing. Several people had not yet returned home, others, still awake, heard ominous crackings and were able to escape death by seconds.

The tragedy of Paisley Close finally awoke the middle classes of Edinburgh to the scandalous housing conditions in the city. Public meetings were held, attended by ministers, architects, doctors, lawyers. The facts of overcrowding, lack of sanitation, high rents, disease and the moral effects of life in such squalor were laid bare in plain terms. No one ever forgot the disaster, and no one after it could plead ignorance of the realities of existence in the Old Town. A Medical Officer for the city was appointed, Housing Associations were set up, planning controls were tightened. The long, slow process of improvement began.

Gavin Greenshields gave important evidence at the official enquiry into the fall, and was highly commended. His employer dismissed him for having disobeyed orders in speaking about the events leading up to the tragedy.

No legal proceedings were taken as a result of the enquiry. It was concluded that the fall had been caused by a series of alterations made in the two shops flanking Paisley Close, which fatally weakened a weight-bearing wall.

In addition to the human survivors a cat and a dog were rescued from the ruins, and two caged birds: a linnet, which survived, and a canary, which died.

472